ALSO BY JO NESBØ

Headhunters

The Son

Blood on Snow

Midnight Sun

Macbeth

The Kingdom

BOOKS IN THE HARRY HOLE SERIES

The Bat

Cockroaches

The Redbreast

Nemesis

The Devil's Star

The Redeemer

The Snowman

The Leopard

Phantom

Police

The Thirst

Knife

THE JEALOUSY MAN

AND OTHER STORIES

Jo Nesbø

THE JEALOUSY MAN

AND OTHER STORIES

Translated from the Norwegian
by Robert Ferguson

Alfred A. Knopf   New York   2021

CONTENTS

Part One: Jealousy

London   3

The Jealousy Man   23

The Line   119

Trash   125

The Confession   145

Odd   155

The Earring   189

Part Two: Power

Rat Island   209

The Shredder   317

The Cicadas   357

The Antidote   435

Black Knight   457

PART ONE

Jealousy

LONDON

I'M NOT AFRAID OF FLYING. The chances of dying in a plane crash for the average frequent flyer are one in eleven million. To put it another way: your chances of dying of a heart attack in your seat are eight times higher.

I waited until the plane took off and levelled out before leaning to one side and in a low and hopefully reassuring voice passed this statistic on to the sobbing, shaking woman in the window seat.

'But of course, statistics don't mean much when you're afraid,' I added. 'I say this because I know exactly how you feel.'

You – who until now had been staring fixedly out of the window – turned slowly and looked at me – as though you had only now discovered someone was sitting in the seat next to yours. The thing about business class is that the extra centimetres between the seats mean that with a slight effort of concentration it's possible to persuade yourself that you are alone. And there is a common understanding between business-class passengers that one should not break this illusion by exchanging anything beyond brief courtesies and any practical matters that have to be dealt with ('Is it OK if I pull down the blind?'). And since the extra space in the footwells makes it possible to pass each other if needing to use the toilet, the overhead lockers and so on without requiring a coordinated operation, it is, in practice, quite possible to ignore one another completely, even on a flight that lasts half a day.

From the expression on your face I gathered that you were mildly surprised at my having broken the first rule of travelling business class. Something about the effortless elegance of your outfit – trousers and a pullover in colours which I wasn't completely convinced were matching but which do so nevertheless, I guess because of the person who is wearing them – told me that it was quite a while since you had travelled economy class, if indeed you had ever done so. And yet you had been crying, so wasn't it actually you who had broken through that implied wall? On the other hand, you had done your crying turned away from me, clearly showing that this wasn't something you wanted to share with your fellow passengers.

Well, not to have offered a few words of comfort would have been bordering on the cold, so I could only hope that you would understand the dilemma facing me.

Your face was pale and tear-stained, but still remarkable, with a kind of elvish beauty. Or was it actually the pallor and the tear stains that made you so beautiful? I have always had a weakness for the vulnerable and sensitive. I offered you the serviette the stewardess had placed under our tumblers of water before take-off.

'Thank you,' you said, taking the serviette. You managed a smile and pressed the serviette against the mascara running down under one eye. 'But I don't believe it.' Then you turned back to the window, pressed your forehead against the Plexiglas as though to hide yourself, and again the sobs shook your body. You don't believe what? That I know how you're feeling? Whatever, I had done my bit and from here on, of course, made up my mind to leave you in peace. I intended to watch half a film and then try to sleep, even though I reckoned I would get an hour at most, I rarely manage to sleep, no matter how long the flight, and especially when I know I need to sleep. I would be spending only six hours in London, and then it was back to New York.

The *Fasten your seat belt* light went off and a stewardess came up, refreshed the empty glasses that stood on the broad, solid armrest between us. Before take-off the captain had informed us that tonight's flight from New York to London would take five hours and ten minutes. Some of those around us had already lowered their seatbacks and wrapped blankets around themselves, others sat with faces lit by the video screens in front of them and waited for their meal. Both I and the woman next to me had said no thanks when the stewardess came round with the menu before take-off. I had been pleased to find a film in the Classics section – *Strangers on a Train* – and was about to put my headphones on when I heard your voice:

'It's my husband.'

Still holding the headphones in my hands I turned to her.

The mascara had stopped running and now outlined your eyes like stage make-up. 'He's cheating on me with my best friend.'

I don't know whether you realised yourself that it was strange to be still referring to this person as your best friend, but I couldn't see that it was any of my business to point it out to you.

'I'm sorry,' I said instead. 'I didn't intend to pry . . .'

'Don't apologise, it's nice when someone cares. Far too few do. We're so terrified of anything upsetting and sad.'

'You're right there,' I said, unsure whether to put the headphones aside or not.

'I expect they're in bed with each other right now,' you said. 'Robert's always horny. And Melissa too. They're fucking each other between *my* silk sheets right at this very moment.'

My brain at once conjured up a picture of a married couple in their thirties. He earned the money, a lot of money, and you got to choose the bedlinen. Our brains are expert at formulating stereotypes. Now and then they're wrong. Now and then they're right.

'That must be terrible,' I said, trying not to sound too dramatic.

'I just want to die,' you said. 'So you're mistaken about the plane. I hope it *does* crash.'

'But I've got so much still left to do,' I said, putting a worried look on my face.

For a moment you just stared at me. Maybe it was a bad joke, or at the very least bad timing, and under the circumstances maybe too flippant. After all, you had just said you wanted to die, and had even given me a credible reason for saying it. The joke could be taken either as inappropriate and insensitive or as a liberating distraction from the undeniable bleakness of the moment. *Comic relief,* as people call it. At least when it works. Whatever, I regretted the remark, and was actually holding my breath. And then you smiled. Just a tiny wavelet on a slushy puddle, gone in the same instant; but I breathed out again.

'Relax,' you said quietly. 'I'm the only one who's going to die.'

I looked quizzically at you, but you avoided my eyes, instead looked past me and into the cabin.

'There's a baby over there on the second row,' you said. 'A baby in business class that might be crying all night; what d'you think of that?'

'What *is* there to think?'

'You could say that the parents should understand that people who have paid extra to sit here do so because they need the sleep. Maybe they're going straight to work, or they have a meeting first thing in the morning.'

'Well, maybe. But as long as the airline doesn't ban babies in business class then you can't really expect parents not to take advantage.'

'Then the airline should be punished for tricking us.' You dabbed carefully under the other eye, having exchanged the serviette I had handed you for a Kleenex of your own. 'The business-class adverts show pictures of the passengers blissfully sleeping.'

'In the long run the company'll get its just deserts. We don't like paying for something we don't get.'

'But why do they do it?'

'The parents or the airline?'

'I understand the parents do it because they've got more money than they have shame. But surely the airline has to be losing money if their business-class offer is being degraded?'

'But it'll also damage their reputation if they get publicly shamed for not being child-friendly.'

'The child doesn't give a damn if it's crying in business or economy class.'

'You're right, I meant for not being parent-of-small-child-friendly.' I smiled. 'The airlines are probably worried it'll look like a kind of apartheid. Of course, the problem could be solved if anyone crying in the business section was made to sit in the economy section and had to give up their seat to a smiling, easy-going person with a cheap ticket.'

Your laughter was soft and attractive, and this time it got as far as your eyes. It's easy to think – and I did think – that it's incomprehensible how anyone could be unfaithful to a woman as beautiful as you, but that's how it is: it isn't about external beauty. Nor inner beauty either.

'What line of work are you in?' you asked.

'I'm a psychologist and researcher.'

'And what are you researching?'

'People.'

'Of course. And what are your findings?'

'That Freud was right.'

'About what?'

'That people, with just a few exceptions, are pretty much worthless.'

You laughed. 'Amen to that, Mr . . .'

'Call me Shaun.'

'Maria. But you don't really believe that, Shaun, do you?'

'That with a few exceptions people are worthless? Why shouldn't I believe that?'

'You've shown that you're compassionate, and to a genuine misanthropist compassion means nothing.'

'I see. So why should I lie about it?'

'For the same reason, because you're a compassionate person. You play up to me discreetly by claiming to be afraid of flying, same as me. When I tell you I'm being betrayed you comfort me by telling me how the world is full of bad people.'

'Wow. And I thought I was supposed to be the psychologist here.'

'See, even your choice of career betrays you. You might as well just admit it, you're the best proof against your own proposition. You're a worthwhile person.'

'I wish that were the case, Maria, but I'm afraid my apparent compassion is merely the result of a bourgeois English upbringing, and that I'm not worth much to anyone other than myself.'

You turned your body a couple of almost imperceptible degrees closer to me. 'Then it's your upbringing that gives you worth, Shaun. So what? It's what you do, not what you think and feel, that gives you value.'

'I think you're exaggerating. My upbringing means only that I don't like to break the rules for what is considered acceptable behaviour, I don't make any genuine sacrifices. I adapt, and I avoid unpleasantness.'

'Well, at least as a psychologist you have value.'

'I'm a disappointment there too, I'm afraid. I'm not intelligent or industrious enough ever to discover a cure for schizophrenia. If the plane went down now all the world would lose would be a rather boring article on confirmation bias in a scientific periodical read by a handful of psychologists, that's all.'

'Are you being coy?'

'Yes, I'm coy too. That's another of my vices.'

By now you were laughing brightly. 'Not even your wife and children would miss you if you disappeared?'

'No,' I answered abruptly. Since I had the aisle seat I couldn't just end the conversation by turning to the window and pretending to have spotted something interesting in the dead of the night down there in the Atlantic. To pull the magazine out of the seat pocket in front of me would seem too obvious.

'Sorry,' you said quietly.

'It's OK,' I said. 'What did you mean when you said you were going to die?'

Our eyes met and for the first time we *saw* each other. And though this might be with the benefit of hindsight, I think we both caught a glimpse of something that told us, even then, that this was a meeting that just might change everything. Indeed, that had already changed everything. Perhaps you were thinking that too but then were distracted as you leaned over the armrest towards me and noticed how I stiffened.

The scent of your perfume had made me think of her. That it was her smell, that she had come back. So you leaned back in your seat and looked at me.

'I'm going to kill myself,' you whispered.

Then you leaned back in your seat and studied me.

I don't know what my face expressed, but I knew you weren't lying.

'How do you propose to do it?' was all I could think to say.

'Shall I tell you?' you asked with an impenetrable, almost amused smile.

I thought about it. Did I want to know?

'Anyway it's not really true,' you said. 'In the first place, I'm not *going* to kill myself, I've already done it. And in the second place, it's not *me* who's killing myself, it's them.'

'*Them?*'

'Yes. I signed the agreement about . . .' You looked at your watch, a Cartier. I guessed it was a present from this Robert. Before or after he was unfaithful? After. This Melissa wasn't the first, he'd been unfaithful from the beginning. '. . . four hours ago.'

'*Them?*' I repeated.

'The suicide agency.'

'You mean . . . like in Switzerland? As in, assisted suicide?'

'Yes, only with more assistance. The difference is that they kill you in such a way that it doesn't look like suicide.'

'Really?'

'You look as if you don't believe me.'

'I . . . oh yes, yes I do. I'm just very surprised.'

'I can understand that. And this has to be just between us, because there's a confidentiality clause in the contract, so I'm not actually supposed to talk to anyone about it. It's just . . .' You smiled, at the same time as the tears welled up in your eyes again. '. . . so intolerably lonely. And you are a stranger. And a psychologist. You're pledged to confidentiality, right?'

I coughed. 'In regard to patients, yes.'

'Well then, I'm your patient. I can see you have a vacant appointment right now. What is your fee, doctor?'

'I'm afraid we can't do it like that, Maria.'

'Of course not, that would be against the rules of the profession. But surely you can just listen as a private individual?'

'You must understand that it presents ethical problems for me as a psychologist if someone with suicidal tendencies confides in me without my doing anything about it.'

'You don't understand. It's too late to do anything about it, I am already dead.'

'You're dead?'

'The contract is non-reversible, I will be killed within three weeks. They explain to you in advance, that once you've signed your name to the contract, there is no panic button, that if they allowed that it might create all kinds of legal complications afterwards. You're sitting next to a corpse, Shaun.' She laughed, but now her laughter was hard and bitter. 'Surely you can have a drink with me and listen for a while?' You raised a long, slender arm to the service button and its sonar ping rang through the darkness of the cabin.

'Fair enough,' I said. 'But I am not going to give you any advice.'

'Fine. And you promise not to talk about it later, even after I'm dead?'

'I promise,' I said. 'Although I can't see what difference it would make to you.'

'Oh it would. If I break the confidentiality clause in the contract they can sue my estate for a fortune, and that would leave almost nothing for the organisation I'm leaving the money to.'

'How can I help?' asked the stewardess who had soundlessly materialised beside us. You leaned across me and ordered gin and tonics for both of us. The neck of your pullover fell forward slightly, and I saw the naked, pale skin and realised that you did not have her smell. Your smell was faintly sweet, aromatic, like petrol. Yes, petrol. And a kind of tree the name of which I could not recall. It was an almost masculine smell.

After the stewardess had turned off the service light and disappeared, you kicked off your shoes and stretched out a pair of narrow, nylon-clad ankles that made me think of the ballet.

'The suicide agency has very impressive offices in Manhattan,' you said. 'It's a law firm, they claim that everything is legal and above board, and I don't doubt it. For example, they won't take the life of anyone who is mentally disturbed. You have to submit to a thorough psychiatric examination before signing the contract. And you also have to cancel any insurance policies you might have so that they can't be sued by insurance companies. There are a lot of other conditional clauses too, but the most important is the confidentiality clause. In the USA the rights of two adult parties voluntarily to enter into an agreement go further than in most other countries; but if their practice became known, and there was publicity, they are, of course, afraid that the response would lead politicians to put a stop to them anyway. They don't advertise their services, their clients are exclusively wealthy people who learn of their existence word-of-mouth.'

'Well then, yes, I can see why they would want to keep a low profile.'

'And their clients obviously require discretion; there's something shameful about suicide, after all. Like abortion. Abortion clinics don't operate illegally, but they don't exactly advertise their business over the main entrance.'

'That's true.'

'And of course, discretion and shame are what lie behind the whole business concept. Their clients are willing to pay large sums of money to be eliminated in a way that is physically and psychologically as pleasant and unexpected as possible. But the most important thing of all is that it happens in such a way that neither family, friends nor the world at large have any reason at all to suspect suicide.'

'And how do they manage that?'

'We're never told, of course. Only that there are countless ways, and that it will happen within three weeks of the contract being signed. We're not given any examples either, because that way we would, consciously or not, avoid certain situations, and that would generate an unnecessary degree of fear. All we are told is that it will be completely painless, and that we really won't see it coming.'

'I can understand why it's important for some people to hide the fact that they've taken their own lives, but why is it for you? On the contrary, wouldn't it be a way of taking your revenge?'

'On Robert and Melissa you mean?'

'If you died in a way that was obviously suicide it wouldn't just be about shame. Robert and Melissa would blame themselves, and also more or less consciously blame each other. This is something we see time and time again. Have you ever, for example, studied the divorce rate among parents of children who have taken their own lives? Or the figures for suicide among the parents?'

You just looked at me.

'I'm sorry,' I said and felt myself turning a little red. 'I'm imputing a desire for revenge to you simply because I'm sure that's what I would have felt myself in your position.'

'You think you showed yourself up there, Shaun.'

'Yes.'

You gave a brief, hard laugh. 'That's all right, because of course I want revenge. But you don't know Robert and Melissa. If I were to kill myself and leave a note in which I said it was because Robert was unfaithful, he would of course deny it. He would point out that I had been treated for depression, which is true, and that towards the end I had also clearly developed paranoia. He and Melissa have been very discreet, so perhaps no one knows about them. I would guess that for about six months after the funeral, for the sake of appearances, she would date one of the other finance guys in Robert's circle. They all drool over her, and she's always got away with being the cockteaser she is. And after that she and Robert would announce they were a couple and explain that what brought them together was a shared grief over my death.'

'OK, you're probably even more of a misanthropist than me.'

'I don't doubt it. And the really nauseating thing is that deep down, Robert would feel a certain pride.'

'Pride?'

'Over the fact that a woman didn't want to live if she couldn't have him all to herself. That's how he would look at it. And that's how Melissa would look at it too. My suicide would raise his stock even higher and end up making them happier.'

'You believe that?'

'Sure I do. Aren't you familiar with René Girard's theory about *mimetic desires*?'

'No.'

'Girard's theory is that beyond satisfying our basic needs we don't know what it is we want. So we mimic our surroundings, we value what other people value. If enough people around you say Mick Jagger is sexy, you'll end up wanting him yourself, even if in the first place you think he looks awful. If Robert's stock goes up because of my suicide, Melissa will want him even more, and they'll be even happier together.'

'I understand. And if it looks as though you died in an accident or died some other form of natural death?'

'Then it has the opposite effect. I become the one whom chance or fate took. And Robert will think differently about my death and about me as a person. Slowly but distinctly I'll develop a saintly aura. And when the day comes when Melissa starts to annoy Robert – and she will – he'll just remember all the good things about me and miss what we had together. I wrote him a letter two days ago telling him I'm leaving him because I need to be free.'

'Does that mean he doesn't know that you know he's been messing about with Melissa?'

'I've read all their text messages on his phone and never said a word to anyone before now, before you.'

'And the purpose of the letter?'

'In the beginning he'll feel it's a relief not to have to be the one who leaves. It'll save him money in the divorce settlement and leave him looking like the good guy, even if he does hook up with Melissa shortly afterwards. But after a while the seed planted in that letter will grow. That I left him to be free, yes. But also because I must have thought I could meet someone better than him. That there might even have been someone even before I left. Someone who wanted me. And as soon as Robert thinks that . . .'

'. . . that means you're the one with the mimetic desires. And that's why you went to the suicide agency.'

You shrugged. 'So then what is the divorce rate among the parents of children who take their own lives?'

'What?'

'And which parent is it that takes their own life? The mother, am I right?'

'Well, you tell me,' I said, fixing my gaze on the back of the seat in front of me. But I could feel your eyes on me as you waited for a more detailed answer.

I was rescued by the arrival of two glasses that appeared as if by magic from the darkness and landed on the armrest between us.

I coughed. 'Isn't it intolerable to have to wait so long? Wake up every morning and think, perhaps today I'll be murdered?'

You hesitated; you didn't want to let me off that easily. But in the end you let it go and answered: 'Not if the thought that perhaps today I won't be murdered feels worse. Even if, naturally, we are sometimes overcome by panic about dying, and a survival instinct we never asked for, the fear of dying is no greater than the fear of living. But that's something that you as a psychologist are familiar with.' You put a slightly exaggerated stress on *psychologist*.

'True enough,' I said. 'But studies have been made into nomadic tribes in Paraguay where the tribal council decides that someone has grown so old and weak that they've become a burden to the tribe and have to be killed. The person in question doesn't know either when or how it's going to happen, but they accept that that's the way things are. After all, the tribe has managed in an environment with little food and long, arduous wandering because they sacrificed the weak so they can take care of the healthy and ensure that the tribe survives. Maybe in their younger days those now under sentence of death themselves had to swing the club over the head of some frail old great-aunt one dark evening outside the cabin. And yet the research shows that for the members of the tribe the uncertainty creates a high level of stress and that in itself is a probable cause of the short life expectancy among these tribes.'

'Of course there's stress,' you said, yawning as you stretched your stockinged foot so that it touched my knee. 'I would have preferred it to take less than three weeks, but I presume it takes time to find the best and most secure method. For example, if it's to look like an accident and at the same time be painless, that probably requires a lot of careful planning.'

'Do you get your money back if this plane goes down?' I asked and took a sip of the gin and tonic.

'No. They said that because their expenses are so high for each client, and the clients are, after all, suicidal, they have to insure themselves against the client getting in before them, intentionally or not.'

'Hm. So, at most you have twenty-one days left to live.'

'Soon just twenty and a half.'

'Right. And what do you intend to do with them?'

'Do what I've never done before. Talk and drink with strangers.'

You emptied your glass in one long swallow. And my heart began to pound as though it knew already what was going to happen. You put the glass down and laid a hand on my arm. 'And I want to make love with you.'

I had no idea how to respond.

'I'm going to the toilet now,' you said. 'If you follow in two minutes, I'll still be there.'

I felt something happen. An inner rejoicing that wasn't merely desire, but something affecting my whole body, a feeling of being reborn I had not had in a long, long time, and, if the truth be known, I had never expected to feel again. You had positioned the palms of your hands on the armrests as though about to rise from the seat, but you remained seated.

'I guess I'm not that tough,' you sighed. 'I need to know whether you're actually coming.'

I took another sip to give me a moment. She looked at my glass as she waited.

'What if I have someone?' I said, and could hear that my voice sounded hoarse.

'But you don't.'

'What if I don't find you attractive? Or I'm gay?'

'Are you afraid?'

'Yes. Women who take the sexual initiative frighten me.'

You studied my face as though searching for something. 'OK,' you said. 'I'll buy that. I'm sorry, it really isn't my style, but I don't have time to pussyfoot around. So what are we going to do?'

I could feel myself calming down. My heart was still beating too fast, but the panic and the instinct for flight were gone. I turned the glass in my hand. 'Do you have a connecting flight from London?'

You nodded. 'Reykjavik. It leaves an hour after we land. What were you thinking of?'

'A hotel in London.'

'Which one?'

'The Langdon.'

'The Langdon's good. If you stay there more than twenty-four hours the staff know your name. Unless they suspect it's an illicit affair, in which case their memories are Teflon-coated. But anyway, we won't be staying there more than twenty-four hours.'

'You mean . . .'

'I can rebook the Reykjavik flight for tomorrow.'

'Are you sure?'

'Yes. Does that please you?'

I thought about it. I wasn't pleased. 'But what if . . .' I began, but then stopped.

'Are you worried they might do it while you're with me?' you asked, and chinked your glass brightly against mine. 'That you find yourself with a corpse on your hands?'

'No.' I smiled. 'I mean, what if we fall in love? And you've signed a contract saying you want to die. An unbreakable contract.'

'It's too late,' you said, and laid your hand over mine on the armrest.

'Yes, that's what I'm saying.'

'No, I mean the other thing is too late. We've already fallen in love.'

'Have we?'

'A bit. Enough.' You squeezed my hand, stood up and said you would be back in a moment. 'Enough for me to be glad I have maybe three weeks.'

While you were away in the toilet the stewardess came by and took our glasses and I asked if we could have two extra pillows.

When you came back you had put fresh make-up on.

'It's not for you,' you said, clearly reading my thoughts. 'You liked the way it was a bit smeared, didn't you?'

'I like it both ways,' I said. 'So then who is the make-up for?'

'Who do you think?'

'For them?' I asked and nodded in the direction of the cabin.

You shook your head. 'I recently commissioned a survey in which the majority of women asked replied that they wore make-up to feel good. But what do they mean by good? Is it just the absence of feeling uncomfortable? Uncomfortable at being seen as they really are? Is make-up really just our own self-imposed version of a burka?'

'Isn't make-up used as much to accentuate as to hide?' I asked.

'You accentuate something and you hide something else. All editing – at the same time as it clarifies – involves a cover-up. A woman applying make-up wants to attract attention to her lovely eyes so that no one notices her nose is much too big.'

'But is that a burka? Don't we all want to be seen?'

'Not all. And no one wants to be seen as they really are. Incidentally, did you know that in the course of a lifetime a woman spends as much time putting on make-up as the entire duration of conscription for men in countries like Israel and South Korea?'

'No, but that sounds like a comparison involving a random collection of information.'

'Exactly. But not involving a random collection.'

'Oh no?'

'The comparison is one chosen by me and naturally, it is, in itself, a valid observation. Fake news doesn't necessarily mean fake facts, it can involve manipulative editing. What does the comparison tell you about my view of sexual politics? Am I saying that men have to serve their country and risk their lives while women prefer to beautify themselves? Maybe. But a little verbal editing is all it would take for that same comparison to show that women are as afraid of being seen as they really are as nations are of being conquered by enemy forces.'

'Are you a journalist?' I asked.

'I edit a magazine that isn't worth the paper it's printed on.'

'It's a woman's magazine?'

'Yes, and in the worst possible sense of those words. Do you have any baggage?'

I hesitated.

'I mean, when we land in London, can we take a taxi straight away?'

'Just hand baggage,' I said. 'You still haven't told me why you put on make-up?'

She lifted a hand and stroked my cheek with her index finger, just under my eye, as though I too had been crying.

'Here's another comparison involving random facts,' she said. 'More people die every year from suicide than from war, terrorism, crimes of passion, in fact all murders, combined. Beyond any doubt, you are the most likely murderer of yourself. That's the reason I put on make-up. I looked in the mirror and could not bear the sight of the naked face of my own killer. Not now that I'm in love.'

We looked at each other. And as I raised my hand to take hers she took mine. Our fingers intertwined.

'Isn't there something we can do?' I whispered, suddenly breathless, as though I were already running. 'Can't we buy you out of this contract?'

She put her head on one side, as though to observe me from another angle. 'If it were possible, then it's not certain we would have fallen in love,' she said. 'The fact that we are unobtainable for each other is an important part of the attraction, don't you think? Did she die too?'

'What?'

'The other one. The one you wouldn't talk about when I asked if you had a wife and children. The kind of loss that leaves you afraid to fall in love again with someone you're going to lose. The thing that made you hesitate when I asked if you have any baggage. Do you want to talk about it?'

I looked at you. Did I?

'Are you sure you want to . . . ?'

'Yes, I want to hear,' you said.

'How long do you have?'

'Ha ha.'

We ordered another round of drinks and I told my story.

When I was finished it was already growing light outside the window, because we were flying towards the sun, towards a new day.

And you wept again.

'That's so sad,' you said, and laid your head against my shoulder.

'Yes,' I said.

'Does it still hurt?'

'Not all the time. I tell myself that since she didn't want to live, then the choice she made was probably better.'

'Do you believe that?'

'You believe it too, don't you?'

'Maybe,' you said. 'But I really don't know. I'm like Hamlet, a doubter. Maybe the kingdom of death is even worse than the vale of tears.'

'Tell me about yourself.'

'What do you want to know?'

'Everything. Just begin, and where I want to know more, I'll ask.'

'OK.'

You told your story. And the picture of the girl gradually revealed was even clearer than that of the person who sat leaned into me, her hand beneath my arm. At one point a pocket of turbulence shook the aircraft. It was like riding across a series of small, sharp waves and gave your voice a comic vibrato that made us both laugh.

'We can make a run for it,' I said when you had finished.

You looked at me. 'How?'

'You book into a single room at the Langdon. This evening you leave a note at Reception for the hotel manager. In it you tell him you're going to drown yourself in the Thames. You walk down there this evening, to a place where no one can see you. You take off your shoes and leave them on the embankment. I come and pick you up in a hire car. We drive to France and take a plane from Paris to Cape Town.'

'Passport,' was all you said.

'I can arrange that.'

'You can?' You continued to stare at me. 'Just what kind of psychologist are you, exactly?'

'I'm not a psychologist.'

'You're not?'

'No.'

'What are you?'

'What do you think?'

'You're the man who's going to kill me,' you said.

'Yes,' I said.

'You had the seat beside me booked even before I came to New York to sign the contract.'

'Yes.'

'But you really have fallen in love with me?'

'Yes.'

You nodded slowly, holding on tightly to my arm as though you were afraid of falling.

'How was it supposed to happen?'

'In the passport queue. A needle. The active ingredient disappears completely or is camouflaged in the blood within an hour. The autopsy will indicate that you died of an ordinary heart attack. Heart attack has been the most common cause of death in your family, and the tests we did indicate that you are at risk of the same thing.'

You nodded. 'If we run, will they come after you as well?'

'Yes. There's a lot of money involved, for all parties, including those of us who carry out the assignments. It means that they require us to sign a contract too, with a three-week deadline.'

'A suicide contract?'

'It allows them to kill us at any time, with no legal risk attached. It's understood that if we are disloyal then they will activate the clause.'

'But will they find us in Cape Town?'

'They'll pick up our trail, they're expert at that, and that will lead them to Cape Town. But we won't be there.'

'Where will we be?'

'Is it all right if I wait before telling you that? I promise you it's a nice place. Sunshine, rain, not too cold, not too hot. And most people there understand English.'

'Why are you doing this?'

'Same reason as you.'

'But you're not suicidal, you probably earn a fortune doing what you do, and now you're prepared to risk your own life.'

I tried to smile. 'What life?'

You looked around, leaned forward and kissed me on the lips. 'What if you don't enjoy our lovemaking?'

'Then I'll dump you in the Thames,' I said.

You laughed and kissed me again. A little longer this time, lips a little wider apart.

'You will enjoy it,' you whispered in my ear.

'Yes, I'm afraid I will,' I said.

You slept there, with your head against my shoulder. I put your seat back and spread a blanket over you. Then I put my own seat back, turned off the overhead light and tried to sleep.

When we landed in London I had put your seatback in an upright position and fastened your seat belt. You looked like a little child, asleep on Christmas Eve, with that little smile on your lips. The stewardess came round and collected the same glasses of water that had been standing on the shared armrest between us since before we took off from JFK, when you stared weeping through the window and we were strangers.

I was standing in front of the customs officer in bay 6 when I saw people in high-visibility jackets with red crosses running towards the gates and pushing a stretcher. I looked at my watch. The powder I emptied into your glass before we took off from JFK worked slowly but it was reliable. You had been dead for almost two hours now, and the autopsy would indicate a heart attack and not much else. I felt like crying, as I did almost every time. At the same time I was happy. It was meaningful work. I would never forget you, you were special.

'Please look at the camera,' the customs officer said to me.

I had to blink away a few tears first.

'Welcome to London,' said the customs officer.

THE JEALOUSY MAN

I GLANCED OUT AT THE propeller on the wing of the forty-seater ATR-72 plane. Beneath us, bathed in sea and sunshine, lay a sandy-coloured island. No visible vegetation, only yellowish-white chalk. Kalymnos.

The captain warned us we might be in for a rough landing. I closed my eyes and leaned back in my seat. Ever since I was a child I have known I was going to die in a fall. Or to be more precise, that I was going to fall from the sky into the sea and drown there. I can even recall the day on which this certainty came to me.

My father was one of the assistant directors in the family firm of which his older brother, Uncle Hector, was head. We children loved Uncle Hector because he always brought presents when he came to see us, and let us ride in his car, the only Rolls-Royce cabriolet in all Athens. My father usually returned from work after I had gone to bed, but this particular evening he was early. He looked worn out, and after tea he had a long, long telephone conversation with my grandfather in his study. I could hear that he was very angry. When I went to bed he sat on the edge of it and I asked him to tell me a story. He thought about

23

it for a bit, then he told the tale of Icarus and his father. They lived in Athens, but they were on the island of Crete when his father, a wealthy and celebrated craftsman, made a pair of wings from feathers and wax with which he was able to fly through the sky. People were mightily impressed by this, and the father and his whole family were everywhere regarded with great respect. When the father gave the wings to Icarus, he urged his son to do exactly as he had done, and follow exactly the same route, and everything would be all right. But Icarus wanted to fly to new places, and to fly even higher than his father. And once he was airborne, intoxicated at finding himself so high above the ground as well as by the onlookers, he forgot that it wasn't because of his supernatural ability to fly but because of the wings his father had given him. In his overweening self-confidence he flew higher than his father and came too close to the sun, and the sun melted the wax that held the wings in place. And with that Icarus fell into the sea. Where he drowned.

As I was growing up it always seemed to me that my father's lightly adapted version of the Icarus myth was intended as an early warning to his oldest son. Hector was childless, and it was presumed that I would succeed him when the time came. Not until I was grown up did I learn that at around that time the firm had almost gone bankrupt as a result of Hector's reckless gambling on the price of gold, that my grandfather had fired him, but for the sake of appearances allowed him to keep his title and office. In practice it was my father who ran the firm thereafter. I never found out whether the bedtime story he told me that evening referred to me or to Uncle Hector, but it must have made a deep impression on me because ever since I have had nightmares that involve falling and drowning. Actually, on some nights the dream seems like something warm and pleasant, a sleep in which everything painful ceases to exist. Who says you can't dream of dying?

The plane shook and I heard gasps from the other passengers as we sank through so-called air pockets. For a moment or two I felt something like weightlessness. And that my hour had come. But it hadn't, of course.

The Greek flag was blowing straight out from the flagpole by the little terminal building as we left the plane. As I passed the cockpit I heard the pilot say to the stewardess that the airport had just closed and that it was unlikely they would be able to return to Athens.

I followed the queue of passengers into the terminal building. A man wearing a blue police uniform stood with arms folded in front of the luggage belt and studied us. As I headed towards him he gave me a quizzical look and I nodded my confirmation.

'George Kostopoulos,' he said, holding out a large hand, the back of it covered with long black hairs. His grip was firm, but not exaggeratedly so, as is sometimes the case when provincial colleagues feel they're in competition with the capital.

'Thank you for coming at such short notice, Inspector Balli.'

'Call me Nikos,' I said.

'Sorry I didn't recognise you, but there aren't many pictures of you, and I thought you were . . . er, older.'

I had inherited – probably from my mother's side – the kind of looks that don't age particularly with the years. My hair was grey and the curls gone, and I had maintained a fighting weight of seventy-five kilos, though nowadays less of it was muscle.

'You don't think fifty-nine is old enough?'

'Well, goodness me yes, of course.' He spoke in a voice that I was guessing was a little deeper than his natural register and smiled wryly beneath a moustache of the type men in Athens had shaved off some twenty years earlier. But the eyes were mild, and I knew I wouldn't be getting any trouble from George Kostopoulos.

'It's just that I've been hearing about you ever since I was at the Police Academy, and that seems like a pretty long time ago to me. Any more baggage I can help you with?'

He glanced at the bag I was carrying. And yet I had the feeling he was asking about something more than what I was actually bringing with me in a physical sense. Not that I would have been able to answer him. I carry more with me on my travels than most men, but my baggage is the type that is carried alone.

'Only hand baggage,' I said.

'We've got Franz Schmid, the brother of the missing man, at the station in Pothia,' said George as we left the terminal building and crossed to a small, dust-coated Fiat with a stained windscreen. I guessed he had parked beneath some stone pines to keep out of the direct sunlight and instead got a dose of that sticky sap that in the end you have to scrap off with a knife. That's the way it is. You raise your guard to protect your face and you leave your heart exposed. And vice versa.

'I read the report on the plane,' I said, putting my bag on the back seat. 'Has he said anything else?'

'No, he's sticking to his story. His brother Julian left their room at six in the morning and never returned.'

'It said Julian went for a swim?'

'That's what Franz says.'

'But you don't believe him?'

'No.'

'Surely drownings can't be all that unusual on a holiday island like Kalymnos?'

'No. And I would have believed Franz if it hadn't been for the fact that he and Julian had a fight the previous evening, in the presence of witnesses.'

'Yes, I noticed that.'

We turned down a narrow, pitted track with bare olive trees and small white stone houses on both sides of what must have been the main road.

'They just closed the airport,' I said. 'I suppose that's because of the wind.'

'It happens all the time,' said George. 'That's the trouble with having the airport on the highest point of an island.'

I could see what he meant. As soon as we got between the mountains the flags hung limply down from the flagpoles.

'Fortunately my evening flight leaves from Kos,' I said. The secretary in the Homicide Department had checked the travel itinerary before my boss had given me permission to make the trip. Even though we give priority to the very few cases involving foreign tourists, a condition of the permission was that I was to spend only one working day on it. Usually I was given free rein, but even the legendary Detective Inspector Balli was subject to budget cuts. And as my boss put it: this was a case with no body, no media interest and not even reasonable grounds to suspect a murder.

There were no return flights from Kalymnos in the evening, but there was one from the international airport on the island of Kos, a forty-minute ferry ride from Kalymnos, so he had grunted his assent, reminding me as he did so of the cutback on travel expenses and that I should avoid the overpriced tourist restaurants unless I wanted to pay out of my own pocket.

'I'm afraid the boats to Kos won't be going either in this weather,' said George.

'This weather? The sun is shining and there's hardly a breath of wind, except up there.'

'I know it seems unlikely from here, but there's a stretch of open sea before you reach Kos and there have been a number of accidents in sunny weather just like this. We'll book a hotel room for you. Maybe the wind will have eased off by tomorrow.'

For him to say the wind would 'maybe' ease off instead of the more typically overoptimistic 'bound to have eased off' suggested to me that the weather forecast didn't favour either me or my boss. I thought disconsolately of the inadequate contents of my bag, and a little less disconsolately of my boss. Perhaps I might be able to get a little well-earned rest out here. I'm the type who has to be forced to take a holiday, even when I know I need one. Maybe being both childless and wifeless is what makes me so bad at holidays. They feel like a waste of time and serve only to reinforce what is an admittedly voluntary loneliness.

'What's that?' I asked, pointing towards the other side of the car. Surrounded on all sides by steep inclines lay what looked like a village. But there were no signs of life. It looked like a model someone had carved from grey rock, a gathering of small houses like Lego blocks, with a wall enclosing the whole, all of it in the same monotonous grey.

'That's Palechora,' said George. 'Twelfth century. Byzantine. If the inhabitants of Kalymnos spotted hostile ships approaching they would flee up there and barricade themselves. People hid up there when the Italians invaded in 1912 and when the Allies bombed Kalymnos, when it was used as a German base during the Second World War.'

'Obviously a must-see,' I said, without adding that neither the houses nor the fortifications looked especially Byzantine.

'Hm,' said George. 'Or actually no. It looks better from a distance. The last time it was repaired was by the Knights Hospitaller in the sixteenth century. It's overgrown, there's rubbish, goats, even the chapels are used as latrines. You could get up there if you could manage the stone steps, but there was a landslide and now the climb is even more strenuous. But if you're really interested I could get a guide for you. I can promise you you'll have the entire stone village all to yourself.'

I shook my head. But I was, of course, tempted. I always find myself tempted by what rejects me, shuts me out. Unreliable narrators. Women. Logical problems. Human conduct. Murder cases. All the things I don't understand. I am a man of limited intellect but limitless curiosity. It is, unfortunately, a frustrating combination.

Pothia turned out to be a lively labyrinth of houses, narrow one-way streets and alleys. Even though November was approaching, and the tourist season had ended some time ago, the streets were crowded with people.

We parked outside a two-storey house in the harbour area where fishing boats and yachts that were not too extravagantly luxurious lay alongside one another. A small car ferry and a speedboat with seating for passengers underneath and up the top were tethered to the quayside. Further along the quay stood a group of people, obviously foreign tourists, discussing something with a man in some kind of naval uniform.

Some of the tourists had rucksacks with coils of rope sticking out from each side of the top flap. Several of those I had travelled on the plane with had been similarly equipped. Climbers. Over the last fifteen years, Kalymnos had changed from being a sun-and-surf island to a destination for sports climbers from all over Europe; but that happened after I had hung up my climbing boots. The man in the seagoing uniform spread his arms wide as though to protest that there was nothing he could do about it, pointing to the sea. There were white crests here and there but, as I far as I could see, the waves weren't dangerously high.

'As I said, the problems arise further out, you can't see from here,' said George, who had obviously read the look on my face.

'That's often the case,' I said with a sigh, and tried to come to terms with the fact that, for the time being at least, I was trapped on this little island which, for some reason or other, seemed even smaller now than it did from the air.

George entered the police station ahead of me, passed a counter, and I nodded greetings left and right as we made out way through a cramped and overcrowded open-plan office where not only the furniture seemed outdated but also the bulky computer screens, the coffee machine and the oversized photocopier.

'George!' called a woman from behind a partition. 'A journalist from *Kathimerini* rang. They want to know if it's true that we've arrested the brother of the missing man. I told them I would ask you to ring them.'

'Call them yourself, Christine. Say there have been no arrests in the case and that at this moment in time we have no comment.'

I understood, of course. George wanted to work in peace and to keep hysterical journalists and other distracting elements at bay. Or did he perhaps just want to show me, the guy from the big city, that out here in the provinces they were professionals too? Best for our working relationship if that was the case, so I wouldn't have to use my experience to explain to him that pedantic points of detail were, as a rule, a bad strategy to adopt when dealing with the press. And of course, since Franz Schmid voluntarily made himself available for questioning, he was not technically under arrest – indeed, had not even been apprehended. But once it emerged – and here there was no 'if'' about it – that Franz was being held behind closed doors at the station for hours and the police gave the impression of wanting to keep quiet about it, it would give rise to the type of speculations that were meat and drink to journalists. In that case, better to give a more open and friendly reply, something to the effect that the police were, of course, talking to anyone who could give them a better picture of what might have happened, and that included the missing man's brother.

'Cup of coffee and something to eat?' asked George.

'Thanks, but I'd rather get going straight away.'

George nodded and stopped in front of a door. 'Franz Schmid's in there,' he whispered.

'OK,' I said, lowering my voice but not whispering. 'Has the word "lawyer" been mentioned yet?'

George shook his head. 'We asked if he wanted to call the embassy or the German consul on Kos, but, as he put it, "What can they do to help find my brother?"'

'Does that mean you haven't confronted him with your suspicions?'

'I asked him about the fight, but that's all. But he probably realises that we've asked him to wait here until you come for a reason.'

'And who did you say I was?'

'A specialist from Athens.'

'Specialist in what? Finding missing persons? Or finding killers?'

'I didn't specify, and he didn't ask.'

I nodded. George remained standing there for a couple of seconds before it dawned on him that I wasn't going to enter until he had left.

The room I stepped into was about three metres by three. The only light came from two narrow windows high up on a wall. The person in the room was sitting at a small, square table on which stood a jug of water and a glass. There was a tall man man seated at it. Both forearms were resting on the blue-painted wooden tabletop, his elbows making ninety-degree angles. How tall? Maybe one ninety? He was slender, with a face aged beyond what his twenty-eight years might suggest, one that conveyed the spontaneous impression of a sensitive nature. Or maybe it was rather the fact that he seemed calm and content just to sit there, bolt upright, as though his head were so full of thoughts and feelings that he had no need of external stimuli. On his head he wore a cap with horizontal stripes in Rasta colours, with a discreet little skull on the rim. Dark curls protruded from beneath the cap, such as I once had. The eyes were so deep-set I couldn't immediately fathom them. And at the same moment it dawned on me that there was something familiar here. It took a second for my brain to dig it up. The cover of a record Monique had at her room in Oxford. Townes van Zandt. He's seated at a similar table, posed in almost the same way, and with a similarly expressionless face that still managed to seem sensitive, so naked and unprotected.

'*Kalimera*,' I said.

'*Kalimera*,' he replied.

'Not bad, Mr . . .' I glanced at the folder I had removed from my bag and placed in front of me on the table. 'Franz Schmid. Does that mean you speak Greek?' I asked in my very British English, and he gave the expected reply.

'Unfortunately no.'

I hoped that with my question I had established our starting point. That I was *tabula rasa*, I knew nothing about him, I had no reason to have any preconceived notions about him and that he could – if he so wished – change his story for this new listener.

'My name is Nikos Balli, I am an inspector from the Homicide Department in Athens. I am here hopefully to remove any suspicion that your brother has been the victim of criminal activity.'

'Is that what you think has happened?' The question was posed in a neutral and straightforward way. He struck me at once as a practical man who simply wanted to acquaint himself with the facts. Or wished to give that impression.

'I have no idea what the local police think, I can only speak for myself, and at this moment in time I don't believe anything. What I do know is that murders are rare occurrences. But any murder is so harmful to Greece as a holiday destination that when one does occur, it is our duty to show the rest of the world that this is something we take very seriously indeed. As in the case of plane crashes, we have to find the cause and solve the mystery, because we know that whole airlines have gone bankrupt over a single unexplained crash. I'm saying that to explain why I might be asking you about details which might seem irritatingly irrelevant, especially to someone who has recently lost his brother. And that it might sound as though I am convinced that you or others are responsible for killing him. But be aware that, as a homicide investigator, it is my task to test out the hypothesis that a murder may have been committed, and that it will be a mark of my success if I am able to dispense with any such hypothesis. And that, regardless of the outcome, we might be a step closer to finding your brother. All right?'

Franz Schmid gave a small smile that didn't quite reach to his eyes. 'Sounds like my grandfather.'

'Sorry?'

'Scientific approach. Programming of the object. He was one of the German scientists who fled Hitler and helped the USA develop the atom bomb. We . . .' He stopped and wiped his hand across his face. 'I'm sorry, I'm wasting your time, Inspector. Fire away.'

Franz Schmid's gaze met mine. He seemed tired, but alert. I couldn't tell just how far he had seen through me, but it was a keen gaze that – as far as I could judge – signalled intelligence. When he said 'programming of the object' he was clearly referring to the fact that I had formulated his motivation for helping me; that it might help us to find his brother. It was standard manipulation, no more than expected. But I suspected that Franz Schmid had also spotted the more obscure manipulation involved, part of the interrogator's method of getting the person being interrogated to lower their guard. The reason I almost apologised in advance for the aggressive tone of the interrogation that was about to follow and laid the blame on the economic cynicism of the Greek authorities. It was to make me appear to be the decent, honest cop. Someone in whom Franz Schmid could safely confide.

'Let's begin with yesterday morning, when your brother disappeared.'

As I listened to Franz Schmid's story I observed his body language. He seemed patient, didn't lean forward and talk rapidly and loudly, the way people do when they unconsciously feel that their explanation is the key to the solution of a case they would like to see solved, or to prove their own innocence. But the opposite wasn't the case either. He didn't tiptoe around as though he were navigating a minefield, didn't hesitate. His explanation came in a calm, steady stream. Maybe it was because he had been able to rehearse it in conversation with others. In any case that didn't tell me much; the performance of the guilty is often more precise and convincing than that of the innocent. The reason might be that the guilty come well prepared and have a story ready, whereas the innocent tell the story as it comes to them then and there. So even though I observed and analysed, body language was a secondary issue for me. Stories are my field, my speciality.

Even though I concentrated on his story, my brain also drew conclusions based on other observations. Such as that Franz Schmid, in spite of being clean-shaven, seemed to be a certain type of hipster, the type that wears a cap and a thick flannel shirt indoors even when it's hot. A jacket hung on the hook behind him, and to judge by the size it was his. The sleeves of the flannel shirt were rolled up and the bare forearms seemed disproportionately muscular when compared to the rest of his body. As he spoke he now and then scrutinised his fingertips and carefully squeezed the joints of his fingers, which seemed thicker than average. The watch on his left wrist was a Tissot T-touch which I knew had a barometer and an altimeter. In other words, Franz Schmid was a climber.

According to the case notes both Franz and Julian Schmid were American citizens, resident in San Francisco, unmarried, with Franz working as a programmer for an IT firm and Julian in marketing for a well-known producer of climbing equipment. As I listened to him I thought how his American English had taken over the world. How my fourteen-year-old niece sounded like something out of an American teens' film when she talked to her foreign friends at the International School in Athens.

Franz Schmid told me he had woken at six in the morning in the room he and his brother Julian had rented in a house right by the beach in Massouri, a town about a fifteen-minute drive from Pothia. Julian was already up and about to go out, that was what had woken Franz. As usual, Julian intended to swim the eight hundred metres to the neighbouring island of Telendos, something he did every morning, there and back. The reason he did this so early was, in the first place, because it gave the brothers enough time to climb the best rock faces before the sun hit them from midday onwards. Secondly, Julian liked to swim naked, and it didn't begin to get light until around six thirty. Thirdly, Julian felt that the dangerous undercurrents in the sound were less strong before sunrise and before the wind got up. Usually Julian would be back and ready for breakfast by seven, but on this particular day he simply never showed up again.

Franz made his way down the steps to the small, crumbling stone jetty that lay in a little bay directly below the house. The large towel his brother usually took with him lay at the end of the jetty, a stone on top of it to stop it blowing away. Franz felt it with his hand. It was dry. He scanned the water, called to a fishing boat that was chugging up the sound, but no one on board seems to have heard him. Then he ran back up to the house and got the landlord to ring the police in Pothia.

First on the scene were the mountain rescue team, a group of men in orange shirts who, mixing professional seriousness with a friendly, bantering tone, at once got two boats out on the water and commenced the search. Next came the divers. And finally the police. The police got Franz to check that none of Julian's clothes were missing and satisfied themselves that Julian could not have gone to his room unseen by Franz – who was eating breakfast in the basement – dressed, and left the house.

After scouring the beach on the Kalymnos side, Franz and some of his climbing friends rented a boat and crossed over to Telendos. The police searched from the boat along the shoreline, where the waves broke against jagged rocks, while Franz and his friends visited the houses scattered across the mountainside, asking if anyone had seen a naked swimmer come ashore.

After returning from the failed search Franz spent the rest of the evening calling family and friends to explain the situation. He was contacted on the phone by journalists, some of them German, and spoke briefly to them about what had happened. That they were still hopeful, and so on. He hardly slept that night and at daybreak the police telephoned and asked if he could come to the station to assist them. Naturally he had done so and that was now – Franz Schmid looked at his Tissot watch – eight and a half hours ago.

'The fight,' I said. 'Tell me about the fighting the night before.'

Franz shook his head. 'It was just a stupid quarrel. We were in a bar at the Hemisphere and playing billiards. We were all a bit drunk. Julian started shooting his mouth off, I had a go back at him, and next thing I know I've thrown a billiard ball at him and hit him on the head. Down he went, and when he came to he was nauseous and throwing up. I thought concussion, so I got him in the car to drive him to the hospital in Pothia.

'Do you often fight?'

'When we were kids yeah. Now, no.' He rubbed the stubble on his chin. 'But we don't always take our drink that well.'

'I see. Well, that was brotherly of you to take him to the hospital.'

Franz snorted briefly. 'Sheer egoism. I wanted to get him checked so we would know if we could go ahead with the long multi-pitch we planned to climb the next day.'

'So you drove to the hospital.'

'Yes. Or actually, no.'

'No?'

'We were some distance out of Massouri, and Julian insisted he was feeling better and that we should turn round. I said it would do no harm to check, but he said that in Pothia we risked being stopped by the police

35

and they'd suspect me of driving under the influence, I'd end up in a cell and he wouldn't have anyone to climb with. It was hard to argue against that, so we turned round and drove back to our place in Massouri.'

'Did anyone see you come back?'

Franz carried on scratching his jaw. 'Someone's bound to have. It was late at night, but we parked on the main road, where all the restaurants are, and there are always people there.'

'Good. Did you meet anyone you think can help us so we can get independent confirmation of this?'

Franz took his hand away from his chin. I don't know whether it was because he realised the rubbing might be interpreted as nerves or because it simply wasn't itching any more. 'We didn't meet anyone we know, I don't think. And when I think about it, it was actually fairly quiet. The bar at the Hemisphere was possibly still open, but all the restaurants were probably closed for the evening. Now in the autumn it's mostly climbers in Massouri, and climbers go to bed early.'

'So no one saw you.'

Franz sat up straight in his chair. 'I'm sure you know what you're doing, Inspector, but can you tell me what this has to do with my brother's disappearance?' His voice was still calm and controlled, but for the first time I saw something that might have been tension in the look on his face.

'Yes I can,' I said. 'But I'm pretty sure you can work it out for yourself.' I nodded towards the folder on the table in front of me. 'It says in there that the landlord says he was woken by the sound of one or several loud voices coming from your room, and that he heard chairs being dragged about. Were you still quarrelling?'

I saw a slight twitch pass across Franz Schmid's face. Was it because I reminded him that the last words that had passed between the brothers had been hard?

'As I told you, we weren't exactly sober,' he said quietly. 'But we were friends by the time we fell asleep.'

'What were you quarrelling about?'

'Just some nonsense.'

'Tell me.'

He took hold of the glass of water in front of him as though it were a lifebelt. Drank. A postponement that gave him time to work out how much he should tell me, and what he should leave out. I folded my arms and waited. I knew of course what he was thinking, but he seemed sharp enough to know that if I didn't get the information from him then I would get it from witnesses to the quarrel. What he didn't know was that George Kostopoulos already had this from the one of the witnesses. That this was what caused George to ring the Homicide Department in Athens. And why it had ended up on my desk. The Jealousy Man's desk.

'A dame,' said Franz.

I tried to work out the significance – if any – the use of this word had for him. In British English dame was an honorary form of address, an aristocratic title. But in America, dame was Chandleresque slang, as in a chick, a broad, a bird, not exactly derogatory, but then not a hundred per cent respectful either. Meaning someone a guy could have, or someone he better watch out for. But in Franz's native language dame had an entirely neutral ring, like the way I interpret it in Heinrich Böll's *Gruppenbild mit Dame*.

'Whose dame?' I asked to get to the heart of the thing as quickly as possible.

Again that slight smile, a flicker and then gone. 'That's exactly what the discussion was about.'

'I understand, Franz. Can you give me the details there too?'

Franz looked at me. Hesitated. I had already used his forename, which is an obvious and yet surprisingly efficient way of creating intimacy with someone you're interrogating. And now I gave him the look and the body language that gets murder suspects to open their hearts to the Jealousy Man, Phthonus.

The murder rate in Greece is low. So low that a lot of people wonder how it's possible in a crisis-ridden country with high unemployment, corruption and social unrest. The smart answer is that rather than kill

37

someone they hate, Greeks allow the victim to go on living in Greece. Another that we don't have organised crime because we're incapable of the organisation required. But of course we have blood that is capable of boiling. We have *crime passionnel*. And I'm the man they call in when there's a suggestion that jealousy is the motive behind a murder. They say I can smell jealousy. That's not true of course. Jealousy has no distinct smell, colour or sound. But it has a story. And it's listening to this story, what is told as well as what is left out, that enables me to know whether I am sitting in the presence of a desperate, wounded animal. I listen and know. Know because it is me, Nikos Balli, I am listening for. Know, because I am myself a wounded animal.

And Franz told me his story. He told it because this – this bit of the truth – is always good to tell. To get it out, to air the unjust defeat and the hate that are the story's natural consequences. For there is, of course, nothing perverse in wanting to kill whatever might stand in the way of our primary function as biological creations; to mate, in order to propagate our unique genes. It is the opposite that is perverse; to allow ourselves to be hindered in this by a morality that we have been indoctrinated to believe is natural or divine in origin but which is, in the final analysis, merely a matter of practical rules dictated by what are, at any given time, the needs of the community at large.

On one of their rest days from climbing Franz had rented a moped and ridden to the northern side of Kalymnos. In the country village of Emporio he met Helena, who waited tables in her father's restaurant. He fell hard for her, overcame his natural shyness and got her phone number. Three dates and six days later they became lovers in the cloister ruins of Palechora. Because she was under strict instructions from home not to get involved with guests, and foreign tourists in particular, Helena insisted their meetings be kept secret and involve just the two of them, because on the northern side of Kalymnos everyone knew her father. So they were discreet; but of course, Franz kept his brother informed of events from the moment of that first meeting at the restaurant; every word they exchanged, every look, every touch, the first kiss. Franz showed

Julian pictures of her, a video of her sitting on the castle wall and looking down at the sunset.

They had done this ever since childhood, shared every tiny detail, so that all experiences became shared experiences. For example, Julian – who was, according to Franz, the more extrovert of the two – had shown Franz a video he had made in secret a few days earlier of himself having sex with a girl in her apartment in Pothia.

'As a joke Julian suggested I visit her, pretend to be him, and see if she noticed any difference between us as lovers. An exciting idea, of course, but . . .'

'But you said no.'

'Well, I'd already met Helena, I was already so much in love that I couldn't think or talk about anything else. So maybe it wasn't so surprising that Julian was attracted to Helena too. And then fell in love.'

'Without ever even having met her?'

Franz nodded slowly. 'At least, I didn't think he'd ever met her. I had told Helena I had a brother, but not that we were identical twins, exact physical copies of each other. We don't usually do that.'

'Why not?'

Franz shrugged. 'Some people think it's weird that you come in two identical copies. So we usually wait a bit before mentioning it or introducing each other.'

'I understand. Please continue.'

'Three days ago my phone suddenly went missing. I looked everywhere for it, it was the only place I had Helena's number and she and I exchanged text messages all the time, she was bound to be thinking I was through with her. I made up my mind to drive to Emporio but the following morning heard it vibrating in the pocket of Julian's jacket while he was out swimming. It was a text message from Helena thanking him for a nice evening and hoping they could meet again soon. And so of course I realised what had happened.'

He noticed my – probably badly acted – expression of puzzlement.

'Julian had taken my phone,' he said, sounding almost impatient when

I apparently still failed to get it. 'He found her number among my contacts, called her on my phone so she assumed it was me when she saw the caller ID. They arranged to meet and even after they met it didn't occur to her that the person wasn't me but Julian.'

'Aha,' I said.

'I confronted him when he returned from his swim, and he admitted everything. I was furious, so I went off climbing with some others. We didn't meet again until the evening, at that bar, and then Julian claimed that he'd called Helena, explained everything, that she'd forgiven him for tricking her and that they were in love with each other. I was furious, of course and . . . and yes, so we started arguing again.'

I nodded. There were a number of different ways of interpreting Franz's honest account. It might be that the pressures of jealousy were so intense that the humiliating truth simply had to be told, even if it cast him in a suspicious light now that his brother had gone missing. If that was the case – and if he had killed his brother – the combined pressure of his guilt and his lack of self-control would produce the same result: he would confess.

Then you had the more intricate interpretation: that he guessed I would interpret his openness in precisely this fashion, that I would suppose he found the inner pressures irresistible, so that if, after these confessions, he did not crack up and admit the murder, I would be the more willing to believe in his innocence.

Finally, the most likely interpretation. That he was innocent and therefore had no need to consider the consequences of telling all.

A guitar riff. I recognised it immediately. 'Black Dog'. Led Zeppelin.

Without rising from his seat Franz Schmid turned and took a phone from a pocket of the jacket hanging on the wall behind him. Studied the display as the riff went into a variation after the third repetition, the one where Bonham's drums and Jimmy Page's guitar just don't go, and yet go together so perfectly. Trevor, a friend who had the room next to mine at Oxford, wrote a mathematical paper about the intricate rhythmic figures in 'Black Dog', about the paradox that was John Bonham, Led

Zeppelin's drummer, better known for his ability as a drinker and wrecker of hotel rooms than for his intelligence, in which he compared him to the semi-literate and apparently simple-minded chess genius in Stefan Zweig's 'Chess'. Was Franz Schmid that kind of drummer, that kind of chess player? Franz Schmid touched the display, the riff stopped, and he held the phone to his ear.

'Yes?' he said. Listened. 'One moment.' He held the phone out to me. I took it.

'Inspector Balli,' I said.

'This is Arnold Schmid, uncle to Frank and Julian,' said a guttural voice in that much-parodied German-accented English. 'I am a lawyer. I would like to know on what grounds you are holding Franz.'

'We are not holding him, Mr Schmid. He has expressed a willingness to assist us in the search for his brother, and we are taking advantage of that offer as long as it remains open.'

'Put Franz back on the line.'

Franz listened for a while. Then he touched the screen and placed the phone on the table between us with his hand on top of it. I looked at it as he told me he was tired, he wanted to get back to the house now, but that we were to call him if anything turned up.

Like a question? I wondered. Or a body?

'The phone,' I said. 'Do you mind if we take a look at it?'

'I gave it to the policeman I was talking to. With the PIN code.'

'I don't mean your brother's, I mean yours.'

'Mine?' The sinewy hand tightened like a claw around the black object on the table. 'Er, will this take long?'

'Not the actual phone,' I said. 'Of course, I realise you must have it with you under the present circumstances. So what I'm asking for is formal permission to access the call log and text messages that have been registered on your phone over the last ten days. All we need is your signature on a standard release form to acquire the information from the telephone company.' I smiled as though it was a regrettable necessity. 'It will help me to cross your name off the list of possible leads we need to follow.'

Franz Schmid looked at me. And in the light coming from the windows above I could see his pupils distend. Distension of the pupils, allowing more light to enter, can have a number of causes, such as fear, or lust. On this occasion it seemed to me to indicate only heightened concentration. As when a chess opponent makes an unexpected move.

It was as though I could feel the thoughts racing through his head.

He'd been prepared for us to want to check his phone, so he'd deleted the calls and text messages he didn't want us to see. But maybe nothing got deleted at the telephone provider, he thought, or – shit! – how did it work? He could of course refuse. He could ring his uncle now and get confirmation that there was no difference under Greek, American or German law, he was not obliged to give the police anything at all so long as they had no legal right to demand it. But how would it look if he made things difficult? In that case I was hardly going to cross his name off the list, he was probably thinking. I saw what looked like the onset of panic in his eyes.

'Of course,' he said. 'Where do I sign?'

His pupils were already contracting. His brain had scanned the messages. Nothing crucial there, probably. He hadn't shown me his cards, but for one revelatory moment he had at least lost his poker face.

We left the room together and were on our way through the open-plan offices looking out for George when a dog, a friendly-looking golden retriever, slipped out from between two partitions and jumped up barking happily at Franz Schmid.

'Well, hey there!' he cried spontaneously, squatting to scratch the dog behind the ear in the practised way of people with a genuine love of animals, something which the animal instinctively seems to realise; it was probably the reason it had chosen Franz and not me. The big dog's tail whirled like a rotor as it tried to lick Franz's face.

'Animals are better than people, don't you think?' he said as he looked up at me. His face was radiant; suddenly he looked like a different person to the man who had been sitting opposite me.

'Odin!' cried a sharp voice from between the walls of the partition, the same voice as had told George that a journalist had called. She emerged and grabbed the dog by the collar.

'I'm sorry,' she said in Greek. 'He knows he's not allowed to do that.'

She looked to be about thirty. She was small and compact, athletic-looking in a uniform with the white ribbon of the tourist police. She raised her head. She was red around the eyes, and when she saw us her cheeks turned the same colour. Odin's claws scraped against the floor covering as she dragged the whimpering dog back behind the partitions. I heard a sniffle.

'I need help to print out a warrant to check the contents of a phone,' I said, addressing the partition. 'It's on the home page of –'

Her voice interrupted me. 'Just go to the printer at the end of the corridor, Inspector Balli.'

'Well?' said George Kostopoulos as I poked my head in between the partition walls around his desk.

'The suspect is on a moped on his way back to Massouri,' I said, handing him the sheet of paper with Franz Schmid's signature. 'And I'm afraid he suspects that we're on to him and could do a runner.'

'No danger of that. We're on an island, and the forecast is for the wind to increase. Are you saying that you . . . ?'

'Yes. I think he killed his brother. Can you mail me the printouts as soon as you get them from the telephone company?'

'Yes. Shall I ask them to send Julian Schmid's text messages and call logs too?'

'Unfortunately that requires a court order so long as he's not officially confirmed dead. But you've got his phone?'

'Sure have,' said George and opened a drawer.

I took the phone, sat in a chair at his desk and tapped in the PIN code written on the Post-it note on the back. Browsed through the calls logs and text messages.

I saw nothing of immediate relevance to the case. Just a message about a climbing route that had been 'Sent', which in climber's lingo means that it has been climbed and which automatically made my palms begin to sweat. Mutual congratulations exchanged. Dinners arranged, the name of the restaurant where 'the gang' were gathering and the time. But by the look of it, no conflict and no romance.

I jumped as the phone began to vibrate in my hand at the same time as a male vocalist started singing in the kind of pathos-filled and passionately choked-up falsetto that shows you're a devotee of mainstream pop from the 2000s. I hesitated. If I answered I would probably have to explain to a friend, a colleague or relative that Julian was missing and presumed drowned on a climbing holiday in Greece. I took a deep breath and pressed ACCEPT.

'Julian?' whispered a female voice before I had time to say anything.

'This is the police,' I said in English and then stopped. I wanted to let it hang there. Allow the realisation that something had happened to sink in.

'Sorry,' said the female voice with resignation. 'I was hoping it might be Julian, but . . . any news?'

'Who is this?'

'Victoria Hässel. A climbing friend. I didn't want to bother Franz and . . . yeah. Thanks.'

She hung up and I took a note of the number.

'That ringtone,' I said. 'What was it?'

'No idea,' said George.

'Ed Sheeran,' came the voice of the dog owner from the other side of the partition. ' "Happier".'

'Thanks,' I called back.

'Anything else we can do?' asked George.

I folded my arms and thought it over. 'No. Or actually yes. He was drinking from a glass in there. Can you get it fingerprinted? And DNA if there's any saliva on the rim.'

George cleared his throat. I knew what he was going to say. That this would require the permission of the person involved, or a court order.

'I suspect the glass might have been at a crime scene,' I said.

'Sorry?'

'If in the DNA report you don't link the DNA to a named individual but simply to the glass, the date and the place, that'll be OK. It might not be admissible in a court of law, but it could be useful for you and me.'

George raised one of his chaotic eyebrows.

'That's the way we do it in Athens,' I lied. The truth is that sometimes that's the way *I* do it in Athens.

'Christine,' he said.

'Yes?' There was the scraping of a chair and the girl in the tourist-police uniform peered over the divider.

'Can you send the glass in the interrogation room for analysis?'

'Really? Do we have permission from –'

'It's a crime scene,' he said.

'Crime scene?'

'Yes,' said George, without taking his gaze from me. 'Apparently that's the way we do things here now.'

It was seven in the evening and I was lying on the bed in the hotel room in Massouri. The hotels in Pothia were all full, probably because of the weather. That was OK by me, I was nearer the centre of things here. High above me, on the hills on the other side of the road, yellow-white limestone rock rose up. Mysteriously beautiful and inviting in the moonlight. There had been a fatal accident on the island in the summer, the newspapers had written about it. I remember I hadn't wanted to read about it but did so anyway.

On the other side of the hotel the mountainside plunged more or less straight down into the sea.

The second day of searching was over, the waters in the sound between Kalymnos and Telendos had been calmer further out. But, given the forecast for tomorrow, there wasn't going to be any third day, I was told. In any event, when someone is believed to have been lost at sea, the search is limited to two days, American or not. The wind rattled the windowpanes and I could hear the sound of the waves breaking against the rocks out there.

My task – to make a diagnosis, to decide whether jealousy of a homicidal nature was involved – was over. The next step – the tactical and technical investigation – wasn't my strongest suit. My colleagues from Athens would take care of that. Now the weather had postponed the changing of the guards, and it emphasised and even exposed my inadequacies as a homicide detective. I simply lacked the imaginative ability to see how a murderer might have set about killing someone and then hiding his tracks. My chief said it was because what I possessed in the way of emotional intelligence I lacked in practical imagination. That's why he called me the jealousy investigator, that's the reason I was sent in as a scout and pulled out as soon as I had given the case the red or green light.

There's something called the eighty per cent rule in murder cases. In eighty per cent of cases the guilty party is closely related to the victim, in eighty per cent of cases the guilty party is the husband or boyfriend, and in a further eighty per cent of these the motive is jealousy. It means that as soon as we answer a call in the Homicide Department and hear the word 'murder' at the other end of the line, we know there's a fifty-one per cent chance that the motive is jealousy. This is what makes me, in spite of my limitations, an important man.

I can pinpoint exactly when it was I learned to read other people's jealousy. It was when I realised that Monique was in love with someone else. I went through all the agonies of jealousy, from disbelief, via despair, to rage, self-contempt and finally depression. And perhaps because I had never before in my life been exposed to such emotional torture, I discovered that, at the same time as the pain was all-consuming, it was like observing oneself from the outside. I was a patient lying without an anaesthetic on the operating table at the same time as I was a spectator in the gallery, a young medical student getting his first lessons in what happens when a person has the heart cut out of their breast. It might seem strange that the extreme subjectivity of jealousy can go hand

46

in hand with that kind of cold, observational objectivity. My only explanation is that I, as the jealous one, took steps that made me a stranger
in my own eyes, to such an extent that it forced me into the position of
the frightened observer of myself. I had lived enough to see the self-
destruction in others but had never thought the poison might lie within
me too. I was mistaken. And what was surprising was that the curiosity
and fascination were almost as strong as the hate, the pain and the self-
contempt. Like a leper who watches as his own face dissolves, sees the
diseased flesh, his own rotten interior manifest itself in all its grotesque
and disgusting and terrifying horror. I emerged from my own leprosy
permanently damaged, that much is clear, but it also rendered me
immune. I can never again experience jealousy, not in that way. If that
also means I can never love anyone, not in that way, I really don't know.
Maybe there were other things my life besides jealousy that led to my
never having felt the same about anyone as I felt about Monique. On
the other hand: she made me what I have become in my professional
life. The Jealousy Man.

From childhood onwards I have had a striking ability to become deeply
engaged in stories. Family and friends described it as everything from
remarkable and moving to pathetic and unmanly. To me it was a gift. I
wasn't a part of Huckleberry Finn's adventures; I *was* Huckleberry Finn.
And Tom Sawyer. And, when I started at school and learned how to be
Greek, the *Odyssey*, of course. Naturally, they don't have to be the great
tales of world literature. A very simple, even badly told story about infi-
delity, real or imagined, it doesn't matter which, will do. I am inside the
story. From the first sentence I am a part of it. It's like turning on a
switch. And it also means that I am able to spot quickly any false notes.
Not because I have a unique talent for reading body language, the timbre
of a voice or the automatic rhetorical strategies of self-defence. It's the
story. Even in a crudely and very obviously falsely conceived character I
am able to read the main themes, the person's probable motivation and
place in the story, and on the basis of this I know what inexorably leads
to what in this character. Because I have been there myself. Because our

jealousy evens out the difference between you and me, beyond the barriers of class, sex, religion, education, IQ, culture, upbringing, our behaviour begins to resemble each other's, the way drug addicts resemble each other in their behaviour. We are all of us living dead who rave through the streets driven on by this single need: to fill the enormous black hole that is inside us.

One more thing. The power of imaginative projection is not the same as empathy. 'That I understand doesn't mean I care,' as Homer says. Homer Simpson, that is. But in my case it is, unfortunately, one and the same thing. I suffer, suffer, with the jealous one. And that's why I hate my job.

The wind pulled at the window sash, trying to open it. Wanting to show me something.

I fell asleep and dreamed of falling from a great height. And woke an hour later when the falling man hit the ground, so to speak.

I had mail on my phone. It contained a printout of Franz Schmid's deleted SMSs and call logs. The night before his brother went missing he had, according to the log, called a certain Victoria Hässel eight times without reply. I checked the number and was able to confirm that it was the same Victoria I had briefly spoken to on Julian's phone. But the feeling of someone hitting the ground from a great height, the distinct shiver, the sound of flesh against stone that you never, never forget, that didn't come until I read the text message Franz had sent to a Greek number registered to Helena Ambrosia.

I have killed Julian.

Emporio was a tiny hamlet at the north end of Kalymnos where the main road simply came to a halt. The girl who came to my restaurant table reminded me of Monique. For a while, a few years, I saw Monique everywhere, in the features and eyes of every woman, in the smooth back of every girl, heard her in every word spoken to me by a stranger of the opposite sex. But with time the ghost had paled beneath the constant daylight of time. And after a few years I was able to get up and walk the streets of Athens and know it would leave me in peace. Until darkness fell again.

This girl was pretty too, although not of course as pretty. But in fact yes, she was. Slim, long-legged, with naturally graceful movements. Brown, soft eyes. But her complexion was spoiled by impurities, and she had no chin. What was it Monique lacked? I could no longer remember. Decency, maybe.

'How can I be of service, sir?'

The slightly exaggerated courtesy of the phrase – which I had grown so used to hearing expressed with just a hint of ironic condescension from waiters in England – sounded touchingly honest in the mouth of this pure young Greek girl. She and I were the only ones in the charming little family restaurant.

'Are you Helena Ambrosia?'

She blushed when she heard me speaking Greek and nodded in reply. I introduced myself and explained that I was there in connection with the missing Julian Schmid and saw the consternation that spread across her face as I told her what I knew of her association with Franz Schmid. At regular intervals she glanced over her shoulder as if to make sure no one came out from the kitchen and overheard us.

'Yes yes, but what does this have to do with the one who's missing?' she whispered quickly, angry and flushed with shame.

'You've been with them both.'

'What? No!' She got carried away and raised her voice, then lowered it once more to an angry whisper. 'Who says so?'

'Franz. When you met his twin brother Julian in the stone city Julian pretended he was Franz.'

'Twin?'

'Identical,' I said.

The confusion was plain to see in her face. 'But . . .' I could see her running through the sequence of events in her head, see her confusion change to disbelief and change again to outrage.

'I've . . . I've been with two brothers?' she stammered.

49

'Didn't you know?'

'How could I? If there really are two of them then they're exactly alike.' She pressed her hands to her temples as though to prevent her head exploding.

'So Julian was lying when he told his brother he phoned you in the evening on the day after you met him in the stone city and explained everything to you, and said that you forgave him?'

'I haven't spoken to either one of them since then!'

'What about that message you got from Franz. "I have killed Julian."'

She blinked and blinked. 'I didn't understand that message. Franz had told me he had a brother, but not that they were twins or that his name was Julian. When I read the text I thought maybe Julian was the name of a route he'd climbed, or a name he'd given to a cockroach in his room, something like that, that I was bound to get the explanation later. But we had just closed for the evening and I was very busy clearing up, so all I did was send a smiley in reply.'

'I've read the texts you sent to Franz's phone. All of them are fairly short answers to long messages. The text you sent the morning after you met Julian is the only one where you take the initiative, the only one where I notice, on your side, a certain . . . affection?'

She bit her lower lip. Nodded. Her eyes brimmed with tears.

'So even though Julian lied about having told you he wasn't Franz, it wasn't until you met Julian that you fell in love?'

'I . . .' All the energy seemed to drain from her body and she slumped into a chair opposite me. 'When I met . . . the one called Franz, I was very excited. And flattered, I guess. We met up at Palechora, where there are hardly ever any people, and certainly no one from this island who would know my family. It was very innocent, but the last time I let him kiss me goodnight. Even though I wasn't in love, not really. So when he . . . that is, it must have been Julian, texted me and asked to see me, I said no. I had made up my mind to stop while the going was good. But he insisted in a way that . . . like he'd never done before. He was funny. Being self-deprecating So I agreed to a final, short meeting. And when we met at Palechora it was as though everything had changed. Him, me, the way we talked together, the way he held me. He was so much more relaxed and playful. And it was infectious. We laughed a lot more. And I thought it was because we had got to know each other better, that we were more relaxed.'

'Did you and Julian have sex?'

'We . . .' She tensed and her face flushed. 'Do I have to answer?'

'You don't have to answer anything at all, Helena, but the more I know, the easier it will be for me to solve the case.'

'And find Julian?'

'Yes.'

She closed her eyes. Looked as though she was concentrating hard. 'Yes, yes, we did. And it was . . . very good. When I returned home that evening, I knew that I had been mistaken, that I really was in love and that I had to see him again. And now he's . . .'

Helena buried her face in her hands. A sob came from behind the fingers. Fingers that were long and thin, like Monique's, who used to hold them up and say they looked like spider's legs.

I asked Helena a few more questions she answered honestly and straightforwardly.

She had seen neither Franz nor anyone pretending to be him after that last date at the fortress; she confirmed that she sent a text message to Franz's number the morning after she'd been with Julian saying she hoped they could meet again soon but got no reply. Not until the evening when she received that short, enigmatic message 'I have killed Julian', to which she sent a smiley in reply. It was obvious she had not attempted to make any further contact, since she was the one who had sent the last message.

I nodded, mildly surprised to learn that the rules of the game remained unchanged since the days of my own youth and was able to confirm that the way she answered told me she had nothing to hide. Or more accurately, she was hiding nothing. She had the lover's freedom from shame, in the belief that love is elevated above all else. Love really is the sweetest psychosis, but in her case it had now turned into the worst form of torture. It had been held out to her, and as quickly taken away.

I gave her my number and she promised to ring if she remembered something she wanted to tell me, or if one of the brothers got in touch. I saw how her face lit up when I held out this hope that Julian might still be alive; but by the time I left she was crying again.

'Victoria.' The voice sounded out of breath. Like someone who has just rappelled down after an ascent and hurried to the rucksack where the phone is ringing.

'Nikos Balli, I'm a detective with the police,' I said as I swung the hire car carefully around a flock of goats that had taken up residence on the asphalt outside Emporio. 'We spoke briefly on Julian Schmid's phone. There are a few questions I'd like to ask you.'

'Unfortunately I'm on the peak right now. Can it wait until –'

'Which peak?'

'It's called Odysseus.'

'I'll come there if that's OK.'

She explained the route to me. Between Arginonta and Massouri, a turn-off to the left just before the hairpin bend. Park at the end of the gravel track by the climbers' mopeds. Follow the track – or the other climbers – up the mountainside, eight or ten minutes' walk to the lower part of the face, I'll see her and her climbing partner on a broad ledge five or six metres above the ground, the natural footholds in the mountain will lead me up there.

Twenty minutes later I stood on a track on a barren mountainside with a couple of thyme plants the only vegetation, wiped the sweat from my brow and looked up at a limestone rock face about a hundred metres wide and some forty to fifty metres high that cut diagonally across the hillside like a wall. Spread out along the base of the wall I saw at least twenty ropes that ran between the anchors on the ground and the climbers on the wall. This was a type of sport climbing that, put simply, goes something like this: before the team of two starts out, the one who's climbing first attaches one end of the rope to his harness, which also holds the number of carabiners he's going to need on the route, often around a dozen. At intervals across the route metal bolts have been fastened to the rock face. When the climber reaches one of these he fastens a carabiner to the bolt and then fastens the rope to the carabiner. The second member of the team, the anchor on the ground, has a rope lock fastened to his climbing harness and the rope runs through this rope lock, in much the same way as the seat belt in a car runs between rollers. The anchor carefully pays out the rope as the climber ascends, the way you have to pull out a car safety belt slowly so that it doesn't lock. Should the climber fall, the rope is pulled so swiftly that the lock clamps over the rope, unless the anchor has disengaged it completely. So if the climber falls, then he won't fall much beyond the last carabiner to which he fastened the rope and be stopped there by the lock and the body weight of the anchor. In other words, the most common form of sport climbing is relatively free from danger, by comparison with, for example, free soloing, which involves climbing without ropes or any other form of security. Unlike the sport climber, the free solo climber has a life expectation shorter than that of a heroin addict, which is incidentally a fairly apt comparison. All the same, as I stood there, I felt myself shaking. Because nothing is completely safe, and sooner or later whatever can go wrong will go wrong. Some people think that's a joke along the lines of Murphy's Law, but it isn't. It's a matter of simple mathematics and logic. Absolutely everything that can happen according to physical law will, sooner or later, happen. It's just a question of when.

I walked the last few metres up to the wall and located the ledge where a woman stood holding a rope that ran up the wall to a climber ten metres above her. I scrambled up to her using hands and feet.

'Victoria Hässel?' I asked, panting.

'Welcome aboard,' she answered without taking her eyes off the climber.

'Thanks for giving me a moment of your time.' I held on tight to a deep crack in the wall, leaned out cautiously and peered down. Only six metres and yet I felt the pull.

'Afraid of heights?' asked Victoria Hässel, still without having looked at me as far as I could tell.

'Isn't everybody?' I asked.

'Some more than others.'

I looked up at her climbing partner. A boy who looked to be quite a bit younger than her. And – judging by his uncertain footwork and the firm grip she kept on the belay device and rope – he had rather more to learn from her about climbing than the other way round. It was hard to judge Victoria Hässel's own age – anything from thirty-five to forty-five. She certainly looked strong. Almost skinny, long-limbed, but with a muscular back under the taut training top. Sinewy underarms, resin on her hands and wearing climbing breeches. She had given my suit and brown leather shoes a rather disapproving look. I could feel my hair being blown about in the wind. Her own was held under a knitted cap.

'Lot of climbers,' I said with a nod in the direction of the wall.

'Usually more,' said Victoria, and focused her gaze on her climber again. 'But there's too much wind today, a lot of people sitting in the cafes.' She nodded in the direction of the white-whipped sea.

From here we had a view of pretty much everything. The main road, the cars, Massouri centre, people like tiny black ants down there. Along the bare hillside below us I could see climbers approaching along the track.

'You might not believe this,' said Victoria, 'but when the wind's like this the ropes can blow right up and end high up in the mountain and snag up there.'

'If you say so then I'll believe it.'

'Believe it,' she said. 'What's this about, Mr Balli?'

'Oh, that can wait until your climber is down.'

'It's an easy passage, go ahead, talk.'

'I seem to remember hearing there's a rule that you should concentrate on your climber when you're securing the rope.'

54

'Thanks for the advice,' she said with a crooked smile. 'But why not just leave that to me?'

'Fair enough,' I said. 'But can I point out that your climber just clipped the wrong way round onto that last carabiner?'

Victoria Hässel looked sharply at me. Looked up at the carabiner I was talking about. Realised I was right and that the rope was running in the wrong direction. If he fell and he was unlucky the rope could slip out of the carabiner and he would keep on falling.

'I saw that,' she lied. 'Any moment now he'll hook the rope into the next carabiner and then he'll be secure.'

I coughed. 'Looks like the crux is coming up now, and if you ask me it looks as if it might give him trouble. If he falls there and the carabiner doesn't take the fall, then the next one's so low it won't stop him before he hits the ground. Agree?'

'Alex!' she shouted.

'Yes?'

'You've threaded the rope the wrong way round on the previous carabiner. Don't go any higher. Try to climb down and clip it on right!'

'I think I better carry on up to the next bolt and clip on the right way there.'

'No, Alex, don't . . .'

But Alex had already moved away from the good fingertip holds and was on his way up to a large downward sloping hold which probably looked good to him but which, to the trained eye, appeared to have too much resin over it from where climbers before him had tried and failed to get a hold. And from where he was dangling there were no possibilities of retreat. His trouser legs flapped. Not because of the wind but as a result of the stress reaction climbers call 'the sewing machine' which, sooner or later, affects everybody. I watched as Victoria took up as much of the rope as she could to make it as short as possible, but it was too little, Alex would hit our shelf.

'Alex, you have a foothold up on the right!' shouted Victoria, who had also realised what was about to happen. But it was too late, Alex was about to get chicken wings, the elbows rose up, a sure sign that his strength had given out.

'He's falling, you've got to jump,' I said quietly.

'Alex!' she called, paying no attention to me. 'Get your foot up, then you'll make it!'

I grabbed hold of her harness with both hands.

'What the fuck are you –' she snarled, half turning towards me.

My gaze was fixed on Alex. He screamed. And fell. I dragged Victoria backwards, spun her round me like a hammer thrower and tossed her off the shelf. Her short sharp shriek drowned out Alex's longer howl. The logic was simple: I had to get her somewhere lower as quickly as possible so that her body weight could arrest his fall before he hit the ground.

Both the part of the rope on its way up and the part travelling down tensed, and then suddenly all was silence. The screams, the shouts exchanged between the other climbers, the very wind itself seemed to be holding its breath.

I looked up.

Alex was hanging in the rope some way up the face. The reverse-mounted hook had held him after all. OK, so today I didn't save anybody's life. I stepped to the edge of the ledge and looked down at Victoria Hässel. She was dangling on her harness on the rope below the locking mechanism two metres below me and staring up, her eyes dark with shock.

'Sorry,' I said.

'Thanks,' I said to Victoria as she poured coffee from a Thermos into two plastic cups and handed one to me.

She had sent Alex to join a team higher up the mountain while she and I remained sitting on the ledge.

'I'm the one who should say thanks.'

'For what? The hook held the rope, so it would have worked out all right anyway. And you banged your knee.'

'But you did the right thing.'

I shrugged. 'We'll let that be our consolation, right?'

She gave a crooked smile and blew on her coffee. 'So you're a climber?'

'Was,' I said. 'Haven't touched stone in almost forty years.'

'Forty years is a long time. What happened?'

'Yeah, what happened? What happened here, by the way? I read there was a fatal accident.'

As unpleasant as the subject was, Victoria Hässel grabbed the chance to talk about something she knew wasn't what I had come to talk to her about.

'It was a classic mistake. They forgot to check the length of the route against the length of the rope, and not even put a knot in the end of the rope. On the way down the safety man didn't notice there was no more rope left until it was too late. With no knot in the end of the rope it ran out through the belay device, leaving the climber in free fall. Eight metres, you might think you would survive that. But he landed head first on the stone and in that case even two metres can be enough.'

'Human error,' I said.

'Isn't it always? When was the last time you heard it was the rope that broke or the bolts that came loose from the rock?'

'True enough.'

'It's just too fucking awful.' She shook her head. 'But all the same. I read somewhere that in places where there's been a climbing fatality, you often see a marked increase in the number of climbers there.'

'Really?'

'Not many people say it out loud. But if there wasn't a certain amount of risk involved, you wouldn't get many people climbing.'

'Adrenaline junkies?'

'Yes and no. I don't think it's fear we become addicted to but control. The feeling of mastering danger, mastering our own fate. Of exerting a control we don't have over the rest of our lives. We are slightly heroic because we don't make mistakes in critical situations.'

'Right up until the day we lose control and make that mistake,' I said and took a sip of coffee. It was good. 'If, that is, it is a mistake.'

'Yes,' she said quietly.

'Franz rang you eight times that night after he and Julian had quarrelled. The next day Julian was missing. What did he want?'

'I don't know. Arrange a climb maybe. Maybe he didn't have a partner after the quarrel.'

'According to his call log you never rang back. But you rang Julian's phone. Why?'

She pulled on a fleece jumper and warmed her hands around the coffee cup. She nodded slowly. 'They are similar, Franz and Julian. And yet different. Julian is easier to talk to. But I called just to make sure people hadn't forgotten the most obvious possibility, that Julian might be somewhere and have his phone with him.'

'Of course,' I said. 'Sure, they're similar and yet different. They obviously have different tastes in music. Led Zeppelin and . . .' I had already forgotten that crooner's name. 'But they like the same girl.'

'Guess they do.'

I looked at her. My jealousy radar wasn't picking up anything. So this wasn't about romance, she wasn't in love with Julian, or having a relationship with him. Franz had not been trying to get in touch with Victoria to ask for help in trying to spoil things for Julian and Helena. So what was it then?

'What do you think has happened?' she asked. 'Did Julian go for a swim and get into difficulties? Maybe on account of the concussion he suffered in the bar?'

I realised she was testing me. That my reply would determine the nature of her next move.

'I don't think so,' I said. 'I think Franz killed him.'

I looked at her. And as I half expected, she looked less shocked than she should have done if she knew nothing. She took a large mouthful of coffee, as though to hide the fact that, nevertheless, she still had to swallow.

'Well?' I said.

She looked around. The four members of the other rope team were well out of earshot in the wind. 'I saw Franz come home that evening.'

Here it was.

'I couldn't sleep and was sitting out on the balcony of my room on the other side of the road. I saw Franz park and get out of the car alone. Julian wasn't with him. Franz was carrying something, it looked like clothes. When he unlocked the door he looked round and I think he spotted me. I think he knew that I saw him. I think that's why he rang. He wanted to explain.'

'You didn't want to hear the explanation?'

'I didn't want to get involved. Not until we knew more, not until Julian had been found.'

'And then?'

She sighed. 'I thought that if Julian wasn't found, or he was found dead, then I'd come and tell you. Before would only complicate things. It would look as if I was accusing Franz of something criminal. We're a group of climbers who are friends, we trust one another, every day we trust each other with our lives. I might have ruined all that if I'd acted impulsively. Understand?'

'I understand.'

'Fuck.'

I followed her gaze down the mountainside. A person was on his way up the track from the road down there.

'It's Franz,' she said, standing up and waving.

I peered down. 'Sure?'

'You can tell by the Gay Rights hat.'

I peered again. Gay rights. The rainbow flag, not the Rastafarian.

'I thought he was hetero,' I said.

'You know you can support other people's rights besides your own?'

'And Franz Schmid does?'

'Don't know,' she said. 'But at least he follows St Pauli and the Bundesliga.'

'Sorry?'

'Football. His grandparents come from my city, Hamburg, and we've got two rival clubs. You've got HSV, which is the big, friendly, straight

59

rich club that Julian and I support. Then you've got the angry little lefty punk club St Pauli, with skull and crossbones as their badge, who openly support gay rights and everything else that irritates the Hamburg bourgeoisie. That seems to attract Franz.'

The figure down below had stopped and was looking up at us. I stood up, as though to make it clear this wasn't an ambush. He remained where he was and appeared to be studying us. I guessed that he had seen that the person waving was his climbing companion Victoria and was wondering who the other person was. Maybe he recognised the suit. He was probably expecting me to pop up again after I had read the text message that said straight out he had killed Julian. He had had enough time to find an explanation. I was anticipating something along the lines of that he had intended to arouse Helena's curiosity before telling her that it was a slight exaggeration, that in fact all he'd done was hit his brother on the head with a billiard ball. But now, seeing me with Victoria, it perhaps dawned on him that that wouldn't be enough.

The figure was in motion again, heading downwards.

'He probably thinks it's too windy,' said Victoria.

'Yes,' I said.

I saw him get into the hire car, saw the dust swirl up from the gravel track as the car disappeared. I sat down again and looked out over the sea. The white looked like frost roses on the windows in Oxford. Even up here you could taste the salt in the gusts of wind. Let him run, he wasn't going anywhere.

I was still at the station when Franz Schmid rang just before midnight.

'Where are you?' I asked, crossed to the partition and signalled to George that I had him on the line. 'You haven't answered my calls.'

'Signal's weak,' said Franz.

'So I hear,' I said.

I had called the public prosecutor in Athens who had issued an arrest warrant for Franz Schmid, but we hadn't found Franz in his rented room, or on the beach, or in any of the restaurants, and no one knew where he was. George had only two patrol cars and four policemen at his disposal, and until the weather improved we wouldn't be getting any reinforcements from the police on Kos, so I suggested we use base stations to locate Franz's mobile phone. But as George explained, there were so few base stations on Kalymnos they wouldn't do much to narrow down the search area.

'I paid a visit to Helena's restaurant,' said Franz. 'But her father was there and said I couldn't see her. Does that have anything to do with you?'

'Yes. I've told Helena and the family to keep away from you until this is over.'

'I told her father that my intentions were honourable, that I want to marry Helena.'

'We know that. He called us after you'd been there.'

'Did he tell you he gave me a letter from Helena?'

'He mentioned that too, yes.'

'You want to hear what she says?' Franz started to read without waiting for a reply: '"Dear Franz. Maybe for everyone there is one person in this life who is meant just for us, and who we only meet just the one time. You and I were never meant for each other, Franz, but I pray to God that you haven't killed Julian. Now that I know that he's the one for me I ask you on bended knees: if it is within your power, save Julian. Helena." You seem to have persuaded her that I am behind his disappearance, Balli. That I might have killed him. Do you realise that what you are doing is ruining my life? I love Helena more than I have ever loved anything, more than my own self. I just can't imagine a life without her.'

I listened. Though the wind was crackling in his phone I could hear waves. Could be anywhere on the island, of course.

'The best thing now would be for you to hand yourself in to us in Pothia, Franz. If you are innocent it would be in your own best interests.'

'And if I'm guilty?'

'Then it will still be in your own best interests to hand yourself in. No matter what, you can't get away, you're on an island.'

In the silence that followed I listened to the waves. They sounded different to the waves below my hotel room – but different in what way?

'Julian isn't innocent either,' said Franz.

I exchanged a look with George. We had both heard it. Is, not was. But a clue like that isn't reliable. I have heard several killers refer to their victims as though they were still alive, and perhaps they still are for them. Or more accurately: I know that a dead man can be the constant companion of his killer.

'Julian lied. He claimed he'd been in touch with Helena earlier that evening using his own phone, told her everything, and that the two of them were now in love. He wanted me to give her up without a fight. I know, of course, that Julian is a liar and a womaniser, that he'll stab you in the back to get what he wants, but this time he made me so angry. So angry, you have no idea how it feels . . .'

I didn't respond.

'Julian robbed me of the best thing I ever had,' said Franz. 'Because I haven't had that, Mr Balli. He was always the one who got them. Don't ask me why, we were born identical, but all the same he had something I didn't. Something he picked up along the way, a crossroads where he was given light and I got darkness, and then we went our separate ways. And he had to have even her . . .'

The waves were breaking in the same brutal way as they did against the rocks outside my hotel. The sound was more long-drawn-out, that was the difference. The waves rolled. Franz Schmid was on a beach.

'So I condemned him,' he said. 'But I'm a Californian, so I didn't condemn him to death, but to life imprisonment. Isn't that a suitable punishment for ruining a life? Isn't that the punishment you would have handed out yourself, Balli? Yes? No? Or aren't you an opponent of the death penalty?'

I didn't reply. Noticed George was looking at me.

'I'm letting Julian rot in his own little love-prison,' said Franz. 'And I've thrown the key away. Although life sentence . . . The kind of life he has now, that won't last long.'

'Where is he?'

'What you said about me not being able to get away . . .'

'Where is he, Franz?'

'. . . that isn't quite accurate. I'm about to fly out of here on flight nine nineteen, so farewell, Nikos Balli.'

'Franz, tell us where – Franz? Franz!'

'Did he hang up?' asked George, who was on his feet.

I shook my head. Listened. Nothing but wind and waves now.

'The airport is still closed?' I asked.

'Of course.'

'Have you heard of flight nine nineteen?'

George Kostopoulos shook his head.

'He's alone on a beach,' I said.

'Kalymnos is full of beaches. And at night when it's stormy you won't find a single person on any of them.'

'A long, shallow beach. It sounds as though the waves are breaking far out and rolling in for some distance.'

'I'll call Christine and ask her, she's a surfer.'

The car that had been rented in Franz Schmid's name was found next morning.

It was parked in a turning circle by a sandy beach midway between Pothia and Massouri. A trail of footprints, still visible despite the wind, led from the driver's side directly into the sea. George and I stood in the gusting wind and watched the divers struggling against the breakers. At the southern end of the beach the waves washed up against sloping, slippery rocks which, further inland, reared up in a vertical wall, a yellow-brown limestone wall that reached all the way to the top where the airport was. Further along the beach, Christine with her golden retriever was trying to pick up a trail. The dog had been born with only one working eye, she had told me during a coffee break at the station, that's why she named him Odin. And when I asked her why she had chosen Odin instead of something one-eyed from our own mythology, such as Polyphemus, she looked at me and said: 'Odin is shorter.'

According to George, Odin was a good tracker. Christine had taken him into Franz and Julian's room so he would know which scent to follow, and when we reached the beach he ran straight over to the car and stood there barking until George managed to get the door open. Inside the car we found Franz Schmid's clothes: shoes, trousers, underwear, the rainbow-patterned St Pauli cap and a jacket with his phone and wallet.

'So he was right,' said George. 'He did manage to get away.'

'Yes,' I said as my gaze glided over the foaming breakers. George had got hold of two divers from the local club. One of them was signalling with his hand to the other and trying to say something, but the sound of the waves drowned him out.

'You think this is where he dumped Julian's body?' asked George.

'Maybe. If he killed him.'

'You're thinking about what he said about imprisoning his brother for life instead?'

'Maybe he did. Or maybe not. Maybe he exposed Julian to a situation in which he knew that Julian would not just die but suffer first.'

'For example?'

'I don't know. The rage of jealousy is like love. It's a madness that can make people do things they would normally never dream of doing.'

My gaze switched to the rocks, sloping and polished smooth by the waves. Franz could have waded over there, come ashore again someplace that left no footprints and got away. On flight nine nineteen? What did that mean? To get up to the airport he would have had to either return to the road or climb straight up.

Without a rope.

Free solo.

I couldn't help it; I closed my eyes and saw Trevor fall.

Opened them again quickly so as not to see him hit the ground.

Concentrated.

Franz Schmid had perhaps stood here too, seen and thought the same as me. That the airport is closed. That every exit route is blocked. Apart from this one. The last one. But it's difficult to just swim out to sea and drown yourself. It takes time, it takes willpower not to submit to the survival instinct and turn.

'We found this in the shallows.'

George and I turned. It was one of the divers. He was holding up a gun.

George took it, turned it over a couple of times. 'Looks old,' he said, prodding at the underside where the magazine was.

'Luger, Second World War,' I said and took the gun from him. There was no rust on it, and the way the water pearled on it showed that it was still well oiled, so it couldn't have been lying long in the sea. I pressed the release catch on the side of the trigger guard, removed the magazine and handed it to George. 'Eight if it's full.'

George squeezed out the bullets. 'Seven,' he said.

I nodded. Felt an infinite sadness come over me. The wind was forecast to ease by tomorrow evening, and the sun to go on shining, but inside me it had clouded over. I could usually tell whether it was just passing, or a new period of darkness was on its way. But right at that moment I didn't know.

'Flight nine nineteen,' I said.

'What?'

'That's the calibre of those bullets you're holding in your hand.'

When I rang my chief in the Homicide Department with my report, he told me that the press in Athens were on the case, a number of journalists and photographers were in Kos and just waiting for the weather to fair up enough for a boat to take them over.

I headed back to my hotel in Massouri and ordered a bottle of ouzo for my room. I drink any brand apart from the now unfortunately commercialised and watered-down Ouzo 12, but I was pleased when I saw they actually had my favourite Pitsiladi.

As I drank I reflected over how strange it had all been. A murder case with two dead, but no bodies. No invasive press, no harassed chief and no stressed investigating groups. No vague lab technicians and pathologists, no hysterical next of kin. Only a storm and silence. I hoped that storm could last forever.

After I'd drunk almost half the bottle I went down to the bar so as not to drink the rest. I saw Victoria Hässel sitting at a table with some people from the other climbing group I had seen the previous day. I sat at the bar and ordered a beer.

'Excuse me?'

British accent. I half turned. A man, smiling, check shirt, white hair but in good shape for his age, around sixty. I'd seen several like him here, English climbers of the old school. They grew up climbing trad, meaning routes without bolts permanently fixed to the mountain, where they had to provide for their own safety in cracks and holes. On gritstone in the Lake District, where the routes were graded not only by how hard they were to climb but also how great the danger to life was. Where it rained, or was too cold, or was so hot that the eggs of a particularly bloodthirsty type of mosquito hatched and ate you alive. Englishmen loved it.

'Do you remember me?' said the man. 'We were in the same rope team near Sheffield. Must have been in '85 or '86.'

I shook my head.

'Come on,' he said with a laugh. 'I can't recall your name but I remember you were climbing with Trevor Biggs, he's a local lad. And that French girl who just flew up those slopes the rest of us had such a struggle with.' His face suddenly became serious as if something had occurred to him. 'Bloody back luck about Trevor, by the way.'

'I think you're getting me mixed up with someone else, sir.'

For a moment the Englishman stood there, open-mouthed and with an expression of mild surprise on his face. I could see his brain feverishly scanning his book of memories in search of his mistake. Then, as though he had found it, he nodded slowly. 'My apologies.'

I turned back to the bar and in the mirror saw that he sat down with his climbing companions and their climbing wives. Said something and nodded in my direction. They resumed their conversation and they passed around the local guidebook with the climbing routes marked. It looked like a good life.

My gaze moved on to one of the other tables and met Victoria Hässel's.

She sat there dressed in the climber's evening outfit: clean climbing clothes. Her hair, which had earlier in the day been hidden under her cap, was blonde, long and flowing. She sat turned towards me, looked as though she had temporarily absented herself from the conversation. She held my gaze. I don't know if she was waiting for something. A signal. Information about the Schmid case. Or just a nod of recognition.

I saw that she was on the point of standing up, but I was ahead of her and had already placed my euros on the bar. I slipped off the bar stool and left. Back in my room I locked the door.

In the middle of the night I was awoken by a loud bang, like a gunshot. I sat up in bed, my heart beating furiously. It was the window sash; a gust of wind must finally have torn it loose. I lay awake and thought of Monique. Monique and Trevor. I didn't finally get back to sleep until daylight.

'The forecast is for the wind to drop,' said George and poured a coffee for me. 'You'll probably be able to make it over to Kos tomorrow.'

I nodded and looked out of the station window. Harbour life seemed strangely unaffected by the fact that the island was to all intents and purposes cut off for the third day running. But that's how it is, life goes on, even – or perhaps especially – when you think it unliveable.

Christine and one of the constables entered and joined us.

'You were right, George,' she said. 'Schmid bought the Luger from Marinetti. He recognised Franz from the photo and says he was in the shop in the afternoon the day before Julian was reported missing. He got the impression Franz was a collector. He bought the Luger and a pair of Italian handcuffs left over from the war. Marinetti swears, of course, that he thought the Luger had been spiked.'

George nodded and looked contented rather than annoyed. When I'd wondered how and not least why Franz had managed to carry a handgun with him on the plane from California, George had suggested we check Marinetti's antique shop in Pothia. According to George, Marinetti had a cellar so full of antiques dating from the long years of the Italian and then the German occupation of Kalymnos that he hardly knew just exactly what he had.

'Can we say the case is solved now?' enquired Christine.

George turned to me as though forwarding the question.

'Case closed,' I said. 'But not solved.'

'No?'

I shrugged. 'We have, for example, no body to give us final proof of what we think has happened. Maybe the two brothers are sitting on a plane back to the USA and laughing at us after the greatest practical joke ever.'

'You don't believe that,' said George.

'Absolutely not. But as long as there are other possibilities, there will always be a doubt. The physicist Richard Feynman says we can't be absolutely certain about anything at all, the best we can do is presume with varying degrees of certainty.'

'But if there is a doubt, what do we do about it?' asked Christine, who actually looked quite upset about it.

'Nothing,' I said. 'We content ourselves with a reasonable degree of certainty and set to work on the next case.'

'Doesn't that leave you –' Christine stopped, looked as though she was afraid she might be about to go too far.

'Frustrated?' I asked.

'Yes.'

I had to smile. 'Remember, I'm the Jealousy Man. Usually I'm around for the first or second day of a murder investigation. I'm the man with the divining rod, the one who indicates the spot on the ground where water might be found, and then leaves the digging to others. I've had lots of training in leaving cases behind me without getting all the answers.'

Christine looked to be assessing me. I could see she didn't believe me.

'Am I jealous?' she asked, putting her hands on her hips and adopting a provocative expression.

'I don't know. You would have to tell me something first.'

'Such as what?'

'What you think might have made you jealous, for example.'

'What if I don't want to, what if it hurts me too much?'

'Then I would have no way of knowing,' I said, and clapped my hands together. 'And now, people, how about we get something to eat?'

'Right!' said George. But Christine carried on looking at me. She probably knew that I knew. The story behind those red eyes. She was jealous.

For the remainder of the day I wandered along narrow paths on the mountain on the southern side of the beach where we had found Franz Schmid's car and gun. The high, inaccessible limestone walls reminded me of the vaulted ceilings in Christ Church Cathedral in Oxford which, in their dark, English seriousness were so different from, for example, the exuberant brightness of the Mitropoli Cathedral in Athens. Maybe that's why – despite the fact that I am an atheist – I felt more at home in Christ Church. I spoke to my boss on the phone. He said they would send a detective and two techs the next day if the wind had dropped, and that he wanted me back, a woman had been murdered in Tzitzifies, and her husband couldn't provide an alibi. I advised him to put someone else on the case.

'The victim's family say they want you,' said my boss.

'Surely that's for us to decide.'

He said the name of the family. One of the shipping dynasties. I gave a sigh and hung up. I love my country, but some things just never change.

My eye caught an unusually broad overhang. Or more accurately: it was the overhang that caught my eye. I saw an elegant line running from a cleared belay station in towards the rock face. Here and there light from a metal glue-in bolt reflected the sunlight. Because of the overhang I couldn't quite locate the anchor, and because the mountains fell directly into the sea right next to the path and the belay station, I was unable to step any further out. But it had to be a long route, at least forty metres.

I looked down fifty or sixty metres to where the waves broke against the rocks. When the climber was lowered down from the anchor, he or she would have to swing back and forth so as to reach the belay station and not be lowered straight down into the sea. But what a beautiful route it was! In due course, as my gaze moved upward, my brain began automatically to analyse, to visualise the climbing movements the holds and contours would require. It was like turning over the ignition in a machine unearthed after being buried beneath ruins for years. Did it still work? I turned the key, pressed the accelerator. The climbing motor whined reluctantly, coughed, protested. But then it started. And the protests stopped. Now the muscles remembered and glowed with pleasure as the brain recalled climbing. I could see no other routes in the vicinity and guessed that most climbers thought it was a long way to travel just to climb one – even though spectacular – route. But I would have done it, even if it was the last route in my life.

The imaginary climb was still a presence in my body in the evening. I had ordered another bottle of Pitsiladi to my room. The wind had eased off slightly, the waves didn't beat quite so fiercely against the limestone, and in isolated pockets of complete silence I could hear music coming from down in the bar. I guessed Victoria Hässel would be there. I sat there. It was ten o'clock, and I had drunk enough to be able to go to bed.

On waking the next day, I could no longer hear the wind and the discordant fluting sounds from the cracks and pipes and chimneys I had become so used to.

I threw open the window. The sea was blue, no trace of white, and it was no longer raging but groaned. Pumped heavy, lazy rollers across the body of the land, like a lover after orgasm. The sea was tired. Like me.

I got back into bed and called down to Reception.

The ferry was running again, said the receptionist. The next departure was in one hour, and that would give me plenty of time to make the next plane to Athens, which left at three – should he order a taxi for me?

I closed my eyes. 'Let me order . . .' I began.

'Time?'

'No taxi. Two bottles of Pitsiladi.'

There was a brief silence.

'I'm afraid we've run out of that brand, Mr Balli. But we do have Ouzo 12.'

'No thanks,' I said and hung up.

I lay there for a while listening to the sea before calling down again.

'Have them sent up,' I said.

I drank slowly but steadily. My eyes followed the shadows in Telendos, how they moved, grew shorter, and then – as the afternoon came – stretched out again in what looked almost like a gesture of triumph. I thought of all the stories I had listened to in the course of my work. That it was true what they said, a confession is a story that's just waiting for an audience.

When darkness fell I went down into the bar. As I had expected, Victoria Hässel was sitting there.

I met Monique in Oxford. She was studying literature and history, like me, but she was in the year above me so we didn't attend the same lectures. But in places like that the foreigners gather and are drawn together, and soon we had met each other so many times socially that I plucked up the courage to ask her out for a beer.

She made a face. 'Well, it'll have to be a Guinness.'

'You like Guinness?'

'Probably not, I hate beer. But if we have to drink beer then it's got to be Guinness. It's supposed to be the worst of the lot, but I promise I'll be more positive than I sound.'

Monique's logic was that everything ought to be tried, and with an open mind; that way it can be dismissed afterwards with new insight and a good conscience. That went for everything; ideas, literature, music, food and drink. And me, I have thought with hindsight. For we were as different as can be imagined. Monique was the sweetest, most captivating girl I had ever met. She was bubbly and good-humoured, and so kind to everyone around her that all I could do was give up and accept the role of bad cop. She was so unaffected by her upper-class background, her matchless intelligence and almost irritatingly flawless beauty that you had no option but to like her in spite of it all. And when she looked at you, looked at *you*, then of course there was nothing for it but just to give up. Abandon all resistance and fall head over heels in love. She treated her many suitors with a sweet mixture of tactful consideration and mild rejection that made you feel that, behind her principle of trying everything there was something else, something that was natural and not principled. Monique was saving herself for the right man, she was a virgin not from conviction but by inclination.

With me it was the other way round. I despised my promiscuous inclinations but couldn't resist them. Despite the fact that I was shy, creepy in the opinion of some, and with my rather rigid and stiff formality could seem more English than Greek, my appearance was obviously attractive to members of the opposite sex. English girls especially fell for what they called my Cat Stevens looks, meaning the dark curls and brown eyes. But in addition to that – and I think it was this more than my appearance that caused them to open both their hearts and bedroom doors to me – was the fact that I had the ability to listen. Or more accurately, I was interested in listening. For me, who lived and breathed for all stories save my own, it was no great sacrifice to listen to young women's long monologues on privileged upbringings, the difficult relationship with Mother, doubts about their sexual orientation, the most recent unhappy love story, the flat in London she couldn't use any more now that Father had installed his young lover there, fake dilemmas and those hideous backstabbing friends who had gone off to St-Tropez without telling her. Or else – if I was a little luckier – about the longing to commit suicide, the existential compulsive-obsessive thoughts and the secret ambitions to write. Afterwards many of them wanted to have sex with me, especially if I had hardly opened my mouth. It was as though silence always worked to my advantage, being interpreted in the most favourable way possible. But these sexual intermezzos did nothing to improve my self-confidence. On the contrary, they only heightened my self-contempt. These girls went to bed with me because my silence meant that they could imagine me in whatever way they wanted. I had everything to lose by revealing who I was; a shy whoremonger devoid of self-confidence, substance or spine, just a pair of brown eyes and long ears. And before long they noticed how my gloominess, my natural darkness, extinguished the light in the room so that they had to get out, away. I can't blame them.

With Monique all that changed. I was changed. For example, I began to talk. From the moment we helped each other to drink that first nasty-tasting Guinness we had conversations, with the accent on *we*, and not those monologues I had grown used to. And the topics were different too. We talked about matters outside ourselves, like the self-preserving mechanisms of poverty, like the human belief that morality – meaning, in particular, one's own morality – represented some kind of permanent quality. Or how we more or less consciously avoid learning anything that might upset our political and religious convictions. Books we'd read, we'd not read, ought to read because they were good. Or overrated. Or simply bad but useful.

In the degree to which we spoke of ourselves and our own lives, it was always related to the general, to an idea or a conception, to *la condition humaine*, as Monique called it, referring not to my own favourite French writer André Malraux but to the political philosopher Hannah Arendt. We tossed these and other writers at each other not in any competitive sense but as a way of testing out one's own original thinking on a person you trusted enough to dare to be mistaken, and to admit as much. The sparks could really fly, and it was after one such furious disagreement that she, late one night and after a few glasses of wine in her room, took a swipe at me, and then put her arms around me, and for the first time we kissed.

The following day she gave me an ultimatum. If I wouldn't be her boyfriend then we couldn't go on meeting. It wasn't because she was desperate or in love with me, but because an arrangement such as that involved a mutual sexual exclusivity, something that was a non-negotiable demand for her, in that she was pathologically frightened of sexual diseases, so afraid, in fact, that there was a fair chance the fear would spoil and shorten her life sooner than any sexual disease. I laughed, she laughed, and I accepted her ultimatum.

It was Monique who introduced me to climbing. She had a father who from an early age would take her to classic modern sports climbing locations in Verdon and Céüse.

In all honesty in England there isn't much climbing, and certainly not in and around Oxford, but my fellow Led Zeppelin fan Trevor Biggs, the slightly chubby, good-natured, red-haired son of a factory worker from Sheffield, told me of friends that climbed in the Peak District close to his home town. Trevor turned into a kind of regular wingman for me. With his outgoing manner and warm sense of humour he attracted people – guys as well as girls – who would join us at our table. Often it was these girls who, after a time, turned their attention to me. Trevor also owned a run-down but still functioning Toyota HiAce van, the outstanding virtue of which was that it had seat warmers. When I suggested to him that he could combine climbing with visits to his parents and in addition share the petrol costs with two others he went for the idea immediately.

That was the start of three years of weekend trips and climbing. The drive didn't take more than two and a half hours, but to get as much climbing as possible out of the weekends we spent the nights in a tent, in the van or – if the weather was particularly bad – at Trevor's parents' house.

In the course of that first year I soon became better than Trevor, perhaps because I was more dedicated and more concerned to impress – or at least not to disappoint – Monique. She was and remained far superior to us. Not because she was particularly strong, but that small, neat body flew up the walls with the technique, balance and footwork of a ballet dancer. She understood climbing in a way that Trevor and I could only dream of. I, and in due course Trevor, did not really begin to get going until we were able to find sites where the climbing was done in handholds and ledges, where what was needed was brute physical strength. But it was Monique's advice, her encouragement and her ability to share in our joys and minor triumphs that kept me and Trevor going. And the sound of her sparkling, happy laughter echoing between the rock faces because Trevor or I had once again fallen and dangled there at the end of a rope, cursing in frustration and asking to be lowered. Not because we wanted to give up but so we could attempt the whole thing once again, from the bottom up.

At times – perhaps because Monique felt he needed it more than me – it seemed as though she were a touch more enthusiastic in her praise when it was Trevor who managed something new rather than me. But that was fine. The fact that she was like that was one of the reasons I loved her so much.

It was in our third year that I realised Trevor had begun to take his climbing seriously. I had mounted a so-called fingerboard above the door to strengthen my fingers. Trevor never touched it. But now, quite often, I would see him dangling there. Sometimes it almost felt as though I caught him doing it red-handed, as though he didn't want me to know that he was practising as much as he was. But his body betrayed him. When the sun shone and it became so hot on those Peak District rock faces that Trevor and I pulled off our T-shirts, I could see that his formerly chubby upper body was still a dazzling milk-white, but now all the fat was gone. Well-defined muscles rippled like steel cables under his skin when he, in his almost robotic way, forced a way up the overhangs on routes where even Monique herself had to admit defeat. I still had the advantage on him on the vertical routes because I had been careful to study Monique's technique, but there was no doubt about it, the competition between Trevor and me had grown much more even. Because that's what it had become: a competition.

It was also around this time that I began partying a little too much. Meaning, of course, I did too much social drinking. My father was a recovering alcoholic. It was something I had known about since childhood, and he had tried to warn me off it. But his warning had been to avoid drink when I was feeling bad, not happy, like I was now. Whatever it was, the combination of a lot of climbing, a lot of Monique and a lot of 'partying' began to affect my studies. Monique was the first to point it out, and this became the occasion of our first quarrel. Which I won. Or at least, she was crying when she left because I'd got the last word.

Next day I apologised to her, laid the blame on Greek social norms for my use of exaggeratedly harsh words, and promised to party less and study more.

For a while I kept that promise. I even dropped a weekend in the Peak District to catch up on my studies. It was tough, but it had to be done, the exam was just round the corner and I knew my father was expecting results at the very least the equal of my older brother's, who he had got into Yale and who was now sat on the board of the family business. All the same, this enforced swotting made me almost hate the things I actually loved, literature in particular. I envied Monique and Trevor their days off and was almost relieved when they came back early on the Saturday evening because of the rain and said that they'd hardly climbed a metre.

I continued to give priority to my studies, so much so that at one point Monique complained. It pleased me, but it was a strange pleasure, and had an even stranger side effect. From the start I felt Monique had more power over me than I had over her. It was something I accepted and attributed to the fact that she was a greater catch for me than I was for her. So I came out on top there too. What was interesting now was that the less time I spent with her, the more that seemed to even out the balance of power between us. So I buried myself again, redoubled my studies, and when the day of the big exam came along and I left the exam room after five hours, I knew that what I had handed in was something that would make not just my tutor and father proud, but Monique too. I bought a bottle of cheap champagne and ran to her room on the first floor of her hall of residence. Led Zeppelin's 'Whole Lotta Love' was playing so loudly when I knocked that she didn't hear me. Overjoyed – because it was I who had given her that record, and if there was anything I felt at that moment it was a whole lotta love! – I ran round to the back. Even with the bottle of champagne in one hand I easily climbed the tree that was outside her window. Once I was high enough to see inside I waved the bottle and was on the point of calling her name and telling her I loved her, but the words stuck in my throat.

Monique was always thrillingly vocal when we made love, and the walls between the rooms so thin we used to play music to cover the sounds.

I saw Monique, but she didn't see me, her eyes were closed.

Trevor didn't see me either because he had his back to me. That milky-white, now muscular back. His hips were moving, pumping up and down almost in time to 'Whole Lotta Love'.

I remained in a trance until I heard a crash and, looking down, saw the champagne bottle had smashed against the cobblestones below. Shards of glass protruded from a white, bubbling puddle. I don't know why the thought that someone might see me caused me to panic, but I slid rather than climbed down, and the moment my feet hit the ground I ran, I fled.

I ran all the way back to the shop where I had bought the champagne, bought two bottles of Johnnie Walker with the last of the money my mother had sent me and ran to my hall of residence. Locked myself in my room and began to drink.

It was dark outside when Monique knocked on my door. I didn't open, called out that I was in bed, could it wait until tomorrow? She said there was something she had to talk to me about, but I said I didn't want to take the chance of her catching what I had. Terrified of infection as she was she left, after asking me, through the door, how the exam had gone.

Trevor knocked on my door too. When I called out that I was ill, and he asked if there was anything I needed, I whispered 'a friend', turned over in bed and called out 'No thanks'.

'Hope you'll be better for our climbing trip on Friday,' said Trevor.

Friday. That gave me three days. Three days to dive down into a darkness I didn't even know existed. Three days in the grip of jealousy. Each time I breathed out it tightened its grip a little more, made it harder to breathe in fresh air. Because that's what jealousy is, it's a boa constrictor. When I was a kid and my father took me to the cinema to see the Disney version of *The Jungle Book*, I got very confused because in the Rudyard Kipling book my mother read to me so many, many times Kaa the snake was nice! My father explained that all creatures have two faces, it's just that we can't always see the other one, not even in ourselves. But I had begun to see my other face. Because as the lack of oxygen over these three days destroyed my brain I began to think thoughts I had no idea were inside me, but which must have been there all the time, in the dregs of my personality. And I saw the other face of the good snake Kaa. The jealousy that tempted, manipulated, hypnotised with wild fantasies of revenge that sent thrilling shivers through the body and needed only another swig of whisky to keep it going.

When Friday came along and I shook off my depression, pronounced myself recovered and rose as though from the dead, I was no longer the same Nikos Balli. No one could see it in me, not even Trevor and Monique when I greeted them at lunch as though nothing had happened and said the weather forecast for the weekend looked great, we would have a fantastic weekend. As we ate I didn't listen to Trevor and Monique as they spoke in codes they thought I couldn't understand, instead I listened to a couple of girls on the other side of the table who were talking about one of their friends' new boyfriend. I listened to the words they chose, the adjective that was a little too strong, the slightly too pleased response when one spoke disapprovingly to the other of their mutual friend, the anger that made the sentences shorter, more biting, without the flow that comes with calm thought. They were jealous. It was so simple. And I was not basing my new instinct on psychoanalysis but on pure, concrete verbal analysis. No, I was no longer the same. I had been somewhere. I had seen things there. Seen and learned. I had become the Jealousy Man.

'Pretty sad story that,' said Victoria Hässel as she pulled on her panties and started looking round for the rest of her clothes. 'Did the two of them become a couple?'

'No,' I said. I turned in the bed and lifted first an empty then an almost empty bottle of Ouzo 12 from the bedside table and filled the dram glass. 'It was Monique's last year and her final exam was just a few days away. She didn't do very well, but after that she went back home to France, and neither Trevor nor I ever saw her again. She married a Frenchman, had kids, and as far as I know lives somewhere in Brittany.'

'And you – who studied literature and history – you became a policeman?'

I shrugged. 'I had a year left at Oxford, but when I went back for the autumn the partying thing got out of hand again.'

'Broken heart?'

'Maybe. Maybe it was just that the closeness of the memories was too strong. Whatever, the only thing that seemed to matter was to keep getting smashed. Once I even thought of flight nine nineteen.'

'Sorry?'

'When things were at their worst I would squeeze this stone I had picked up from the ground somewhere in the Peak District.' I held up a clenched fist to demonstrate. 'Concentrated on transferring the pain into the stone, let it suck it all out.'

'Did that help?'

'At least I didn't take flight nine nineteen.' I emptied the dram glass. 'Instead I dropped out in the middle of the autumn term and took a flight to Athens. Worked for a while in my father's firm, and then enrolled at the Police Academy. My father and the rest of the family thought it was some kind of delayed adolescent rebellion. But I knew that I had been given something, a gift, or a curse, something that might possibly be of some use to me. And the discipline and training at the Academy helped keep me away from . . .' I nodded towards the bottle of ouzo. 'But that's enough about me. Tell me about yourself.'

Victoria Hässel straightened up at the end of the bed and buttoned up a pair of freshly washed climbing pants and looked at me in disbelief. 'In the first place I'm going climbing now. In the second place you got me to talk about myself and nothing else but myself for over four hours in the bar yesterday. Have you really forgotten that?'

I shook my head, smiling as I tried in vain to recall it. 'I just wanted to know more,' I lied, and saw that she knew I was lying.

'Cute,' she said, walked round the bed and kissed me on my high forehead. 'Later, maybe. You smell of my perfume, just so you know.'

'My sense of smell is terrible.'

'And mine is wonderful. But don't worry, I come out easily in the wash. See you later today? Adio.'

I wondered whether to tell her that finally, two days after the ferry and the planes had begun to leave Kalymnos again, I had booked a seat on a flight to Athens. But it wouldn't have changed anything, would just have meant a little more play-acting.

'Adio, Victoria.'

George picked me up as arranged an hour before my flight departed. It was a ten- or twelve-minute drive, and I still only had hand luggage.

'Better now?' he asked as I got into the car.

I had called Athens and explained that I was sick, that they should put someone else on the Tzitzifies case. I rubbed my face.

'Yes,' I said, and it was true, I didn't feel at all bad. Maybe Ouzo 12 does taste like crap, but I'll give it this, the hangover is nothing like as bad as you get with Pitsiladi. And I had drunk myself clear. For a while, the clouds were gone.

I asked him to drive slowly. I wanted to enjoy my last view of Kalymnos. It really was lovely here.

'You should come in the spring, when the flowers bloom, and there's more life and colour in the mountains.'

'I like it the way it is,' I said.

When we reached the airport, George announced that the plane from Athens was delayed, since there was no sign of it on the runway. He parked, and suggested we sit in his car until we saw the plane land.

We sat in silence and looked out on Palechora, the town made of stone.

'People from Kalymnos used to hide out up there sometimes in the old days,' said George. 'From pirates. Sieges could last for weeks, months. They had to sneak out at night to fetch water from camouflaged wells. They say children were conceived and born up there. But it was a prison, no question about it.'

A swishing in the air above us. A swishing through my head.

The ATR-72 and the thought arrived at the same moment.

'The prison of love,' I said.

'What?'

'Both Franz and Julian had dates with Helena in one of the buildings in Palechora. Franz said he had sentenced his brother to life imprisonment in his own prison of love. That could mean . . .'

The brief roaring of the propellers drowned out my words as the plane landed and was waved in behind us, but from the look on George's face I could see he had already understood where I was heading.

'I guess this means,' he said, 'that you won't be taking the plane to Athens after all?'

'Call Christine. Tell her to bring Odin with her.'

From a distance Palechora looked like a true ghost town. Grey-black, lifeless and petrified, something the Medusa had looked at. But now, close up – as happens in murder cases too – the details, the nuances and colours began to appear. And the smell.

George and I hurried through the ruins towards one of the houses that was still more or less intact. Christine was standing in the doorway holding Odin, who was barking and keen to get inside. She had been the first to arrive, along with two members of the mountain rescue team, and we'd been communicating over the walkie-talkie. We had stepped up our pace after she reported her find but still had a hundred-metre climb before we were there. They made the discovery in what was probably Palechora's only cellar. Later I learned that the cellar had been used to store dead bodies in during sieges, since the soil inside the fortress walls wasn't deep enough to bury them.

The first thing that struck me when George and I bent down and entered the low-ceilinged cellar, and before my eyes had adapted to the dark, was the stench.

Maybe my old eyes take a little longer to get dark-adapted than they used to, maybe that was why I was able to control my feelings as the sight of Julian Schmid gradually took shape in front of me, his naked body still partially covered by a dirty woollen blanket. One of the mountain rescue men was squatting beside him, but there was little he could do. Julian's arms reached stiffly above his head, hands clasped as though in prayer, fastened by handcuffs to an iron bolt in the stone wall.

'We're waiting for Teodore,' whispered George, as though this were an autopsy or a church service. 'He's bringing something to cut the handcuffs.'

I looked at the floor. A pool of faeces, vomit and urine. That was the source of the smell.

The figure on the floor coughed. 'Water,' he whispered.

Someone from the mountain rescue team had obviously already given him all he had, so I stepped forward and pressed my bottle against the dry lips. It was like seeing a half-dead mirror image of Franz. Or rather: Julian Schmid seemed thinner than his twin brother, had a large blue mark on his forehead, perhaps from that billiard ball, and his voice sounded different. Was it because his brother was an exact copy of himself that Franz was unable to kill Julian? Indeed, had it even made it easier for Franz to take his own life? I had my own reasons for think-ing so.

'Franz?' whispered Julian.

'He's gone,' I said.

'Gone?'

'Disappeared.'

'And Helena?'

'She's somewhere safe.'

'Can . . . one of you tell her? That I'm OK?'

George and I exchanged glances. I nodded to Julian.

'Thank you,' he said, and drank again. And as though the water ran straight through his head, tears began to trickle from his eyes. 'He didn't mean it.'

'What?'

'Franz. He . . . he just went crazy. I know it. It sometimes happens to him.'

'Maybe,' I said.

A crackle came from George's walkie-talkie and he went outside.

A moment later he put his head back in. 'The ambulance has arrived. It's waiting down on the road.' He disappeared again. The stench really was overpowering.

'I think that deep down Franz wanted you to be found,' I said quietly.

'You think so?' said Julian.

I knew then that he knew Franz was dead. And that this was the prayer he looked as though he had been praying, that I would tell him what he needed to hear. What he had to hear if he was ever to be whole again. So I did.

'He regretted it,' I said. 'He actually told me that you were here. He wanted me to rescue you. He had no way of knowing how slow on the uptake I was.'

'It hurts so much,' he said.

'I know,' I said.

'What can you do?'

I looked around. Picked up a grey stone from the ground and pressed it into his hands. 'You squeeze that. Imagine that it's drawing all the pain out of you.'

The bolt cutters arrived and Julian was taken away.

I called Helena and gave her the news that Julian had been found alive. As we were talking it struck me that never before had I, as a detective, broken the news to someone that a loved one had been found alive. But Helena's reaction wasn't dissimilar to what usually happened when I broke the news of a death: a few seconds silence while the brain probably searched for the reason for this misunderstanding, the reason why this couldn't possibly be true. And then – not finding one – the tears as the reality of the situation dawned on them. Even those who in time turned out to be the jealous guilty party would start to cry, often more disconsolate than the shocked innocent. But Helena's tears were different. They were tears of joy. A sunlit downpour. It stirred something within me, some vague memory, and I felt a lump in my throat. And as she sobbed her gratitude I had to cough in order to keep my voice steady.

In the afternoon, when I arrived at the hospital in Pothia, Helena was by the bedside and holding the hand of a Julian who was already looking better. Helena seemed to assume it was my razor-sharp intelligence that was responsible for his being saved. I didn't mention that it was probably my lack of imagination that meant he almost died.

I asked for a few words alone with Julian, and Helena grabbed my hand and kissed it before she left us.

Julian's account of the sequence of events was pretty much what I had been expecting.

On the way to hospital after the fight in the bar the quarrel with Franz flared up again. 'I lied,' said Julian. 'I said I had talked to Helena and told her everything, and she forgave me and told me she loved me. That he should just give up and forget about her as soon as he could. Yes, it was a lie, but I thought I would call Helena afterwards, and the result would in any case turn out to be the same. But Franz screamed that it was a lie, pulled in at the side of the road, opened the glove compartment and took out the pistol he had bought in Pothia.'

'Had you seen him like that before?'

'I have seen him furious, and we have fought, but I have never seen him like that, never so . . . crazy.' Julian's eyes were bright. 'But I don't blame him. I had fallen in love with that girl because he had told me about her, shown me pictures, praised her and built her up to the skies. And I stole her. There's no other way to put it. I betrayed them both, him and her. I would have done the same to him. No, I would have shot, I would have killed. Instead he forced me to drive to Chora and from there up to Palechora with a gun in my back. He had obviously had a look round when he was up here and found that cellar. And he chained me up there with the handcuffs he'd bought in Pothia.'

'And then he left you to die?'

'He said I could stay there until I rotted, then he left. Of course, I was terrified, but at that particular point in time I was more afraid for Helena than myself. Because he always came back.'

'What do you mean?'

'When we used to fight as kids he was always just that little bit stronger than me. Sometimes he would lock me up. In a room, or a cupboard. Once it was a chest. Said I would die there. But he always came back. He was so sorry, though of course he never showed it. And I was certain the same thing would happen this time too. Right up until about two or three days ago. I suddenly woke up and . . .' He looked at me. 'Well, I'm not the type that believes in spiritism, but from what me and Franz have experienced I'd be curious to find out what we know about telepathic communion between twins in a hundred years' time. Whatever, I simply knew something had happened to Franz. And when the hours and days went by and he didn't come back, I began to think I really was going to die there. You saved me, Mr Balli. I'll be forever in your debt.'

Julian extended a hand from under the duvet and took mine. I felt the stone I had given him pressed into my palm. 'In case you too should ever feel pain,' he said.

In the hospital corridor on the way out Helena stopped me and asked if she might invite me to dinner at their restaurant. I thanked her but explained that I was taking the last evening flight out of Kos.

It left me with a couple of hours left to kill before the ferry so I accompanied Christine to Julian's room in Massouri to fetch his clothes.

I stood in the street by the police car and watched the lovely sunset behind Telendos while Christine was inside the house. An elderly woman in a flowery dress carrying bags of shopping limped by and stopped.

'I hear you found one of the twins,' she said. 'The nice one.'

'Nice?'

'I do the cleaning and make the beds every morning at nine.' She nodded towards the house. 'Most of them have gone off climbing by then, but sometimes I woke the two of them. One was always grumpy, the other one just smiled and laughed and said I could come back and do it tomorrow. Julian, that was the nice one's name. I never found out what the other one was called.'

'Franz.'

'Franz.' She savoured the name.

'It's German,' I said.

'Well, apart from that Julian I don't like Germans. They screwed us during the war and they're screwing us again now. Treat us like we're bad tenants in their Europe who haven't paid the rent in a while.'

'Not a bad image,' I said, thinking as much of my own native country as of Germany.

'They act like they've changed,' she scoffed. 'A woman leader and all that stuff. But they're Nazis and they always will be.' She shook her head. 'One morning I saw handcuffs on the bedside table. No idea what that Franz used them for, something fascist I expect. Is he dead?'

'Maybe,' I said. 'Probably. Almost definitely.'

'Almost?' She looked at me, still a trace of that contempt for all Germans in her face. 'Isn't it the police's job to know?'

'Yes it is,' I said. 'And we know nothing.'

She waddled away, and I heard laughter from the other side of the road.

I turned and there, sitting on a veranda beneath a cypress tree, sat Victoria with her feet on the railings and a cigarette in the corner of her mouth.

'You get screwed?' she said with a laugh, puffing out smoke into the still dusk.

'You understand Greek?'

'No, but I understand body language.' With a slow, languorous gesture she tapped ash from her cigarette. 'Don't you?'

I thought of the night. I sobered up in the course of those hours. It was good. We were good to each other. A bit mean, but mostly good. 'Yes I do, I do.'

'See you later in the bar?'

I shook my head. 'I'm flying to Athens tonight.'

'Like a visit?'

From the look on her face I realised the question had just popped out. And she understood – or misunderstood – my hesitation in replying.

'Forget it.' She laughed again, and drew hard on her cigarette. 'You're married with kids and a dog in Athens. You don't want trouble and you won't get any.'

I realised she hadn't asked anything about my life now, and that I had spoken about the only thing that mattered to me: the past.

'I'm not all that afraid of trouble,' I said. 'But I'm old. Whereas you've got your whole life in front of you.'

'Yep, I'm a better deal for you than you would have been for me.'

'I would have ended up ahead,' I said and smiled.

'Adio again, Nikos.'

'Adio again, Monique.'

Not until I got into the car did I realise my slip of the tongue.

It was gone midnight by the time I let myself into my flat.

'I'm home,' I called out into the dark, dropped my bag onto the floor, went to the kitchen section of the big, open-plan room with its glass walls and its views of Kolonaki, one of the more fashionable districts of central Athens.

Took out the little box I had in my pocket, opened it and looked at the grey stone lying inside, like a jewel in a goldsmith's box.

I got a glass, opened the fridge, and the light fell across the parquet floor and reached across to the bookshelves and the heavy teak writing desk with the big Apple screen.

Inherited money.

I filled the glass with the freshly pressed juice my housekeeper makes, crossed to the computer and touched the keyboard. A big picture of three young people in front of a rock face in the Lake District appeared.

I clicked on the icons and checked the websites of the largest newspapers. All of them had extensive covering of developments in the Kalymnos murder case. My name didn't appear in any of them. Good.

I kissed my index finger and placed it on the cheek of the girl between the two boys on the screen and said aloud that now I was off to bed.

In the bedroom I put the box with the grey stone on the shelf above the bed, next to the other stone that lay there. The bed was so big and empty, the silk sheets looked so chilly that as I lay down I had the feeling I was about to swim out to sea.

Two weeks later I received a phone call from George Kostopoulos.

'A body's been found in the sea not far from the beach where Franz disappeared,' he said. 'Or actually, on land – the body was speared on one of the rocks where the waves break. It's exposed and people don't go there much, but it looks as though someone has started climbing along a route fifty or sixty metres above the rocks and fallen. A climber called it in.'

'I think I know where it is,' I said. 'Has the body been identified?'

'Not yet. It's so badly smashed up from lying there that I'm surprised the climber was even able to recognise it as human. My own first impression was that it was a dead dolphin. Skin, face, ears, sexual organs, all gone. But there's a hole in the skull that can hardly be anything but a bullet-hole.'

'It could still be a refugee from a boat.'

'I know, we had a few washed up here last year, but I doubt it. I've sent a DNA sample from the body, so we'll get the answer in a couple of days. I was just wondering . . .'

'Yeah?'

'If it matches the DNA profile from the saliva sample we took from Franz Schmid's water glass, what do we say?'

'We say we have made a positive identification.'

'But remember, we got that DNA through a . . . in an unauthorised manner.'

'Oh? As far as I remember we asked Franz Schmid and he gave it to us of his own free will.'

It was silent at the other end.

'Is that the way . . .' he began.

'Yes,' I said. 'That's the way we do it in Athens.'

The results arrived three days later.

According to the report, the DNA from the human remains on the rocks matched that voluntarily given to detectives by Franz Schmid in Pothia. My name was not mentioned.

I held the phone below the tablecloth as I read the news in order not to distract the woman who was in the process of telling me that she believed her husband's overdose must have been because he'd got his heart pills and his other medication mixed up, maybe because he was so confused by the young trainee at work he was planning to leave his family for.

I stifled a yawn and thought about that climbing route out there south of the beach. I had obtained a copy of the climbers' guide to Kalymnos and discovered that the route was called Where Eagles Dare, grade 7b. Even in the picture it looked fantastic. If I was ever going to get in good enough shape to climb it, it would take training and I would need to lose a few kilos. And for me to have time for that people would either have to take a break from killing each other, or else I would have to take a break. A long one.

Five Years Later

I looked out of the plane window. The island beneath was unchanged. A yellow block of limestone dropped into the sea by Poseidon to make the earth tremble.

But the skies were clouded over.

The weather was less stable in spring, the taxi driver told me on my way into Emporio, I would do better to come in the autumn. I smiled as I looked at the oleander bushes in full bloom on the hillsides and breathed in the scent of thyme.

Helena and Julian were standing on the steps of the restaurant with little Ferdinand as I emerged from the taxi. Julian smiled broadly while Helena embraced me as though she would never let go. We had exchanged emails regularly, by which I mean she told me how things were going, and I read her messages. Read the way I listened, and replied briefly, mostly follow-up questions, as was my habit when in conversation.

It hadn't been easy in the beginning, she wrote. Julian was more affected by what had happened than was initially apparent. After the euphoria of being rescued and being back with her had passed he became dark, closed-off and difficult, a different man from the one she had fallen in love with, it seemed to her. And he spoke so much of his brother. He excused Franz. It seemed important to Julian that she, and her parents too, should understand that Franz wasn't evil, he had simply been very, very much in love.

In fact it got so bad she was thinking about leaving him, until something happened that changed everything: she had become pregnant.

And from that day on it was as though Julian had woken up and become again the Julian she could scarcely remember now from the single night they had spent together before he went missing. Happy, good, kind, warm, loving. Maybe he never became quite as full of life and crazy as she remembered from that night, but what of it? Don't all women think their husbands were a little more exciting in the early days? And what more can one ask of a man than that he is faithful, loving, and works hard for the family? Even Helena's father had to admit that she had got a husband who was a hard worker and reliable, someone he could safely hand the restaurant on to when that time came.

According to Helena, Julian had cried like a child himself on Ferdinand's arrival. Like his father the boy radiated love. 'Like some kind of heater,' she wrote. 'And when the winter storms batter Kalymnos you couldn't wish for anything better.'

'So you think you're ready for Where Eagles Dare,' said a smiling Julian once I was installed in my room and we were seated at lunch in the restaurant. Grilled octopus. It was their speciality, and it really did taste fabulous. I noticed that Julian didn't eat it and wondered if it might have something to do with the myth that octopuses feeds on corpses. Not a myth, of course. Every creature in the sea feeds on the drowned when the chance comes along.

'I don't know,' I said. 'But at least I've done a little climbing on the crags around Athens.'

'Then we'll start out early tomorrow,' he said.

'It's an extremely long route,' I said. 'Forty metres.'

'No problem, I have an eighty-metre rope lying around somewhere.'

'Excellent.'

The ringtone on his phone played. He was about to take the call when he stopped and looked at me.

'You look so pale, Nikos? Is everything OK?'

'Of course,' I lied, and managed to return his smile. My stomach was twisting, and I could feel the sweat breaking out all over my body. 'Take the call.'

He gave me a long, searching look. He perhaps thought it was the height of the route that had caused my reaction.

He picked up the phone and finally the tune stopped playing.

Whole Lotta Love.

Same thing as usual. The song not only took me forty years back in time, to a tree in a yard in Oxford, it actually made me feel physically ill.

Julian must have realised it wasn't the climbing. 'Didn't you like the music?' he asked once his call was finished.

'It's a long story,' I said, and laughed now that I had had time to compose myself. 'But I thought you didn't like Led Zeppelin. I seem to remember you had something a bit softer on your phone.'

'Did I?'

'Yes, some Ed something. Ed Cheap. Ed Sheep . . .'

'Ed Sheeran!' cried Helena.

'That's it,' I said and looked at Julian.

'I love Sheeran,' said Helena.

'How about you, Julian?'

Julian Schmid raised his glass of water. 'It's quite possible to like both Zeppelin and Sheeran.'

He drank for a long time without taking his eyes off me.

'I just thought of something,' he said when finally he put his glass down again. 'The weather forecast for tomorrow says there might be rain, it's actually impossible to know whether the cloud fronts round here are going to hit the island or not. Even though the route is overhanging, the wind will drive in so much rain that the wall will get soaked, so why don't we head out there now? You're here for such a short time, this way we can be sure you'll be able to have a crack at it before you have to leave.'

'Yes, it would be a real bore for you to have come all this way just to see me and Ferdinand,' said Helena.

I smiled.

We finished the meal and I went up to my room to get ready. As I packed my climbing gear, through the window I could see Julian playing with Ferdinand. The boy ran laughing around his father, and each time Julian grabbed hold of him and swung him round so that his little blue-and-white cap fell off the boy shrieked with joy. It was like a dance. Not a dance I had ever danced with my own father. Or had I? If so I had forgotten it.

'Excited?' asked Julian as we parked after our silent drive out to the spot where we had found Franz's car.

I nodded as I gazed out across the beach. Looked different today. No sun. Waves that whispered peacefully as they rolled onto the sand without breaking.

After a brisk twenty-minute walk we were out on the point and looking up at Where Eagles Dare. It looked more intimidating with the steel-grey clouds hanging over it. We put on our climbing harnesses and Julian handed me two bunches of quickdraws.

'I imagine you probably want to climb it *onsight*,' he said.

'Thanks, you overestimate me, but I'll see how far I get.' I clipped the quickdraws into the harness, attached myself to the rope, pulled on the old but comfortable climbing shoes I had used in the Lake District and dipped my hands into the bag of resin fastened on a cord around my waist. Instead of stepping the two paces to the wall, I walked out to the edge of the path and looked down.

'That's where they found him,' I said, nodding down towards the breakers. They were calmer today but the sound still reached up to us after a short delay. 'But you already knew that.'

'Yes, I knew,' said the voice behind me. 'How long have you known?'

'Known what?'

I turned to face him. He was pale. Maybe it was just the light, but for a moment that almost white pallor made me think of Trevor. But there again, nowadays I think quite often of Trevor.

'Nothing,' he said, his face and voice expressionless as he threaded the rope through the manual ATC brake fastened to his halter and ritually checked his equipment list. 'You're in, the carabiner is fastened, the rope is long enough, and your knot looks fine.'

I nodded.

Placed one foot in the overhanging wall and gripped into the first obvious handhold. Tensed my body and got my other foot up.

The first ten metres of the climb were fine. I moved easily. Losing those kilos and getting the muscles back had made all the difference. And my climber's psyche was in good shape too. The previous year I had fallen several times on routes that were minimally bolted, and when the rope stopped my swaying fall after some eight or ten metres I didn't even feel relief, only a mild disappointment that I hadn't managed the route without a fall. But here the permanent bolts were close together, and in the event of a fall the drop would be short. I actually began to wonder if I had brought along enough quickdraws as I fastened them to the bolts and clipped in the rope.

I heard a gull screech at the same instant as my thin limestone hold broke away. I fell. It lasted only a moment, that state so often and so inaccurately described as weightlessness. Then the rope and the harness tensed around my waist and thighs. A short, hard fall. I looked down at Julian who was standing on the ground with the rope tensioning out from the brake in the harness.

'Sorry,' he shouted. 'You fell so quickly I didn't have time to take your fall.'

'Don't worry,' I shouted back, and since I couldn't get close enough to the overhanging rock face I started to pull myself up the rope using just the muscle power of my arms. Even though it was barely three metres and Julian used his body weight to pull in the slack, the climbing rope was so thin and slippery that by the time I reached the bolt from which the rope hung I was completely exhausted. I looked at my hands. I had already worn off a lot of skin.

After a rest I continued climbing. I had to grab hold of one of the quickdraws at the crux, the toughest point of the route, but apart from that I felt the coming of the flow, when there's no need to think, the hands and feet seem to solve the stream of equations with one and two unknowns all by themselves. Reaching the top fifteen metres later I clipped the rope into the anchor with a sense of inner content that was deep and calm. I hadn't managed it without a fall, but the climb had been magical nevertheless. I turned to take in the view. According to George, on a clear day you could see the coast of Turkey from Kalymnos, but today I saw only: the sea, myself, the route. And the rope that ran down to the man I had saved, and who would save me.

'Ready!' I shouted. 'You can lower me down!'

I sank down through the still, heavy afternoon air. Daylight was already fading; once Julian had tried the route we would have to head back if we were to avoid walking along the steep, stony path in the dark. But something told me that Julian wouldn't be making the climb when, after a few metres in which I lowered myself, I suddenly saw the dark section on the yellow rope passing inside me on its way up to the anchor.

The midpoint marker.

'The rope's too short!' I shouted.

Even though there was no wind, it might well have been the case that the surf, the crying of the gulls or simple absent-mindedness meant that he didn't hear me and continued to haul me down.

'Julian!'

But he continued to pay out the rope, faster now.

I looked down at the sea, then in towards the path where the rest of the rope snaked its way up, like a cobra dancing to a flute. And I could see it now, there was no knot in the loose end of the rope.

'Julian!' I shouted again. I was so close to him I could the deadness in his facial expression. He was going to kill me, there were only a few seconds remaining before the end of the rope slid unhindered right through the brake, and I would fall.

'Franz!'

The elasticated rope was pulled tight and tensed above the drop. My harness was pressing into the small of my back. My descent had stopped, I swayed up and down in the empty air. It was just two or three metres down to Julian, but since I was hanging vertically from the anchor at the top, I dangled over the edge where the track ran. If the rope passed through the brake I would fall past Julian and all the fifty or sixty metres down to the rocks where the waves frothed like the contents of a smashed champagne bottle.

'Looks like the rope isn't eighty metres after all,' said Julian. 'Sorry – to err is human.' His face didn't look as if he was sorry.

It was his endgame now. That end was located twenty centimetres below the brake and his hand. Right now it was the only thing holding me. Owing to the angle and the friction in the brake it wasn't hard for him to hold me there. On the other hand, he couldn't do it forever. And when he let go it wouldn't look like a murder but like an all too common type of climbing accident: the rope was too short.

I nodded. 'You're right, Franz . . .'

He didn't respond.

'. . . it is human to err.'

We studied each other. Him half standing on the track, half sitting on the halter and the rope, me dangling directly above him, over the abyss.

'Paradox,' he said at length. 'That's a Greek word, isn't it? Like when Ferdinand is afraid of the dark when it's bedtime and he wants Daddy to tell him fairy stories until he's asleep. But he insists that they're scary stories. Isn't that a paradox?'

'Perhaps,' I said. 'Perhaps not.'

'In any case, you can see the darkness coming, maybe you should tell a scary story now, Nikos. And then maybe you and I won't be so afraid.'

'How about we resolve this situation here first?'

He loosened his grip on the rope, let it slip a few centimetres closer to the brake.

'I think,' he said, 'that the resolution will lie in the story you tell.'

I swallowed. Looked down. A fall of sixty metres doesn't take long. But you can get through quite a lot of thinking in the time it does take. Unfortunately you also have time to reach a speed of 123.5 kilometres an hour. Would I hit the water, just about survive the fall and drown? Or would I hit the rock and die an instantaneous and pain-free death? I had seen that one close up. The stillness and the absence of drama had been the most striking thing, even in the seconds after he hit the ground, before everybody began to scream and run around. It had turned cold, and yet I could feel the sweat running like molten wax. I had not planned to expose the fake Julian in this way, with my whole life quite literally in his hands. On the other hand it was logical. Indeed, in a way it made everything easier. The ultimatum would be clearer.

'OK,' I said. 'Are you ready?'

'I'm ready.'

'Once upon a time . . .' I took a deep breath. 'Once upon a time there was a man named Franz who was so jealous that he killed his twin brother Julian, so that he could have the lovely Helena all to himself. He took his brother down to a beach, shot him in the head and threw the body into the sea. But when Franz realised that Helena loved Julian, and only Julian, and that she didn't want Franz, Franz arranged things in such a way that it looked as though it was him and not Julian who had ended up in the sea with a bullet through the head. Afterwards he chained himself up in a cellar, and when he was found he pretended to be Julian, and to have been there ever since Julian had been reported missing. Everyone believed him, everyone believed he was Julian, and so Franz did get his Helena, and they all lived happily ever after. Satisfied?'

He shook his head but still held on to the rope. 'You're not a born storyteller, Nikos.'

'True.'

'You have, for example, no proof.'

'What makes you think that?'

'With proof you wouldn't have come here alone, and I would have been arrested a long time ago. And I happen to know that you've left the police force. These days you spend your time sitting in the National Library reading books, am I right?'

'No,' I said. 'I use the Gennadius Library.'

'So then what's this visit all about? Is this the old man come to pursue the case that won't give him any peace because he no longer feels certain he discovered the truth?'

'It's true I'm not at peace,' I said. 'Though it's not about this case. But it is not true that I'm here in search of proof, because I already have proof.'

'You're lying.' The knuckles of the hand holding the rope whitened.

'No,' I said. 'When the DNA from the body in the sea matched what we got from Franz during the interrogation, everybody thought that wrapped things up. But of course there was one more possibility. Because identical twins come from the same egg and share a genetic heritage, they also have the same DNA profile. So in theory the body we found could just as well have been Julian as Franz.'

'So what? Just as well is not the same as proof that it wasn't Franz.'

'Correct. I didn't get my proof until I received the fingerprints that you, Franz, left on the glass you drank from during our conversation at the police station in Pothia. I compared them with the prints I had at home in Athens.'

'Athens?'

'To be precise, on a box on a shelf above my bed. On the stone you gave me at the hospital. Yes, paradox is Greek, and the paradox here is that even though twins have identical DNA profiles, their fingerprints are not identical.'

'That's not true. We compared fingerprints, and they are the same.'

'Almost the same.'

'We have the same DNA, so how is that possible?'

'Because fingerprints are not decided one hundred per cent by genetics. They're also affected by your surroundings in the womb. The position one foetus lies in in relation to the other. The difference in the length of the umbilical cord which, in turn, creates a difference in the bloodstream and the access to nourishment which, again, determines how quickly the fingers grow. By the time your fingerprints are fully formed, which is at some point between week thirteen and week nineteen of the pregnancy, small differences have arisen which are detectable on close examination. I gave them a close examination. And guess what? The fingerprints on the stone I got from you at the hospital when you were claiming to be

Julian, and on the glass that you, Franz, drank from at the police station, were identical. In a nutshell, the two people were . . .'

'. . . one and the same.'

'Yes, Franz.'

Maybe it was just the onset of darkness, maybe just our always biased gaze that adjusts its bias on the basis of every new item of information received, but it seemed to me I could see Franz emerge in the person beneath me, see him throw away his mask and step out of the role he had been playing all these years.

'And you are the only one who knows this?' he said quietly.

'That's correct.'

From out at sea came the single, pained cry of a gull.

It really was true, the work I had done in reconstructing the crime and the identity switch had been done in isolation, and with no other tools but these fingerprints, my halting logic, and my vivid powers of imagination.

He killed Julian the night they drove to the hospital, probably while they were still quarrelling and in a moment of jealous rage. I presumed it was true that in an effort to get Franz to give up Helena, Julian claimed to have been in touch with her that same day, revealed that he was the twin brother and had tricked her, and that Helena nevertheless said that it was him, Julian, that she wanted. Julian lied to Franz; Helena didn't know she had been with both twins until I told her. And yet Julian knew he was right, that she would prefer him, because when it came to capturing a woman's heart he would always win out over his gloomy brother. I guessed that Franz, maddened by jealousy, pulled out the Luger and shot his brother there and then. And that in that same blind rage, with no thought for the consequences, sent that text message to Helena saying he had killed Julian, the one he thought she had promised herself to. But then Franz regained his composure. And it became clear to him that, if he played his cards right, Helena might still be his. He found a spot where he could drive all the way down to the sea, undressed the body and threw it into the sea. After that Franz drove back to Massouri, returned Julian's clothes, phone and other personal items to the room, and reported him missing the following morning, saying he had gone out before daybreak for a swim. Even though it was credible that Julian had drowned, Franz knew that if we found out about their quarrel the previous evening, it might make us take a closer look at him, so he deleted the message he had sent to Helena. He also deleted the log that showed he had made eight attempts to call Victoria, who had seen him return home alone that night. Probably he wanted to talk to Victoria to explain it away, and to persuade her not to complicate matters by telling the police. But after talking to me at the police station in Pothia he realised that we could trace the log and the text messages through the phone company. He also learned that I had spoken with Helena, and while on his way to the rock face at Odysseus he had seen me talking to Victoria. Franz realised that the net was closing in on him.

And was desperate.

The only card he still held was that Julian's body had not yet been found. And that he and Julian had the same DNA, so that if Julian's body was found, it might be possible to fool us into believing it was Franz.

Franz Schmid's only hope was to disappear, to cease to exist. So he staged his own suicide. Called me from the beach and announced it in such a way as to leave no doubt about it. Planted the idea that maybe Julian wasn't dead, that he might yet be found in his 'prison of love'. He had to express it like that to give himself time to get up to Palechora before we solved his riddle, but he probably hadn't reckoned on my taking several days to do it. After his phone conversation with me he left his clothes and mobile phone in the car, walked barefoot out into the waves and threw away the Luger so that if we found it that would strengthen the likelihood of suicide. Climbed ashore again on the rocks and from there made his way to Palechora, it can't have taken him much more than an hour. It was night, there was a storm, so he knew the chances of encountering anyone or at least anyone who would recognise him were minimal.

'You had a woollen blanket with you but you must have had clothing and shoes to get up to Palechora,' I said. 'Where did you get rid of them?'

I could see Franz loosening his hold, saw the yellow-taped end slide up towards his hand.

'In Chora,' he said. 'In a rubbish bin below the fortress walls. Along with the packaging for the emetic and the laxatives I took so that it would look as though I had been chained there for a long time before you found me. I made it up to the cellar, and then I shat and puked like a pig. I really thought it wouldn't take you long to find me.'

'You stayed in the cellar the whole time?'

'During daylight hours yes, otherwise I risked being seen from Chora, or by tourists. But I went out at night to get some fresh air.'

'And of course, you didn't chain yourself to the wall until you knew that "rescue" wasn't far away. The key to the handcuffs, where did you hide that?'

'I swallowed it.'

'And that was all you ate while you were there? No wonder you looked a good deal thinner.'

Franz Schmid laughed. 'Four kilos. It shows, when you're already thin to begin with. I got a bit desperate when I realised you weren't taking the hint. I started shouting for help. And when I finally heard people walking out there, I had shouted myself hoarse and almost lost my voice.'

'That's why your voice was different,' I said. 'You had just shouted until you were hoarse.'

'No one heard me,' said Franz.

'No one heard you,' I repeated.

I took a deep breath. The climbing harness tightened, constricting the circulation, and my feet were already beginning to contract. I knew, of course, that he might have two reasons for confessing. One was that, come what may, he intended to let me drop into the abyss. The other, that it feels good to confess. To shift the burden over onto someone else. It's the reason that confession is one of the church's most popular attractions.

'So you assumed the life of your own brother,' I said.

Franz Schmid shrugged. 'Julian and I knew each other's lives inside out, so it was easier than you might think. I promised Helena I would soon be back, then I travelled home. I kept away from people who knew us too well, like family and friends, and Julian's work colleagues. The isolation and a couple of other strange situations were excused as loss of memory as a result of the trauma I had been through. The hardest thing was the funeral, when my mother said she was convinced that I was Franz, and that grief must have driven her mad. And the speeches, when I realised how many people loved me. After the burial I left my job, meaning Julian's job, and came back here to Kalymnos. Helena and I had a small wedding – only Mother was invited from my side. But she wouldn't come. She thinks I stole Helena from Franz, and that Helena has betrayed Franz. We had almost no contact until the birth of Ferdinand. But since I sent a few pictures of Ferdinand we've spoken on the phone. So we'll see how it works out.'

'And Helena . . . does she know anything?'

Franz Schmid shook his head. 'Why are you doing this?' he asked. 'You give me a rope and tie yourself to the other end and tell me that if I kill you no one will know anything.'

'Let me ask you instead, Franz, isn't it terrible to have to bear the weight of this alone?'

He didn't reply.

'If you kill me now, you'll still be alone. With not just a murder committed in blind rage but a cold-blooded murder. Is that what you want?'

'You leave me with no choice, Nikos.'

'A man always has a choice.'

'When it comes to his own life maybe. But now I have a family to consider. I love them, they love me, and I am willing to make any sacrifice for them. Peace in my soul. Your life. Do you really think that's so strange?'

I fell. I caught a glimpse of the end of the rope as it disappeared into Franz's hand and knew it was all over. But then the harness tightened around my thighs and back again and I swayed lightly on the elasticated rope.

'Not strange in any way,' I said. My pulse dropped, the worst was over, I was no longer so afraid to die. 'Because that's what I've come here to offer you. Peace in your soul.'

'Not possible.'

'I know I can't give you perfect peace. After all, you killed your brother. But I can offer you peace from the fear of being exposed, of having to look over your shoulder the whole time.'

He gave a quick laugh. 'Because now it's all over, and I'm about to be arrested?'

'You're not going to be arrested. At least not by me.'

Franz Schmid leaned backwards. With the end of the rope now in his hand it was just a question of how long he could hold on. That was OK. I was prepared for it to end this way. It was one of the only two ways out that were acceptable to me.

'And why aren't you going to arrest me?' asked Franz.

'Because I want the same thing in return.'

'The same thing?'

'Peace in my soul. It means I can't arrest you without doing the same thing to myself.'

I saw the sinews and the veins move beneath the skin of the back of his hand. His neck muscles tensed, and he breathed more heavily. I understood I only had seconds left. Seconds, a sentence or two to tell the story of the day that had shaped the rest of my life.

'So what plans have you got for the summer?' I asked Trevor as I raised the Thermos cup to my mouth.

Trevor, Monique and I were sitting on separate stones and facing each other. Behind us was a wall some twenty metres high, and before us a softly undulating landscape of meadows. Most of it was uncultivated, here and there we saw cows. On clear days like today, from the top of the wall, you could see the smoke from the factory chimneys hovering over Sheffield. We had finished climbing, the sun was already low in the sky, and we were just taking a short break for food before heading back. The hot cup scorched my raw fingertips, and the cup felt slippery because I had just rubbed Elizabeth Arden's Eight Hour Cream into my fingers – that's a ladies' cosmetic first produced in the 1930s, but as I and hundreds of other climbers had discovered, it was much better for rebuilding new skin than any patented climbers' cream.

'Don't know,' Trevor answered.

It was difficult to get him talking today. Same with Monique. On the drive from Oxford, and also while we were climbing it was me – the one with the broken heart – who did the talking. Joked. Kept the spirits up. Of course I saw them exchanging looks that said who's going to tell him, you or me? But I adroitly avoided giving them a suitable opening. I had filled any silences in the car with meaningless chitchat that would almost certainly have sounded frenetic had it not been on the subject of climbing, where all talk sounds frenetic. This was to be a one-day trip, since Monique needed the rest of the weekend to prepare for her finals, so perhaps they intended to wait until we were almost home so that they wouldn't have to spend hours in the car with me after dropping the bombshell. On the other hand, they were probably desperate to get it over with, confess their sins, swear it would never happen again, accept my disappointment, even, perhaps, my tears. But after that my forgiveness too, my magnanimous promise that yes, we could pretend it had never happened and continue as before. Yes, and perhaps grow even closer now that we had a foretaste of what it was we risked losing: each other.

We climbed trad-routes only the whole day, meaning we had to fasten our own bolts in places the mountain allowed it. Naturally it's a much riskier way of climbing than using permanent bolts, since a wedge you've just pushed into a crack can easily be jerked out if you fall. But strangely enough, given my disturbed state of mind, I had climbed well. And very relaxed, almost oblivious to danger the harder it became to fix good, secure supports. Things seemed the other way round for Trevor and

Monique, Trevor especially. Suddenly he wanted bolts knocked in every-where, even on the easier passages, which meant the climbing took an irritatingly long time.

'What about your summer plans?' asked Trevor and took a bite of his sandwich.

'Work a bit for my father in Athens,' I said. 'Earn enough to visit Monique in France and finally get to say hello to her family.'

I smiled at Monique, who returned my smile awkwardly. She has probably forgotten, though it was only three months ago that the two of us had pored over the map, picking out vineyards and small peaks and pleasurably going over a few practical details as though we were plan-ning an expedition to the Himalayas.

'We'd better tell you,' said Trevor in a low voice, staring down at the ground.

I felt myself grow cold, felt my heart sink in my chest.

'I'm planning a trip to France too in the summer.' Trevor went on chewing.

What the hell did he mean? Weren't they going to tell me what had happened? About this slip-up that was behind them now, Monique who had been feeling so alone because I had been neglecting her, Trevor who had succumbed to a moment of weakness, no excuses, of course, but the remorse they felt, the promise that, of course, it would never happen again – wasn't any of this going to come out? Trevor was going to France. Did the two of them . . . were the two of them, were they going to follow the route Monique and I had planned?

I looked at Monique, but her gaze too was fixed to the ground. It dawned on me. It dawned on me that I had been blind. But I had been blind because the two of them had put my eyes out. Something big and evil and black surged up inside me. It couldn't be stopped, it was as though my stomach twisted and a stinking, yellow-green spew was trying to force its way out. There was no way out; mouth, nose, ears, the sockets of my eyes, they were all sewn shut. So the spew filled my head, driving out every sensible thought, surging and bursting inside me.

I could see Trevor preparing for it. For the crux. He took a deep breath, his new broad shoulders and his back swelled up. That white back I had seen through the window. He opened his mouth.

'You know what?' I said hurriedly. 'I'd like to climb one route more before we go.'

Trevor and Monique exchanged confused glances.

'I . . .' Monique began.

'It shouldn't take long,' I said. 'Only Exodus.'

'Why?' said Monique. 'You've already climbed it today.'

'Because I want to climb free solo,' I said.

The two of them stared at me. The silence was so complete we could follow the conversation going on between the climber and his anchor a hundred metres further along the rock face. I pulled on my climbing shoes.

'Don't mess about,' said Trevor with a strained laugh.

I saw from Monique's look that she knew I wasn't messing about.

I wiped my slippery, greasy fingertips dry against my climbing trousers, stood up and walked over to the face. Exodus was a route we knew inside out. We'd climbed it dozens of times with ropes. It was easy all the way up to a marked crux – the most difficult point – near the end where you need to commit fully, abandon your balance and throw your left hand out towards a little handhold that slopes slightly downwards, meaning that the only thing that stops you falling is the friction on the rock. And because it's about friction, we could see from the ground that the handhold was white with the resin of climbers who had dipped their hands in their bags directly before the move so their skin would be as dry as possible.

If you were left hanging your only option was to move your right hand to a large handhold, get your feet up on the ledge and climb the remaining few, easy metres. Once at the top there was a simple descent without ropes down a slope on the rear of the crag.

'Nikos . . .' Monique said, but I had already started climbing.

Ten seconds later I was high up the crag. I heard the conversation further along the face suddenly stop and knew they had realised I was climbing free solo. That means climbing without rope, with no security of any kind. I heard one of them curse quietly. But on I climbed. On up past the point where it might have been possible for me to think better of it and climb down again. Because it was fantastic. The rock. Death. It was better than all the whisky in the world, it really did make me lock everything else out, forget everything else. For the first time since I sat in that tree and saw Trevor and Monique fucking I was free of pain. I was now so high that if I made a single mistake, if I slipped, became exhausted or a handhold broke, I wouldn't just fall and hurt myself. I would die. I have heard that those who climb free solo programme themselves not to think about death, because if you do all your muscles will stiffen, your supply of oxygen will be blocked, the lactic acid will build up and you will fall. It was the other way round for me that day. The more I thought about death, the easier the climbing seemed to be.

I was at the crux. All I had to do was let my body drop to the left and arrest the fall with my left hand on that single, small handhold. I stopped. Not because I hesitated, but to enjoy the moment. Enjoy their fear.

I stood on my left big toe, let my right foot dangle under me as a counterbalance, leaned over to the left. Heard a little scream from Monique and felt a delicious hollowness in my body as I tipped off balance, out of control and abandoned myself to gravity. I threw out my left hand. Found the ledge and gripped hard. The fall was arrested almost before it had begun. I moved my right hand to the firm, big hold and got my feet up on the ledge. I was safe. And felt almost immediately a strange disappointment. The two other climbers, two elderly Englishmen, had made their way over to Trevor and Monique, and now that they saw I was no longer in danger of falling they began to give vocal expression to their anger. I heard them say the usual things, how free soloing should be banned, that climbing is about risk-management, not about challenging death, that people such as me set a bad example to the younger climbers. I heard Monique defending me, saying there were no young climbers here today, if they didn't mind her saying so. Trevor said nothing.

Standing steady now, as a way of resting and to get the lactic acid out of my muscles for the final few metres, I used a familiar climber's technique, alternately turning the right hip and the left in towards the rock face against which I was standing, holding on with my left and then right hand as I did so. As the left hip brushed against the rock, I felt something prick me in the thigh. It was the tube of Elizabeth Arden cream I had in my trouser pocket.

In later years I have tried to reconstruct it, tried to spool back through my own mind, but it's impossible. All I can conclude is that we are to a quite surprising degree incapable of recalling what we think, that, as is the case with dreams, it slips away, and that we work out what we must have thought from what we in actual, historical fact did do, nothing else.

And what I did that Friday afternoon in the Peak District in England, standing firm and steady and holding on to the rock with my right hand, was stick my left hand into my trouser pocket. As I was standing with my left side and hip twisted towards the rock face, my left hand and pocket were hidden from view to those standing below on the ground, moreover they were preoccupied with discussing the ethical dilemmas associated with suicide climbing. With my hand in my pocket I unscrewed the cap, squeezed the tube, held the thick, fatty cream between two fingers. Continuing to hold on with my right hand I placed my left hand back on that handhold at the crux, seemingly attempting to adjust slightly the position of my feet and smeared off the white cream. Established that it was impossible to distinguish it from the white resin that had been there before. I wiped my hand dry on the inside of my thigh where I knew that the smears of cream would not be seen if I stood with my legs together. I then climbed the last few steps to the summit.

By the time I had descended the rear of the crag and walked round to the front the two other climbers had gone. I could see them walking along the path through the fields. Clouds were moving in from the west.

'You idiot,' hissed Monique, who stood there with her rucksack on her back ready to leave.

'I love you too,' I said and took off my shoes. 'Your turn, Trevor.'

He stared at me in disbelief.

In fiction great narrative power is often vested in a single look. In a literary sense the convention helps the writer tell his story well, and sometimes to great effect. But since I am not, as I have said, a specialist in the interpretation of body language, or more sensitive to atmosphere than others, I can only conclude, based on what he did, that he knew. He knew that I knew. And that this would be his way of doing penance; to challenge death, in the same way as I had just done. That this was now the only way he could show his respect for me and have any hope of my forgiveness.

'You won't make your idiotic action any less idiotic by persuading him to do something just as idiotic!' hissed Monique. There were tears in her eyes. Maybe that's why I didn't hear the rest of her tirade. I stared at those tears and wondered if they were for me. For us. Or were they for the moral trap she and Trevor had fallen into, which was so contrary to everything she thought she stood for? Or for the knife that was about to be plunged into me, and which seemed to call for more courage than they possessed? But after a while I stopped thinking about that too.

And when Monique realised I was no longer listening and that I was no longer looking at her but at something behind and now above her she turned, and saw Trevor on his way up the crag. She screamed. But Trevor was beyond the point at which he could regret it and turn back. Beyond the point at which I could regret it.

No, that's not true. I could have warned him. Tried to get him to find another way, look for other handholds that would get him past the crux. I could have. Did I consider it? I don't remember. I know I thought it, but did I think it then, or later? What hoops has my memory jumped through, in order to if not exonerate me then at least offer me extenuating circumstances? Again, I don't know. And which pain would be the greater? The one I would have to live with if Trevor had travelled to France that summer and maybe spent the rest of his life with Monique? Or the one I was fated to live with – to lose both of them anyway? And would any of those pains have been worse than to have lived with Monique, lived a lie, lived in denial, knowing that our marriage was false and based not on mutual love but on mutual guilt? That its foundation stone was the gravestone of the man she had loved more than me?

I could have warned him but I didn't.

Because back then I would have chosen the same as I would today – to live a life of lies, denial and guilt with her. And had I known there and then that such a thing was impossible I would have wished that it were me who had fallen. But I didn't. I had to live on. Until today.

I remember little of the rest of that day. Meaning that it is, of course, archived somewhere, but in a drawer I never opened.

What I do remember is something from the drive back to Oxford. It's night, and several hours since Trevor's body has been brought down, since Monique and I have given our statements to the police and tried to explain to Trevor's distraught mother while his father's sobs of pain cut through the air.

I'm driving, Monique is silent, we're on the M1 somewhere between Nottingham and Leicester. The temperature had plummeted with the coming of rain, so I've turned on the seat warmers and windscreen wipers, thinking that now it will all have been washed away, the proof against me on the crux. And in the warm interior Monique suddenly says she can smell perfume, and from the corner of my eye I see her turning towards me and glancing down into my lap. 'You've got something white on the inside of your thigh.'

'Resin,' I say quickly, without taking my eyes off the road. As though I had known she would point this out and had my explanation ready.

We drove the rest of the way in silence.

'You killed your best friend,' said Franz Schmid.

The tone was neither shocked nor accusing. He was simply stating a fact.

'Now you know as much about me as I know about you,' I said.

He looked up at me. A breath of wind lifted his quiff. 'And you think that means I've nothing to fear from you. But your crime is beyond the statute of limitations now. You can't be punished for it.'

'Don't you think I've been punished, Franz?' I closed my eyes. It didn't really matter if he let go of the rope or not, I had made my confession. Naturally he couldn't give me any kind of absolution. But he could – *we* could – give each other a story that said that we were not alone, not the only sinner. It doesn't make it forgivable, but it makes it human. Turns it into a human failing. The failure is always human. And that at least makes me human. And Franz too. Did he understand that? That I had come to turn him into a human being? And myself too? That I was his rescuer, and he mine? I opened my eyes again. Looked at his hand.

By the time we headed back down it was so dark that Franz had to go first with me coming along close behind. As I concentrated on following in his footsteps along the narrow, steep track I heard the surf muttering and snorting beneath us, like a beast of prey disappointed that its prey has got away.

'Careful here,' said Franz, although I still stumbled against the large loose rock he had stepped over. I heard it rolling down the mountainside but said nothing. An optician once told me that among the most predictable statistics regarding the human body is that by the time we're approaching sixty our eyes have lost something like twenty-five of their sensitivity to light. So my sight was worse now. But it could also be that my sight was better now. At the very least I understood my own story better. We walked on, and as we rounded the point I saw the lights from the houses down on the beach.

Franz got me down from Where Eagles Dare by using his feet and the rock face to approach a little closer to the first bolt, at the same time hauling in enough rope to enable him to grab it and tied a knot in the end. With a bit of scrabbling and swinging I managed to scramble onto the protruding lip of the ledge just as the last of the daylight faded.

As soon as we reached the turning circle and were inside the car Franz called Helena.

'We're both fine, darling, the climbing just took a little longer than expected,' he said. Pause. A smile spread over his face. 'Tell him Daddy will be home soon and I'll read to him. Tell him I love you both.'

I looked out to sea. Sometimes it seems as though life is full of impossible choices. But perhaps that's because we don't recognise the easy choices as choices. It is the dilemmas, the unmarked crossroads that occupy our thoughts. At Oxford, in a discussion about Robert Frost's famous poem 'The Road Not Taken', I once maintained, not without a certain youthful arrogance, that the poem was clearly in praise of individualism, advice to us young to take 'the one less travelled by' because 'that has made all the difference', as the poet says in the final two lines. But our sixty-year-old professor smiled and said it was precisely this kind of naive, optimistic misunderstanding that has dragged Robert Frost's poem down to the level of Khalil Gibran and Paulo Coelho and made it so beloved of the masses. That the poem's weakness is the final verse, because it is ambivalent and can be read as a failed attempt to sum up what the rest of the poem is actually about; that you must choose. That you know nothing of the road, not even which of them is 'less travelled by' since, according to the poem, these seem to be the same as far as the eye can see. And that you won't even know where the one you didn't take leads to. Because – as the poet says – the road you travel leads to new roads and will never return to this particular crossroads. Therein lies the poetry, our professor maintained. The melancholy. The poem is not about the road you took, but about the one you didn't take.

'The title makes that very plain,' said the professor. 'But the world, and we as individuals, interpret everything according to our needs. The victors write the history of the war and cast themselves as the ones with right on their side. Theologians read the Bible in such a way as to give the Church as much power as possible, and we use a poem to tell ourselves that we don't need to feel that we have failed, even if we never lived up to our parents' expectations nor followed in their footsteps. The actual progress of the war, the actual biblical text, the poet's actual intentions are secondary. Am I right or am I right?'

Franz put the phone back in the mid-seat console. But he didn't turn on the ignition. Instead he sat there looking out at the sea, like me.

'I still don't understand it,' he said. 'I mean, you're a policeman.'

'No,' I said. 'I'm not a policeman for the simple reason that I never was a policeman, I just worked as one. You've got to understand that in the story about me, I am you, Franz. Julian betrayed you the way Trevor betrayed me. And the disease of jealousy made killers out of both of us. Life imprisonment in Greece means you can get released on parole after sixteen years. I've served more than twice that. I wouldn't want the same thing to happen to you.'

'You can't even know whether or not I feel regret,' said Franz. 'Maybe I didn't need to confess to find peace. And as for you, you could have gone to a priest and confessed.'

'I had another reason for coming,' I said.

'And that is?'

'You're the road I never took. I had to see it.'

'What do you mean?'

'You chose her, you chose the one who – innocently or not – was the reason you killed your own brother. Is it possible to live with that? That's what I wanted to know. Can you live in happiness with the one you killed for in the shadow of that gravestone? I have always believed that was impossible for me.'

'And now that you've seen the other road and know that it's possible, what are you going to do about it?'

'That is another story, Franz.'

'Will I get to hear it some day?'

'Maybe.'

Franz drove me to the airport two days later. We didn't talk much during that time; it was as though both of us were empty. Most of my conversation had been with Helena and Ferdinand, and on my last evening Ferdinand insisted I tell him a bedtime story. I saw no sign of jealousy in Franz as he stood in the doorway, smiling contentedly, probably amused at the way little Ferdinand was already bossing me about. So once Ferdinand had kissed his parents goodnight I sat on the side of his bed and told him the story of Icarus and his father. But, just as my father had done, I made my own version of the story, this time with a happy ending in which both of them got away from the prison on Crete.

There was a downpour just as we pulled up in front of the terminal building and we sat in the car to wait it out. Palechoa was swathed in grey cloud. Franz was wearing the same flannel shirt as when I had seen him for the first time, at the police station five years earlier. Maybe it was the shirt that made me notice but now I could see he was getting older too. He sat with both hands on the wheel, looking out through the windscreen as though summoning up the courage to say something. I was hoping it wouldn't be anything too big and dark. When he did finally begin he spoke without looking at me.

'Ferdinand asked me this morning where your children and their mother were,' said Franz. 'When I said you didn't have any, he asked me to give you this.' Franz pulled a worn little teddy bear up out of his jacket pocket and handed it to me.

His gaze met mine. We both laughed.

'And this,' he added.

It was a photograph they had evidently printed out on photo paper. It showed me swinging Ferdinand round just the same way I had seen his father do.

'Thanks,' I said.

'I think you'll make a good grandpa.'

I looked at the picture. Helena had taken it. 'Will you ever tell her? What really happened?'

'Helena?' Franz shook his head. 'In the beginning I could have done, ought to have done, of course. But now I no longer have the right to spoil the story she believes in. Because, of course, she has based a life and a family on it.'

I nodded. 'The story,' I repeated.

'But . . .' he started, and then stopped.

'But?'

He sighed. 'Sometimes I get the feeling she knows.'

'Really?'

'It's something she said once. She said she loved me, and I said I loved her, and then she asked if I loved her so much that I would have killed someone I loved only a little bit less in order to have her. There was something about the way she said it. Then before I could answer she kissed me and started talking about something else.'

'Who knows?' I said. 'And who needs to know?'

The rain stopped.

By the time I boarded the plane the cloud cover had broken.

When I went to bed in my Athens apartment that evening I put the teddy bear on the shelf above the bed and took down an opened envelope lying there. It was postmarked Paris and dated two months ago. I took the letter out and read it one more time. Her handwriting hadn't changed after all these years.

It was late at night before I finally managed to get to sleep.

Three months later

'Thank you for a perfect day,' said Victoria Hässel and raised her wine glass. 'Who would have thought there was such good climbing to be had in Athens. And you with such powers of endurance.'

She winked as though to make certain I got the double meaning.

Victoria had contacted me a few days after I returned home from Kalymnos, and we corresponded at least once a week after that. Maybe it was the distance and the fact that we had no mutual friends and didn't know each other very well that made it so easy for me to confide in her. Not about murder but about love. And on my part that meant Monique. Her own love life was a little richer and more varied, and when she wrote that she was going to meet her latest flame, a French climber, in Sardinia, and was planning to travel via Athens, I was genuinely not sure whether it was such a good idea. I wrote, telling her that I liked the distance, the feeling of talking to a confessor who couldn't see my face.

'I can always wear a paper bag over my head,' she wrote back. 'But I won't be wearing much more than that.'

'Is your brother's flat as posh as this?' Victoria asked as I cleared the table and carried our dishes over to the worktop.

'Posher and bigger.'

'Does that make you envious?'

'No. I'm . . .'

'Happy?'

'I was about to say, content.'

'Me too. So content it's almost a pity I have to travel on to Sardinia tomorrow.'

'You've got someone waiting for you, and I hear the climbing there is fantastic too.'

'You're not jealous?'

'Of the climbing, or of your boyfriend? In that case it's his job to be jealous of me.'

'I was single that time in Kalymnos.'

'You told me. And I'm a lucky man who's been able to borrow you for a while.'

We took our wine glasses out onto the balcony.

'Have you come to any decision regarding Monique?' she asked as we looked out across Kolonaki, with the sounds of the diners at the pavement restaurants rising up to us like monotonous but happy music.

I had told Victoria about the letter I had received just after I arrived back from Kalymnos. That Monique was now a widow and had moved to Paris. And how she had written that she thought about me a lot and wanted me to go over and meet her.

'Yes,' I said. 'I'm going over.'

'It'll be fantastic,' she said as she raised her glass.

'Well, I'm not too sure about that,' I said as I put my glass down on the little table.

'Why not?'

'Because it's probably too late. We're different people now from what we were then.'

'If you're so pessimistic, why go?'

'Because I need to know.'

'Know what?'

'Where the other road leads to, the one we didn't take. Know whether happiness would have been possible in the shadow of a gravestone.'

'I've no idea what you're talking about. But *is* it?'

I thought about it for a moment. 'Let me show you something,' I said.

I came back with the bear and the photograph of me with Ferdinand.

'Cute,' she said. 'Who's the boy?'

'He's the son of . . .' I took a deep breath to make quite sure I got this right. 'Julian Schmid.'

'Of course,' she said.

'Ah, so you see the likeness?'

'No, but I can see the cap.'

'The cap?'

She pointed to Ferdinand's blue-and-white cap. 'The club colours. And that square in the front is HSV's club badge. My club, and Julian's club.'

I nodded. A sudden thought flitted through my head, but I rejected it, and it disappeared. And instead thought of this: that Franz had probably already changed the Zeppelin ringtone on his phone for something a little more easy-going that didn't reveal the real him. The same way he had chucked out his St Pauli rainbow cap and put on his brother's clothes and accoutrements and lied to everyone around him, all day, every day. I couldn't do that. It wasn't that I had moral scruples. I simply didn't have the talent or the patience to carry it out. If I went to Paris, I would have to tell Monique what I did that day in the Peak District.

I walked Victoria back to her hotel, her departure was at the crack of dawn next day. Then I headed back home. Athens is what the English call an acquired taste. But I took a long detour through neighbourhoods rougher than Kolonaki because I knew I wouldn't be able to sleep.

Maybe Monique suspected all along. Maybe the remark she passed about the stain on my thigh when the seat warmers had caused the Elizabeth Arden cream to smell so strongly was just her way of letting me know. That she knew, and that she also knew that, on account of her betrayal, in some way she shared the guilt, and that our ways must part here.

But now, late in life, it could be that we had actually found our way back to that crossroads where we had took leave of one another. Now – if we wanted to, if we dared – we could take that other road. Me, a murderer. But I had served my time, hadn't I? I was able to feel good about Franz and about his happiness. Might I also be able to feel good about my own?

At a corner I couldn't recall ever having passed before a stray dog sauntered across the street, glancing neither to right nor left. It looked as though it had caught the scent of something.

THE LINE

I HATE PEOPLE WHO CUT in lines.

Must be because I've spent far too many of my thirty-nine years standing in lines.

So even though there are only two people in my 7-Eleven, and the old lady is having trouble finding her purse, I stare coldly at the boy who has just pushed in front of her. He's wearing a quilted jacket which I recognise as a Moncler because I've looked at one myself and realised I'm never going to be able to afford it. The coat I bought at the Salvation Army shop just before the winter came is fine. But I can't seem to get rid of the smell of the woman who owned it before me. Who was ahead of me in the line.

It isn't often people sneak in lines here, unless it's at night, and they're drunk. In the main the people in this country are polite. The last time someone did so as blatantly as this was two months ago. A stylishly dressed woman who denied it when I accused her of cutting in line threatened to speak to my boss and get me sacked.

The boy meets my eyes. I see the hint of a smile. He feels no shame. And he's not wearing a mask either.

'I only want a tin of General snuff,' he says, as though the 'only' justified cutting in line.

'You'll have to wait your turn,' I say into my mask.

'It's right behind you. It'll only take five seconds.' He points.

'You'll have to wait your turn,' I say again.

'If you'd just given it to me I would have been out of here by now.'

'You'll have to wait your turn.'

'You'll have to wait your turn,' he imitates, exaggerating my accent. 'Come on, bitch.' His smile broadens, as though it's a joke. Maybe he thinks he can talk to me like that because I'm a woman, I'm in a low-paid job, an immigrant with a different skin colour from his chalky white. Maybe he's borrowing from a tribal language he thinks I speak. Or maybe he's being ironic and this is his parody of being a bad boy. After a closer look at him I reject this last possibility. It's too complex for him.

'Move aside,' I say.

'I've got a train to catch. Come on.'

'Maybe if you'd asked the person in front of you if it was OK?'

'My train . . .'

'The trains run all day,' I say to the accompaniment of the steady rumbling from the metro two staircases below. When I started working here my little sister asked if I wasn't worried about terrorists and sarin. In the civil war, before we got out, sarin was what everyone was afraid of. Afraid that the guerrillas would release the poison gas the way we'd heard a Japanese sect had done in the Tokyo underground sometime back in the nineties. My sister was nine years old and had nightmares every night about poison gas and underground stations.

'There's only one every fifteen minutes on my line,' he hisses. 'I've got a meeting, OK?'

'All the more reason to ask her nicely,' I say, with a nod in the direction of the lady behind him who has finally found her credit card and is ready to pay for the three items lying on the counter in front of me. The boy – I'd put his age in the mid-twenties and guess he's a regular at the training centre, mostly weights and explosive workouts – loses the patience he clearly feels he's been showing.

'Now, you nignog!'

My heart starts beating faster, but not so much because he's trying to offend me. I don't know whether the guy's a racist or is just trying to get at me in the way he thinks will hurt and provoke me most, the way he would have called me dwarf if I was short, or porkie if I was fat. I don't care what his prejudices are; my heart is beating faster because I'm afraid. Because in the course of just a few seconds this overgrown child standing in my shop has crossed a line, meaning probably he has problems with his self-control. I can't see anything in his pupils or his body language to indicate that he's high on something, the way the soldiers often were, although of course anabolic steroids could be in there somewhere. My ex-husband says that, because I'm a chemist, I'm always trying to explain the world by reference to chemistry. Like that proverb about the man with the hammer who sees every problem in terms of nails.

So, yes, I'm scared, but I've been more scared. And I'm angry, but I've been angrier.

'No,' I say calmly.

'You sure?'

He takes something from the pocket of his nice, warm Moncler jacket.

A red Swiss Army knife. Flips out the big blade. No, it's the nail file. Raises his hand, sticks his middle finger up in the air and starts to file a nail, laughing in my direction. One of his front teeth has a big dark stain on it. Could be from methamphetamine, which contains chemicals such as anhydrous ammonia and red phosphorous that eat up the enamel. But of course it could just be a case of bad dental hygiene.

He turns to the woman behind him. 'Hey, missus – OK by you if I do a bit of shopping?'

The woman stares open-mouthed at the knife and looks as though she's trying to say something, but not a sound comes out. Instead she nods, quick as a woodpecker, and makes noises like she's having trouble breathing. Above the mask her glasses mist over.

The boy turns back to me. 'There, see? Come on.'

I take a deep breath. Maybe I've underestimated the boy. At least he's street-smart enough to know that the CCTV cameras in 7-Eleven shops record pictures but not sound, so that in a court case there would be no indisputable proof that he'd actually said 'nignog' or anything like it that could be called hate speech. Unless the elderly lady behind him has better hearing than I think. And there's no law against filing your nails.

I turn slowly and take down the packet of snuff, thinking the situation over.

As I say, I've been standing in lines since I was born and I can remember them all. The food lines I stood in with Mamma when I was little. The line around the UN lorries when the fighting first started. The line at the health station where my sister was diagnosed with tuberculosis. The staff line at the university toilets because the chemistry department didn't have separate toilets for female students. The line of refugees leaving town when the war broke out. My sister and me in the line to board the boat and take the places for which Mamma had sold everything we owned. More food lines in a refugee camp where the chances of being raped were about as high as they were back home in the war zone. The line and the waiting to be sent to another country, to a refugee centre that held out hopes of a better life. The line to be allowed to leave the centre, get a job and contribute to this country that has taken us in and that I love. I love it so much that one of the three pictures hanging above the bed in the little flat my sister and I share was of the king and queen, along with Mamma and Madame Curie, my two other heroes.

I put the tin of snuff in the counter and the boy holds his credit card over the card reader.

As we wait for the card reader to confirm the purchase I open a drawer on my side of the counter. Inside is a box of fresh masks. I open the little bottle standing beside the box, take out a mask and drip a drop onto it. While doing this I'm thinking about my sister. She took down the picture of the royal couple yesterday. She said they'd cut in line. A newspaper wrote that the king and queen had already had the vaccination the rest of the country was waiting for. Without going public about it the government had offered the royal couple first place in the lifeboats, before it was their turn according to the rules that applied for the rest of the population.

And the two in the picture had accepted. Two people whose only real duty was to be symbols, to unite the country in times of war and crisis, had been given the opportunity to perform that duty in a really meaningful way, by showing a good example to people when it came to following the call from the authorities to show solidarity and discipline and to wait patiently in line. But the royals, the privileged royals, didn't take the opportunity. Instead they took the opportunity to jump the line. I asked my sister whether she wouldn't have done the same thing. She said yes. But that she wasn't the ship's captain. I said perhaps the royals did it to show a good example, to show people it was safe to be vaccinated. My sister said I was naive, that this was the same excuse the Algerian captain had used when the boatload of refugees capsized and he was the first into the lifeboat.

The card reader confirms the purchase.

I take the mask out of the drawer and offer it to him.

He looks at me uncomprehendingly as he stuffs the tin of snuff into his jacket pocket.

'You'll need it on the train,' I say. 'It's mandatory now.'

'I don't have time to –'

'It's free.'

With a mocking smile the boy grabs the mask and runs off.

'Now it's us,' I say with a smile to the elderly lady.

It's almost eleven in the evening by the time I get home to our one-room flat. It's ice-cold, because I only turn the radiators on at night, when I'm home, and when the electricity is cheaper.

I'm tired and I don't turn on any of the lights, just the little TV set. I keep the sound low. I don't see my sister, but she's sitting somewhere in the dark and her voice fills the room. She says it's dangerous where I work. That two months ago a woman died on the train and in her blood they found traces of an organophosphorus compound used in insect sprays, not unlike sarin. And now the same thing has happened to this boy. My sister points to the TV screen where a news anchor looks gravely into the camera.

As I follow her desultory thoughts I make myself something to eat, by which I mean I warm up the leftovers from yesterday. I don't make anything for her. My sister hasn't eaten since she was ten years old and died of tuberculosis while waiting in a line of patients who had been promised treatment. Last year as many people in the world died of tuberculosis as of this new infection. But of course, there's nothing about tuberculosis on the news, because that's not a problem here in the wealthy world.

'Poor thing,' says my sister with a sob as the TV shows a photograph of the boy, taken on a summer's day aboard a sailing boat with some friends. He's smiling broadly and I notice he doesn't have a dark stain on his front tooth.

'Look at him,' she snuffles. 'It's so meaningless when someone dies so young.'

'Yes,' I say as I unfasten the top buttons of my coat. 'Even there he's cutting in line.'

TRASH

SOMEONE HAS TO DO THE cleaning up.

Apart from the fact that I pick up the garbage here in the city I can't think why that sentence occurred to me on that particular morning. I had the feeling it was something that came to me during the night; but I get blackouts sometimes when I've had too much and last night was one of those nights.

The garbage truck stopped with a wheeze and I jumped down from the rear ladder. Saw one of Pijus's eyes in the mirror before I walked across to the bin outside the apartment block. In the old days I always used to run. That was when the bosses at head office didn't much care if we got through the round well before the end of the stipulated time between six and one thirty and went home an hour or two early. Or if we managed the round for the whole week in four days so that we could have Friday off. But that was before. Now we had to follow the Oslo municipal council's rules for regular hours of work, so if you finished early you just had to have a cup of coffee or play with your mobile phone in the office, you couldn't just go home and screw the wife or cut the grass, if you get my meaning.

So I didn't run, didn't even jog, I walked. Walked shivering in the summer dawn towards the green wheelie bin, a lightweight two-wheeler, rolled it over to the truck, hitched it to the bin tipper and watched the plastic bin rise up into the air accompanied by the repetitive hymn of the hydraulics and electricity, followed by the thud as the container was whipped over and the trash hit the metal floor and the compactor began compressing it. Then I wheeled the bin back into place, being careful it was well out the way of the garage door, there had been complaints before from the residents. Fuck you, as far as I'm concerned, but recently there'd been a few too many. Not that it's all that easy to get sacked as what they call a *refuse disposal officer*, but some people say I've got an anger management problem. OK, so I've got an anger management problem. So I'm worried that if the boss turns up one more time in the mess room and gives me a bollocking in front of the other guys (OK, there's *one* girl, out of 150 employees) I just might punch his lights out. And that would mean my job, no two ways about it.

I sat in the passenger seat next to Pijus. Rubbed my hands together in front of the heater. Even thought it was July and summer holidays, Oslo at six o'clock in the morning was still so cold that I didn't ride outside on the ladder until I'd built up a bit of body heat. And anyway, Pijus was a guy you could talk to and that isn't always the case with the other guys on the trucks. Mostly it's Estonian, Latvian, Romanian, Serbian, Hungarian and all that, with maybe just a smattering of English. But Pijus spoke Norwegian. He claimed he'd worked as a psychologist before moving to Norway, but we've heard that one before. But whatever he used to do, the truth was he was smarter than the rest of us (Pijus called it having a *higher level of intellectual ambition*), and he had a vocabulary as big and stiff as a lexicon. But it was Norwegian, and that was probably why the boss had us working together on the same truck. Not that there's really all that much needs to be said on a garbage truck, you both know what the job involves, but the boss thought there would be less arguing and misunderstandings if the lads at least spoke the same language. And he probably also thought Pijus would be able to keep me out of trouble.

'What is the cause of the wound on your forehead?' Pijus asked in his stilted but somehow unimpeachable Norwegian.

I glanced at myself in the mirror. The cut ran like a crack in the ice directly above one eyebrow.

'Dunno,' I said, which was the truth. As I say, I have trouble with blackouts and I couldn't remember a thing about last night, only that I woke up in bed with my wife lying with her back to me. I must have forgotten to set the alarm, just woken up out of habit but a bit later than usual, realised I was still too drunk to drive the Corolla to work and just thrown on my clothes and off out the house to catch the first bus. So obviously, I hadn't had time to peruse my ugly mug in the bathroom mirror.

'Have you been brawling again, Ivar?'

'No, I spent last night at home with the missus,' I said, running a finger over the cut. Damp. Fresh. I did remember me and the missus having a couple of drinks. Or no, actually, Lisa decided she was going to give up drinking altogether. So *I* had had a couple of drinks. And then a couple more, apparently.

Pijus stopped the truck and we jumped down. At this address there were two big four-wheeled bins to go out, and that needed two of us. Otherwise it's the driver who's the boss, he can sit and relax behind the wheel with his HGV driving licence and his wage packet three grades higher than the mate's. But Pijus is well aware of the fact that when he came here from his shit little country I was the one who was doing the driving, and he was the driver's mate. I lost my licence, but that's another long and boring story about booze and a loudmouth traffic cop with a breathalyser who turned up in court with a black eye and claimed it was completely unprovoked.

I pulled out the enormous bunch of keys and found the right one. Apparently there are around 7,000 keys covering the whole of Oslo at the depot. I hope they take good care of them.

'So you were fighting with your little wife,' said Pijus.

'Eh?'

'Why were you fighting? Unfaithful? Women who have been cheated on can be just as aggressive as men. Especially if they have children. But in that case they usually turn on the intruder. That's the way oxytocin works. The woman gets pregnant and the chemistry makes them more monogamous, more empathic and kinder. But at the same time they get more hostile in the face of potential threats.'

'Wrong, wrong and wrong again,' I said, and began pushing one of the bins in the yard towards the gate. 'We don't have kids, and I haven't screwed anyone. And women aren't monogamous.'

'Aha, so she's the one who's been unfaithful.'

'What the hell are you talking about?' I let go of my bin right in front of the gate and Pijus had to stop his to avoid crashing into me.

He shrugged. 'That's why you were fighting. You felt your position was threatened. Your amygdala was activated. Fight, flight or freeze. She's small, so you chose to fight. It's only natural.'

I could already feel the blood sort of tightening in my head. It's a much too familiar feeling. The pressure rises and to stop my head exploding I need to open a valve, find some other way out, because otherwise it'll burst open and little yellow bits of brain go whirling through the air and land on walls and bicycles, prams and letter boxes and some little guy trying to kid people into believing he's a fucking psychologist.

As a rule the solution is to open my mouth and even out the pressure that way, same as when you're on a plane. I just have to roar. Roar something.

'My amagy . . .' I began. I was calm. Pretty calm. OK, I raised my voice a bit.

'Amygdala,' said Pijus with a little and very fucking irritating grin. 'Think of it like a woman's name, Amy G—'

That did it for me.

'Don't talk to me like that, you fucking nazibastardcunt!' I pushed the container as hard as I could so the bloody Latvian was sandwiched between the two bins, and I was on my way round to give him a good kicking when a voice cut through the morning air in the yard.

'We are trying to sleep!'

I looked up. There was a woman standing on a second-floor balcony. She was probably only in her forties but she'd let herself go and looked more like fifty. I can say that because she was completely naked.

'Shut up and put some clothes on, you dirty old slag!' I yelled. 'OK?'

The woman laughed, a piercing wail of a sound, raised both arms in the air, lifted one knee and twisted her hip into a grotesque glamour-model pose. 'I'll ring your boss!' she shrieked. 'This time tomorrow, gentleman, you'll both be on the dole!'

And through the red curtain of my rage I could see it all. The boss giving me the message he'd been waiting so long for the opportunity to give me: *Svendsen, you are so fucking fired!*

I could feel the bin against my stomach. Pijus was pushing at the other end, nodding towards the gate, signalling that we should get out.

'Think she'll do it?' I asked as the wheels rattled across the asphalt outside.

'Yes,' said Pijus.

'Very fucking inconvenient,' I said.

'Oh yes?'

'The Corolla's due for its EU test and I've promised the missus a holiday in the Canaries this Christmas. What about you?'

Pijus shrugged. 'I send money to my parents. They get by, but without the money they won't eat well and they won't be able to pay for the electricity.'

I helped him hook the container onto the hydraulics. 'I shouldn't complain, is that what you're saying?'

'No, I'm just saying we all have our problems, Ivar.'

Maybe we do. My problem was that when I got angry I couldn't keep things separate any more. I should have had optical detectors that did it for me, like they have at the dump out at Klementsrud. We just offloaded into this sort of unmanned factory of a place and all the trash waltzes off on a conveyor belt with robots sorting out the big bits from the little bits and sending the organic stuff to the incinerators, the glass, plastic and metal for recirculating, and so on. If only I could learn to just let some things go.

I calmed down, and as we emptied the containers tried again to remember. What the fuck actually happened last night? All I knew was that it must have been a lot, because when I woke up I wasn't just hungover, I felt like I'd just run two marathons. Did I fight with Lisa? Had I – who in all the thirty years of our marriage never laid a hand on her – had I done something to her? She was lying on her side in the bed with her back to me when we woke up. That was in itself a bit weird because usually she slept flat on her back. But a fight, a fist fight? I couldn't see that. But what I did see now, now that I thought about it, was that we had quarrelled. It was as if the echo of harsh and ugly words was only just now reaching me from the night before. And I'd used one of them again just a couple of minutes ago. Slag. I'd called Lisa a couple of things over the years, but never slag.

We wheeled the bins back into the yard. The lady on the balcony was gone.

'She's inside calling the boss,' I said.

'He's not up,' said Pijus. 'Not yet.' He looked up the facade, nodding, his lips moving as though he was counting something. 'Come on, Ivar.'

I followed Pijus out and over to the entrance to the block, where he stood and studied the list of residents' names.

'Second floor, second door on the right,' he muttered, and rang the bell. Waited, looking at me with that little smile, but it wasn't quite so annoying this time.

A voice crackled over the speakerphone. 'Hello?' said a piercing voice.

'Good morning, fru Malvik,' said Pijus, sounding like he was trying to imitate someone. Someone who spoke better Norwegian than he did. 'My name is Iversen, I'm from the Oslo police. We've just had a call from the Oslo city sanitation services. They're reporting an incident involving indecent exposure by someone on the second floor. Since we were on patrol in the area we've been asked to look into it. I am aware that there are several people living on the second floor, but let me ask you first: is this something you have any knowledge of, fru Malvik?

There was a long pause.

'Fru Malvik?'

'No. No, I don't know anything about that.'

'No? Well, in that case I won't trouble you any further for the time being.'

There was a scraping sound as the woman hung up her entryphone and Pijus looked at me. We hurried out to the truck so the woman wouldn't have time to look out her window into the street and see that it was us. We didn't start laughing until we were up and driving. And then I laughed so hard I cried.

'Something wrong, Ivar?' asked Pijus, who had stopped laughing a long time ago.

'Just hung-over,' I said as I wiped my nose on my sleeve. 'No way is that woman gonna call the boss now.'

'No,' said Pijus, stopping outside the 7-Eleven where we usually bought a coffee and took our first smoke break.

'One question,' I said, after I'd bought a large coffee and poured half of it into the extra paper cup I'd taken and handed it to Pijus. 'If you can imitate someone who speaks better Norwegian than yourself, why don't you do it all the time?'

Pijus blew on his coffee, but still pulled a face as he took the first swig.

'Because I'm just imitating.'

'Well, we all do that,' I said. 'That's how we learn to speak.'

'True,' said Pijus. 'So I don't know. Because it feels fake, maybe. Phoney. As if it's a deception. I'm a Latvian who has learned Norwegian, and that's what I want to sound like, not like an impostor. If I speak so well you believe I am Norwegian, and then make some little phonetic or grammatical mistake that lets me down, then consciously or unconsciously people are going to feel they've been tricked and they won't trust me any more. See? Best just to relax and speak my own version of New Norwegian.'

I nodded. That's what they called it at work. Not to be confused with the actual New Norwegian people in the country districts of Norway speak, but a catch-all term covering all that Kebab-Norwegian, Norwenglish, Russian-Norwegian and all the rest of that weird jabberwock the immigrant workers here speak.

'Why did you really come to Norway?' I asked.

We'd be working together for nearly a year now and it was the first time I'd asked. Well, sure, I had asked before, but the difference this time was that *really*. I was asking for something more than the standard response, about the money being better, that it was hard even to find a job where he came from. Which was probably true, but not necessarily the whole truth. So this was the first time I'd asked out of genuine interest.

He didn't answer immediately. 'I had affairs with some of my patients.' Took a deep breath and, as though wanting to make sure I didn't get too alarmed, added: '*Female* patients. They opened themselves to their psychologist, they were vulnerable, and I exploited that.'

'Not good,' I said.

'No,' he said. 'Some of them were lonely and unhappy. But so was I, my wife had just died from cancer. I didn't manage to resist the invitations from these women. We needed each other.'

'So what was the problem?'

'In the first place, a psychologist is not allowed to have romantic liaisons with his patients, no matter what his civil status. And in the second place, some of the women were married.'

'Oh, I *see* . . .' I said slowly.

He glanced over at me. 'Someone talked,' he said. 'It came out and I was dismissed. I could always have got myself another job, for example lecturing at the university in Riga. But some of the husbands didn't think they'd had enough revenge and hired a couple of Siberians to make sure I ended up in a wheelchair. One of the women warned me and I had no choice but to get out. Latvia is a small country.'

'So you're the type who burns the candle at both ends and then lays the blame for it all on a tragic tale.'

'Yes,' said Pijus. 'I'm the bad version of a bad person, the kind who makes excuses for his own sleazy behaviour. If you look at it like that you're a better person than me, Ivar.'

'Oh?'

'Your self-contempt is more honest than mine.'

I hadn't a clue what he was talking about and concentrated on my coffee.

'So who is it your wife's been cheating on you with?' he asked and I spluttered coffee all over the dashboard. The pressure in the head came straight back. 'Easy now,' he said. 'Use your frontal lobe. That will tell you that I'm here to help. And that the best thing you can do is tell me. Remember, I've sworn an oath of confidentiality.'

'Confidentiality!' I said, the coffee cup in my hand trembling.

'All psychologists have to.'

'I know that, but you aren't my shrink.'

'Well, yes, I am not,' said Pijus as he handed me the roll of paper we always kept between the seats.

I wiped the coffee from my hands, my chin, the dashboard. Crumpled the paper into a ball and hissed between my teeth. 'Her boss at work. Nasty bastard. Ugly too. Trash, the whole man.'

'So you know him?'

'No.' What the hell had I just said? That Lisa had been cheating on me with her boss at the sorting office? Had she? Was that what we had quarrelled about?

'Never met him?' asked Pijus.

'No. Or actually yes. Or . . .' I thought about it. Lisa had talked a lot about Ludvigsen, so much that I perhaps just had the feeling of having met him. Her new boss praised her for the job she was doing, something her old boss never did. And Lisa bloomed. She'd always been susceptible to flattery, so desperate for it you had to keep it under control so she didn't get used to a level that was impossible for a husband or a boss to sustain. But Ludvigsen had just piled it on, and I'd probably thought that he wasn't doing it just to inspire the workers. Besides being a lot sweeter than I could remember her being, Lisa had got herself a new, short hairdo, taken off a few kilos and stayed out late in the evenings going to all sorts of different cultural things with friends I didn't even know she had. It was as though she'd suddenly got a life from which I was excluded, and that was probably why I checked her mobile phone. And found a message from this Ludvigsen. Or Stefan, which was how Lisa had him listed in her Contacts.

And so I sat there and told Pijus about it.

'What did it say in the message?' asked Pijus.

'I MUST see you again.'

'With the stress on must?'

'In capital letters.'

'Other messages?'

'No.'

'No?'

'She'd probably deleted them. The one I found was only a day old.'

'And her reply?'

'Nothing. Or else she'd deleted that.'

'If she was afraid of someone seeing the reply she would probably have deleted his message too.'

'Maybe she didn't have time to reply.'

'In a day? Hm. Or maybe she had no reason to feel guilty, maybe that was why she didn't delete anything. Maybe he came on to her, but she wasn't interested and didn't answer his message either.'

'That's exactly what she said, the fucking –' I took a breath. Slag. That's the kind of word, once it's out the bag, you can't get it back in again.

'You're afraid,' said Pijus.

'Afraid?'

'Maybe you should tell me what happened last night.'

'Duh, now you sound more like a cop than a psychologist.'

Pijus smiled. 'So then don't tell me.'

'Even if I wanted to I can't remember. Booze.'

'Or repression. Try.'

I looked at my watch. We were still well ahead of schedule, and as I say: we no longer had any reason to hurry on and get finished before one thirty.

So I tried. Because actually he was right, I was afraid. Was it because Lisa was lying on her side? Damned if I know, but there was something wrong, I just knew it. Something that had to come out, just like when the pressure rose in my head. I started to tell the story, but soon came to a halt.

'Take it easy and start from the beginning,' said Pijus. 'Include all the details. Memory is like winding up a ball of yarn, one association leads to the next.'

I did as he suggested, and damned if he wasn't right.

As I say, we were having a couple of drinks and Lisa suddenly said she was going out at the weekend. And I blew up and confronted her about the text message. I actually intended to let it go and just see what happened, but instead I lost it and began shouting that I knew her and Ludvigsen had something going on. She denied it, but she's had so little practice at lying it was almost pathetic. I put a bit of pressure on and she cracked, sobbing and admitting that on the firm's outing to Helsinki in the spring there was a lot of drinking and things happened. She claimed that was the reason she'd decided to give up drinking completely, so nothing like it would ever happen again. And I asked her if this wasn't a MeToo thing. If it wasn't Ludvigsen – who was her boss after all – who should take all the blame and not just half of it. And Lisa said well, yeah, maybe he was a little bit more to blame, because according to one of her colleagues he'd been plying her with drinks all evening. By this time I was really pissed off. I mean, you don't spit in your glass when the boss offers to buy you a drink, do you? Getting it down is more or less part of the job.

'And after that?'

'He's invited me to his house.'

'And where's that?'

'Kjelsåsveien 612.'

'So you've been there!'

'No!'

'Then how d'you know the address?'

'Because he told me of course.'

'But remembering it was 612, I mean, that's really ... it's very suspicious.'

She started laughing, and that was when I called her a slag, grabbed the car keys and stormed out before I could do anything worse.

'You mean worse than driving while intoxicated?' asked Pijus.

'Yes, worse than that,' I said.

'Please continue.'

'I drove around and yes, I did think about driving back home and killing her.'

'But you didn't do that?'

'That's what ...' I raised my hand to my chin, squeezed my cheek between thumb and forefinger. My voice was thick and trembling. 'That's exactly what I do not know, Pijus.'

I don't know if I'd ever called him by his name before. I'd thought of his name several times, must've done, but said it out loud? No, I'm pretty damn sure I never did.

'But you feel you might have done?'

The stomach pains came so suddenly and so violently that I instinctively bent forward.

I remained doubled over for a while before I felt his hand on my back.

'Come on now, Ivar, it'll be all right.'

'Will it?' I gasped. Completely fucking out of control.

'I could tell when you came to work today that something had happened. But I don't believe you've killed your little wife.'

'What the hell would you know about it?' I bellowed from between my legs.

'You walked away from your wife because you didn't want to do anything rash,' he said. 'And that was after you'd received confirmation of something you'd suspected for some time. You left to give your frontal lobe a chance to process something you knew your amygdala couldn't handle in the appropriate manner. That was a mature act, Ivar. It shows that you are beginning to understand how to deal with your anger. I think maybe you should call home and check your wife's OK, OK?'

I lifted my head and looked at him. 'Why do you care?'

'Because you cared?'

'Eh?'

'When I had just started and was the driver's mate on your truck. You helped me, told me in English what to do. Even though I could tell you hated speaking English.'

'I don't hate English, I'm just not good at it.'

Pijus smiled. 'Exactly, Ivar. You were willing to seem a little stupid in order to help me be a little less stupid.'

'Steady now, all I wanted was a driver's mate who knew what to do, or it would have meant long days and hard work for me, understand?'

'I understand. More than you know, maybe. You can tell when people are willing to help you. Don't you notice it now? Or do you think I only want to help because I don't want my driver's mate to screw everything up for me?'

I shook my head. Sure, I knew Pijus was helping me. The way he always did. Today with that crazy old baggage on the balcony wasn't the first time he'd covered for me. It's just that it's so fucking annoying when a foreigner comes and doesn't just take your job but ends up your boss. It just doesn't seem right. A guy can't just come along and take over something he has no right to. Something I have a right to. That means war. Someone has to die. OK, OK, you're not supposed to think like that, that's the kind of thinking that gets me in trouble, I know, I know. But what the fuck.

'I've got too much testerone,' I said.

'Testosterone,' said Pijus. OK, so he said it with that irritating grin of his.

'It makes you aggressive,' I said.

'Not necessarily,' said Pijus.

'More aggressive than horny, anyway. Maybe not surprising Lisa went looking somewhere else.'

'Wrong, wrong and wrong again,' said Pijus, and oh yeah, I could hear he was imitating me. 'When tests done on animals seem to show that testosterone exclusively promotes aggression, that's because the animals that have been given the testosterone are the ones that resort to aggression when a crisis occurs. But that's because the animal brain doesn't necessarily see any alternative solution. More up-to-date research actually shows that testosterone's function is more general than that. It prepares you to do whatever is necessary in critical situations. Whether than means aggression and anger or the opposite.'

'The opposite?'

'Suppose there's a diplomatic crisis that threatens world peace. What's needed then is not aggression but a rapid changeover to self-negating generosity and empathy directed towards someone you actually hate. Or say your job is to control a rocket landing on the moon. The computer fails and you have to work out the speed, the angle of approach and the distance in your head. Anger isn't the thing. And yet it's testosterone that comes to our aid in such situations.'

'Come on, you're making this up,' I said.

Pijus shrugged. 'Remember up by Storo?'

'Storo?'

'The freezing rain. We'd reversed up to the wall and were about to empty the bins there.'

He looked at me. I shook my head.

'Come on, Ivar. The truck was on a slope, and it began to slide down?'

I just shook my head again.

'Ivar, I was standing with my back to the truck and I would have been crushed to death if you hadn't lightning-quick turned the biggest wheelie bin up on its side between the truck and the wall.'

'Oh, that. Well, you wouldn't exactly have been crushed to death.'

'My point is that you showed you are capable of reacting both spontaneously and rationally at the same time. It is not the case that you *have to* lose your head when you feel the rush of adrenaline and testosterone. Don't worry, you're smarter than you think, Ivar. So call her. Use your testosterone to show empathy. And calculation.'

Well, I'll be damned. So I did call her.

No answer.

'She's probably asleep,' said Pijus.

I looked at my watch. Eight. Of course it could be that she was on the bus on the way to work, she wouldn't take the call then. I sent a text message. My feet were beating like drumsticks against the floor as I waited. The sun rose and was shining through the windscreen. It was going to be a hot day. A hot day in hell, I thought as I pulled off my jacket.

'We better get moving,' said Pijus and turned the key in the ignition.

I met Lisa at a party at a friend's place when I was at training college.

I had a go at this guy from Ljan who thought there was something he could teach me about respect. I knew he'd provoked me because he'd heard I was easy to wind up and I knew he did it because he was a good fighter and wanted to show off in front of the girls there. But knowing all that is no help at all, not when the guy in question came out with the type of stuff that was just asking for a sock on the jaw. To make a short story even shorter, the guy beat me up. Lisa wiped the blood from my nose with a toilet roll, helped me to my feet and walked home with me to the students' lodgings I had in Sogn. And stayed the night. And the next day. And the next week. In a word, she stayed.

We never had time to fall in love, never had time for the painful but at the same time wonderful uncertainty about whether or not the other one really does want you. The game, the doubt, the ecstasies – we gave it all a miss. We were a couple. Say no more. Some thought I'd got a woman who was too good for me, at least that's what they thought as time went by, because Lisa was actually in those early days quiet and sort of mousy, without the figure she acquired later when she put on a few kilos, and without that radiance that others besides me noticed she had once she got over the worst of her shyness.

They said she was good for me, that I'd quietened down, that I didn't seem so *volatile*, as the child psychiatrist called it, since he didn't dare call me unstable. And it's true, Lisa knew how to calm me, it was when she wasn't around or if I'd had one too many that things spiralled out of control. I was done once or twice for grievous bodily harm, but only served a couple of short stretches. And as I say, I had never laid a hand on Lisa. Never had any reason to. Not until now. I don't think she was ever scared of me, not once in her life. Scared for others maybe, friends and relations, if they said the wrong thing to me. And I suspect she was halfway relieved when the doctor told us we couldn't have kids. Shit, I was relieved myself, but of course I didn't say that. But Lisa was never afraid for her own safety, and that was probably why she'd dared to admit that stuff about Ludvigsen. But how could she kid herself she knew my limits when I didn't bloody know them myself and was sitting here wondering exactly what the fuck I might have done?

When I was ten years old my big brother and me were each given a glass of lemonade before our parents went out on a Saturday night. But the moment they were out the door my big brother spat in them both, two big, slimy blobs, and probably figured that now both drinks were his. But the thing is, you can't drink out of a glass with a busted jaw, and at the hospital all he got through the straw was water.

Anyway, what had happened now was that Lisa was like one of those glasses of lemonade. Spat on, spoiled. There was no other way I could look at it. I'd lost what I'd been given, and all that was left after that was useless retaliation, the levelling out of the pressure. Fuck you. Fuck me.

And now I felt it coming back. The pulsing in my temples.

Maybe because we were in Kjelsåsveien and had just passed number 600.

As we moved between houses and bins I was sometimes in and out of the cab, sometimes standing on the ladder at the back. Checking the mobile every time.

Maybe she was at a meeting.

With Ludvigsen.

OK, I mustn't think like that. And anyway, she wasn't. I don't know how come I was so certain about that, but I was.

And then there we were, Kjelsåsveien 612.

It was a villa, no more and no less flashy than any of the others in that area. The kind you don't have to be rich to live in if you'd inherited it from your parents, and they didn't need to have been rich either. But if you wanted to buy one now, it would set you back a few hundred thousand. Orchards cost money, even in the east end of town, where I live.

I noticed that the outside light above the porch was on. Either Stefan Ludvigsen didn't care about the cost of electricity, or he was the forgetful type. Or maybe he wasn't at work but still at home. Was that what had my pulse hammering away as I walked towards the garage? That he was going to come out, tell me that he hadn't been able to get hold of Lisa on the phone and that he'd called the police and they were on their way to our place? And it wasn't just the pounding of my heart that told me, I knew it with a sudden and absolute certainty: I'd done a murder last night. I felt it not just in my aching forearms, in my fingertips, in the thumbs that had pressed against the little larynx, but deep inside me. I was a killer. I saw the bulging eyes, the pleading, dying gaze up at me in resignation and despair before out they went, like red warning lights when the current's turned off.

Did he know, Ludvigsen? Was he sitting behind a window somewhere in there, looking at me? Maybe he didn't dare come out but was just sat there waiting for the police to arrive? I listened out through the quiet of the summer morning for the sound of sirens before opening the unlocked door to the garage where his four-wheel bin was. And there was a car. A spanking-new black BMW. Villains drive BMWs, right? Only I was the villain here. I wheeled the bin out; it was so heavy the wheels sank into the gravel and I had to push hard. I hooked it onto the hydraulics and met Pijus's gaze in the mirror. He shouted something, but it was lost beneath the whirring of the lift.

'Eh?' I shouted back.

'Isn't that your car?' I heard him say.

'I don't have any bloody BMW.

'Not that one!' shouted Pijus. 'That one.'

I saw he was pointing further up the road. And there, fifty metres in front of us, stood a white Corolla. A car due any time now its EU check. A car that had a prominent dent in the bonnet from where a fist had landed to emphasise a point in a discussion with a traffic warden.

It dawned on me. I think 'dawned' is the right word, because it means something that happens very slowly. It happened slowly because it was so hard for me to understand that Lisa would do something like that to me. There was the BMW that Ludvigsen should've gone to work in, and there was the Corolla that should've been at home in my garage. In other words Lisa had got up, seen the car was in the garage and driven it up here to where Ludvigsen was waiting for her.

I stared up at the house. They were inside. What were they doing now? I tried to blank out the images but I couldn't fucking do it. I wanted to kill somone. As in, murder them. As in, take someone's life and take the punishment for doing it. And it wasn't anger that was talking now. Or actually, it was. But it was the kind of anger I knew I'd never be able just to walk off. It had to come out. There was no other way for it. I had to get rid of Ludvigsen. Lisa . . . I couldn't finish the thought. Because even though I had this image of them on my brain, both naked in a big, hideous four-poster, there was something about the picture that didn't add up. Something that doesn't make sense. Like something you know you've forgotten someplace or other but you just can't remember where.

Anyway, soon as I was finished emptying this bin I was going to get the jack from the toolkit, march up to his house, get inside and become a killer. Now the decision was taken I felt a strange lightness in my head, as though the tension had already smoothed itself out. I was watching the bin rise when up the phone rang. I answered.

'Hi,' said Lisa.

I froze. I recognised the sounds in the background. She was in the Distribution Centre. She was at work.

'I see you've tried to call me several time,' she said. 'Sorry, but it's all a bit chaotic here today, no one knows where Ludvigsen is. Can we talk later?'

'Sure,' I said, watching as the bin reached the top of its arc. 'I love you.'

In the silence that followed I could sense her confusion.

'You're not . . .' she began.

'Oh yes,' I said. 'I'm hurt and upset.' The bin began to empty. 'But I love you.'

I hung up and looked at the Corolla. It was standing in shadow and still had dew on the windscreen. It must have been there all night.

The contents of the green wheelie bin came sliding out, and something hit the metal bottom of the hopper with a soft splash. I looked inside. There, between the bulging and knotted plastic bags and empty pizza cartons, lay a pale, plump body in blue pyjamas. And I must have met Stefan Ludvigsen before, because I recognised him. His staring, ruptured eyes looked straight past me. The marks on the throat had turned black. And it was like when the fog first starts to lift and the sun breaks through and suddenly seems twice as strong. Like ice melting from around the poles, the landscape of memories emerged with accelerating speed.

I recalled his sobbing and choked confession. His excuse was that he was recently divorced, he'd made a mistake. The kitchen knife he grabbed and began waving about in my face, thinking probably I was too drunk to be able to react quickly enough. He'd caught me one nick in the forehead before I knocked the knife out of his hand. The knife was good, it was what got me fired up. Gave me an excuse. Self-defence, for fuck's sake. So I'd squeezed the life out of him. Not too quickly and not too slowly. Not saying I enjoyed it, that would be an exaggeration, but at least it gave him time to understand. Time to regret. Time to suffer. Just like I did.

I watched as the compressor squeezed the half-naked body into something like a foetal position.

Standing on the ladder I turned and looked at the gravel pathway leading to the front door. No drag marks. I had tidied up after me, got rid of any possible traces I'd left, inside and out.

If I was drunk when I jumped into the Corolla and drove up here in the middle of the night and rang on his bell I sobered up instantly the moment I saw him lying dead on the kitchen floor. And sober enough to realise that if I got stopped for driving under the influence on the way home I would be on record, and later on it could be connected to Ludvigsen's disappearance. Because he had to disappear. Vanish, actually. Had I planned it all even before I rang his doorbell? Because Pijus, Pijus was right. I *did* have the ability to act quickly and at the same time be rational.

I went up to the cab and climbed in.

'Well?' said Pijus, looking at me.

'Well what?' I asked.

'Anything you want to tell me? As I told you, I've taken an oath of confidentiality.'

What the hell was I supposed to say to that? I looked eastward, to where the sun had risen over the ridge. The round would soon be over, and we would be heading that way, to the waste disposal centre at Klementsrud where the robot scanners would sort Ludvigsen away as the organic waste he was, and the conveyer belt transport him to the hell he deserved, where every trace, every memory, everything that lay behind us would be annihilated, and nothing of what we have lost will be recycled.

And I found the words, the ones that usually get stuck somewhere on the way out; this time they flowed from the tongue like music.

'Someone has to do the cleaning up,' I said.

'Amen to that,' said Pijus.

And the garbage truck shivered into life and set off down the road.

THE CONFESSION

'AM I BEING OF ANY help, officer?'

I put Simone's coffee cup down on the tablecloth on her coffee table. Her coffee cup. Her tablecloth. Her coffee table. Even the dish of chocolates in the middle of the table is hers. Things. Strange how little things mean once you're dead. One way or another.

Not that things were so important for her when she was alive either. I've just been explaining all this to the officer. That she told me I could take anything I wanted when she threw me out – the stereo, the TV, books, kitchen equipment, *you name it*. She was ready for it. She'd decided this was going to be a civilised break-up.

'In our family we don't argue over teaspoons,' she said.

I didn't argue either. Just stared at her, trying to discover the real reason hidden behind those vapid clichés she'd been spouting: 'Best for us both', 'moving in different directions' and 'time to move on'. And so on.

Then she put a sheet of paper down on the table and asked me to tick off whatever I wanted.

'It's just an inventory I've made. Don't let your feelings get in the way of common sense now, Arne. Try to see this as a controlled liquidation.'

She said. As though it was one of her father's subsidiary companies and not a marriage she was talking about. Naturally, I had been much too proud to even look at her list. Too hurt to take anything at all from the overgrown villa in Vinderen where we had shared both the good and – the way I remembered it – the very few bad days.

Maybe it was a bit hasty of me to just give up everything like that. After all, she was a wealthy young woman, good for fourteen million, whereas I am a debt-ridden photographer with a little too much faith in his own business skills. Simone supported my idea of starting my own studio along with six other photographers. If not financially then at least morally.

'Father doesn't see the economic benefits,' she said. 'I think you should back yourself, Arne. Show him what you can do, he's bound to invest in the project once he sees.'

On paper the money was hers, but it was her father who pulled the strings. The insistence on a prenup when we got married was, of course, his idea. He probably saw it all, how she'd soon grow out of her long-haired young photographer with his lofty dreams and his 'artistic ambitions'.

So I went for it, aggrieved and determined to show how wrong he was about me. Took the gold medal for borrowing at a time when banks were chucking money after you if you had anything at all that looked like a business idea. It took me six months to prove that Simone's father was right. As a rule it's hard to pinpoint the exact moment at which a woman stops loving you. With Simone it's easy. It happened when she opened the front door and the man standing on the steps told her he was from the enforcement court with a demand for the seizure of my assets. She treated the man with an icy politeness, wrote out a cheque, and we kept the car. She employed that same icy politeness when she asked me to take what I wanted when I left. I took my clothes, some bedlinen and a personal debt of just over one million kroner.

I should have taken the coffee table. Because I like this coffee table. I like the small dents on its surface, souvenirs of our wild parties, the paint splashes from the time I decided to paint everything in the living room green, and the one leg that was ever so slightly crooked from the first and only time we ever made love on it.

The investigating officer sits in an armchair facing me, and the notebook lies untouched on the table in front of him.

'I read that she was found on this sofa,' I say as I raise my coffee cup.

An unnecessary detail, of course. It was on all the front pages. The police couldn't rule out suspicious circumstances, and her family name was enough to arouse media interest. According to the coroner's report the cause of death was cyanide poisoning. At one time Simone took a course in goldsmithing with the idea of taking over her father's chain of shops, but as so often before she soon got bored with it. The bottles of cyanide she had smuggled out of the workshop were still down in the cellar. For the thrill of it, she maintained. But since there was nothing to suggest the poison came from her own bottles and no indication of how she had ingested it, the police were unwilling to conclude without further investigation that it was suicide.

'I know what you're thinking, officer.'

I can feel the springs beneath the sofa cover against my thighs. An old rococo sofa, her style. Had he had her on this sofa, her new guy, the architect? He moved in just a few weeks after I moved out. For all I know he was screwing her on the sofa while I was still living in the house. The officer doesn't ask me to explain what I mean when I say I know what they're thinking, so I go ahead on my own initiative:

'You're thinking she wasn't the type to take her own life. And you're absolutely right. Don't ask me how, officer, but I know she was murdered.'

He doesn't appear to be all that interested in my observations.

'And I also know that murder is bound to look bad for me as the scorned husband. It gives me a motive. I could have come to see her, I knew where she kept the poison, I could have slipped it into her coffee and then left. I imagine that's why you've been to my place, to see if there's a match between any of my clothes and the fibres you found here in Simone's house.'

The officer doesn't respond. I sigh.

'But since neither the fibres nor the footprints or fingerprints are mine you have no definite proof against me. So some bright spark has suggested bringing me here to the villa to see how I deal with being back at the scene of the crime. A little bit of psychological warfare. Am I right?'

Still no response.

'The reason you haven't found anything is simple. I haven't been here, officer. At least not this past year. And the housekeeper does a thorough job with her vacuum cleaner.'

I put down my coffee cup and take a Twist from the dish of chocolates. Coconut. Not my favourite, but perfectly acceptable.

'It's almost sad, officer. The way all traces of a person can be removed so quickly and so easily. As though one had never existed.'

The chocolate spins round four times when I pull on the ends of the wrapper. I remove the silver foil, fold it four times, run a fingernail over the folds and put it on the coffee table. Then I close my eyes and pop the chocolate into my mouth. Holy Communion. The absolution of sins.

Simone loved chocolates. Especially Twist. Every Saturday when I did the shopping at Kiwi I used to buy a big bag of them. It was one of our few routines. It was a sort of anchor in a life based on opportunism, whims, the occasional evening meal together and, as a rule, waking up in the same bed. We blamed our jobs, and I believed that everything would be different once we had a child. That would bring us together. A child. I remember how shaken she was the first time I brought it up.

I open my eyes again.

'We were the perfect Twist couple, Simone and I,' I say, and halfway expect the officer to raise one eyebrow and give me a puzzled look. 'I'm not thinking of the dance but the chocolate,' I explain. The officer evidently doesn't have a sense of humour. 'I like liquorice and nougat and

I hate banana creams. As it happens she loved the banana creams. You know, the ones with the yellow-and-green wrapping. Oh yes, of course, you've already . . . If ever we had guests I had to take them all out before I put the dish out, so she could have them herself the next day.'

I think about adding a light laugh, but instead – and quite unexpectedly – the little anecdote gives rise to an emotional avalanche. I feel something swelling in my throat. I've no intention of saying anything at all but then I hear my own tormented whisper:

'We loved each other, officer. We more than loved each other. We were the air each other breathed, we kept each other alive, do you understand? No, of course, why should you?'

By this time I'm almost angry. Here I sit, exposing my most private and painful thoughts to him, fighting back the tears, and the officer just sits there completely expressionless. He might at the very least offer a nod of commiseration or pretend to be taking a note.

'Until she met me Simone's life was meaningless and directionless, she was on the skids. On the surface everything seemed fine – the looks, the money, the so-called friends – but there was no substance, no direction, you understand? I call it the terror of things. Because things can be lost, and the more things you have the more afraid you are of losing them. She was drowning in her own affluence, she couldn't breathe. I came along and gave her space. Gave her air.'

I stop. In front of me the officer's face has started swimming.

'Air. The opposite of cyanide, officer. Cyanide paralyses the cells in the respiratory organs, you can't breathe and in a matter of seconds you choke to death. But I'm sure you know that?'

That's better. Talk about something else. I swallow, pull myself together and continue.

'This architect, Henrik Bakke, I don't know how she met him. She always said she met him after I moved out, and at first I believed her. But friends have told me how naive I was, pointing out that the guy moved in almost immediately. Before my side of the bed was even cold, as one of my friends put it. And yet, officer – and I know this may sound strange – it's actually a sort of comfort to know that it was her feelings for someone else that ruined everything for us. That what Simone and I had wasn't the kind of thing that just burns itself out of its own accord. That it took love to conquer love.'

I cast a quick glance at the officer but look away when his eyes meet mine. I'm usually careful when it comes to talking about feelings, especially my own. But there's something inside me now that has its own momentum and I can't stop. Maybe don't even want to stop.

'I think I'm a normally jealous guy. Maybe Simone wasn't a classic beauty, but she had an animal quality that made her beautiful in a dangerous way. She had a way of looking at you that could make you feel like the goldfish alone at home with the cat. But the men swarmed around her. Like crocodile birds around the mouth of the crocodile. She did something to their heads, she . . . well, you've seen her yourself. My black angel of death, I used to call her. I used to joke that she'd be the death of me, that one of her fanatical admirers would decide to do away with me. But deep down that didn't frighten me as much as the thought that one day she'd fall for one of those insistent suitors of hers. Like I say, I'm a normally jealous man.'

The officer has slumped deeper into the armchair. Not surprising really; so far I've said nothing of interest to the investigation. But he shows no sign of wanting to stop me either.

'And yet I've never been jealous of Henrik Bakke. Isn't that funny? At least not in the sense of hating him or having a grudge against him. I think the way I looked at it was that he was just another guy same as me, he loved Simone more than anything else on earth. I actually thought of him more as someone in the same boat as me than as a rival.'

I fish around with my tongue in the corner of my mouth where a shred of coconut has got stuck and feel a momentary stab of discomfort. The officer's silence is deafening.

'OK. So that wasn't exactly true. I *was* jealous of Henrik Bakke. At least the first time I met him. Let me explain. One day he called me at my office and asked if we could meet, he had some papers for me from

Simone. I knew these must be the divorce papers, and even though it was, of course, unspeakable of her to use her new lover to deliver them I was curious to know who he was and so I agreed to a meeting at a restaurant. I presume he was just as curious about me.

'Anyway, he turned out to be a really nice person – polite without being servile, intelligent but in a discreet way, and with a humorous appreciation of the comical aspect of our situation. We drank a couple of beers, and when he began after a while to talk about Simone it didn't take long for me to realise that he was having exactly the same trouble with her as I had had. She was a cat. She came and went as she pleased, she was spoiled and moody, and loyalty was not her most outstanding quality. If I can put it like that. He complained of all the men friends she had and wondered why she couldn't have female friends like other women. Talked about the nights she'd come home drunk after he'd gone to bed, and all the new and exciting people she'd met who she was so keen to tell him about. In a sort of aside he asked if I'd seen her since we'd split up and I'd moved out, and with a smile I had to tell him no. The smile was because I had realised that he was probably more jealous of me than I was of him. Isn't that something of a paradox, officer?'

The officer opens his mouth but then he changes his mind and leaves his jaw hanging half open. It looks very silly. Actually I had decided not to say too much, but it's funny how another person's silence can affect you. To start with I experienced it as threatening, but I can see now that it isn't what you might describe as a *speaking* silence. Not that the officer looks especially interested or attentive; what he exudes is more a sort of neutral nothingness. It's an absence of speech, a vacant space that operates like a vacuum sucking up my own words.

'We had another beer and a few good laughs as we swapped stories about some of her foibles. Such as how she always changed her mind after she ordered the food, so you had to get the waiter over and change the order. Or the way she always had to go to the toilet after she'd turned out the light and said 'goodnight'. And of course the Saturday shopping expedition and what a catastrophe it was if you forgot to buy the Twists.

'So I wasn't all that surprised to meet Bakke again at the Kiwi store on Saturday morning a couple of weeks later. We both laughed when I looked in a very demonstrative way at the bag of Twists in his shopping trolley. And he asked about the divorce papers, he said Simone's lawyer was waiting for them. I said I'd had a lot to do but that I would see to it next week. I was perhaps a little annoyed with him for bringing it up. I mean, what was the rush? He'd taken my place in her bed, surely that was enough to be going on with? It almost seemed as though he could hardly wait to get married to her. And her millions. So I asked him straight out if they were planning to get married. He looked bewildered, so I repeated my question. He smiled wanly and shook his head. And then I got the picture.'

I straighten the liquorice wrapper between my fingers. 'Lakris – lakrits – lakrids' it says. Danish and Swedish as well as Norwegian. Easy to understand anyway. It's good when neighbours speak almost the same language.

'There was something in his eyes, a pain I recognised from my own reflection in the mirror back then. Bakke was on his way out. Simone was bored. It was just a question of time, and he knew it, already he could taste the bitter fruits of defeat. Have you investigated that, officer? Asked her girlfriends if she had any such plans? You ought to, because that could give him a motive, don't you think? *Crime passionnel*, isn't that what you call it?'

Is that a smile I see curling the officer's lips? He doesn't respond. Of course not, he's under an oath of silence as regards anything to do with the investigation. All the same, at the thought of Henrik Bakke being a suspect I can't help but smile as well. I don't even try to hide it. We smile.

'Quite a paradox, isn't it? I never did get round to sending in those divorce papers, so Simone and I were still man and wife when she died. That makes me the sole heir, officer. So if it really was Henrik Bakke who killed her, what that means is that the man who stole the love of my life from me has made me a millionaire. Me. How's that for one of life's little ironies?'

My laughter echoes back at me from the flock wallpaper and the oak parquet flooring. I exaggerate it slightly, slap my thighs and put my head back. Then I see the officer's eyes. Cold, like a shark's. They nail me to the sofa. I stop instantly. Has he realised? I take another chocolate, a Daim, have already unwrapped it, but then change my mind and take a Nougat Bali instead. I repack the Daim in its wrapper. Must think. No, no need to think. One look at the officer is enough.

'The good thing about Twist is the wrapping,' I say. 'That you can change your mind. You can wrap it up again without anyone's being able to see it's been opened. Unlike most other things. Confessions, for example. Once a confession has been so to speak unwrapped then that's it, it's too late.'

The officer nods his head. It's more like a bow.

'OK,' I say. 'No more games.'

I say this as though I've just made up my mind here and now, but of course that's not the case. For several minutes now I've just been waiting for the right moment. And the right moment is now.

'You found those little bottles of cyanide solution in the cellar, didn't you, officer?' The chocolate melts on my tongue, and I can feel the hard centre against my soft palate. 'One was missing. I took that with me when I was thrown out. Not really sure why. I was pretty far down, maybe I had some idea of doing away with myself. You make hydrocyanic acid from cyanide, but you probably know that?'

My fingers sift through the chocolate bowl and find a banana cream but then put it straight back. Old habits.

'A couple of days after I met Bakke at the Kiwi store I bought a bag of Twists. At a chemist's I bought a disposable syringe which I filled with cyanide when I got home. I then opened the bag of chocolates, took out the banana creams and carefully unwrapped them, injected the poison, wrapped them again and put them back in the bag. The rest was simplicity itself. The following Saturday I waited outside the Kiwi store until Bakke pulled up in Simone's Porsche, slipped into the store in front of him with the bag of Twists under my coat, placed the bag at the front of the shelf with the Twists and from my position behind the shelving was able to see that he had picked the right bag.'

The officer sits with head bowed. As though he's the one confessing to murder by poison rather than me.

'I read that when Henrik Bakke found her he thought at first she was asleep. Pity he wasn't there when she died. He might have learned something. I mean, it must be fascinating to study a human being in transit between life and death, don't you think?'

The officer looks as though he might be preparing a response, a long and complex response that's going to require a lot of thought. I continue.

'I counted on you arresting Henrik Bakke as soon as you had the results of the autopsy. I presumed it would be an easy matter to work out that the cyanide came from the chocolates that Bakke had indisputably brought into the house.

'But you didn't, officer. You didn't manage to connect the poison to the remains of chocolate you found in her stomach because the chocolate had already melted and dissolved. So I began to worry that Henrik Bakke might get away with it.'

I drink what's left of my coffee. The officer's cup is still there, untouched.

'But once a second body arrives on his slab I'm pretty sure the coroner is going to be able work it out, don't you think? That the murder weapon was right there in front of you the whole time?'

I point to the dish of chocolates and fix him with a smile. No response.

'One last Twist before I raise the alarm, officer?' In the ensuing silence I can hear the faint crackling of a banana cream wrapper as it slowly begins to unfold like a yellow-and-green rose on the coffee table in front of him. That beautiful coffee table.

ODD

ODD WAS — SEEN FROM THE AUDITORIUM — standing in the wings on the right-hand side.

He tried to breathe normally.

How many times had he stood like that, dreading the prospect of making his entrance in front of a crowd as he listened to the person who was going to interview him build him up, ratchet up the expectations? And this evening they would already be high, given that tickets to enter cost twenty-five pounds, more than the price of any of his slender books. With the possible exception of English first editions of his debut book, which could no longer be found in the second-hand bookshops and was selling for three hundred pounds on the net.

Was that what made it so difficult to breathe? The fear that, as himself, the actual flesh-and-blood Odd Rimmen, he wouldn't live up to the hype? *Couldn't* live up to the hype. After all, they'd turned him into a kind of superman, a psychic intellectual who hadn't just analysed the human condition but also predicted sociocultural trends and diagnosed the problems of modern man. Didn't they understand that it was just *writing*?

And yes, naturally, an author's thought always had a subtext the author himself didn't necessarily understand or see. That applied even to those authors whom he himself admired. Camus, Saramago – he suspected that even Sartre hadn't fully plumbed his own depths, being more concerned with the external sex appeal of formulation.

Face-to-face with the page's – the computer's – neutral surface and the option of retreat it offered, he could be Odd Rimmen, the man whom the reviewer in the *Boston Globe* had, with the greatest respect, dubbed Odd Dreamin', a nickname that had stuck. But in person he was just Odd, a guy waiting to be exposed as a man of average intelligence with a slightly above average gift for language, and a distinctly below average control of his self-criticism and impulses. And he thought it was this latter – his lack of impulse control – that had led him to expose his emotional life so recklessly in front of thousands, indeed hundreds of thousands (not millions) of readers. Because even though the page/screen offered the option of retreat, the opportunity to regret and make changes, he never did so if he saw that it was *good*. His literary calling took precedence over his personal comfort. He could defy the weakness in his own character and move out of his comfort zone, as long as it all happened on the page, in his imagination, his dreams and his writing which, no matter what the theme or the degree of intimacy, was a comfort zone all its own, securely cut off from the life out there. He could write anything at all, and tell himself it was bound for the bottom drawer of his desk and would never be published. And then, once Sophie, his editor, had read it and massaged his writer's ego to the point at which he believed her claim that it would be a literary crime to deprive readers of this, it was just a question of closing the eyes, trembling and drinking alone, and letting it all happen.

But not with an interview onstage.

Esther Abbot's voice reached him like a far-off rumbling, a storm approaching across the stage. She was standing at a podium, with the armchairs they were to sit in ranged behind her. As though the creation of a setting that looked vaguely like a living room could make him feel more relaxed. An electric chair placed in a meadow full of flowers. Screw them.

'He has given his readers a new vantage point from which to view ourselves, our own lives, the lives of those closest to us, the world about us,' the voice said.

He could just about make out the English words. He preferred to be interviewed in English rather than his native language, exaggerating his accent so that the audience would suppose his inability to formulate himself clearly was an obvious result of the fact that he had to speak in a foreign language, and not the fact that in every oral encounter, even when speaking his own language, he became a clown who stumbled his way through even the simplest sentences.

'He is one of the most acute and uncompromising observers of our time, of our society, and ourselves as individuals.'

What rubbish, Odd Rimmen thought, drying the palms of his hands against the thighs of his G-Star jeans. He was a writer who had achieved a commercial breakthrough entirely on the basis of his descriptions of sexual fantasies that balanced so delicately on the edge of what was acceptable that they were described as controversial and brave, but were not *so* on the edge that they really did shock and upset anyone, at the same time as it was all therapy for any feelings of shame readers might have experienced at having entertained the same fantasies as the author. As he presently realised, the rest of what he wrote rode on the back of these sex descriptions. And Odd Rimmen knew – as did his editor, even though they had never talked about it – that in the books that followed he had gone on to offer variations on these sexual fantasies, despite the fact that they were, thematically speaking, alien elements. They were like long, misplaced guitar solos, with no other relevance than that they were something the public expected, and even demanded of him. A provocation that had become so normal it ought to have occasioned a yawn rather than a gasp, a routine that almost made him throw up, but that he excused by telling himself it was the wheels the rest of the text needed, the element that could deliver his real message to a larger readership than he would otherwise have reached. But he had been mistaken. He had sold his soul, and as an artist he had been damaged by it. Well, then let there be an end to it.

In the novel he was currently working on, and which he had not yet shown to his editor, he had weeded out everything that smacked of a commercial sell-out and cultivated only the poetic, the dreamlike vision, the real. The painful. No more compromises.

Nevertheless, here he was, and in a few seconds he would be brought onstage to deafening applause from a packed Charles Dickens Theatre, an audience that even before he opened his mouth had made up its mind that it loved him, just as it loved his books, as though the two were one and the same thing, as though his writing and his lies had told them all they needed to know about him long ago.

Worst of all was that he needed it. He actually needed their ill-founded admiration and unconditional love. He had become addicted to it, because what he saw in their eyes, the stolen goods he made away with, was like heroin. He knew that it was destroying him, corrupting him as an artist; and yet he *had* to have it.

'. . . translated into forty languages, read all over the world, crossing cultural barriers . . .'

Charles Dickens himself must have been the same kind of heroin addict. Not only had he published many of his novels chapter by chapter, and closely studied the public's response before starting on the next one, he had also undertaken tours in which he read from his own books, and not with the shy distance to his own text of the intellectual author, the lovable diffidence of the humble man, but with a shameless passion that exposed not just his thespian ambitions and, as far as that went, his acting talent too, but also the avidity of his desire to seduce the masses, both high and low, regardless of their position and intellect. And had not that same Charles Dickens – the social reformer, the defender of the poor – been every bit as interested in money and social status as some of his own, less sympathetic characters? And yet it wasn't this, as such, that Odd Rimmen objected to in Charles Dickens. It was that he had *performed* his art. Performed in the worst sense of the word. A combination of street trader and dancing bear, kept in chains by its owner so that it looks dangerous when, in reality, its testicles, claws and teeth have all been removed. Charles Dickens had given his public what it wanted, and what the public wanted at that particular point in time was social criticism.

Would Charles Dickens's writing have been better – or let's say even better – had he kept to the straight and narrow path of art?

Odd Rimmen had read *David Copperfield* and thought at the time he could have made a better job of it himself. Not a lot better, but better. But was that still the case? Or had his pen, his claws and his teeth lost the edge needed to create an art for posterity as a result of his submission to this circus? And if that were indeed the case, was there any way back?

Yes, he told himself. Because the new novel he was working was exactly that, wasn't it?

Nevertheless, here he was, with seconds to go before he was due onstage, about to bask in the admiring gazes, and the spotlights, milking the applause as he mechanically delivered his truisms; in a word, get his shot for the evening.

'Ladies and gentlemen, you've been waiting for him, and now here he is . . .'

Just do it. Not only was this the best slogan ever for trainers – or for any other product – it was also the answer he always gave whenever young people asked for his advice on how to start writing. That there was no reason to postpone it, no preparations needed, it was just about putting pen to paper, and not metaphorically but quite literally. He told them they should start writing that evening. Anything, anything at all, but it had to be now, that very evening.

It had been like that with Aurora, when he finally managed to leave her, after the endless rounds of discussions, tears and reunions that always ended with him back at Start. It had been about just doing it. Physically walking out the door and never returning. So simple, and yet so difficult. When you're addicted you can't just cut down on it and take a *little* heroin. Odd had seen his own brother try that, with fatal results. There was only one way out, and that was to go cold turkey. This evening. Now. Because it won't be better or easier tomorrow. It'll be harder. Postpone things and you end up standing even deeper in shit. What difference is it going to make to put things off for another day?

From the wings Odd Rimmen stared into the blinding backlight out there. He couldn't see the audience, just a wall of blackness. Maybe they weren't there. Maybe they didn't exist. And for all they knew, maybe he didn't exist either.

And there it was. The liberating, redemptive thought. His horse. It was standing there in front of him. All he had to do was put one foot in the stirrup and mount up. Just do it. The other option was not to do it. These were in fact his only alternatives. Or alternative, if he was going to be grammatically strict about it. And from now on he would be. Strict. Truthful. Uncompromising.

Odd Rimmen turned and walked away. He removed the microphone and transmitter from around his neck and handed them to a technician who looked up in bewilderment as he walked past him. He went down the stairs to the dressing room where he, the interviewer Esther Abbot and the publisher's PR had gone through some of the questions. Now the room was empty, and the only sound was Esther's voice from up there, a wordless, hollow booming that echoed through the ceiling. He grabbed the jacket he had left hanging over the chair, an apple from the fruit bowl, and headed out towards the performers' exit. Pushed it open and breathed in the London air of the narrow alleyway, a combination of exhaust fumes, burnt metal and cheese from the restaurant's extractor fan. Odd Rimmen had never smelled freer, fresher air.

Odd Rimmen had nowhere to go.

Odd Rimmen had everywhere to go.

One could say that it all began with Odd Rimmen leaving the Charles Dickens Theatre just seconds before he was due onstage to talk about his most recent publication, *The Hill*.

Or that it began with the *Guardian* writing about it, and saying he had let the paying public down, the arrangers of the Camden Literature Festival and Esther Abbot, the young journalist who had arranged the interview and said how much she had been looking forward to it. Or you could claim it started when the *New Yorker* contacted Rimmen's publisher and asked for an interview. When the publisher's press office told them that, unfortunately, Odd Rimmen didn't do interviews any more, the magazine had asked for his telephone number, hoping to try to get him to change his mind, only to learn that he no longer had a telephone. Indeed, that the publishing house didn't actually know where Rimmen was. No one had heard from him after he left the Charles Dickens Theatre that evening.

This was only partly true, but the *New Yorker* wrote an article about Odd Rimmen *in absentia* in which other writers, literary critics and cultural personalities spoke of their attitude to the author in general and to *The Hill* in particular. Living at his parents' summer place in France, Odd Rimmen could only react with astonishment at the list of famous names who suddenly seemed not only to have read him but to know him personally. That they should lie about their knowledge of his output in order to see their names in the pages of the prestigious *New Yorker* was perhaps no great surprise. And with a couple of days' warning they had naturally had time to glance through a couple of the books in order to get the feel of them, or skim the outlines on some website aimed at students. But that they should also express themselves on his *enigmatic personality* and his *very special charisma* was more surprising, since he could just about remember having met these people in a professional setting – at festivals, book fairs, prize-givings – and exchanged professional courtesies in a business in which courtesy borders on paranoia. (Odd Rimmen's theory was that writers are terrified of offending other writers because better than anyone else they know that a sensitive mind armed with a pen is like a child equipped with an Uzi.)

But in the light of the promise Odd Rimmen had made to himself to be ascetic and pure and to refrain from anything that might be construed as (correction: that might *be*) selling out, intellectual swindle or self-aggrandisement, he had denied himself the right to correct the impression readers of the *New Yorker* might form of him as a kind of literary cult figure.

Regardless of where it began, it continued. And that was what his editor told him when she called him at his remote village home.

'Something's happened, Odd. And it's not stopping, it's just getting bigger.'

Sophie Hall was referring not just to the sales figures but to all the requests for interviews, the invitations to festivals, the pleas from foreign publishers that he visit them for the launch of *The Hill*.

'It's just crazy,' she said. 'After that thing in the *New Yorker* –'

'It'll blow over,' he said. 'One piece in a magazine doesn't change the world.'

'You've cut yourself off so you don't know what's happening. Everyone's talking about you, Odd. *Everyone*.'

'Oh really? And what are they saying?'

'That you . . .' She gave a little laugh. 'That you're slightly crazy.'

'Crazy? *In a good way?*'

'*In a very good way.*'

He knew exactly what she meant. They had talked about it. That the writers who fascinate us are the ones who describe a world that is easy enough to recognise but one viewed through glasses that are very slightly different from the ones we wear. Or they wear, thought Odd Rimmen, since what his editor was telling him was that he had now been promoted to the league for those who see things differently, the intellectually eccentric. But did he belong there? Had he always done so? Or was he a bluff, a conventional wannabe who acted weird just for effect? As he listened to his editor describing the interest in Odd Rimmen, could he not also hear a greater respect in her voice? As though not even she, who had followed him so closely, from sentence to sentence so to speak, was immune to this sudden change of mood, all brought on by a single event: that, almost on impulse, he had run out on an interview just before he was due onstage. Now she was telling him she had just reread *The Hill* and been struck by how good the book they had worked on together *really was*. And even though Odd Rimmen suspected she had merely read the book in another light – the light of the admiration of others – he said nothing.

'What is this about, Sophie?' he asked when she paused for breath.

'Warner Brothers have been in touch,' she said. 'They want to buy an option on *The Hill*.'

'You're kidding.'

'They want to get Terrence Malick or Paul Thomas Anderson to direct.'

'They *want* to?'

'They're wondering if you'd be happy with either of them.'

Would I be happy with Malick or Anderson? thought Odd Rimmen? *Thin Red Line. Magnolia*. Here were two top-quality directors who had managed the almost impossible feat of getting the public at large to go to art films.

'What do you say?' Sophie's voice had the whining overtones of a fourteen-year-old, as though she herself could hardly believe what she was telling him.

'I would've been very happy with either of them,' he said.

'Great, I'll call Warner Brothers and –' She stopped. She had probably heard it.

Conditional sentence, type 2. *Would've been*. Which, as she had once pointed out to him, was actually a verbal contraction of *I would have been*, but one which the copy editor had let pass. Nevertheless, the Conditional. Something that would have happened, had certain conditions been fulfilled. And now she was wondering what the conditions might be. So he told her.

'If I'd've wanted to sell the film rights.'

'You ... you don't *want* to?' The whining overtone was gone. Now she definitely sounded as though she couldn't believe what she herself was saying.

'I like *The Hill* fine just the way it is,' he said. 'As a book. As you said yourself, just lately the book seems to have turned out to be *really* quite good.'

He didn't know if she registered the irony in what he had just said. Normally she would have done. Sophie had a good ear, but right now she was so shaken by everything that was happening that he wasn't so sure.

'Have you thought this through properly, Odd?'

'Yes,' he said. That was the strangest thing. Less than a minute ago he'd been told that one of the biggest film companies in the world wanted to ask two of the world's best directors to direct *The Hill* and make a film, something that would boost not just this book but every book with Odd Rimmen's name on it, past and present, and turn him into a global superstar. But he had thought through the possibility of getting a really big film offer. Daydreamed about it would be a more accurate description. Because apart from the aforementioned sex scenes there was nothing filmatic about Odd Rimmen's novels. Rather the opposite, in fact. They were largely interior monologues with few external events and little conventional dramaturgical structure. And yet still he had thought it through. Only as a hypothetical possibility, naturally, a thought experiment, in which he weighed the arguments against each other while gazing out over the Bay of Biscay. Charles Dickens wouldn't just have yelled out a jubilant Yes! The old ham would have insisted on playing at least one of the main characters himself.

The old, pre-Charles Dickens Theatre Odd Rimmen would have said yes as well but it would have left a bad taste in his mouth. He would have justified himself by saying that in an ideal world he would have said no thanks and kept his book pure. Reserved it for the patient reader, the reader who did not accept simplifications, who would take each sentence at his own pace, guided by the speed of the eye, the maturing of contemplation. But in world ruled by money and vacuous entertainment he could not say no to the kind of attention his type of book (serious, literary) was being offered here, since he was under an obligation to spread the (literary) word, not just to himself, but to everyone who was actually trying to say something in their writing.

Yes, that's what he would have said, and in secret savoured all the attention garnered by the film, the book, and by his own apparent dilemma.

But the new Odd Rimmen rejected that type of hypocrisy. And because he had thought it through, and reality was turning out not to be all that different from the daydream, he was specific about it to his incredulous editor.

'I've thought it through, Sophie, and the answer's no, I'm not going to let *The Hill* get cut down to a two-hour synopsis.'

'But it's so short anyway. Have you seen *No Country For Old Men?*'

Naturally Odd Rimmen had seen this, and naturally she would mention it, he thought. Sophie knew that he loved Cormac McCarthy, knew that he knew that the Coen brothers had managed to *film* that short novel in a one-to-one correlation unlike any other film he could think of. And Sophie also knew that Odd Rimmen also knew what that film had meant for the spread of the books of a writer who had until then been a literary cult figure – and without doing (too) much apparent damage to his reputation among the literary elite.

'Cormac wrote it first time around as a screenplay,' he said. 'The Coen brothers themselves said that when they were writing the screenplay one of them held the book open while the other copied from it. That won't work with *The Hill*. Anyway, I'm in the middle of something in the new book, I'm going to have to hang up now and get back to the writing.'

'What? Odd, don't . . .'

Odd Rimmen was standing in the queue outside the Louvre in Paris when he saw her coming out. Esther Abbot looked as though she wanted to pretend she hadn't seen him but must have known that her surprised expression gave her away.

'So, we meet again,' she said. She was walking arm in arm with a man whom she pulled in closer, as though the mere sight of Odd Rimmen was a reminder that men could disappear at any moment unless she kept a close eye on them.

'I'm sorry,' said Odd Rimmen. 'I never got the chance to apologise.'

'*Never?* Was there someone or something preventing you?'

'No, not really. I apologise.'

'Perhaps you should have saved it for all those people who turned up to hear you.'

'Absolutely. You're right.'

He thought she looked good. Better than he remembered her from the theatre. He thought that perhaps then she had been concentrating too much on the job. Too ingratiating for her to have aroused the seducer in him, the way prey will play dead until the predator loses interest. But standing here now, with a summer tan, slightly angry, with the wind in her hair and a man on her arm, she was quite simply attractive. So attractive that it seemed strange to Rimmen that she had automatically drawn the man she was with closer to her as soon as she saw him. It should really have been the other way round, with the male discreetly marking his territory when confronted by another male of about his own age, and one of a presumably higher social status now, following that article in the *New Yorker*.

'Could I buy you both a glass of wine to show that I mean it?' asked Odd Rimmen. He looked enquiringly at the man, who seemed to be looking for a polite way to decline the offer when Esther Abbot said she thought that sounded nice.

Her companion smiled like a man with a drawing pin in his shoe.

'Some other time, perhaps,' he said. 'You're on your way in, and the Louvre is so big.'

Odd Rimmen studied the ill-matched couple; her bright and light with the sun in her eyes, him as dark and heavy as a trough of low pressure. How could such an attractive woman fall for something as charmless as that? Had she no idea of her own market value? Indeed she did. He could see that, and it struck him that Esther had pulled her boyfriend/husband/lover closer to show him that this Rimmen wasn't something he had to consider a threat. And why did her man need this kind of reassurance? Did she have a history of promiscuity, of being unfaithful?

Or had they talked about him, this unpredictable author? Had Esther somehow indicated to the man at her side that he had reason to fear competition from Odd Rimmen? Was that what lay behind the expression of mingled hatred and fear he saw in the other man's gaze?

'I often go to the Louvre, I've seen most of what's worth seeing,' said Odd, responding to the gaze with a friendly calm. 'Come on, I know a place where they serve a good burgundy.'

'Perfect,' said Esther.

They found the restaurant and even before the first glass had arrived Esther had started to ask questions that Odd suspected were left over from the interview that had never been. Where did Odd get his inspiration from? How far were the main characters based on himself? Were the sex scenes based on personal experience or were they fantasies? At this last question Odd saw the man's face twitch. (His name turned out to be Ryan and he worked at the Embassy in Paris). Odd replied but made no attempt to improvise or be amusing as he usually did (often successfully) when 'performing'. When he *did* perform. But in due course he turned the conversation around to Esther and Ryan.

Ryan seemed to make a point of not revealing what his job at the Embassy actually involved and in doing so clearly hinted that it was something secret and important. Instead he spoke of how the techniques of international diplomacy had been influenced by research done by the psychologist Daniel Kahneman on 'priming' – the idea that by using simple means you can place a thought or an idea in a competitor's head without their being aware of it. That if you show people a poster with the letters E A T and then S O _ P and asked them to fill in the blank, far more of them will write SOUP rather than SOAP by comparison with those in a research group who have not been previously shown E A T.

Odd could see that Ryan was making a real effort to be interesting, but since the pop psychology he was dishing up was already stale news Odd presently turned his attention to Esther. She said she lived in London, where she worked as a freelance culture journalist but that she and

Ryan commuted to see each other 'as often as they could'. Odd noticed that she seemed to be directing this more to Ryan than to him, perhaps with a subtext along the lines of: Do you hear that, Ryan? I'm describing things as though we still have a passionate relationship, that all we wish was that we could spend more time together. Happy now, you fucking boring *whitewasher*?

Odd guessed all of this must be just one of Odd Dreamin's excursions. But maybe it wasn't so far off the mark either?

'Why have you just stopped?' Esther asked as the waiter poured out a third glass.

'I haven't. I'm writing more than ever. And better, I hope.'

'You know what I mean.'

He shrugged. 'Everything I have to say is on the pages of the books. The rest is just distraction and bluff. I'm a sad and pathetic clown. Exposing myself as a person doesn't do my work any favours.'

'No, on the contrary, it seems,' said Esther and raised her glass. 'It seems like the less people see of you, the more you get talked about.'

'My books, I hope you mean.'

'No, you.' Her eyes lingered a little too long on his. 'And, as a result of this, your books, naturally. You're in the process of turning from a cult-cult writer into a mainstream-cult writer.'

Odd Rimmen savoured the wine. And the characterisation. Licked his lips. Hm. Could already feel himself wanting more. More of everything.

When Ryan left to go to the toilet he leaned forward and put his hand over Esther's.

'I'm a little bit in love with you,' he said.

'I know,' she said. And he thought she couldn't possibly know, because until that very moment he hadn't been. Or had he – unlike her – simply not realised it until now?

'What if it's just the wine?' he said. 'Or that with Ryan sitting there you're unattainable?'

'Does it make any difference?' she asked. 'If it's because you're lonely or because I happen to have been born with a symmetrical face? Our reasons for falling in love are banal. It doesn't make falling any the less delightful, does it?'

'Perhaps not. Are you in love with me?'

'Why should I be?'

'I'm a famous writer. Isn't that banal enough?'

'You're a *nearly*-famous writer, Odd Rimmen. You aren't rich. You left me just when I needed you most. And I've a feeling you could do it again if you got the chance.'

'So you *are* in love with me?'

'I was in love with you before I met you.'

Both raised their glasses and drank without taking their eyes off each other.

'It's just incredible,' Sophie almost shouted into the phone. 'Stephen Colbert!'

'Is that big?' Odd Rimmen leaned back and the rickety wooden chair gave a warning groan. He looked out at the old apple trees that his mother claimed she could remember bearing fruit. The air smelled of wild, neglected garden and of the sea, borne on the pleasantly cooling Atlantic breeze from the Bay of Biscay.

'Big?' gasped Odd Rimmen's editor. 'He's overtaken Jimmy Fallon! You've been invited onto the biggest talk show there is, Odd!'

'Because . . . ?'

'Because of the filming of *The Hill*.'

'I don't understand. I said no to the film.'

'That's *exactly* it! Everyone's talking about it on social media, Odd. Everyone's raving about your integrity. The man who sits in a run-down old house in France and writes a book about nothing, that won't sell any copies, says no to worldly fame and stinking riches in the name of the art of writing. Right at this moment you are the coolest writer in the world, do you realise that?'

'No,' Odd Rimmen lied. Because naturally he had been well aware that the uncompromising and apparently puritanical choices he had been making since that evening at the Charles Dickens Theatre not necessarily *would* but very likely *could* result in exactly the same thing as was happening now.

'Let me think about it.'

'The recording is next week but they need an answer today. I've booked your flight to New York.'

'I'll get back to you.'

'Great. You sound very happy by the way, Odd.'

There was a pause, a moment in which Odd wondered whether she might have unintentionally identified what he was really feeling. Triumph. No, not triumph, for that would suggest a goal he had consciously been aiming for. And all he had been aiming for was to organise things in such a way that he could write truthfully, without worrying about anyone or anything, and certainly not his own so-called popularity.

All the same. He had just been reading the neuroendocrinologist Robert Sapolsky's description of how a recovering alcoholic's reward centre in the brain can be activated simply by walking down the street where his favourite bar from the old days is; even though he has no intention of drinking, the acquired expectation from the days of his drinking will liberate the dopamine. Was that what was happening to him now? Was it the mere prospect of a worldwide attention focused on his person that made the hairs on the back of his neck stand up? And he wasn't sure, but was it maybe panic at the thought of ending up in the same old mess as before that made him grip the phone tighter and say a cold, hard no.

'No?' Sophie repeated, and from the slight confusion in her voice Odd realised she thought he was responding to what she had said about him sounding happy.

'No I won't be going on the talk show,' he specified.

'But . . . your book. Odd, honestly, this is a fantastic opportunity to tell the world that it exists. That real literature does exist. You've got to do it!'

'If I did do it then I would have betrayed my vow of silence. I would have betrayed all those who, according to you, praise me for my integrity. I would have become the clown again.' (He noticed that he was using the Conditional.)

'In the first place there's no one to betray, Odd. You're the only one who's committed to your silence. And as for being a clown that's your vanity talking, not the man to whom literature is a *calling*.'

There was an edge to the editor's tone Odd Rimmen hadn't heard before. As though she'd just about had enough. Had already had enough. She simply didn't believe he was being honest. That he, with his anti-Charles Dickens attitude, had become more like Charles Dickens than Dickens himself. Was that it? Was he just playing the part of the principled artist? Well, yes and no. His frontal lobe, the part of the brain that, according to Sapolsky, was responsible for considered decisions, that was probably honest. But what about the nucleus accumbens, the pleasure centre that demanded enjoyment and immediate reward? If the two of them were devil and angel, one on each shoulder whispering into his ears, it wasn't easy to know which he was listening to, which was his true master. All Odd Rimmen could say with certainty was that he had been honest that evening he left the theatre. But hadn't something happened once he discovered that his steadfast resistance to being publicly promoted had resulted in exactly the opposite, that he had become the priest who, with his vow of celibacy, had paradoxically become a sex symbol, and who in all secrecy – secretly even from himself – enjoyed it?

'Odd,' said Sophie, 'you've got to head for the light. D'you hear? Head for the light! Not the darkness.'

Odd coughed. 'I've got a book to write. Tell them that, Sophie. And yes, you're right, I am happy.'

He ended the call. Felt a warm hand touch his neck.

'I'm so proud of you,' said Esther, sitting in the garden chair beside him.

'Are you?' Odd turned and kissed her.

'In an age where all people do is run after the clicks and the likes? You bet I am.' She stretched her arms in the air and yawned, supple as a cat. 'Shall we go into town or just eat home this evening, what d'you think?'

Odd wondered who it was who'd leaked the news that he'd said no to a film of The Hill. Whether it was Sophie. Or whether indirectly he was responsible himself, since he had, after all, mentioned it to several people who might have spread it about.

Going to bed that evening he thought of what Sophie had said about heading for the light. Wasn't that what you said to people who were about to die? That when they reached the other side they would see a bright light and they should turn their steps in that direction? Like a moth to the garden lamp that in another moment would scorch off its wings, Odd thought. But he had another thought too: had Sophie meant that, as a writer, he was dying?

Autumn came, and with it a withering of Odd Rimmen's creativity.

He'd heard other writers talking about writer's block but never quite believed in it himself. At least not for him. He was Odd Dreamin'. The golden goose. The stories just rolled out of him whether he liked it or not. So he assumed it was something that would pass and took the chance to spend more time with Esther. They went for long walks together, discussed literature and films. A couple of times they drove to Paris in Odd's old Mercedes and visited the Louvre.

But the weeks passed and still he couldn't write. His head was empty. Or rather, it was filled with things that didn't make for good literature: good sex, good food, good drink, good conversation, real closeness. The suspicion arose: was it the fault of all this happiness? Had it made him lose the despairing courage that had driven him to explore those dark corners from which he had sent back his reports? But even worse than the euphoric happiness was the sedate security. The feeling each day that nothing was really all that important, just as long as he and Esther had each other.

They had their first quarrels. The way she did the housework. Whereabouts things were kept. Trifles, things that he had never normally bothered with. But enough for her to pack a bag and say she was off to London to spend a few days with her parents.

Odd thought it was a good thing. Now he'd find out if that was enough to get Odd Dreamin' up and about again.

Sunday morning he had moved out from his study to the garden table under the dead apple trees, and then indoors again to the dining-room table. Didn't help. No matter how hard he tried he couldn't manage more than a couple of meaningless sentences.

He considered ringing Esther to tell her he loved her but didn't. Instead he asked himself if he would be willing to exchange happiness and Esther for the ability to write again.

Maybe the answer didn't surprise him, only the speed with which it came: yes, he'd make that trade.

He loved Esther, and right now he hated writing. But he could live without Esther. On the other hand, without writing, he would die, wither and rot.

He heard the door open.

Esther. She must have changed her mind and taken an earlier train. But from the sound of the footsteps Odd knew it couldn't be her.

Someone was standing in the living-room doorway. Long, open raincoat over a suit. Dark hair and a sweaty quiff plastered against his forehead. Panting.

'You stole her from me,' said Ryan, his voice hoarse and quavering. He stepped forward and raised his right hand. Odd saw that it held a gun.

'And for that you want to kill me?' asked Odd. He was a little surprised to hear how matter-of-factly he spoke, but he was only saying what was on his mind. He really was more curious than afraid.

'No,' said Ryan, turning the pistol in his hand and holding it out to Odd. 'I want you to do it yourself.'

Odd, still seated, took the gun and looked down at it. Long lines of numbers – he was reminded of telephone numbers – were engraved along the black steel barrel. And now that he was safe he felt an even stranger sensation. A mild disappointment that the threat had gone as quickly as it had come.

'Like that, you mean?' asked Odd and placed the muzzle of the gun against his temple.

'Exactly like that,' said Ryan. His voice was still quavering, his eyes glazed in a way that made Odd wonder if he might perhaps be under the influence of some chemical substance.

'You know you won't get her back even if I'm gone?' said Odd.

'Yes.'

'So why get rid of me? It's not logical.'

'I insist that you take your own life. All right?'

'What if I refuse?'

'Then you'll have to kill me,' said Ryan. His voice was no longer just hoarse, it was choked with tears.

Odd nodded slowly as he went through it: 'So one of us has to go. Does that mean you can't bear to live in a world in which I exist?'

'Shoot one of us now and get this over with.'

'Or do you want me to kill you so that when Esther finds out she'll leave me and dream of you, the one person she can't have back?'

'Shut up and do it!'

'And if I still refuse?'

'Then I'll kill you.' Ryan reached inside his coat and pulled out a second black gun. The paint on it seemed strangely dull. He squeezed the grip so tightly Odd could hear the plastic crack. Ryan pointed the barrel at Odd, who raised the gun he was holding himself and pulled the trigger.

It happened quickly. Very quickly. So quickly that afterwards Odd Rimmen's defence attorney would have (Conditional) been able to convince a jury that it was only the brain's quicker amygdala, with its fight, flight or freeze response, that had had time to react. That the frontal lobe, the one that says to you *hey, wait a sec, think this through*, had never had time to engage.

Odd Rimmen got up from his chair, walked over to Ryan, looked down at him. At Esther's former boyfriend. At this formerly living human being. At the bullet-hole on the right-hand side of the forehead. And at the toy pistol lying at his side.

Odd bent down and lifted it up. It weighed almost nothing and the butt was cracked.

He'd be able to explain to a jury. But would they believe him? That the dead man had given him his own, real gun and then threatened him with a harmless, broken toy? Maybe. Maybe not. Of course the pain of love can drive a man mad, but a trusted member of the British diplomatic service would hardly have a history of abnormal behavioural or psychiatric problems. No, a defence based on the claim that Ryan had deliberately solicited his own death as a sublime revenge would seem too far-fetched for the average male or female juror to take.

But then something else struck Odd: that reporting it would be a news sensation. And give birth to a thousand myths. Author kills rival in love drama. But this thought at least had time to be processed in the frontal lobe. And there, of course, dismissed.

He crossed to the door and looked out. An unfamiliar Peugeot was parked just outside the gate. The nearest neighbour was so far away that it was unlikely the shot from within the living room had carried. He returned to the corpse, searched the coat pockets and found car keys, a mobile phone, wallet, passport and a pair of sunglasses.

Odd spent the next few hours burying Ryan's body in the garden. Ryan's grave was directly under the largest apple tree, where Odd usually placed the table when he was working, or when he and Esther were eating. He didn't choose the site because he was morbid but because the ground was already well trodden and no one would find a bare patch of grass there unusual. And on the few occasions he had seen dogs on their property it had been on the periphery of the garden, they never ventured that close to the house.

Light rain had started to fall, and by the time he was finished his clothes were wet and dirty. He showered, put his clothes in the washing machine, scrubbed the floor in the living room and waited for night to fall.

When it was dark enough he put on Ryan's coat and sunglasses, his own gloves and a dark cap he found in one of Esther's drawers. He stuffed a lightweight rain jacket into the coat pocket and went out.

In a strangely elated mood he drove Ryan's Peugeot the six kilometres to the clifftop at Vellet. There were often people here during the daytime, especially at weekends, but seldom after dark, and Odd had never seen anyone there when it was raining. He left the car in the car park and walked the hundred metres up to the lookout point. Stood on the very edge of the cliff and looked down at the waves below as they smashed into foaming white surf. He took Ryan's mobile phone from his pocket and dropped it over the edge. Watched it disappear soundlessly into the darkness. Then he pulled the rain jacket out of one coat pocket and made sure the car keys, passport and wallet were still in the other before folding the coat and placing it on the ground, clearly visible and with a stone on top to stop it blowing away.

Then he put on the rain jacket and headed towards home. Thoughts came and went in his head as he walked. Deep down had he always known that the gun Ryan was holding when he shot him was a toy? If so, why had he pulled the trigger anyway? Had his brain had time to consider the alternatives? What would have happened had he *not* shot him? What would Ryan's next move have been? To attack him physically? So that Odd would still have had to shoot him, but it would have left him without the excuse of feeling that his life was threatened?

It was ten o'clock by the time Odd got back to the house and he made himself some coffee. Then he sat down at his computer and wrote. And wrote. He did not return to this world until gone midnight, when he heard the door open.

'Hi,' she said, and just stood there, sort of waiting.

'Hi,' he said, walked over to the woman he loved and kissed her.

'Well, hello,' she said softly as she put her hand against his crotch. 'You *have* been missing me.'

The police made no attempt to hide the fact that they regarded Ryan Bloomberg's disappearance as a suicide. Not just because all the finds and circumstantial evidence pointed in that direction but also because Ryan's close friends and family spoke of his despair following the break-up with Esther, and of how he had voiced suicidal thoughts. The presumption of suicide was further strengthened by the fact that he had recently purchased a Heckler & Koch pistol, and had chosen to kill himself close to where Esther was living with her new love Odd Rimmen.

On the Sunday in question Esther had been in London and not returned home until late, but Odd Rimmen had been at the house and was able to tell police that he had seen a Peugeot parked by the gate outside the house, and that he thought he saw a man sitting inside it, and presumed that he was waiting for someone. This fitted with the police trace on Ryan Bloomberg's mobile, they said. Signals from local base stations enabled them to see how Ryan/Ryan's phone had started moving westward from Paris at first light in the morning, that it had been in the vicinity of Rimmer's house for some hours before the last signal was received close to the clifftop at Vellet.

So police activity in connection with the disappearance was confined to a short and intense search, and no one was surprised – given the strong ocean currents in the area – that no body was found.

After some hesitation Esther decided not to go to the commemorative ceremony in London, fearing it might upset those of Ryan's friends and relatives who blamed her for his death. She told the Bloomberg family of her decision, adding that she would pay her respects later.

Odd Rimmen wrote with renewed zest. And made love with new zest too.

'Let us celebrate this glorious day with a glass of something,' he might say as the sun set in yet another blaze of red, orange and lilac. Then head down into the cellar to fetch one of the dusty bottles of apple wine. And then sometimes he might cross to the small, disused woodstove standing hidden in the darkest and most remote corner. Open the door, poke his hand inside and feel the cold steel of the Heckler & Koch, run his fingertips over the numbers on the barrel.

*

'I'm pregnant,' said Esther.

She stood by the kitchen window with an apple in her hand, looking out across the Bay of Biscay where the livid sky and the whitecaps showed that yet another winter storm was on its way.

Odd put down his pen. He had been writing since morning. He was now several weeks past his deadline. But he was writing again, that was the most important thing. And he was writing well. In fact damned well.

'Are you sure?'

'Pretty sure.' She laid a hand on her stomach as though she could already feel it growing.

'Well, that's . . .' He looked for the word. And suddenly it was as though his writing block had returned. He knew that there was only one, absolutely correct word. Situations were like bolts. There was one, and only one, nut that fitted. It was just a question of rooting around long enough in the drawer until you found it. In recent weeks the words had just come, presented themselves without his having to look; now, suddenly, it was pitch-dark. Was *fantastic* the right word? No, getting pregnant was trivial, something nearly all healthy humans could manage. *Good?* That would sound like a deliberate understatement, ironic and therefore doubly dishonest. During the nine months in which they had lived together he had explained to her that his work was everything; that nothing could be allowed to stand in its way. Not even her, the woman he loved more than anything (more correctly: than any other woman). *Catastrophe?* No. He knew she wanted to have children. If she never said so explicitly the tacit assumption was that they wouldn't be spending the rest of their lives together, that at some point she would have to find someone who would be father to her child/children. Now she'd managed it without that, and she was an independent woman who would be very well able to manage as a single mother. So *inconvenient*, perhaps, but not *catastrophic*.

'Well, that's . . .' he repeated.

Did he suspect that she'd done this on purpose? That she'd been careless with her birth pills in order to test him? And if so: had it worked?

Too bloody right it had. To his own surprise Odd Rimmen realised that he was, if not happy, then at least pleased. A child.

'That's what?' she asked at length. It was clear he'd missed a deadline here too. Odd stood up and crossed to where she was standing by the window. Put his arms around her as he looked out into the garden. At the big apple tree that after twelve barren years had suddenly started to bear fruit again. As they harvested the big red apples and carried them into the kitchen Esther wondered what the cause might be. He replied that the roots were probably getting richer nourishment than usual. He could see she was going to ask him what he meant by that, and to be honest he didn't know what he would have said if she'd done so. But she let it pass.

'That's a miracle,' replied Odd Rimmen. 'Pregnant. A child. It really is a miracle!'

The news that Odd Rimmen had declined the invitation to appear on the world's biggest talk show circulated for a while, but as far as Odd could see it didn't have the same effect as the article in the *New Yorker* and the way he'd turned down the film project. It was as though the story of 'Odd Rimmen: The Recluse' had already been taken on board, and this was just one more version of the same thing.

The reason Odd was able to reach this conclusion was that he had once again started using social media and was keeping up with the news. He told himself it was because as a father-to-be he had to emerge from his self-imposed isolation and *reconnect with the world*, as he put it to Esther.

He travelled with her to London, where she had accepted an invitation to take part in a project aimed at mapping and interviewing the most important female voices in literature, film and music. They lived in a cramped little flat and Odd longed to be back in France.

Each day after Esther left for work he sat down at his laptop and searched out what had been written about him on the internet. In the beginning he had been shocked by how much interest there was, or how much time people obviously had. Not only did they analyse his writing to pieces, they also shared news of where and with whom he had recently been seen (Odd was able to confirm that in ninety per cent of cases it was complete fiction), stories about secret children with secret mothers, what kind of drugs he was into, his probable sexual orientation, and which of his characters was *really* him. He had to admit all that scribbling delighted him. Yes, even those who criticised him or damned him as an arrogant and out-of-touch wannabe artist made him feel . . . what was the word? Alive? No. Relevant? Maybe. Noticed? Yes, that was probably it. He was forced to admit that it was banal, even depressing that he was so uncomplicated. That he should long so greatly for something that he despised so much in others, the insistent and irritating cry of the spoiled child to 'look at me, look at me!' when there was nothing to see beyond a profound egocentricity.

But naturally, these reflections and this (shall we call it?) self-insight did not stop him searching. He told himself it was important to know his status in the world with a new book about to be published. Because not only was it his best book so far – he'd known that for a long time – it was also – and this was something he's only recently come to realise – his masterpiece. The only novel he'd written that might turn out to be of lasting value. And because it was a masterpiece, the obvious problem was that it was also very demanding. It had cost him a lot of hard work, and readers would have to work hard on it too. It wasn't that the writer Odd Rimmen was unaware of the fact that great literature could be exhausting, for he had come close to giving up on both James Joyce's *Ulysses* and David Foster Wallace's *Infinite Jest*. But since the latter had become his favourite novel he knew he would have to do the same thing: aim for the goal without the slightest deviation. But in order to be a masterpiece, a masterpiece must be presented in the correct context. God alone knows how many masterpieces the world has missed out on, forgotten, or not forgotten but never even discovered, disappearing instead beneath the avalanche of the hundreds and thousands of books published every day all over the world. So, to get some idea of what his own contextual status was, Odd Rimmen began going through stuff on social media chronologically from several years back. He noticed that the number of tweets, references to his name and press stories showed a decline over the past year, and that for the most part those writing now were the same old same olds. And most of them didn't get out much either.

The book wasn't due out for another four months (five months to term) and at a meeting at the publishers on Vauxhall Bridge Road Odd Rimmen discussed the launch with Sophie and her very young colleague (Jane something, Odd couldn't remember the surname).

'The bad news is that this is of course a difficult book to promote,' Jane said, as though this was something everybody knew. She adjusted her oversized and presumably trendy spectacles and smiled broadly, showing a lot of gum.

'What do you mean?' said Odd, hoping that he didn't sound as irritated as he was.

'In the first place it's almost impossible to describe what it's about in two or three sentences. Secondly it's difficult to find a target group beyond the very literary-interested and your own regular readers. Which is one and the same thing really. And that is, anyway, a . . .' She exchanged looks with Sophie. '. . . quite small and rather exclusive group.'

She took a deep breath and Odd realised there was a third thing too.

'Thirdly, it's a very dark and empty novel.'

'Empty?' exclaimed Odd Rimmen, who had no problem with its being dark.

'Dystopian,' Sophie added.

'And there are hardly any characters in it,' said Jane. 'At least, not characters the reader can identify with.'

Odd Rimmen realised that the two of them had conferred beforehand. He was at least pleased they hadn't complained that the new book (*Nothing*) was lacking in the sex scenes that had become his trademark. He shrugged. 'It is what it is. Take it or leave it.'

'OK, but we're here to focus on how to get them to take it,' said Sophie. Odd recognised the sharp undertone now.

'The good news,' said Jane, 'is that we have you. *You* are what the media are interested in. The only question is if you're prepared to help your book by making public appearances.'

'Hasn't Sophie explained it to you yet?' asked Odd Rimmen. 'That I help the book by *not* making public appearances? That – for what it's worth – is now my *image*.' He spat the word with all the contempt he could muster. 'Surely the sales department doesn't want to spoil that and ruin the author's *selling point*, do they?'

'Silence can work,' said Jane. 'But only for so long, then it gets boring and counterproductive. Look at it like this: what silence has *sown* we must now *reap*. Every newspaper and magazine will be standing in line for the first, exclusive interview with the man who stopped talking.'

Odd Rimmen thought about what she'd said. There was something a little strange about the words, some kind of hidden contradiction.

'If I'm going to prostitute myself anyway, why do so exclusively?' he asked. 'Why not the full gangbang, total blanket coverage?'

'Fewer column inches,' said Sophie quietly. Her and Jane-something had definitely already talked this over.

'And why not a talk show?' he asked.

Jane sighed. 'Everyone wants to do those, and unless you're a movie star or a famous athlete or reality star it's very, very difficult.'

'But Stephen Colbert . . .' Now it was no longer the irritation but the pathos Odd Rimmen hoped they didn't notice.

'That was then,' said Sophie. 'Doors open, doors close, that's the way of the world.'

Odd Rimmen sat up straight in his chair, raised his chin, directed his gaze at Sophie. 'I take it for granted you understand I'm asking out of curiosity, not because there's any chance of my playing the media clown again. Let the book do its own talking.'

'You can't have your cake and eat it,' said Jane. 'You can't *both* be an icon of cool *and* be read by the masses. Before we decide on a marketing budget for this book we need to know which is most important to you.'

Odd Rimmen turned slowly, almost reluctantly to face her.

'And one more thing,' said Jane-something-or-other. '*Nothing* is a lousy title. No one buys a book about nothing. There's still time to change it. The marketing department suggested *Loneliness*. It's still dark, but at least it's something a reader can identify with.'

Odd Rimmen turned back to Sophie. The look on her face seemed to say that she felt for him, but that Jane was right.

'The title stays,' said Odd Rimmen and got to his feet. Suppressed anger make his voice shake, which made him even more angry, and he decided to shout in order to overcome it. 'And the title also tells you just how much I intend to contribute to this damned commercial media circus. Fuck them. And fuck . . .'

He didn't finish but marched from the room and down the steps, since waiting for a lift that didn't come might possibly spoil his exit, out through Reception and onto Vauxhall Bridge Road where it was, of course, raining. Fucking shit publisher. Shit town. Shit life.

He crossed the road on green.

Shit life?

He was about to publish the best book he'd written, about to become a father, had a woman who loved him (maybe not expressed quite as openly as in their first days together, but everyone knows the strange effect hormone chaos in a pregnant woman can have on her moods and desires), and had the best job a person can have: to express something that is important to him, to be listened to, to be seen – read, for chrissakes!

And that was exactly what they wanted to take away from him. Take away the only thing he had in life. Because it was the only thing. He could pretend all the rest of it was meaningful. Esther, the child, their life together. And of course it was meaningful. Simply not meaningful enough. No, truly not meaningful enough. He needed it all. The cake and eating it. Jam today and jam tomorrow. Overdose on overdose, he needed to kill off this shit life. Now.

Odd Rimmen stopped abruptly. Stood there until he saw the lights change to red and the cars on both sides begin to rev their engines, like beasts ready to attack.

And it occurred to him that it could stop here, like this. That it wouldn't be a bad way of ending the tale. Sure. Great writers before him had chosen such an ending. David Foster Wallace, Édouard Levé, Ernest Hemingway. Virginia Woolf, Richard Brautigan, Sylvia Plath. The list went on. It was long. And strong. Death sells. Gore Vidal called it a 'good career move' when his fellow writer Truman Capote died; but suicide sells better. Who would still be downloading Nick Drake and Kurt Cobain if they hadn't both killed themselves? And had the thought really never occurred to him before? Hadn't it flitted through his mind when Ryan Bloomberg told him to shoot one of them? If only the book had been finished . . .

Odd Rimmen stepped out into the road.

He had time to hear a cry from the person who had been standing next to him on the pavement before it drowned in the roar of the traffic. He saw the wall of cars on its way towards him. Yes, he thought. But not here, not like this, in a banal road accident that could be dismissed as just bad luck.

The amygdala decided on flight and he just reached the pavement on the far side before the cars flashed past him. He didn't stop, carried on running, slipping between people on London's overcrowded pavements, knocking them. Got a few choice swear words in English yelled after him and yelled a few back in French, better ones too. Crossed streets and bridges and open squares, climbed steps. After an hour's running he finally let himself into the cramped and damp apartment. His clothes, even the jacket, were drenched in sweat.

He sat at the kitchen table with pen and paper and wrote a farewell note.

It only took him a couple of minutes. It was a speech he had given to himself so many times before he didn't need to weigh the words, didn't need to edit anything. And on the instant it was back again – the spark. The spark he had lost when Esther entered his life. Rediscovered when he killed Ryan, and almost lost again when Esther got pregnant. And as he placed the suicide note on the kitchen worktop it occurred to him that it was the only absolutely perfect thing he had ever written.

Odd Rimmen packed a small bag and took a taxi to St Pancras, from where an express train to Paris departed every hour.

The house lay dark and silent and waited for him.

He let himself in.

All was as silent as the grave.

He went upstairs, undressed and showered. He thought of Ryan dying on the living-room floor and went to the toilet. He didn't want to be found with his pants full of excrement and piss. Then he put on his best suit, the one he had been wearing that evening at the Charles Dickens Theatre.

He went down into the cellar. It smelled of apples and he stood still in the middle of the floor, the neon tube in the ceiling blinking on and off as though unable to make up its mind.

Once it had stabilised he crossed to the stove, opened the door and took out the pistol.

He'd seen it in films, read it in books, had even himself declaimed Hamlet's thoughts on suicide (*to be or not to be*) when a secondary school student, when he had given a remarkably unsuccessful reading from the play. The hesitation, the doubt, the interior monologue that drags you this way and that. But Odd Rimmen no longer felt any such doubt. One way or another, all roads had been leading here, and this was the right, the only way to end it. So right it wasn't even sad but quite the opposite. A storyteller's last triumph. *Put your gun where your pen is.* And let other so-called writers sit there onstage and bathe in the audience's bargain-price love, lying to themselves and to everyone else there.

Odd Rimmen released the safety catch and pressed the pistol against his temple.

Already he could see the headlines.

And after that: his place in the history books.

No, *Nothing*. The novel's place.

Like that.

He closed his eyes and pressed his index finger against the trigger.

'Odd Rimmen!'

It was Esther's voice.

He hadn't heard her come, but now she was calling his name. She wasn't far away. Maybe up in the living room. And strangely enough calling his full name, as though she wanted *all* of him to step forward and show himself.

Odd fired. There was a crackling sound, like the roaring of a fire. As though time was distended by his senses he could hear the powder ignite and burn in superslow motion, the sounds rising to a crescendo of applause.

Odd Rimmen opened his eyes. At least, he thought he opened his eyes. Leastways, he saw it.

The light.

Head for the light. Sophie's words. The editor he had listened to and trusted all his writing life.

And then he walked towards the light. It blinded him. He saw no one in the darkness behind the light, heard only the crackling applause as it grew even louder.

He bowed slightly and sat down in the chair beside Esther Abbot, the journalist who, despite her rough and almost masculine manner, had a softness about the eyes that he had noticed in the dressing room a few minutes earlier.

'Let's get straight to the point, Mr Rimmen,' said Esther Abbot. 'I'm sitting here with a copy of *The Hill* in my hands and we'll be talking about that. But first: do you think you'll ever be able to write such a good book again?'

Odd Rimmen peered out across the auditorium. He could make out a few individual faces on the first rows. They stared at him, some half smiling, as though they had already discounted any possibility that he might say something funny or brilliant. And he knew that no matter what he said, he would be given the benefit of every doubt. It was like playing on an instrument that half played itself. All you had to do was touch the keys, open your mouth.

'You're the ones who decide what is and isn't good,' he said. 'All I can do is write.'

A sort of sigh passed through the audience. As though they were concentrating in order to penetrate to the *real depths* of what each individual word meant. Jesus Christ.

'And that's exactly what you do, you're Odd Dreamin',' said Esther Abbot as she shuffled her papers. 'Do you write all the time, make things up all the time?'

Odd Rimmen nodded. 'All the time. Every spare moment I get. I was writing just now. Just before I walked out onto the stage.'

'Really? And are you writing this now?'

The audience's laughter dwindled to an expectant silence as Odd Rimmen turned and looked out towards them. Smiled slightly. Waited. These trembling, breathless, holy moments . . .

'I hope not.'

There was a wave of laughter. Odd Rimmen tried not to smile too broadly. But of course it's hard not to, not when you can feel unconditional love being injected directly into your heart.

THE EARRING

'OUCH!'

I looked in the mirror. 'Something wrong?'

'This,' said the fat lady in the back seat, and held up something between her thumb and forefinger.

'What is it?' I asked as I switched my gaze back to the road.

'Can't you see? An earring. I sat down on it.'

'I'm sorry,' I said. 'A passenger must have lost it.'

'Well, of course I realise that. But how?'

'Sorry?'

'An earring doesn't just fall off while you're sitting up straight.'

'I don't know,' I said, braking as we approached a red light at the only junction in town. 'You're my first passenger today, I've only just taken over the car.'

With the cab at a standstill I glanced again at the mirror. The lady was studying the earring. It has probably been lying in the crack between the seats and got squeezed up when her huge arse pressed down the cushions on both sides.

I looked at the earring. And something struck me. I tried to dismiss it at once, because there must have been at least a thousand different varieties of a simple earring like that.

The lady looked up and met my eyes in the mirror. 'It's genuine,' she said, and handed the earring to me. 'You better try to trace the owner.'

I held it up against the grey morning light. The pin was gold. Jesus. I turned it, and sure enough, there was no engraved logo and no manufacturer's name. Told myself not to draw any hasty conclusions, one pearl earring looks pretty much like any other pearl earring.

'It's green,' said the lady.

Palle – who owned the taxi – had taken the night shift, so I waited until ten and the cab was parked up at the rank next to the kiosk steps before I phoned him. Twenty years ago Palle had come here from playing second division football for Grenland to help get our team up out of the third tier. If he didn't manage that then he did manage – at least by his own account – to bed every available female in the town between the ages of eighteen and thirty.

'I think we can safely say I was the team's top scorer,' he said once in the pub, stroking his magnificent blond moustache between thumb and forefinger. Maybe so, I was just a kid in his playing days and knew only that he'd married one of the more obviously available. She was the daughter of the foreman in the taxi owners' union, and when Palle retired from football he got his taxi driver's licence without the waiting period others had to go through. As a subcontracted driver for Palle I'd been waiting five years now with still no sign of that golden ticket.

'Something wrong?' Palle asked in that threatening tone he always used whenever I called him during my shift. He was terrified I might have had a crash or that there was a problem with the car, something I knew he'd halfway blame me for, even if it was someone else crashed into me or some mechanical fault in the worn-out old Mercedes that Palle was too mean to book in for regular servicing.

'Has anyone called in about an earring?' I asked.

'Earring?'

'In the back seat. In the crack between the cushions.'

'No, but I'll let you know if I hear anything.'

'I was wondering . . .'

'Yes?' Palle sounded impatient, as if I'd woken him. The evening shift usually wound down around two o'clock, that being an hour after the two bars closed. After that there was just the one taxi on night shift, a shift that was shared around between the cabs.

'Did Wenche take our taxi yesterday?'

I knew Palle didn't like it when I called it our taxi when in actual fact it was his, but now and then I forgot.

'Is it her earring?' I heard Palle yawn.

'That's what I'm wondering. It's similar.'

'So why not ring her instead of waking me up?'

'Well.'

'Well?'

'An earring doesn't just fall off. Not while you're sitting up straight,' I said.

'It doesn't?'

'That's what people say. Was she in the car yesterday?'

'Let me think.' I heard the click of Palle's lighter at the other end before he continued. 'Not in my car, but I think I saw her in a taxi queue around one, outside Fritt Fall. I can ask around.'

'I'm not wondering which taxi Wenche took, I'm wondering who owns the earring,' I said.

'Well, can't help you there, obviously.'

'You were the one driving.'

'So what? If it was in the crack between the seats it could have been there for days. And I can't be expected to remember the name of every fucking fare I pick up. If the earring's worth something then whoever owns it'll ring. Did you top up the brake fluid? I nearly ended up in the sea when I started work yesterday.'

'I'll do it when things have quietened down a bit,' I said. It was typical of that miserable bugger Palle to send me to the garage instead of going there himself. As a subcontracted driver I wasn't paid an hourly rate, all I got was forty per cent of my takings.

'Remember the hospital pickup at two,' he said.

'Sure sure,' I said and hung up. Studied the earring again. I was hoping like hell I was mistaken.

The rear door opened, and I recognised the smell before I heard the voice. You might think that a taxi driver would get used to the rancid but also sickly-sweet smell that's a combination of stale and fresh booze once the social security money's been picked up, a new round of bottles bought, and everything's set up for a morning session at the home of one of the social security drunks. But the opposite happens. The smell gets worse with each passing year, and nowadays it can really turn my stomach. There was a chinking sound from the off-licence bag and a slurred voice: 'Nergardveien 12. *Chop-chop.*'

I turned the key in the ignition. The brake fluid warning light had been blinking for over a week, and you had to press your foot down a little harder on the pedal, but of course Palle was exaggerating when he said he'd almost rolled into the sea, even if the slope down from his garage to the edge of the quay was steep and dangerous in winter. And yes, when I was sick and tired of Palle giving me all the day shifts at the weekends and the night shifts on the weekdays while he helped himself to every shift it was possible to earn good money on, it did happen – when I parked the car outside his garage some winter night and picked up my own car to drive home – that I offered up a silent prayer that he might skid on the ice and I might jump forward one place in the taxi driver's ticket queue.

'No smoking in the car please,' I said.

'Shut your mouth!' came a bark from the back seat. 'Who's paying for this, you or me?'

That would be me, I thought. I work for forty per cent of the takings, minus forty per cent tax which pays for you to drink yourself to death, and the best I can hope for is that you do it as quickly as possible.

'What did you say?' said the voice from the back seat.

'No smoking,' I said, and pointed at the sign on the dashboard. 'There's a fine of five hundred kroner.'

'Take it easy, son.' Cigarette smoke drifted forward between the seats. 'I've got the cash.'

I lowered the windows front and back and thought how that five hundred wouldn't be on the meter and would go straight into my pocket, because Palle smoked so much there was no chance he would notice the smell. But at the same moment I knew I would actually be a good boy and hand over the five hundred and get nothing myself. Because Palle claimed that it was him who cleaned the inside of the car, something we both knew he never did, that it never happened until it was so filthy inside I ended up doing it because I couldn't stand it any more.

The meter showed 195 when I pulled up on Nergardveien.

The drunk handed me a 200-krone note. 'Keep the change,' he said and was on his way out.

'Hey!' I shouted. 'I want 695.'

'It says 195.'

'You smoked in my cab.'

'I did? Don't remember. All I remember is that fucking draught.'

'You were smoking.'

'Prove it.'

He slammed the door behind him and headed for the entrance to the block to the cheery chinking of the bottles in his bag.

I checked the time. Six hours left of what was already a shitty working day. Then off to my in-laws for dinner. I don't know which I dreaded more. I took the earring out of my pocket and studied it again. A pin sticking out from the round grey pearl, like a balloon on a string. I was reminded of the time when I was too young to join the National Day parade on 17 May and stood watching it with my grandfather. He had bought a balloon for me, and for just a second I must have lost concentration and let go of the string, because suddenly the balloon was floating high above me, and of course, I bawled. Grandad let me cry myself out, and then he explained why he wouldn't buy another one for me. 'It's to teach you that when you're lucky enough to get something you wished for, when you've been given a chance, you've got to hang on to it, because you don't get second chances here in life.'

And maybe he was right. When I hooked up with Wenche I felt as if I'd been given a balloon I'd been longing for and couldn't afford but had been given anyway. A chance. And so I'd held on tight. Not slackened my grip, not even for a second. Maybe I held on a little too tight. Now and then it seemed to me I could feel something tugging at the string. Those earrings had been a slightly-too-expensive Christmas gift, at least compared to the Björn Borg underpants she had bought for me. But was this one of those earrings? It looked like it. It actually looked completely identical as far as I could see, but neither this earring nor the ones I had bought had any particular distinguishing marks that would have told me one way or the other. Wenche came home after I fell asleep last night, she'd been on a long-planned pub crawl with two friends, young mothers who'd finally managed to arrange a kid-free night for themselves.

I took the chance to point out to her that it showed you could still have a life, even with kids; but Wenche had just groaned and told me to stop going on, she just wasn't ready yet. She didn't specify who it was she wasn't ready for, me or the kids. She just left it at that. Wenche needed room to breathe, more room than most. I knew that. Yes, I understood. And I really wanted to give it to her, but somehow I just couldn't. Couldn't quite manage to slacken my grip on that string enough.

An earring doesn't just fall off, not while you're sitting up straight.

If she's been fooling around with some guy in the back seat with Palle driving she must have been well pissed because she knew he was my employer. But then she could do crazy stuff when she'd been drinking. Like the first time we ever screwed, both of us drunk, two in the morning, and she insisted we do it out on the football pitch, up against one of the goalposts. It was only later I found out she'd had an on–off thing with the goalkeeper and he'd just dumped her.

I got her number up onto the screen, stared at it for a moment, then dropped the phone into the console between the seats and turned up the radio.

I parked outside Palle's garage at five. By five thirty I'd showered, changed and was in the hall waiting for Wenche, who was in the bathroom putting on make-up and talking on the phone.

'Yeah yeah yeah!' she said irritably as she emerged and caught sight of me. 'We'll only be even later if you start going on at me.'

I hadn't said a word and knew that the only thing to do was carry on like that. Keep my mouth shut and keep hold of the string of that balloon.

'Do you have to stand there like that?' she groaned as she struggled into her long black boots.

'Like what?'

'With your arms folded.'

I unfolded them.

'And don't look at your watch,' she said.

'I'm not loo—'

'Don't even *think* about it! I've told them we'll be there when we're there. Christ, you do get on my nerves.'

I went outside and sat in the car. She followed, checked her lipstick in the mirror, and for a while we drove in silence.

'Who were you talking to on the phone?' I asked her.

'Mamma,' said Wenche, drawing an index finger beneath her lower lip.

'For so long and just five minutes before you're due to meet?'

'Is there a law against that?'

'Anyone else coming today?'

'Anyone else?'

'Besides your parents and us? Since you're all dolled up.'

'No harm in trying to look smart if you're invited out to dinner. You, for example, you could have worn that black blazer instead of looking like someone off for a holiday in his cabin.'

'Your dad'll be wearing his knitted sweater, so I'm doing the same.'
'He's older than you. It won't do you any harm to show a bit of respect.'
'Respect, yeah,' I said.
'What?'
I shook my head to say it was nothing. Keep a hold of that string.
'Nice earrings,' I said, without taking my eyes off the road.
'Thanks,' she said, in a tone almost of surprise, and from the corner of my eye I saw she automatically raised one hand to her ear.
'But why aren't you wearing the ones I gave you for Christmas?' I asked.
'I wear those all the time.'
'Yes, so why not now?'
'Christ, you do go on.'
I could see she was still fiddling with her earrings. Silvery things.
'I got these from Mum, so maybe she'll think it's nice to see me wearing them. OK?'
'Sure sure,' I said. 'I only asked.'
She sighed, shook her head and didn't have to say it again: I was getting on her nerves.

'So I hear it's soon going to be your turn to get a taxi licence,' said Wenche's father as he poked the big, three-pronged serving fork into one of the dry slices of roast beef and dumped it onto his plate. I hadn't tasted it yet, but knew it was dry, they always had roast beef when I was there, and it was always dry. Sometimes I imagined it might be a kind of test, that they were just waiting for the day I threw the plate at the wall and bellowed that I couldn't fucking stand it any more, not them and not the roast beef and not their daughter. And that they would heave a great sigh of relief.
'Yes,' I said. 'Brorson inherits the licence when his uncle retires this summer, and I'm next on the list after that.'
'And how long do you think that might turn out to be?'
'That depends on when the next taxi owner retires.'

'I understand that, what I'm asking is, when will that be?'

'Well. Ruud is the oldest. He's probably about fifty-five now.'

'Well then, he might carry on driving for at least another ten years.'

'Yes.' I raised the glass of water to my lips, knowing I needed moistening up for the chewing job ahead.

'I was just reading that Norway has the most expensive taxis in the world,' said my father-in-law. 'It's probably not surprising, bearing in mind we also have the world's most dysfunctional taxi business. Idiot politicians who let the villains who run the business rob people who have no alternative form of transport and who in any other country would have something approaching a halfway decent taxi service.'

'You must be thinking of Oslo,' I said. 'And don't forget either, running costs are very high in this country.'

'There are lots of countries more expensive than Norway,' said Wenche's father. 'And the taxis in Norway are not only the dearest in the world, they're in a class of their own completely. I read that, in Oslo, five kilometres during daylight hours costs twenty per cent more than in Zurich, the next dearest, and fifty per cent more than in Luxembourg, which is third. Oh yes, you've got everyone else on the list beaten hands down. Did you know that in Kiev – which is not even the cheapest city in the world – you can, for the price of one taxi in Oslo, hire not just two. Not three. Not five. Not ten. But twenty. I could transport an entire class of schoolchildren in Kiev for what it costs to drive one poor sod here down to the railway station.'

'In Oslo,' I said, and shifted in my seat. The earring in my trouser pocket was sticking into me. 'Not here.'

'So what surprises me,' said Wenche's father as he wiped his thin lips with a serviette while her mother filled his glass of water, 'is why a taxi driver in this country, even if he doesn't own his own car, can't earn himself a decent annual wage.'

'Yeah, you tell me.'

'OK then, I will. In Oslo they issue so many taxi licences that they have to screw up the price to maintain the high standard of living they've become accustomed to, which means fewer customers, so prices have to rise even higher, so in the end it's the handful of people with no alternative form of transport who are being ripped off, so they can keep a whole army of taxi drivers parked up at cab ranks with nothing to do but scratch their arses and complain about people living off unemployment benefit. Whereas in actual fact they're the ones living off unemployment benefits, only it's the passengers who are paying for it. So when Uber comes along and shakes things up a bit in a business that's already a bit shaky, the taxi drivers' union and all its tax-dodging members fly into a rage and insist on keeping their sole right to get paid for just sitting in a parked-up cab. And the only winner is Mercedes, who can sell cars there's no use for.'

His voice hadn't got any louder, only more intense, and I knew that Wenche was looking at me in a sort of amused way. She liked it when her father laid down the law for me like that. She even actually said that the way he acted and spoke was how a real man should, and I should try to learn from him.

'That, at any rate, is the plan,' I said.

'What is?'

'Wait until I get the licence and then buy a Mercedes there's no use for.' I gave a little laugh, but no one else around the table even smiled.

'See, Amund is the same as the taxi drivers in Oslo,' said Wenche. 'He likes to wait in a queue and hope that sooner or later something good will happen. He isn't a doer, like some I could mention.'

Her mother spoke up and changed the subject, I don't remember to what, only that I sat there chewing and chewing on a slice of beef that tasted as though it too had had a tough life. And wondered what Wenche had meant by some she could mention.

'You can drop me off at the pub,' said Wenche as we drove home.

'Now? It's nine o'clock.'

'The girls are there already. We agreed to meet up for a hair of the dog tonight.'

'Sounds like a good idea. Maybe I should come along . . .'

'The whole point is to get away from the husband and kids for a while.'

'I could sit at another table.'

'Amund!'

Don't hold so hard, I thought. Don't get cramp in your hand, you'll lose all feeling, you won't be able to feel the string.

After letting myself into the house alone I went up to the bedroom and began to rummage through the drawer where Wenche kept her trinkets. I opened jewellers' boxes and saw rings and gold chains. One of them looked new and I couldn't remember having seen it before. Then I looked through the earrings. First there was an empty box – that was probably where she kept those silver things she was wearing this evening. Then a pair of unusual-looking pearl earrings with a blue ring that encircled the grey pearls like a narrow equator. She'd got them from her father and called them her Saturn studs. But I didn't find the earrings I had given her, nor the box they came in. I looked in the other drawers. In the wardrobe. Her toilet bag, her handbags, the pockets of her jackets and trousers. Nothing. What could it mean?

I went into the kitchen, took a beer from the fridge and sat at the kitchen table. I had no proof. I couldn't be certain, but all the same I knew there was no way round it now. I would have to look through all those half-thoughts I'd been thinking but dismissing and postponing until I found the box with the other stud in it. Until I could be certain.

It wasn't really the suspicion that Wenche had been fooling around in the back seat that bothered me most. It was Palle denying that Wenche had been in the car at all last night. Why would he lie about that? There were only two possible answers. That he didn't want to gossip, and perhaps she'd even asked him not to. Or that Palle himself had been the other occupant of the back seat. And once that possibility was raised I couldn't block out the rest of it either. I visualised Palle's little arse pumping up and down on Wenche, who was shouting out his name the way she had shouted mine down the football pitch, and continued to do so that first year, until we got married. The mental image made me nauseous. It truly did. Wenche was the best and the worst that had happened to me, but – and this was more important – she was the *only* thing that had happened to me. Not that I'd been a virgin when I met her, but the others had been the ones anyone could have. Wenche had been the only woman who improved my self-image just by allowing me to screw her. As time went by and it became ever clearer to her that she could have done better than me, naturally she made a point of obliging me to ratchet my self-image back down again. But never back down to the level it had been at before I met her. Wenche was and remained my helium balloon. As long as I held on tight to the string I felt a *little* lighter, I had a *little* more lift.

The way I looked at it I had two options. To confront her with the findings and facts. Or keep my mouth shut and just carry on as before. The first option carried the risk of losing both her and the job – at least, if it was Palle who'd been screwing her.

Option two would involve the risk of a loss of self-respect.

My immediate preference was for option two.

But option one, confrontation, naturally also included the possibility that she could invent a completely different explanation for how the earring had ended up between the seats. An explanation I would be able to convince myself was credible. An explanation that meant I wouldn't have to spend the rest of my life imagining Palle's ageing but still firm football arse. And maybe the fact that I had confronted her, shown her that I was willing to risk everything, would make her bloody well understand that I was not just somebody who waited around for things to happen to me, that I could act, I could be master of my own fate. That it wasn't my bloody fault that the licence regulations are the way they are.

Right. I would have to confront her.

I opened another beer and waited. Sweated and waited.

There was a picture of us with our gang on the fridge. It was taken eight years ago, at the wedding, and we all looked so young, younger than those eight years would suggest. Jesus, how proud I was that day. And happy. I believe I can say that: happy. Because I was still at the age when you think that every good thing that happens to you is the start of something, not the end. The thought never occurs that this day, those months, maybe that single year, is all the happiness life has to offer you. I had no fucking idea I was at the top, so I hadn't taken the time to savour the view but carried on in the belief that there were new heights to be reached. I had seen that picture hanging there for a few thousand days, but this evening it made me weep. Yes it did. I wept.

I checked the time. Eleven. Opened another beer. It eased the pain, but only a bit.

I was about to open a fourth when the phone rang.

I answered in a flash, it had to be Wenche.

'Sorry for disturbing you this late,' said a female voice. 'My name is Eirin Hansen. Is this Amund Stenseth, the taxi driver?'

'Yes?'

'I got your number from Palle Ibsen. I believe you might have found the earring I lost in his cab yesterday evening?'

'What kind . . . ?'

'An ordinary pearl stud,' said Eirin Hansen. And if she'd been standing there in my kitchen I would have put my arms around her. My inner jubilation was so great I thought she had to be able to hear it.

'I've got it,' I said.

'Oh, what a relief! It was a present from my mother.'

'Well then, I'm extra pleased I found it,' said I, and thought how fantastic it was that I could be sharing so much joy and relief over the phone with Eirin Hansen, a complete stranger to me.

'Isn't it strange,' I said, 'how when you get bad news one day that turns out to be wrong, the day becomes even better than it was *before* you got the bad news?'

'I've never thought about it but yes, you might be right,' she said with a laugh.

I know it was the euphoria, but I thought Eirin Hansen's laughter sounded so good, she sounded like a nice person. In fact, she even sounded as if she was quite beautiful.

'Where and when can I, er . . . pick up the earring?'

For a moment I was on the point of suggesting I take it to her there and then, wherever she was, before I regained control of the thoughts and feelings that were racing through me.

'I'm driving a day shift tomorrow,' I said. 'Call me and I'll let you know when I'm at the taxi rank by the kiosk near the steps, or at least nearly there.'

'That's wonderful! Thank you so much, Amund!'

'No problem, Eirin.'

We ended the call. And with the joy still singing away inside me I drank the rest of the beer.

It was gone midnight by the time Wenche crept into bed. She probably knew I wasn't asleep, but she kept very quiet and moved around very carefully. I heard her lying down behind my back and sort of hold her breath, as if she was listening to mine. Then I fell asleep.

Next day I woke up bright and raring to go.

'What's up with you?' Wenche asked over breakfast.

'Nothing.' I smiled. 'You're still not wearing my earrings.'

'Will you stop going on about those?' she groaned. 'I lent them to Torill, she thought they looked so good on me and asked if she could borrow them for the office party. I'm meeting her tonight and I'll get them back then, OK?'

'It's nice that other people think they suit you,' I said.

She gave me a funny look as I drained the rest of my coffee and with wings on my heels almost flew out the room.

I felt like a teenager on his first date, excited and afraid at the same time.

After parking at Palle's I got into the taxi and coasted down the slope. I could feel the brake pedal was even slacker and I called the garage and asked Todd if he could fix it tomorrow.

'I could, but if you can bring it in today that gives us more time,' said Todd.

I didn't reply.

'I get it,' Todd said, and I could hear him grinning. 'Palle's driving the day shift tomorrow and you're pissed off it's always you who has to spend his shift at the garage.'

'Thanks,' I said.

At ten the phone rang.

I saw from the display it was Eirin.

'Hi,' was all I said.

'Hi,' she said, as though she knew she didn't have to give her name, that I recognised her number. And didn't her voice sound a little tense, almost nervous? Maybe not, maybe it was just that I wanted her to sound like that.

We agreed to meet at the taxi rank at ten thirty. I did one quick pickup and afterwards parked the taxi and waved Gelbert's and Axelson's cabs in ahead of me. While I was waiting I tried not to think. Because now all the fantasies, all the expectations that had been fighting for a place in my brain were as nothing; soon I would know.

The passenger door opened, and I smelled the perfume before I heard the voice. A meadow in flower outside a cabin in June. Apples in August. The western wind on the sea in October. Sure, I know I'm exaggerating, but those really were the associations I got.

'Hello again.' She sounded slightly out of breath, as if she'd been walking quickly. She was perhaps a little older than I'd imagined. The voice was younger than the face, in a manner of speaking. Maybe she thought something similar about me, that I'd seemed more attractive on the phone, I don't know. But Eirin had been beautiful once, there was no doubt about that. Available, I thought. Yes, I actually did, I thought that word, Palle's word. Doable. Did I want to? Yes, I wanted to.

'Thank you so much for looking after my earring for me, Amund.'

So she got straight to the point. As though she wanted to get it over with. I don't know whether from shyness, nervousness or because I'd been a disappointment to her.

'Here it is,' I said and handed her the stud. 'At least, if it's the right one I found.'

She examined the earring. 'Oh yes,' she said slowly. 'You found the right one.'

'Good,' I said. 'I guess it's so unusual it wouldn't have been easy to find a match for the one that was left.'

'True, true.' She nodded as she stared hard at the earring, as though she didn't dare look at me. As though something she didn't want to happen would happen then.

I said nothing, felt just the hammering of my pulse in my throat, beating so hard that I knew if I tried to talk the tremor in my voice would betray me.

'Well, thanks again,' said Eirin as she fumbled for the door handle. Probably, like me, she'd felt a moment's panic. Naturally. She was sitting there with a wedding ring on her finger. She was wearing make-up, but the morning light was pitiless. She was at least five, perhaps ten years older than me. But certainly still doable. And she would definitely have been doable back when I was a young lad.

'Do you know Palle?' I asked, without a tremor in my voice.

She hesitated. 'Well, know him and know him.'

That was all I needed. *An earring doesn't fall off, not while you're sitting up straight.* I glanced in the wing mirror. It looked as if it had taken a knock and needed tightening.

'Looks like I've got a fare,' I said.

'Ah yes,' she said. 'But thanks again.'

'You're welcome.'

She got out and I watched her as she crossed the square.

She didn't know it, no one knew it, but I had just stepped out of jail. I was outside now, breathing in that unfamiliar air, savouring the new and frightening freedom. Now it was just a question of carrying on, exploiting it, not slipping back into old ways and ending up back inside the walls again. I should probably be able to manage that. And with what I did next I would demonstrate it to myself.

By the time it turned five o'clock I'd had a good day. I'd even got a few tips, something that rarely happened. Was it because of the unusually good mood I was in? The new me, so to speak?

I parked the cab in Palle's garage. He kept his tools hanging on the wall, and it took me twenty minutes to do the job that had to be done.

I got into my own car, called Wenche and told her I'd bought a bottle of white wine to have with dinner, her favourite type.

'What is it with you?' she asked again, only this time without the tone of annoyance she used at breakfast. Almost curious. And why not? Now I was a new me, maybe I could be a new me for her too.

I was humming I drove along, one hand on the wheel. Steering. I liked steering. The other hand was in my trouser pocket and I was thinking about the brake fluid I'd drained back there in the garage. Wondered what it was Palle had on Eirin, or did they have something on each other? Wondered how far back the two of them went. Long enough at least for him to be able to ask her to step up once he realised I was bound to make the connection between him, the earring and Wenche. He'd probably called Wenche immediately after I rang him to ask about the earring. And she'd immediately hidden the box with the one remaining earring. It was a smart move to claim she'd lent them to a friend. She was going out tonight, yes, but she wouldn't be meeting Torill or any of her other friends, she'd be meeting Palle who, according to plan, would have the earring I'd given to Eirin. But Wenche would never get that earring from Palle. And not because Palle had noticed the earrings Wenche was wearing as they lay there in the back seat. There's no way he would have noticed that the earring Eirin handed to him had a narrow band around it, like a blue equator. No way.

No, Palle wouldn't be giving Wenche the Saturn stud. And he wouldn't be giving her any lost earring either. And she would never know they'd been tricked, the pair of them. Because from this afternoon onwards, Palle will no longer be among us, as they say. And she'll have to make do with what she has. Meaning me. But I think she'll get to like me.

The new me. Next in line for a taxi licence following Palle's unexpected demise. I smiled to myself in the mirror, steering with one hand, the other in my pocket, where I held the pin of the pearl earring I had once given Wenche. Held it gently, but firmly. The way you hold a balloon on a string.

PART TWO

Power

RAT ISLAND

I

A HALYARD FLAPS LAZILY AGAINST the flagpole in the wind. I look out over the city. It seems strangely peaceful. But then, from the roof of a ninety-floor skyscraper you don't see the human ants fleeing or hunting through the streets. Hear the cries of those beaten to the ground, the pleas for mercy, the click of the cocked rifle. But you hear the shooting. The growl of a solitary motorcycle. And now that night has fallen you see the fires.

Although from up here most of them look small. The torched cars that look like cheerful lanterns, casting a little light in a city in which it has been over a year since the street lamps stopped working.

I heard a burst of machine-gun fire, not too long. They're young, but they've learned when to stop to prevent the weapon from overheating. They have learned what they need to know in order to survive in these times. Or to be more accurate: to survive a little longer than a person whose needs are the same as yours; food, weapons, shelter, petrol, clothing, drugs and at least one woman who can carry a man's genes into the next generation. To employ a cliché, it's a jungle down there. And the jungle gets closer with each day that passes not with each hour. I'm guessing the building we're standing on now will be part of the jungle by first light.

Up here those who are able to evacuate are doing so. The elite, the richest of the rich, the ones who could afford the ticket out. I stand and study them, the final group of fourteen people, impatiently peering in the direction of the bay from which they expect to see it approach, the military helicopter shuttling back and forth between here and the aircraft carrier the *New Frontier*. The ship has room for three and a half thousand people, food, medicine and everything else necessary for four years on the open sea without needing to visit a harbour. It sails tonight and will be at sea for an indefinite period of time. I don't know what the tickets cost, only that it's slightly less expensive for women since it has been decided that there are to be equal numbers of both sexes on board. No one's saying it out loud, but this is effectively a Noah's Ark for the elite.

My childhood friend Colin Lowe stands in front of me. His wife Liza and daughter Beth are closer to the landing pad, eyes peeled for the helicopter. Colin is one of the country's wealthiest entrepreneurs. He owns internet sites and properties all over the world, including the skyscraper we're standing on. But, as he has just told me, it took them less than thirty minutes to pack.

'You've got everything you need,' I assure him.

The atmosphere up here is nervous, hectic but also strangely excited. Heavily armed and uniformed private militia men, paid for by Colin Lowe Inc., guard the landing pad and the door to the roof. There are more of them on the ground level and around the lifts. Their job is to stop anyone storming the building in the hope of reaching safety before the gangs come. Or even better, of boarding the helicopter out to *New Frontier*. It's hard to blame those who try, and hard to blame those who stop them. We fight for ourselves and those dearest to us, that's the way we're made.

When I arrived at the building earlier in the evening there was a smell of fear and desperation around the gates. I saw a man wearing an expensive suit offer one of the guards at the entrance a briefcase stuffed with notes, but the guard turned him down. Either because there were witnesses, or because no one knows whether that money will be worth anything tomorrow. There was a beautiful, middle-aged woman behind him whom I thought I recognised. As she offered herself to the head guard she reminded him of the names of the films she had acted in.

'We're heading for entropy,' says Colin.

'You know perfectly well I don't know what words like that mean,' I say.

'The Second Law of Thermodynamics.'

'Still blank.'

'Don't you legal people know anything?'

'Only how to clean up after the engineers.'

Colin laughs. I had just summed up the symbiotic nature of our partnership in Lowe Inc. over the last fifteen years.

'Entropy,' says Colin, and looks out over the city's skyline, a jagged silhouette against a sun that is about to disappear into the sea. 'Entropy means that, in a closed system, over the course of time everything will be destroyed. When you leave a sandcastle it will be changed the following day by the weather and the wind. Not replaced by something even more fantastic but just flatter, greyer. Lifeless, soulless. Nothing. That's entropy, Will. It's the most universal natural law of them all.'

'The law of lawlessness,' I say.

'Thus speaks the lawyer.'

'Thus speak the philosophers. According to Hobbes, without laws, without a social contract, we'll be thrown out into a chaos worse than the worst dictatorship. And the way things are looking now, he was right.'

'Leviathan is here,' Colin concurs.

'What's Leviathan?' asks his daughter Beth. Without our noticing it she's come over to join us. She's seventeen, three years younger than her brother Brad, who is out there somewhere. She looks so like my own daughter Amy, but that isn't the only reason I feel the tears welling up when I look at Beth.

'It's the story of a sea monster that doesn't exist,' I tell her when Colin doesn't reply.

'Then how can it be here?'

'It's just an image, darling.' Colin pulls his daughter close. 'A famous philosopher used it to describe a society without law and order.'

'Like this one?' she asks.

A man in military uniform approaches. Colin coughs. 'Go and keep Mum company, Beth, I'll be along soon.'

She obediently runs off.

'Lieutenant?' says Colin.

'Mr Lowe.' The uniformed man has thick, short grey hair and a crackling walkie-talkie from which an agitated voice seems to be trying to contact him. 'My man on the ground floor tells me they're having trouble keeping people out. Should they use live ammunition if . . . ?'

'Are they gangs?'

'Mostly ordinary people hoping to board the helicopter, Mr Lowe.'

'Poor sods. Only shoot as a last resort.'

'Very well, sir.'

'How long until the helicopter gets here?'

'The pilot says in about twenty minutes, sir.'

'OK. Keep us posted when it comes so that everyone is ready to board as soon as it lands.'

'Very good, Mr Lowe.'

As the lieutenant moves away from us I hear him answer the voice on the walkie-talkie. 'I know, sergeant, but our orders are not to use more force than is necessary. Understood? Yes, maintain your position and . . .'

His words fade, leaving behind the soft tapping of the halyard and the siren of a police car that rises up from the dark streets below us. Colin and I both know it isn't the police – it's been over a year since they dared patrol the streets after nightfall – but probably four young men armed with automatic weapons and doped up enough to leave their reflexes intact and hopefully intensified but their inhibitions dulled. Although inhibitions aren't just dulled, they're more or less gone. And not just among these predators but among the population in general.

And maybe that's the only excuse for what I've done.

I can still hear that motorcycle. There must be a hole in the silencer or whatever it's called.

I accelerate down the empty street, through the city, heading southwards, towards the slaughterhouse. It makes a racket from that bullet-hole in the silencer, gotta get that fixed. And I need petrol. The needle's showing red, no bloody way of knowing if I've enough to get there. You definitely do not want to get stranded in the city centre in the middle of the night without your gang, because suddenly you're the prey. But OK, as long as I have petrol, as long as this engine keeps turning then I'm at least partway up the food chain. Because I've found what I was looking for up on the hillside behind me. The opening. The hole in the fortress. Maybe everyone living in the villa will be dead in a few hours' time, maybe not. I'm not the judge here, I'm just the messenger. The sound of the bike echoes round the tall, deserted office blocks. If I ride too hard I might run out of petrol, but the longer I'm still here in the centre the greater my chances of getting in trouble. The mob I just passed up by the Lowe building, for example, when I slowed down a bit one of them tried to grab me to get hold of the bike. People are animals, they're desperate, they're angry and afraid. For fuck's sake. What's happened to this city? What's happened to this big, great country?

II

'Helicopter due in eighteen minutes!' shouts the lieutenant.

'One thousand and eighty seconds,' says Colin, always quicker than me at mental arithmetic.

It didn't take long from the discovery of the virus to the outbreak of the pandemic and the sudden dissolution of everything. People dropped like flies. In the first instance from the disease, then as a result of the collapse of the economy and the social and political institutions. Naturally, the poor were hardest hit by the pandemic; bad news always operates that way. But it was not until food shortages occurred that the situation changed from being something societies tried to tackle together into a struggle between the haves and the have-nots. First pitting the poor against the rich, and then the poor against the poor, until finally the only ones who weren't enemies were family and friends. The food shops were empty, and in due course the gun shops too, although the production of guns and rifles was about the last to stop. The forces of law and order, already breaking down, collapsed. The richest barricaded themselves in behind the walls of their farms and country mansions, preferably on elevated sites which were easier to defend. A few of the very richest, such as Colin Lowe, who had seen the coming of the collapse long before the pandemic, had taken the precaution of acquiring private estates and islands that were self-sufficient and guarded by private militia equipped with the latest in weapons technology. Paradoxically the virus helped them in their struggle against those who posed the greatest threat to them: hordes of the poor and the desperate. Because the virus spread out of control in and around households where people lived in crowded conditions without health insurance and unable to afford to follow the government's quarantine rules. But once the pandemic had levelled off and become less of a threat than the plundering I think the hardest hit were those stuck in the middle. Those with something that could be taken from them but without the means to protect and defend it. And once they had lost everything these people also turned into plunderers. Poverty, desperation, violence, all were contagious.

When the pandemic started I was head of the legal department of Colin's IT company. The virus came from the east, from the other end of the country, but it swept over us – the majority, the safe middle class – before we had time to react.

When Colin first showed me Rat Island five years earlier, a tiny prison island of no more than a hundred hectares not far from the airport, I'd teased him about being a doomsday prepper, one of those paranoid wackos who spends all their time preparing for the worst, for the day when they have no one but themselves to rely on. The reason there are so many of them in our country probably has something to do with the culture of individual liberty here. You make your own luck and no one'll stop you, but no one'll help you either.

'It's just common sense,' was his reply when I suggested that it was bordering on the paranoid. 'I'm an engineer and a programmer, and people like us aren't hysterics who go around thinking the end is nigh. We just reckon on the likelihood of something unlikely happening, same as we do in our work. Because there's one thing you can be sure of, and that is that, given enough time, everything – but absolutely everything – that can happen will happen. The likelihood of the breakdown of society in my lifetime isn't great, but then it isn't negligible either. When I multiply that likelihood by what it would cost me, financially and in terms of quality of life, what that gives me is the price I should be willing to pay for my insurance. This –' he gestured with his hand in the direction of the barren and rocky island with the empty concrete buildings that had once been built to keep killers in, not out – 'is a small price to pay if I want to sleep better at night.'

At that time I was not aware that he already had cabinets full of weapons there. Nor that the reason he and several of his director friends had undergone laser surgery to correct near-sightedness had not been cosmetic but from the knowledge that in a world without law and order it would be difficult to get hold of either spectacles or contact lenses, and that clear eyesight would be critical in a struggle to survive that would have brought us a step closer to the Stone Age.

'No reason not to be prepared, Will. If only for your family's sake.'

But I had not been prepared.

It is not the case that the looting started when the authorities decided to open the prisons which had, in effect, become chambers of death in which isolation was impossible and the virus spread unhindered. The numbers of prisoners released in this way was not sufficient in itself to account for the chaos. It was the feeling it created. A feeling that the authorities were losing control, that law and order were suspended, that soon we would have to grab whatever we could before others grabbed it first. Nor was it that we failed to see or understand what was happening. It was not an irrational fear. We knew that if we could just put this pandemic behind us – and in some countries it was already on the wane – we would be able to return to our normal lives. But we also saw that fear had grown stronger than the common sense of the herd. It wasn't mass hysteria but the lack of a shared common sense. So people made individual choices that were rational and sensible for themselves and those they loved, but catastrophic for the rest of society.

Some became looters and turned to violence out of sheer necessity. Others – like Colin's son Brad – did so because they wanted to.

Brad Lowe's relationship with his father was complicated. As his first-born, Brad was the one Colin expected to take over the business after him. But it wasn't something Brad was cut out for. He lacked his father's intellect and his capacity for work, had neither his vision nor his desire to change the world, and none of his charm or his ability to enthuse others. What he had inherited from his father was an egotism that was at times infinite, and a willingness to sacrifice everything and everyone in pursuit of his goal. It might involve Brad using his father's money to bribe the trainer to pick him for the college football team ahead of others with more talent. Or persuading his father to give him money for a project he and his friends had started to help less fortunate students but which, as it turned out, went towards drugs, women and wild parties in the off-campus house they rented. The final straw that made Colin remove his son from college was when the dean informed him that Brad had physically threatened him after it was discovered he had forged documents to make it look as though he had passed certain exams he had not even taken.

Brad came back home the ultimate loser that summer. And I couldn't help but feel sorry for him. For years our families used to spend mountain holidays in an enormous two-storey cabin we rented together until

Colin bought the place. The bad relationship between father and son made it hard for the rest of us to be around Brad. Because he wasn't a boy without feelings. Quite the contrary, in fact; he had way too many of them. He loved and admired his father. It had always been that way and was something people could see clearly. A lot more clearly than the fact that the father loved his son. Now Brad's emotions veered wildly between despair, anger, an apathetic indifference and an aggression directed against everyone who didn't do what he wanted them to, whether one of his family, one of ours, or one of the employees at the cabin. And that was when I discovered the other Colin inside Brad. The one who appeared when Colin's seductive intelligence and contagious enthusiasm failed to persuade people: the threatening person. The Colin who could almost on a whim buy up some troublesome little competitor, strip its assets and put the workers out of a job. On the couple of occasions when I had trashed Colin's plan on legal grounds he had become so angry that I know he was within a whisker of firing me. I know because I recognised from childhood the black look that came into his eyes when he didn't get his way.

And stayed there until he did.

And I think that's what Brad had discovered. That you can – by the simple act of abandoning a few inhibitions – get your own way through the use of violence, threats and brute force. The way he got the Winston brothers from the neighbouring cabin to join him in setting fire to Ferguson's old garage. Because if they hadn't done so – as the brothers explained later to the police – Brad had threatened to set fire to the Winston cabin while the family was sleeping.

Brad's hapless attempt to court my daughter Amy further demonstrated that he was a boy given to strong feelings. He had been in love with her since they were small children, but instead of growing out of it as is usually the case with childhood infatuations his feelings just seemed to get stronger each summer when they met. Of course it might have been because Amy grew more lovely with each year that passed, but just as likely it was because his feelings weren't reciprocated and her persistent rejection only spurred him on. He seemed to feel as though he had a right to her.

One night I was awoken by the sound of Brad's voice in the corridor outside Amy's room. He was trying to get her to let him in and she was obviously refusing. I heard him say: 'This is our cabin, everything in here is mine, so let me in or else we'll throw you out and your father will lose his job.'

I never told Colin about this – I've done and said a few stupid things myself in the grip of a romantic rejection – and I suspected Colin might come down too hard on his son as a way of showing he wouldn't tolerate that kind of thing. So it wasn't the threats made to Amy but the burning of the garage that tipped things over for Colin. Brad got off with a conditional sentence and the award of hefty damages to Mr Ferguson, paid for by his father, after which Colin put him under house arrest. Two days later Brad left for town on the motorcycle he had been given as an eighteenth birthday present. He took a large amount of cash from his father's safe, and the keys to an apartment in Downtown.

'Well, at least I know where he is,' sighed Colin over breakfast.

Three months later Colin told me he'd heard from the police that the apartment had been completely destroyed in one of the many fires in Downtown, that they hadn't found any bodies inside but that there was no sign of Brad either. Colin had then reported Brad missing and tried to pressurise the police into searching for him, but by that point the police had stopped following up anything other than street violence, arson and murder. We heard from the east coast that in some cities the police had had to barricade themselves inside their police stations as these had become a favourite target of the gangs because of the large numbers of weapons stored there. There were also rumours that in some states the police had stopped turning up for work and were instead operating as highway robbers in order to survive.

After the government had finally declared a state of emergency throughout the whole country and Colin had moved into the abandoned prison on Rat Island with his wife and Beth he told me that he had heard about Brad from other sources. Apparently Colin Lowes's son was now the leader of a gang of looters who called themselves Chaos.

'Why the looting?' said Colin with a shake of the head. 'If he just came to me he'd have everything he needs.'

'Maybe this is what he needs,' I said. 'To show you he can manage on his own. Not only survive without your help in times like these but be a leader. Like you.'

'Hm,' said Colin and looked at me. 'So you don't think it's simply because he likes it?'

'Likes what?'

'The chaos. Looting. He likes . . . destruction.'

'I don't know,' I said.

And it was true.

As the world crumbled around us, Heidi, Amy and I tried to lead as normal a life as possible in Downtown.

Heidi and I had met when we were both law students and it had all happened so smoothly. It took us just two evenings to realise we were meant for each other, and two years to know that we had been right. So there was nothing to discuss. We got married, and Amy arrived three years later. We wanted more children, but it took another fourteen years before little Sam – now nearly four – appeared.

When the virus came along and the city was put on lockdown Heidi's firm went bankrupt. She knew it would be tough to find work in a market in which unemployment had risen from five to thirty per cent, and the economic recession had entered what the experts call critical mass, a state in which a descending spiral had become its own accelerant. So following the pandemic, when people were once again able to move about freely without fear of infection, Heidi started offering legal assistance to the poor. She worked from our kitchen and of course was only rarely paid for the work she did. Luckily money wasn't the biggest problem for our family. Directly before the onset of the pandemic the board of Lowe Inc. had accepted an offer from the country's largest IT company. For me and the other internal shareholders it meant, in principle, that we need never work again as long as we lived. I had given up my job and spent the next few weeks thinking over what I wanted to do with my life. And in the course of those weeks the virus had struck again and decided what it was going to do not only with my life but with the lives of everyone on the planet.

So I had come to the conclusion that the most meaningful thing I could do was help Heidi to help others.

And from that day on not only our kitchen but also the living room and the library had operated as a kind of centre for shipwrecked souls and weird characters of every description. But by now even the legal system had started coming apart at the seams. Even though the government, the national assembly and the courts continued to operate after a fashion, the real question was how much longer we would have a functioning police force capable of administering the law and enforcing the verdicts of the courts, a jail system that could arrange for the serving of sentences, and even a military whose loyalty could be relied on. The national assembly had given the military leaders extended powers to protect property – at least, public property – and in other circumstances this might have been a first step in allowing a group of senior military figures to take over the running of the country. A junta would, after all – according to the social philosophy in *Leviathan* – be preferable to anarchy. But that wasn't what happened. Instead soldiers and officers were recruited to join the private militia established by the wealthy, where they could make five times what they had earned in the regular army.

And those of us who weren't as wealthy had also started to take steps to secure what was ours. What we thought of as ours. Started preparing for the worst.

But nothing could have prepared me for what actually did happen.

And as I stand here on top of the skyscraper listening out for the helicopter I can still feel the taste of the rope in my mouth, still smell the petrol in the garage and hear the screams of those I love inside the house. And the bitter certainty that I would lose everything. Absolutely everything.

'Sixteen minutes!' the lieutenant shouts.

Colin walks to the edge of the roof and looks down into the darkened streets. I can just about hear the sound of a solitary motorcycle. Only a month previously the city was full of motorcycle gangs on the rampage, but now the fuel shortage means most of the robbers are on foot.

'So you don't think Justitia is dead, she just has this hole in her fore-head?' Colin asks.

I look up at him. It's hard to keep up with a mind like his, but since I've been used to following the train of his thoughts ever since we first met in junior school I can sometimes manage it. He hears the motor-cycle and automatically thinks of his son Brad and his gang, Chaos. They wear helmets with a very striking club logo: Justitia, the goddess of justice, the blindfolded woman holding the scales. Only in this ver-sion she has a large, bloody bullet-hole in the middle of her forehead.

'She's down for the count,' I say. 'But I still think the rule of law will reassert itself.'

'And I always thought that was naive. That sooner or later the only ones you can trust are your own close family members. Which of us was right, Will?'

'People will fight back against your entropy, Colin. People want some-thing that's better, they want a civilised society, they want the rule of law.'

'What people want is revenge for an injustice committed. That was what the rule of law was all about. And when that doesn't function any more people arrange for their revenge themselves. Look at history, Will. Blood feuds, vendettas with sons and brothers avenging their fathers and brothers. That's where we come from and that's where we're headed back to. Because that's how we feel. That's what we're like, as human beings. Even you, Will.'

'I hear what you're saying, but I don't agree. I put common sense and humanism above revenge.'

'The hell you do. You might like to pretend you do, but I know what you're feeling inside. And you know as well as I do that feelings will always, always win out over common sense.'

I don't answer. Instead I look down at the street below, tryping to spot the motorcycle. The roar has died away, but I see a cone of light moving and hope that is it. Right now light and hope are what we need. Because he's right. Colin is always right.

III

I slow down. Further down the avenue here there are neither people nor any other traffic on the move, but since I'm driving on sidelights only to attract as little attention as possible I need to keep an eye out for holes in the road. It's crazy, but even though people ran out of petrol long ago they clearly still have plenty of grenades left – the explosions get more frequent by the day.

I brake. Not for a hole but for torchlight. A gang has taken up position at the next crossroads. A car burns soundlessly behind them.

Shit. They've spread spike strips across the whole avenue.

I check my mirror. And sure enough, in the glow from the brake lights I see they're behind me too. They emerge from buildings on both sides, dragging a spike strip behind them to cut off a retreat that way. It takes me two seconds to establish that there are twelve of them, six in front and six behind, that only four of them are visibly armed, that they move like kids and they're not wearing badges or outfits that might tell me which gang they belong to. The bad news for me is that they must have raided a police station for those spike strips, which means they've got guts. Which is another way of saying they're desperate. The good news is that they're ranged in a haphazard and not very practical formation, which tells me that either they don't have much experience, they're stupid, or they think numerical superiority is enough.

I'm still fifty metres away from them when I bring the bike to a complete stop and take off my helmet. Hold it up so they can see.

'Chaos!' I shout, hoping they can see the insignia on the helmet.

'Shit, it's a girl!' I hear someone say.

'All the better,' another laughs.

'Move those strips and let me by and there won't be any trouble!' I shout. As I expected, I get laughter in answer. I switch on the headlight. I can see them better now, ethnicities mixed, clothing mixed too. They look like the leftovers of what no other gang would have. Then I take hold of the Remington rifle fastened to the side of the bike and aim at the biggest one, still blinded by the headlight and as it happens standing directly in front of the spike strip. I think back to the last time I used it, how I made a perfect triangle out of the eyes and the bullet-hole. But of course, then I had the target hanging on a hook right in front of me. I pull the trigger, and the echo bounces around the walls of the houses. The guy falls the right way, backwards onto the spike strip, and I accelerate, aim for the open spread of his legs and manage to slip the rifle back into its holster and get both hands on the handlebars again before the front wheel hits him and I'm riding over him.

No shots from behind me.

These days no one wastes ammunition on lost causes.

I don't know whether it's a conscious decision to ride past Adam's house, but anyway I don't exactly have enough petrol to take any other route. But maybe I need to return to the scene of the crime, to remind myself why I'm doing what I am about to do. Anyway, suddenly I'm there.

Silence. Darkness. I don't stop, just slow down.

The hole in the gate is still there. The hole I made.

I squeezed the handles of the wire cutters and the teeth snapped through the wires in the gate.

I could feel the eyes of all twelve of them behind me, the smell of testosterone, the scuffing of nervous boots unable to keep still on the asphalt.

'Quicker!' whispered Brad excitedly.

I could've asked him what the hurry was, told him there was no way the police might turn up.

I could've asked if he wanted to take over, told him I worked at the speed that suited me best.

Or I could've asked if we shouldn't just drop the whole business and told it like it was: that it was a bad idea.

As Brad's second-in-command it was actually my duty to tell him and to try to get him to give it up. I've thought about that a lot since then. Whether I could have done anything different. Probably not. Because it was Brad's idea, and that mattered more than being a bad idea. In the first place he would not have wanted to lose face in front of the gang by admitting I was right. But I could have done what I usually did, which was to present my arguments as though they were just an interpretation of his own, so that when he realised I was right – and as things turned out he knew I was – he could take the credit for it. That was OK. A stupid leader can manage well enough as long as he is able to distinguish the good advisors from the bad ones. And Brad had that ability. Though he possessed only average intelligence himself, he seemed able instinctively to recognise intelligence in others. He didn't need to be able to understand your reasoning; intelligence was like something that just grew out of your forehead. And it was that, and not my career as a kickboxer, that had led him to appoint a girl as second-in-command of Chaos.

The reason I didn't even try to oppose him or manipulate him was that I knew this robbery was about more than food, weapons, petrol and a generator that may or may not have been in the garage. That Brad knew these people. That they had something he had to have, and nothing would make him change his mind. So I kept my mouth shut. Because I admit it; I don't risk my position in Chaos, which is the only thing keeping me alive, for a bunch of rich whites I don't even bloody well know.

'There!' I said, bending aside the strand of wire and slipping through, feeling the wired ends rasp against my skin and leather jacket.

The others followed. Brad stood there looking up at the darkened house bathed in moonlight. It was two o'clock in the morning. If people ever slept these days, then this was the time when they did it.

We took out our weapons. Sure, there were more heavily armed gangs than ours, especially the breakaway gangs of former policemen or soldiers, or former cartel people who had crossed the border. But by comparison with the usual youth gangs we were a heavyweight militia; each one of us with an AK-47, Glock 17 pistol and combat knife. We'd run out of bazooka grenades but Brad and I had two hand grenades each.

Brad's eyes glowed like those of a man in love. He could almost have been handsome. Maybe he was handsome when he slept. But there was something disturbing about his facial expression and his vibe when he was awake, a fear, as though expecting to be hit, as though he hated you even before you'd done it. And this cold, hard hatred and fear alternated so quickly with what was warm and kind and sensitive that it left you wondering what it must be like to be him from the inside. You really couldn't help but feel sorry for him. And want to help him. And on that particular evening, with the moonlight falling on his long, dirty-blond hair, Brad looked like Kurt Somebody-or-other, a rock star whose records my adoptive dad used to play when he got drunk and started yelling that everybody should do like Kurt, write a couple of great songs and then shoot themselves. But he couldn't create anything at all, my dad, so he just copied the shooting-himself part.

'Ready, Yvonne?' said Brad and looked at me.

The plan was for me to take Dumbo and ring the bell at the main entrance while the rest got in round the back. For what it was worth, I hadn't really understood why we had to wake up a family that was probably sleeping instead of using the element of surprise, but Brad had said that the sight of a Columbian girl and an undersized and retarded lad would make them lower their guard, that that was the kind of people they were. Helpful types, he had called them, his voice filled with contempt.

I nodded, and Brad pulled the balaclava down over my face.

I rang the bell. Must have waited a minute before I saw the little light by the camera above the door go on.

'Yes?' said a drowsy man's voice through the speaker.

'My name's Grace, I was in the same class as Amy,' I said in a tearful voice. I'd got the names from Brad and the acting talent from a Columbian man and woman I never even knew. 'This is my kid brother.'

'What are you doing outside at night and how did you get in?'

'We've been taking some food to my grandma, but now there's a gang in *the street down here and then I remembered Amy's house. We climbed over the barbed wire. Look at Sergio.'*

I pointed to the tears we had made in Dumbo's shirt – although it should have been obvious he hadn't a drop of Latin blood in his veins.

There was a pause. He was probably thinking. It wasn't that unusual to transport food and other stuff between households under cover of darkness.

'Just a moment,' he said.

I listened. Footsteps on the stairs inside, sounded like an adult male. The door opened. Slightly at first, then all the way.

'Come in, I'm Will. Amy's father.'

The man had blue eyes with laugh lines around them, a goatee beard and curly red hair that made him look younger than I guessed he was. Brad was probably right. The types that help people. He was barefoot but had pulled on a pair of worn jeans and a T-shirt with a name on it, probably the university where he was a student. I slipped inside so that I was behind him as he held the door open for Dumbo. Took out my gun and swung the barrel hard against the side of his head. Not to harm him or knock him out – because as tall as I am a kick from my heel to his head would have done the job – but to show him that the girl and the little guy were willing to use violence.

He shouted something and held his hand to the bleeding wound on his forehead. I pointed the gun at him.

'Don't harm my family,' he said. 'Take whatever you want, but don't –'

'If you do exactly as we say no one in the house will get hurt,' I said. And thought I was telling the truth.

IV

Blood ran from the wound in my forehead and down onto my T-shirt as they took me out to the garage and tied me to a chair, which they then tied to the lathe. The girl who said she was a classmate of Amy's – and for all I knew she might have been – examined the diesel generator. It's on wheels, but it weighs 150 kilos, so she was probably trying to figure out how she could take it with them.

My own thoughts were of what Heidi would do now. She'd been woken by the doorbell too and must have realised what had happened. Had she managed to get Amy and Sam to safety in the basement? To what we called the panic room, but which was actually a windowless cellar with stone walls, a solid door that could be locked from the inside, and enough food and water for a week. If the tall girl with the dark hair was as rational as she seemed then they would take just what they needed and could carry and get out of here. The boy with her hadn't said a word, just obeyed the slightest sign from her, and he seemed too harmless to be the type to enjoy hurting people.

It was when I heard Heidi's scream from another part of the house that I realised there were more of them.

'You said –' I began.

'Shut up,' said the girl, and hit me again with the pistol.

The boy looked up at her but she said nothing, just looked at me. It was a look that seemed apologetic.

And then a guy in a white ice-hockey helmet was standing in the garage doorway. The Justitia logo was painted on the front of the helmet.

'He wants you to come in,' he said. There was a repressed laughter in his voice.

Who was *he*? The leader, presumably.

The kid and the girl disappeared and the guy stood in front of me. He was holding a Russian automatic weapon, the type suddenly everyone seems to have, said to be very reliable. A Kalashnikov. In some countries it's part of the national flag, they see it as a symbol in the fight for freedom. But it just makes me shiver. That curved magazine, there's something perverse about it.

'I'll pay you five thousand if you let me and my family go,' I said.

'Which I'll spend where?' asked the guy, laughing. '7-Eleven maybe?'

'I can give you –'

'You don't need to give me anything, Gramps. I take what I want.'

He took down my old motorcycle helmet from a shelf. Took off the hockey helmet and tried it on. Raised and lowered the visor a couple of times. Seemed satisfied, took off the rucksack he was wearing on his back and pushed the helmet down into it.

I heard screams from inside the house again and couldn't breathe. I was the idiot who had opened the door and let Leviathan in. I didn't want to breathe, I wanted to die. But I couldn't die, not now – they needed me. I had to free myself. I tugged on the plastic strips the girl had used to tie me to the chair, felt the skin break and the warm sticky blood running down into my palms.

Heidi screamed again, so loud that I could make out a word. Just the one word. 'No.' Like a desperate and hopeless protest against something she knew was going to happen.

The guy looked at me, put his hand around the barrel of the Kalashnikov and moved it up and down as though masturbating. He grinned at me.

And right there and then, I think, was where it started. When everything I had always thought would be me began to fall apart.

Me and Dumbo stood in the doorway and looked at the dining table. It was made of thick, rough brown planking. Sort of rustic style but you can bet it cost a fortune. Like the one Maria had shown me in some Country Living *kind of magazine and said she wanted a table like that herself. But there was no way I could get that thing on the bike with me. My gaze moved on to the woman. She was lying tied up on the table. They must have found the rope somewhere and tied it round the tabletop and across her neck, chest and stomach. Her legs were tied to the legs of the table and her nightshirt pulled up above her stomach and down below her breasts.*

In front of her I saw the back of a red leather jacket with the embroidered motif of a gaping dragon rearing up out of the sea. Ragnar's jacket. He turned to us.

'There you are.'

Below the smooth brown mane of hair that he would lose before he was thirty Ragnar had these predator's eyes that glowed with something evil and dangerous, even when he smiled. Especially when he smiled. Maybe it wasn't just by chance he referred to the city as 'the savannah' and kept a long metal chain with a hook attached to his bike that he used when he was busy 'separating out the weakest animal in the herd' as he liked to call it.

'Really?' I said.

'Really,' he said, and his smile widened. 'Objections?'

I saw that he saw how I swallowed them down. That's the price you pay for being in a gang. There are rules you must follow. Among other things. But what came next wasn't in the rule book.

'The hour has come, Dumbo,' said Ragnar. 'It's your turn.'

'Eh?'

'Come on. It's nothing to be afraid of.'

Dumbo looked up at me, wide-eyed.

'He doesn't have to,' I said, and I could hear the tightness in my voice.

'Yes, he does.' Ragnar gave me that hostile, challenging look of his, the one that said he should have been Brad's second-in-command, not me. He waited for me to protest so that he could play his ace, but I already knew what it was.

'Brad's orders,' he finally added.

'And where is Brad?' I asked, looking round. Everyone, including Dumbo, was standing with their eyes riveted on the woman on the table. For the first time now I saw the little boy with the large round eyes in an armchair facing the table. He couldn't have been more than three or four years old and he sat there looking at his mother.

'Brad's upstairs,' said Ragnar, and turned to Dumbo. 'You ready, Shorty?'

One of the O'Leary twins sneaked up behind Dumbo and jerked his trousers down. Everyone laughed. Dumbo too, but then he always laughs when the others do so that no one will suspect he hasn't got the joke.

'Hey, hey,' said Ragnar. 'Hey, look at that, the dwarf really is ready!'

More laughter, Dumbo's louder than anyone's.

'Tell Yvonne you're ready, Dumbo!' Ragnar said, looking at me.

'I'm ready!' Dumbo laughed, thrilled to be the centre of attention, his glassy gaze fixed on the woman on the table.

'Jesus, Dumbo,' I said. 'Don't –'

'Insubordination, Yvonne?' Ragnar taunted, laughter in his voice. 'Is this incitement to insubordination we hear?'

'I'm ready!' shouted Dumbo. He liked to repeat sentences he thought he'd got the hang of. And now the others hoisted him onto a chair, turned the music up loud and cheered him on.

I felt my blood boil. But that's when you lose a boxing match, when you let the temperature of your blood decide. So I just said it, quietly, but loudly enough for him to hear me very clearly:

'You will fucking well pay for this, Ragnar.'

There was a scraping of chair legs. The woman was lying with her head turned and looking at the little boy. Tears ran down her face and she was whispering something. And I couldn't help myself, I went closer so I could hear. In spite of the effort she was making to control it her voice was trembling:

'Everything will be fine, Sam. Everything will be fine. Close your eyes now. Think of something nice. Something you'd like us to do tomorrow.'

I stepped forward, took hold of Sam under the arms and lifted him up.

'Let go of him!' the woman shrieked. 'Let go of my son!' I caught her eye.

'He doesn't need to see this,' I said.

Then I hoisted the boy up onto my shoulders, keeping a tight hold of him because he was struggling and squealing like a stuck pig. I headed for the kitchen door but then Ragnar appeared in front of me and blocked the way. Our eyes met. I don't know what he saw in mine but after a couple of seconds he stepped aside.

I heard the mother scream 'No!' as I ducked down through the doorway, walked through the kitchen and out through another door into a corridor. I kept on walking until I found a bathroom. I put the little boy down on the floor and told him his mother would come and fetch him if he kept completely quiet and put his hands over his ears. Then I took the key from the door and locked it from the outside.

I climbed a staircase, passed a couple of open doors and then one that was closed. I opened it carefully.

Light from the corridor entered the room. Brad was sitting beside a bed in which a blonde girl of about my own age lay sleeping. She was still wearing a pair of headphones. I recognised the type, with noise-cancelling so good you could even sleep through the sounds of hand grenades exploding in the streets outside.

Or of your own family being tortured a few metres away.

Brad looked as though he'd been sitting there and looking at her for quite a while. And the girl was nice-looking, in a sort of old-fashioned romantic way, not exactly my type. But obviously Brad's – I'd never seen him like that before, soft and dreamy-eyed, with a small smile on his lips. It struck me that it was the first time I'd ever seen him happy.

The girl in the bed turned away from the light without waking.

'We've got to get out of here,' I whispered. 'We heard the screams even out on the garage – the neighbours might have called the police.'

'We've got time,' said Brad. 'And she's coming with us.'

'Eh?'

'She's mine.'

'Are you out of your fucking mind?'

I don't know if it was because I spoke so loudly, but suddenly the girl in the bed opened her eyes. Brad took the headphones off her head.

'Hi, Amy,' he whispered in a velvety smooth and completely unfamiliar voice.

'Brad?' the girl said, her eyes wide open as she sort of scooted up the bed and away from him.

'Shh,' he said. 'I've come to save you. There's a gang down on the floor below us, they've got your parents and Sam. Stuff a few clothes into a bag and come with me, I've got a ladder outside the window.'

But the girl, Amy, had seen me. 'What are you doing, Brad?'

'Rescuing you,' he repeated in a whisper. 'The others are in the living room.'

Amy blinked and blinked. Got the picture. Got it quick, the way we all had to learn to.

'I'm not leaving Sam,' she said loudly. 'I don't know what's going on, but you can either help me or go.' She looked at me. 'And who are you?'

'Do as he says,' I said, and showed her my gun.

I don't know if that was the right or wrong thing to do – Brad hadn't given any instructions about kidnapping – but as she was about to sit up in the

bed he grabbed hold of her hair, jerked her head backwards and pressed a
cloth against her mouth and nose. She struggled for just a couple of seconds
before her body shuddered and then collapsed into his arms. Chloroform. And
there was me thinking we'd run out of it.

'Help me carry her,' he said as he stuck the cloth into his pocket.
'But what are you going to do with her?'
'Marry her and have children,' said Brad.
Straight away of course I reckoned he'd lost it completely.
'Come on,' he said as he took hold of the limp body under the arms. Looked
at me, eyebrows raised.

I hadn't moved. Didn't know if I was going to be able to either. I looked at
the poster pinned above her bed. Same band as the one I liked listening to.
'That's an order,' said Brad. 'So make up your mind.'
Make up your mind. I knew what that meant, of course. Make up your
mind whether you still want to be a member of the only family you've got.
With the only protection you're ever going to get. Make up your mind now.
So I did manage to move after all. I bent forward. Took hold of her legs.

I heard the sound of several motorcycles fading into the distance as Heidi
staggered into the garage with one of my coats wrapped round her. She
found a knife on the workbench and cut me loose. I put my arms around
her. She was trembling and shivering as she buried her face in my neck,
sobbing as though the tears were choking her.

'They took her,' she said as the tears ran warm against my T-shirt.
'He's taken Amy.'

'He?'

'Brad.'

'Brad?'

'He didn't show his face, but it was Brad Lowe.'

'Are you certain?'

'He was the only one wearing a balaclava and he didn't speak. But he
was in charge and he went upstairs to Amy. And when the girl and the
boy came into the living room one of them said it's Brad's orders.'

'Said what was Brad's orders?'

Heidi didn't reply.

I held Heidi tight. I didn't need to know. Not yet.

The brown-skinned girl had known that our daughter's name was Amy and that she was the same age as her. Brad was a gang leader, that added up. For him to have hidden his face so he couldn't be recognised, that was logical. But the fact that he was still not quite sharp enough to get away with it, that he'd been recognised after all, that was typical of Brad Lowe too.

It was him all right, Brad Lowe. Gone wrong. But lovesick.

So there was a faint hope at least.

V

'So that's nine minutes until the helicopter gets here!' shouts the lieutenant. The halyard is slapping quicker, the wind has got up.

Colin signals to a man who then disappears into a penthouse apartment and re-emerges carrying a champagne cooler with the neck of a green bottle sticking up.

'We might as well say goodbye in style,' smiles Colin. 'The decadents used to say *après moi, le déluge,* but in our case – since the deluge is already upon us – vintage champagne should be popped and drunk by those with the palates – and the throats – to appreciate it. Before their throats get cut.'

'Well,' I say as I accept a glass from the man holding the cooler, 'I'm probably a little more optimistic than that, Colin.'

'You always have been, Will. After all that's happened I can only admire the fact that your faith in the human race remains intact. I wish I had even a fraction of your trust. And your heart. At least you've got that to keep you warm. But all I have is this cold, rational brain. It's like living alone in an enormous stone castle in the dead of winter.'

'Like your prison on Rat Island.'

'Yes,' says Colin. 'And by the way, I've heard a new explanation of why there are so many rats there. In the 1800s before they built the prison, there was an isolation hospital there for people with typhoid fever. They knew that they were going to die, and no one in the city wanted anything to do with a corpse with typhoid fever, not even relatives. And the rats knew it too. After dark they sat would sit squeaking and hissing and chattering and waiting for the fresh corpses to be tossed out of the hospital's back door. If someone died on that island the body would be consumed before sunrise. It was a satisfactory arrangement for all concerned.'

'Do you believe that story? Or do you still think they fled there, the same way you did?'

Colin nods. 'Typhoid from humans can't infect rats but even rats can be infected by our fear. And frightened rats are aggressive, so we're afraid of them and slaughter them indiscriminately. It's not the virus that's going to do for us, Will, but our fear of each other.'

I think of fear. The fear on the night Chaos came to our home. The fear I tried in vain to communicate on the night Heidi and I reported the case, and the following day, when we spoke to detectives at the police station.

The two investigators seated behind the desk no longer looked in my eyes nor in Heidi's but instead down at the notebooks in front of them. I assumed the reason was the horrendous story we had just told them: that our daughter had been kidnapped and my wife raped while I sat tied up in the garage. Not until later did I realise it was because we had just told them we were convinced the gang leader was Brad Lowe, son of the IT entrepreneur Colin Lowe.

'We'll look into it,' said the female investigator who had introduced herself as Chief Inspector Gardell. 'But don't hold your breath.'

'Don't hold your breath? How the hell do you expect us to breathe?' I wasn't aware I was shouting until I felt Heidi's hand on my arm.

'Sorry,' I said. 'But our daughter is out there and we're sitting here and . . . and . . .'

'We understand,' said Gardell. 'I expressed myself badly. What I was trying to say was that it might take time. In the current situation the police simply don't have the resources to investigate all crimes of violence.'

'I realise you must have your priorities,' said Heidi, 'but this is a recent kidnapping, involving a young person, with a perpetrator who we've more or less handed to you on a plate. If anything should have priority . . .'

'We promise to do the best we can,' said Gardell, exchanging looks with her colleague. 'We're on our way out to the scene of a murder, but you'll be hearing from us.'

They stood up, and so did I.

'Aren't you going to take fingerprints?' I said. 'DNA, talk to the neighbours . . .'

'As I say . . .' said Gardell.

For the remainder of the day I tried in vain to get in touch with Colin.

I also drove to the apartment his son had taken the keys to, only to establish the truth of what Colin had said: that all that remained of it was a burned-out shell.

I drove round the streets, almost hoping a gang would try to stop me, I'm not really sure why. But that didn't happen; it looked as though all activity had come to a standstill. Like a truce had been declared.

I drove home and Heidi and I lay with Sam between us. Perhaps it was to give him the feeling of total security we had been unable to give Amy.

At daybreak Sam was sleeping deeply and I asked Heidi if she would tell me the rest of what had happened, the details that had not emerged in the concise description she had provided for the police.

'No,' was her brief answer.

I looked at her and wondered how she could remain so cool and calm. I knew psychological shock could manifest itself as apathy, but that was not what this was. It felt as though she had taken control of her own mind and body and forced herself to assume this chilly calm, the same way certain animals can lower their own body temperature.

'I love you,' I said.

She didn't answer. And I understood. She had blocked out all emotions, chilled her heart to ice so that it wouldn't run out of her and across the table and onto the floor. Because then she wouldn't be any use to either of us. Out of love she now loved us a little less. That had to be the explanation.

'I love you,' he said.

She didn't reply.

I watched them through the keyhole. Saw Brad lean towards the girl, Amy. She sat there on his bed with her head bowed. She was wearing a pair of comically large, checked golf trousers and a man's shirt that Brad must have taken from the wardrobe of the people who lived here before; they hadn't taken much with them when they left.

I looked around carefully, listened out for the others down in the kitchen; I didn't want to be caught in the act of spying on our leader.

Then I put my eye back to the keyhole again.

She was so pretty, even with her hair hanging down and covering most of her face.

Was that why I was spying on them?

After the robbery we'd gone straight home. I rode behind Brad's bike up one of those narrow, deep valleys that cut furrows through the hills at the northern end of town. Once — when this was coyote country — artists and hippies had lived here, people who couldn't afford to live in the city centre. Now it was the other way around: the poor lived in the centre and the rich in big houses with views over the bay and the skyscrapers down there. But many things were going back the other way again. Several of the houses were empty, and we saw more coyotes and wild dogs trotting along the roads in search of something to eat.

Chaos's new clubhouse was directly opposite a house where a gang had killed six people, including the wife of a wealthy film director. That was a long time ago. We moved here after the fire at Brad's apartment in Downtown. It was a villa belonging to one of the partners in Brad's father's company and when the pandemic started Brad heard his father mention that this guy had moved to New Zealand and taken his family with him. It was apparently pretty common for rich doomsday preppers to buy houses down there, a place far enough away to shelter them from all the rest of the world's miseries. Well, you can't get lucky all the time every time and before the TV news channels closed down they were reporting that New Zealand was one of the countries hardest hit by the virus. Brad said that whether the owner was dead or not the big house was standing there so empty it was almost inviting us in.

The whole way here Brad had been holding the girl upright on his bike as we crawled through the curves. I had never seen him riding so carefully.

And now he was sitting there in the big bedroom and telling her he loved her. Which was definitely a new and unknown side to the guy.

I was the only one with my own bedroom; the others shared the five other rooms. Before long the villa was on its way to becoming an uninhabitable pigsty and – to Ragnar's great annoyance – I got Brad's permission to arrange housekeeping duties for everyone.

'Do you hear what I'm saying, Amy?' Brad bent his head in order to catch her gaze. 'I love you.'

Amy lifted her head. 'I don't love you, Brad. I don't even like you, I never have done. Now will you take me home?'

'I understand that you're afraid, Amy, but –'

'I'm not afraid,' she interrupted firmly. 'You're the one that's afraid, Brad.'

He gave a strained laugh. 'What have I got to be afraid of? Are you a kickboxer maybe?'

'Of what you've always been afraid of, little Brad. Your big daddy. You're afraid he's going to punish his snot-nosed little disappointment of a son.'

Brad's face went white. 'He's nothing to worry about because he's not here.'

'Oh, but he is here. He's always up there on your shoulder. When you say –' she put her head on one side and imitated Brad's sincere delivery – '"I love you", that's your father you're talking to.'

There was no way this could end well. But she just kept on:

'But as you can hear, your father is saying he doesn't lo—'

Brad hit out. Just with the flat of his hand, but with enough force to turn her head on that slender, fine neck of hers. She put a hand to her face. Blood was coming from one of her nostrils. I knew Brad, had seen him so many times once he'd lost control, and I was certain that from now on things could only get worse for Amy.

'Don't talk like that,' he said quietly. 'Take off your clothes.'

'What?' She sniffed in contempt. 'Are you going to rape me?'

'Understand one thing, Amy. I am the only one who can protect you from the world out there. And the world out there starts in the kitchen downstairs. If I'm not here to stop them, they'll tear you to pieces. They're a pack of wolves, that's what we are.'

'I'd rather have ten of them than you, Brad.'

He hit her again. This time with his fist. She tried to hit him back but he blocked her arm. He's got quick reflexes, Brad. He's strong and he keeps in shape. If he could only control his emotions then he'd be a good fighter.

He grabbed hold of her blouse and pulled and the buttons flew off and scattered across the parquet floor. Then he stood up and took off his trousers. Amy tried to jump down from the bed and run towards the door but Brad easily stopped her with one arm and pushed her back onto it.

'For your sake I hope you're not a virgin,' said Brad as he sat on her chest so that his legs pinioned her arms.

'I'm not,' she said defiantly, though her voice was trembling now. 'But you are. Since rapes don't count, I mean. And you won't manage it this time either . . .'

Her voice was cut off as Brad clutched her throat. With his other hand he pulled down the baggy trousers and her knickers. He must have relaxed his grip because she managed to splutter: '. . . because I am your father, you're afraid of me too, just wait . . .' before he began to choke her again.

He forced himself in between her thighs. I saw his naked buttocks tense and relax, but from the anxious swearing and the jerky movements I realised he wasn't able to manage it. Either she'd jinxed his erection or else he just couldn't handle the situation. Or else – and this struck me as a third possibility – he really did love the girl.

'Shit!' he yelled and jumped off the bed. Pulled up his trousers and buttoned them as he walked towards the wardrobe and took something from inside. It took me a moment to realise it was a golf club. He held it with both hands above his shoulder as he walked towards Amy.

I put my hand on the doorknob and turned it. Or did I? Maybe I didn't have time, maybe the door was locked on the inside. Maybe I changed my mind. Because one way or the other, what could I have done about it? There was a dull thud, like the sound of a meat-hammer hitting a steak as the head of the club buried itself in her upper body. And a crackling, crunching sound – like when you're frying an egg for breakfast – when the next blow hit her on the forehead. She collapsed silently across the bed.

Brad turned and walked straight towards me. I was just a few metres away down the corridor by the time the door opened, but I managed to turn to make it look as though I was walking towards his bedroom and not away from it by the time he burst out.

'There you are!' he said. 'Get someone to help you carry her down into the basement. Use one of the rooms with thick walls and a decent lock.'

'But . . .'

'Now!'

He carried on past me and down the stairs.

VI

It was now three days since Amy had been kidnapped. Having tried in vain to get hold of Colin by phone, mail and through intermediaries I made my way down to the harbour. The sex clubs there were still open as though nothing had happened, or perhaps because they had. Finally I met in one of them a slightly drunk fisherman who was willing to take me out to Rat Island and asked a ridiculously high price for such a short trip. The stripper onstage gave me a dirty look as I walked off with a third of her audience.

As we neared the island a boat of the same type used by the coast-guards approached us. On reflection it probably was a coastguard boat. A machine gun had been mounted on the foredeck. The boat came alongside us. I shouted across to a guy in uniform the purpose of my visit; he called it in on the radio and a couple of minutes later he waved us in. Colin was standing on the jetty smiling broadly as we lay to.

'This is a pleasant surprise,' he said as he embraced me.

'I've been trying to get in touch with you.'

'Oh, really? The signal out here is even more unreliable than it is in the city. Come on!'

He strode on ahead of me in the direction of the huge building in the centre of the island.

'So?' he said. 'You and the family well?'

I swallowed. 'No.'

'No?' He tried to adopt a quizzical look.

'I'll get to it,' I said. 'So this is your home now?'

'Well, for the time being. Liza hates the place and thinks I should have bought some lovely big island instead of this barren lump of stone. She doesn't understand that the overview is more important than the appearance right now.'

We stopped in front of the building. I put my head back and looked up at the tall, weather-worn concrete wall.

'You feel safe in your home?'

'Here, yes,' said Colin, hitting with concrete with his fist. 'These walls could've stopped the French Revolution. And my snipers can pick off anything that approaches, even at night.'

High above I saw the line of narrow, arrow-slit windows that com-manded unbroken views in all directions. The sea glistened and glinted invitingly around us, as though this were just a normal day. But there wasn't a sailing boat in sight. Just the thick smoke drifting across the surface of the water from the city fires. On the other hand, maybe the sea didn't find this day any more special than one with happy yachts and surfers sailing about. Yep, just any old day with the human race wandering about the surface of planet Earth.

'Let's eat. I asked the kitchen to make some –'

'No,' I said, watching as a brown rat scampered across a sloping rock. 'Let me tell you why I'm here. Brad attacked us in our house.'

'What did you say?'

'He took Amy.'

'What?' He tried to sound as if he was shocked.

'And the police won't – or can't – do anything about it.'

'When . . . ?'

'Three days ago.'

'Why didn't you tell me before? Right, problems with the net.'

Colin has many talents but acting isn't one of them. He made a show of shaking his head as I told him about the nightmare night, in as much detail as Heidi had been willing to share with me. And after that he didn't have to pretend to be horrified any more.

'We told the same story to the police,' I said. 'But once they realised that the man we were talking about was Colin Lowe's son they stopped taking notes.' I took a deep breath. 'It looks to me as though you already know all this, so I'm assuming they contacted you immediately afterwards.'

'The police contacted me?'

'Come on, Colin. I know you too well. And as your lawyer I know all about your connections in the police.'

Colin studied me for a few moments. And, as usual, his assessment was correct.

'What you've got to understand, Will, is that you are my friend, but Brad is my son.'

'I know that and you're forgiven, but he has to let Amy go. And you must get them to arrest Brad.'

'Hang on,' said Colin. 'There's more. The police told me the only evidence they have that it was Brad is that in the course of the evening someone apparently mentioned his name. But that you yourselves did not recognise him. Not recognise a boy who practically grew up with you? Not recognise the body language, the eyes, the voice?'

'What are you saying, Colin?'

'I'm saying that when your daughter gets kidnapped you're desperate. You look and you search until you find something, anything at all. And what you found was the sound of one of the most common names in the city, briefly and in passing. Because it gave you something to hang on to. But I know Brad. God knows he's no angel, but he didn't do this, Will.'

'Then find him. Talk to him!'

'No one knows where he is, no one has any contact with him. Listen, I'm as worried about Brad as you are for –'

'Then let the police send out an alert for him,' I interrupted before he could finish the meaningless sentence.

'But there's no proof, not even a suspicion. And they're the ones saying it, not me. None of us can force them to use resources on a case they don't believe exists.'

'Yes, you can!'

'I can't, my dear Will. Not even if I wanted to.'

'Yes. But you don't want to. You're afraid Brad's guilty.'

'He isn't guilty.'

'Then you're afraid he'll be found guilty.'

'Maybe that has something to do with it, yes.'

I punched the concrete wall in despair. 'The courts are still up and running, Colin. And on my life I swear Brad will get a fair trial. Yes, even if he's killed her. You hear me?'

'And I swear on my life that my son is neither a kidnapper nor a murderer, Will. On my life. You hear me?'

I looked out over the sea again. The silent sea that witnessed fates such as ours being played out each second of each day. And twinkled and sparkled just the same.

'Yes, I hear you,' I said. 'You swear on your life.'

Another rat scampered across the wet, sloping rock, the sun catching on its long tail.

Then – without a word or a gesture of farewell – I walked down to the jetty and the boat that waited for me.

That night I drove through the city streets again, looking for Amy or someone who could tell me something. The following day I was back at the police station in Downtown asking for news, asking them to investigate, trying to persuade them that Brad Lowe was behind it. And again all I met was closed doors and deaf ears, and I was finally asked to leave the station.

As I walked across the large car park outside the shopping mall I saw someone leaned up against my car. It was Chief Inspector Gardell.

'How's the search going?' she asked.

I shook my head.

'Want a tip you didn't get from me?'

I looked at her. Nodded.

She took a sheet of paper out of a folder and handed it to me.

I studied it. An address, with a name I recognised.

'This was one of Lowe's partners,' I said. 'You think Amy might be there?'

Gardell shrugged. 'We've had complaints from the neighbours. Drugs, gunshots and partying late into the night. Seems like Brad Lowe and his gang have moved in there.'

'But you haven't done anything?'

'Complaints about noise aren't a top priority for us right now.'

'But gunfire and illegal occupation, aren't those pretty serious?'

'We've had no complaints from the owner. And for all we know the people living in his house have a firearms licence.'

I nodded. 'I'll get up there and check it.'

'Not sure I would do that,' said Gardell.

'No?'

'With so many weapons around it's not advisable just to turn up and ring on the doorbell. At least not alone.'

I looked at her. 'But you won't help me.'

Gardell took off her sunglasses and squinted with one eye in the sunlight.

'You're not the only one saying that these past few months.'

'I'm not?'

'No.' She handed me the folder. I opened it and flipped through the documents. They were reports. Armed robbery. Causing bodily harm. Grievous bodily harm. Rape. Twenty, maybe thirty of them.

'And what is the connection?'

'Brad Lowe and his gang,' said Gardell. 'This is just a selection, but I think it might interest you.'

I looked at her again. 'I think I know what you're risking by doing this, Chief Inspector. So why are you doing it?'

She sighed. Put the sunglasses on again. 'Why do we do anything at all in this fucked-up world?'

Then she left.

In the course of that afternoon I spoke to most of those who had signed the complaints in the folder.

The ones I contacted first were those who had been raped. On the assumption that they, or their fathers or brothers, would be most highly motivated and easiest to persuade. But presently I realised that what Gardell had given me was already some kind of shortlist of names of people who not only had good reasons to want revenge but were physically and mentally capable of getting it. At least if they weren't acting alone.

'You mean vigilantes?' said one of those I spoke to.

I savoured the word. It represented everything I was against. At least, in a society in which there was an already functioning judicial system it did. But in the absence of such a thing then it wasn't vigilante activity as such but the best alternative means of getting justice. That was the way to look at it: not as breaking the law but as a kind of emergency supplement to the law.

I tried to explain this to the person involved, but the legal terms I used might have made it difficult to follow my reasoning.

'Sounds like vigilantes to me,' he said. 'I'm in.'

By that evening I was able to tell Heidi that I had the backing of fifteen grown men. And that one of them had undertaken to provide us with weapons.

I had expected her to be pleased – or at least to snap out of that darkly apathetic mood she'd sunk into since the attack – but instead she just stared at me as though I were a stranger.

'Find Amy,' was all she said, and closed the door to our bedroom.

I slept in the living room and heard an animal howling and howling out there in the night, and the dull thuds of exploding grenades that might have been a block away or ten blocks away, it was impossible to tell. I don't know what kind of animal it was, but it sounded big. I'd heard about the fire in the zoological gardens the previous night and how they had had to release the animals to save them. Good idea, I thought. But if that particular animal was edible . . . I didn't have time to complete the thought before I heard a shot and the howling came to an abrupt halt.

'What you see here represents my most fundamental rights,' said the bald-headed man as he gestured with his hand towards something that reminded me more than anything else of a collection of insects mounted on pins, only magnified and more grotesque. The wall was covered with handguns. Pistols, rifles, automatic weapons, machine pistols, even a large machine gun mounted on a tripod that looked like someone kneeling.

'The freedom to defend myself.'

The bald-headed man gave us a pleased smile. He wanted to remain anonymous and had asked us just to call him Fatman. Of the fifteen who had signed up two days earlier three had pulled out. It wasn't surprising. Initial enthusiasm at the chance for revenge had given way to more rational considerations: other than a short-lived emotional satisfaction, how would it benefit me personally? And what was I risking? When the courts punish criminals the overwhelming power they have access to means they risk little; but what about us? What happens when revenge is taken for revenge?

'They knew we had weapons, that was why they came,' said Fatman. 'But they didn't find this secret room, so all they got were the Kalashnikovs and the hand grenades. Help yourselves, gentlemen.'

'What did they do to you and yours?' asked Larsen – an African American music teacher wearing a freshly pressed blue shirt – as Fatman showed him how to load, prime and change the magazine on the weapon he had chosen.

'I just told you,' said Fatman.

'They . . . er, stole some rifles?'

'And my hand grenades.'

'Grenades. And that was enough to leave you wanting revenge?'

'Who said anything about revenge? I just want to shoot some bad guys, and now I've got a bloody good reason, right?'

'Nice one,' said Larsen quietly.

Fatman flushed. 'How about you?' he snorted. 'They take your Volvo?'

I cursed inwardly and closed my eyes. I needed these men to work together, not this. I'd read the reports carefully and knew what was coming.

'They killed my wife,' said Larsen.

It went very quiet in this damp basement room. When I opened my eyes again I saw everyone had their gaze fixed on the man in the blue shirt and suit trousers. In the report, Larsen had written that he and his wife were standing on the pavement outside a secret food depot with the food they'd bought. They'd gone there with eight adult relatives; it was the usual thing to move around in packs, it was reckoned to be safer. A motorcycle gang had come at them and the men pulled out the few weapons they had – knives and an old rifle. But the bikes had passed them without slowing down. They thought the danger was over until the last rider tossed out a chain with a hook on it that embedded itself in Larsen's wife's thigh and dragged her off down the street, and while the men rushed to her assistance the gang stopped and picked up their bags of food.

'An artery in her thigh was punctured,' said Larsen. 'She bled to death in the street while those bandits picked up the hams and the tins.'

The only sounds that could be heard were Larsen's hoarse breathing and swallowing.

'And they had . . . ?' said a cautious voice.

'Yes,' said Larsen, who had regained control of his voice. 'They were wearing helmets with dead Justitia.'

The men in the room nodded.

One of them coughed.

'Tell me, that machine gun . . . does it work?'

Two days later we were ready.

We'd had shooting practice at a rifle range under the direction of Pete Downing, a former Marine who had been involved in house-to-house fighting in Basra in Iraq. Him, me and Chung, a construction engineer, had gone over the drawings of the place Chung had obtained through a contact in the Planning and Building Services Department. Downing had drafted a plan of attack that he went through with us in a room we had rented in the basement of the rifle range. He pointed out that there could be several kidnap victims in the house, playing down in this way the fact that the focus of the action was primarily on Amy and me. The funny thing was that once he was done he turned and spoke to me.

'Well, Will Adams, think that sounds OK?'

I nodded.

'Thank you,' said Downing as he rolled up the large sheets of paper he had drawn on.

I stood up. 'Then we meet here at midnight,' I said. 'Remember, dark clothing.'

The men stood up and filed out. Several of them nodded as they passed me, from which I realised that they regarded me as the leader of the operation. Was that just because I had taken the initiative? Or was something more involved? Was it because of the way I had described not just the practical side of our intended operation but also its moral and socially responsible dimensions? Had my simple remarks about justice not being something you get but something you take given them a thirst for battle they hadn't been able to feel when they were alone, but that they realised they had been missing now that they had been given a morally acceptable motivation? Maybe. Because maybe they had noticed that I meant every word of what I was saying. That it is every-one's responsibility to cut the head of the Leviathan, the sea monster, before it grows so big it devours us all.

But I don't think that was on anyone's mind as our column of three cars crawled up the narrow, twisting road heading towards the villa on the hill. I sat squashed between two others in the back seat and thought only of what I was to do, my own practical role in the planned operation. And that I didn't want to die. The smell I recognised through the sweat from the others in the car was probably the same as I was giving off myself. Fear.

VII

I awaken to the sounds of shots, people shouting, running footsteps along the corridor.

My first thought was that it was just another party that had got out of hand, that someone had started a fight, probably with Ragnar.

I heard someone try the door of my room. It was locked, the way it always is. It's not from the fear that someone will come in and rape me. In the first place I know I could take them, and in the second place Brad would chop their head off, and in the third place, you become sort of demagnetised as a sex object for guys when they realise you're into the same thing as they are: girls. But I also know that the way the drug-taking has, to put it mildly, esca-lated these days it's just a question of time before someone tries it. And that will mean so much trouble for them that there's no reason not to lock the door. But from my point of view they're the ones who are locked in, not me.

I swung my legs over the side of the bed and grabbed the Kalashnikov lying underneath it. Because the voices out in the corridor didn't belong to any of the boys, and now I heard two loud bangs from shock grenades. Oscar was on watch tonight; what the hell was going on? Had he fallen asleep on the job?

No one trying the doorknob any more – have they moved on? Just then I heard the dull thud of a shot from the other side of the door and the whiplash as the bullet passed my head and hit the wall.

I raised the gun, pushed the security catch into automatic and fired. Even in the half-dark I could see how the salvo perforated the door and the white splinters of wood flaring. Outside, someone fell heavily and began to scream. I pulled on my shoes, trousers and jacket and crossed to the window. Down on the lawn Oscar was lying splayed out on his back in an X-shape, the Kalashnikov beside him, as though he was sunbathing in the moonlight. I made a quick calculation. I didn't know how many of them there were, but they'd taken out Oscar before he had a chance to raise the alarm, and they had shock grenades. So not just a bunch of amateurs. And who were we? A gang of doped-up kids who knew how to attack but hadn't had any practice in how to defend. If I didn't take a decision quickly it was going to be taken for me.

I had the bike key in my pocket.

Shit, I even had a place to go: Maria had asked me to move in with her on a permanent basis. And hadn't I even considered it, independently of this? OK, Chaos had saved me once, but wasn't it true that we had all saved each other? That it was the pack, the twelve of us together, that protected us? And not loyalty, or some code of honour. Fuck that. Had anyone here ever sacrificed anything for me? No way.

I got the window open and climbed out, hung from the ledge by my arms and then let go. The roses in the bed below were dead and gone long ago, but not the bramble bushes that had replaced them, big and ugly. It was like rolling around in barbed wire.

I took a deep breath, pulled the pin on the shock grenade and nodded to Downing. He nodded back, turned the handle on the door I had pointed out on the plans as the master bedroom, and pushed it slightly open.

I did as he had shown me, bent low and rolled the grenade along the parquet flooring so that it made as little sound as possible. Downing closed the door again and counted to four.

Even through the closed door the sound was deafening and a flash of light blitzed out through the keyhole.

Downing kicked the door open and we went in, positioning ourselves on each side of the doorway as he had shown us.

My pulse was racing as the beam of my torch searched the room for Amy. It flashed across the window, and on the lawn outside I saw a figure running towards a parked motorcycle. I moved the beam on until it caught something that at first I thought was a sculpture. A boy with pale white skin sat bolt upright in bed, staring as though paralysed. That's the effect the shock grenade has, Downing had explained.

It was Brad.

Downing yelled at him to put his hands up, but Brad was probably still deaf from the bang and he just stared at us in bewilderment. Downing hit him across the face with the butt of his gun, and a slimy blob of blood and spittle flew through the cone of light.

I pushed Brad backwards onto the bed and sat on top of him. He didn't struggle.

'It's me,' I said. 'Will. Where is Amy?'

He blinked up at me.

I repeated the question, at the same time pressing the barrel of the pistol I had chosen against his forehead.

'We know it was you,' I said. 'Your sentry's dead. You want to be next, Brad?'

'She . . .' he began.

It took him two long seconds, time enough for me to start shaking like a leaf on a tree, before he was able to continue:

'She isn't here. We let her go as soon as we left Downtown. Didn't she turn up?'

I don't know whether it was because he had inherited his father's repertoire of facial expressions, but I knew he was lying.

I hit him with my gun. And again. Apparently. Because by the time Downing stopped me and I was in control of myself again Brad's face was a grotesque bloody mask beneath me.

'She's dead,' I said.

'You don't know that.'

I closed my eyes. 'He wouldn't have lied if she wasn't dead.'

I climbed on my motorcycle that was standing beneath the large garage over-hang. From where I sat I could see across the lawn and into Brad's room and the dancing light beam of a torch.

They'd got him.

I was about to start the engine. I would have been out of there in seconds flat, but a thought stopped me. The thought of leaving Dumbo, just abandon-ing him. I glanced at the room he shared with Herbert, the only Black guy in the gang. The light was on inside. Maybe they hadn't reached them yet. I climbed back off the bike and sprinted across the lawn and over to their win-dow. Stretched up on tiptoes and peered in. Dumbo was sitting on the bed in his underpants and T-shirt, feet dangling as he stared at the door. Herbert was nowhere in sight. I tapped on the glass and Dumbo jumped, but when he saw my face pressed against the windowpane he smiled.

He opened the window. 'Herbert went out to see what's going on,' he said. 'Do you know –'

'Put your shoes on!' I whispered. 'We're getting out of here!'

'But –'

'Now!'

Dumbo disappeared.

I saw him fiddling with his shoelaces as I counted the seconds. I should have got him shoes with Velcro.

'Freeze,' I heard a voice say right behind me.

I turned round. A bald-headed man holding a rifle with telescopic sights was standing there. I continued to turn.

'Didn't you hear –' he began to say, then dropped the rifle and stopped speaking and breathing after my kick hit him between the legs. I saw him

collapse to the ground, then turned back to the window. Dumbo was standing
on the ledge.

'Jump!' I said.

I took his fall, but he was so heavy we both tumbled over onto the grass.
Then we were on our feet and he was running after me towards the bikes.

I'd heard Fatman's voice outside the window and looked out.

A long-legged girl and a small, bow-legged boy were running across
the lawn. It was them. I was certain of it. Everything about them – faces,
bodies, their way of moving – was etched fast in my memory from when
I sat tied up in the garage. They reached the motorcycles and the girl
sat on one of them while the boy climbed up behind her. She fiddled
about in her pockets looking for something, keys probably. I saw a red
dot dancing on the white T-shirt under her jacket.

Laser.

I opened the window. Fatman was lying on the lawn below, the butt
of the rifle to his cheek.

'Don't shoot!' I shouted. 'We're not killers.'

'Shut up,' he grunted without looking up.

'That's an order!'

'Sorry, but this is my bad guy.'

'If you shoot, so will I,' I said. Quietly. That was probably why he
stopped and looked up. Saw the pistol pointing at him. Stared as we
heard the roar of the motorbike rise, fall and then disappear as it went
through the gate and headed down towards the valley.

I lowered the pistol. I don't know why, but a small part of me had
wanted him to shoot them. Because then I could have shot him.

'The helicopter will be here in four minutes!' shouts the lieutenant.
'Everyone who's boarding, get ready now!'

I only half hear him. Because standing here on the roof of the skyscraper and waiting to say goodbye I'm thinking now about something
else: that I had wanted to shoot someone. That I had wanted

circumstances to give me an excuse to become a person I don't believe myself to be. That perhaps I no longer know who I am. I look at the lucky ones, standing there listening out for the helicopter. I look for signs of guilty conscience among them. I don't see any.

We were all gathered in the living room as Downing and Larsen cleared the rest of the house.

We had one man badly wounded, they had one dead – the sentry – and four wounded.

'We've got to get him to hospital,' said Chung, meaning the man who had been wounded by the shots through the door.

'No way. That was the agreement,' said Fatman, who seemed to be suffering discomfort in his groin.

'But –' said Chung.

'Forget it. We don't want the police breathing down our necks,' said Fatman with finality.

'Drive him to hospital,' I said.

Fatman turned towards me, his face flushed with anger. 'Says you, yeah, who let one of the bastards escape.'

'There was no reason to kill her, she was running away.'

'We're here to exact punishment, Adams. You're just here to find your daughter, and you're using us to help you do it. Fair enough, but don't go playing the Good Samaritan at our expense. Try telling Simon here that that girl didn't deserve a bullet.'

I looked at Simon. A chubby, softly spoken chef with kind eyes and an infectious laugh. Yes, we'd had laughs together too. Simon and his family had been visited by a gang with dead Justitia on their helmets. They'd launched grenades from a bazooka and within seconds the house had turned into a blazing inferno. His wife and son were still in hospital, so badly burned no one could tell him whether or not they would survive.

'What d'you think, Simon?' I said. 'Should I have let him kill her?'

Simon looked at me for a long time. 'I don't know,' he said at last.

'Will you help Chung get Ruben to the hospital?' I asked.

He nodded.

Downing and Larsen came in.

'Find anything?' asked Fatman.

They didn't answer. They couldn't look me in the eye, and whatever slender hope I might still have been clinging to vanished.

Amy was in the basement, lying on a filthy mattress in a locked room. Not to stop her running away, but to hide the body. I stared at her. My heart was switched off. My brain simply registered what I saw. Unless something else had killed her first, the cause of death was obvious. Her forehead had been smashed in.

I went down the basement corridor where Larsen and Downing stood waiting.

'We'll interrogate them,' I said, nodding up at the ceiling and the next floor above where the gang members were, sitting on the floor of the room, their hands strip-tied.

'You don't think first we should –' Larsen began to say.

'No,' I interrupted. 'Let's get started.'

The question of guilt was soon established. We used an old trick, simple but effective. In my professional capacity as a lawyer I had often criticised the police for using it.

We placed the gang members in separate rooms, left them there for a while before two of us went in and pretended we had already spoken to the others. I did the talking, and my opening was the same every time:

'I'm not saying who, but one of your gang has just identified you as the person who killed my daughter Amy. I'm sure you can guess who that is. I will shoot you, personally and with great pleasure, unless you can persuade me within the next five minutes that it was someone else.'

The bluff is so obvious that some of them will see through it immediately. But they can never be completely certain. And they definitely can't be certain that the others will see through it too. So the maths goes like this: why should I keep quiet and take the chance of this being a bluff when someone else is bound to snitch anyway?

After four interrogations two had identified Brad. After six we knew it had happened with a golf club in the bedroom. I went to one of the two offices where Brad was sitting and confronted him with what we had found out.

He leaned back in the leather chair, hands behind his back in the plastic cable ties, and yawned. 'Well then, I guess you'd better shoot me.'

I swallowed and waited. And waited. Then came the tears. Not mine, his. They dripped down on the aged grey teak of the desk. I saw them soak into the wood.

'I didn't mean it, Mr Adams,' he snuffled. 'I loved Amy. Always have done. But she . . .' He took a deep, quivering breath. 'She despised me, she didn't think I was good enough for her.' He gave a quick laugh. 'Me, son and heir of the second-richest man in the city. What do you think of that?'

I said nothing. He raised his gaze and looked at me.

'She said she hated me, Mr Adams. And you know what, that's one feeling we do share. I hated me too.'

'Is this your idea of a confession, Brad?'

He looked at me. Nodded. I looked at Larsen who nodded briefly to indicate that he'd seen it the same way as me. We stood up and went outside to where Downing was waiting.

'Confession,' I said.

'What are you going to do?' asked Larsen.

I took a deep breath. 'Put him in jail.'

'Jail?' snorted Downing. 'He's gotta hang!'

'Have you thought this through, Will?' asked Larsen. 'You know as well as I do that if you hand him over to the police he'll be out on the street again by tomorrow morning.'

'Yes, but I'm going to imprison him in his own jail.'

'What d'you mean?'

'Lock him up in the same place where he locked up Amy. He can sit there in custody until I've prepared the case and had him convicted.'

'You're going to . . . put Colin Lowe's son in front of a judge and jury?'

'Of course. Everyone's equal in the eyes of the law. That's the foundation our nation is built on.'

'There I am afraid to say you are mistaken, Adams,' said Downing.

'Oh?'

'Our nation is built on the principle that might is right. That's the way it is now, and that's the way it always has been. The rest is just playing to the gallery.'

'Well,' I said, 'Maybe it's possible for might to be really in the right for once.'

Just then we heard shouting. It was coming from behind the house. We ran outside in time to see that we were too late.

'The Black guy confessed,' said Fatman. He was holding a flaming torch in his hand and the light made the sweat on his forehead glisten. Like us he was staring in the direction of the tall oak tree. The rest of the men stood around us, all of them silent now.

A boy was dangling from the lowest of the branches. There was a noose around his neck. He was tall, thin, maybe sixteen years old and he wearing a T-shirt with 'Chaos' written on it.

'Herbert,' a hoarse voice shouted from a window in the house. I turned but saw no one.

'We've got a confession,' I said. 'You've hanged the wrong person.'

'Not that confession,' said Fatman. 'He confessed to starting that fire. And it wasn't me that hung that guy, it was him.'

He pointed to a man standing directly beneath the hanged boy. Simon, the cook. His hands were pressed together as he looked up at the corpse and he was muttering something. A prayer, maybe. For his family. For the dead. For himself. For all of us.

As a group we had never discussed what we were going to do with the members of Chaos. All our attention had been focused on freeing Amy, and it was pretty obvious that the gang members couldn't expect any mercy if they tried to resist. They would get hurt or be killed. For most of us that would probably be revenge enough. But we hadn't talked about what to do if they surrendered, as they had done now.

Essentially there were only three options. Execute them. Maim them. Or let them go.

Fatman was the only one to vote for execution.

A few thought that some kind of amputation, such as severing the right hand, was in order, but there were no volunteers to perform the amputations. I suspect that the thought of nine mutilated but still fully functional young men wandering about the city with revenge on their minds was not particularly attractive.

Downing's suggestion that they be lashed with a rope seemed to have the most support. It would probably be seen as some kind of let-off and not a motivation for revenge at a later date.

I argued that we shouldn't hand out any punishment at all unless we could give the 'accused' a fair trial. That, I said, was what distinguished us from them. In rejecting revenge we would not only be true to the principles of justice our forefathers had built this land on, we would also be providing a good example for these young people, showing them that it was possible to behave in a civilised fashion in the midst of these chaotic times, that there was a way back to decency. I promised I would personally make sure that, as far as possible, Brad Lowe would be treated in accordance with our most fundamental principles of justice.

I don't know whether it was my words that convinced them. Whether it was the fact that Larsen – the only one of us besides me with a close relative murdered – offered a few short words in support of me. Or whether it was the wind that had made the young Black man in the tree swing back and forth, and the branches to give off a moaning sound that constantly turned our attention in his direction.

Without further discussion we released all of them except Brad.

'We're gonna regret this,' said Fatman as we watched the rear lights of the motorbikes disappear into the deepening darkness of the city night.

VIII

Amy was buried after a ceremony in a church in Downtown. It was sparsely furnished and austerely equipped, yet everything seemed strangely untouched, as though God's house was still holy even to the looters. We didn't advertise the service or invite anyone, and besides Heidi, Sam and me the only others present were Downing, Larsen and Chung.

I spent the remainder of the afternoon trying to persuade Heidi to move to Colin's hillside villa along with Chung, Larsen and Downing's families. I reminded her how easy it had been for Chaos to enter our house, that the same thing not only could but would happen again. And that there was safety in numbers. Heidi said we couldn't, it was someone else's house, someone else's property, even if it was standing empty at the moment. I said that while I had the greatest respect for property rights, at the moment those rights were taking a short break. And we needed somewhere to hold Brad in private custody until the court case against him started.

The following day we moved the few things we needed up the hill and started work on turning the place into a fortress.

The attorney general's large white office building in Downtown had just the right balance of the architectonic pathos that encourages respect, and the dull pedantry that does not provoke when the taxpayer is the one funding it.

Adele Matheson, the attorney general, had the kind of office that's used for working in, not for giving off signals about authority and status to visitors and colleagues. A simple writing desk piled high with documents, a slightly out-of-date computer with cables in all directions, shelves of legal literature and a window that offered light but not a distracting view. And absolutely no family photos that might remind her of things more important in life than work and urge her to stop working and get on home.

Matheson sat in a high-backed leather chair behind the piles of documents and peered at me over the top of her glasses. Though she didn't have the high profile of some of her colleagues the respect she enjoyed from her peers was all the greater. If she was known at all it was for her integrity and her tenacity in hunting down the powerful and those with an aversion to finding themselves exposed in the media. A journalist once wrote that any interview or press conference involving Matheson was confined to a repertoire of four responses: 'Yes', 'No', the slightly longer 'We don't know that', and the really long 'We can't comment on that'.

'You are a lawyer, Mr Adams,' she said when she had listened to me. 'If you believe you have proof that this person killed your daughter, why come here, why not take the case to the police?'

'Because I no longer trust the police.'

'We're living in strange times, no doubt about that. And yet you seem to trust the public prosecutor's office?'

'Going through the attorney general means at least one step less in the process before the case gets to court.'

'You're worried about corruption. Is that it?'

'The boy's father is Colin Lowe.'

'*The* Colin Lowe?'

'Yes.'

She rested a finger on her upper lip then made a note. 'Do you know where the boy is now?'

'Yes.'

'And that is?'

'If I told you he was being held in private custody you would have to prosecute me and that would put the case against the boy in jeopardy, don't you think?'

'Private detention is of course a serious matter and if the confession came as a result of it then the court can simply throw the case out.'

'Fruits of a poisoned tree.'

'Yes, you are of course familiar with the legal principles involved. But if things are as you say, and you have witnesses who can confirm that there was a confession and that it was not coerced, then we have a stronger case.'

I noted that she was now saying 'we' instead of 'you'. Was that because of the name Colin Lowe?

'You will also need to get hold of at least one of the gang members who identified Brad as the killer,' she said.

'That could be difficult. But several of us heard them say that it was Brad.'

'That is indirect information and as a lawyer you are aware that would not be sufficient in a court of law. If I'm going to bring this to court I need to feel at least as sure of getting a conviction as the jury does if they're going to reach a verdict of guilty beyond reasonable doubt.'

I nodded. 'I'll find one of them who identified Brad.'

'Good.' Adele Matheson clapped her hands together. 'I'll get going, so let's stay in touch. This might be a good opportunity to show the world that the rule of law has not broken down completely.'

'I hope so too,' I said, looking at the only picture in the room. It was small and hung slightly sideways. It showed Justitia. Blind, impartial. With no bullet-hole in her forehead.

From the attorney general's office I made my way to the police station in Downtown where I asked to see Chief Inspector Gardell. She accompanied me out to the car park by the shopping mall where I told her I could get Brad Lowe in front of a jury if I could get hold of one of the gang members who had identified him as the killer.

'You had the bastard but you're going to give him his day in court?' she asked, with the same sense of astonishment an atheist might use when asking a Christian if they really believed that business about walking on water.

'I need to find one of the gang,' I said. 'Can you help me?'

She shook her head. I thought it was a no until she said: 'I can certainly keep my ears and eyes open, but don't –' and I knew what was coming next – 'hold your breath.'

I thanked her, and as I walked away it was with a feeling that she was watching me and still shaking her head.

Chung, the structural engineer, was in charge of making the villa impregnable.

The wall surrounding the property was raised, the two gates reinforced, and everything between the house and the wall that could be used as cover or shelter was removed. The windows were fitted with bulletproof metal plates with gun slits, and the walls, doors and roof reinforced to resist grenades. Mines and booby traps with motion sensors were sown across the outer approaches. A control room was established in the basement from where the property could be kept under surveillance, with facilities to operate remotely controlled machine guns and grenade throwers mounted up on the first floor. We also had two drones with cameras that could be remotely controlled from the basement, or the War Room as Downing insisted on calling it.

In essence: anyone wanting to capture the villa would need artillery and bombs.

And if, in spite of all, someone managed to get inside the place, Downing had night-vision goggles. He said that he and his brother soldiers had made an ally of the nights in Iraq by cutting the power before starting the nightly hunt for terrorists in the hostile neighbour-hoods of Basra. Once our families had gone to bed and all the lights were off Larsen, Chung and I practised working with these, but in truth the trials just left me feeling giddy and nauseous. And once, when Chung turned on the light without any warning, it was like staring straight into the sun and I was left half blind for several hours afterwards.

Chung also suggested we dig a tunnel in case we needed to retreat. I thought about it for a long time before saying it would cost too much. I was lying.

Through former colleagues in the Marines Downing had heard about an ammunition depot where we could barter weapons for food and medicine, and this we did. Larsen and I stored the ammunition in an unused washroom with thick stone walls in the basement. When Chung joined us he showed us the hole in the wall where the private sewage pipe he had made ran. If we were under siege and had our water and sewage disposal cut off then we now had a sewage pipe that opened onto a steep, overgrown slope below the property, as well as a water pipe Chung had attached to the mains supply further down the valley. In the unlikely event the besieging force should come across the sewage pipe and identify it as leading to our house there was of course the possibility they could fire a grenade up through it and into the house, but according to Chung it wouldn't do much damage – the walls of the room were just too thick. Unless, of course, high explosives were being stored in there.

He said it in his usual dry, practical way, with no facial expression to indicate whether he was being ironic or humorous. And that's why we laughed, Larsen and I, as Chung looked at us with his sorrowful gaze, which made us laugh all the more.

We decided to move the ammunition to the laundry that was being used as Brad's cell. I had put him there because that was where they had kept Amy's body. I was probably hoping it would serve as a constant reminder to him of what he had done, and would torment his conscience.

When we were finished I stood in the doorway of Brad's new cell where he lay on the mattress reading one of the books I had put in there with him. He was already thin and pale after the short time he had been held in custody, despite the fact that we fed him well and walked him in the garden every day.

'What's this?' he asked, pointing to the hole in the wall beside his head.

'It's for the sewage,' I said.

'You mean like me?' He put down the book, bunched his fist and put his arm in all the way up to his shoulder.

'People aren't sewage,' I said.

'If I slim down enough to wriggle out through it, where would I end up?'

'The slope below the Polanskis' house,' I said. I don't know why I told him that. Or did I actually know, even then? I picked up a plastic tie that had slipped down off one of the boxes of ammunition. Gathered it up and shoved it in my pocket.

Brad smirked. 'So I won't hang myself with it?'

I didn't answer.

He leaned on his elbow. 'Why can't you just execute me and get it over with?'

It was strange. Even though he was lying down and I was standing, he was the one locked up and in my power, it was as though he looked down on me, not the other way round.

'Because we aren't like you,' I said. And I met his gaze.

'You soon will be. If you want to live, I mean.'

'What I hope,' I said, 'is that you'll become like us. Or better than us.'

'How is that going to matter if I'm locked up for the rest of my life?'

'There's no guarantee that you will never again have to make a choice which has consequences for your fellow human beings, Brad.'

'Well then, give me the chance. Let me go. I promise you, my dad will pay whatever you ask. Make that whatever *I* ask!'

I shook my head. 'This is about something bigger than you, Brad.'

'Come on! What could be bigger than my dad's fucking money?'

'Choosing what's good instead of what's evil. That's bigger.'

Brad laughed and shoved the book so that it came skidding across the stone floor towards me. 'Like it says in here. Liberal left-wing piss if you ask me.'

I looked down at the book. Tom Bingham, *The Rule of Law*. Liberal left-wing piss? That meant at least he must have read it to form an opinion on it. Maybe it was true, what I was hoping: that all of us, including me, had underestimated Brad's intellectual capacity?

'You're telling me you don't want revenge?' he asked. 'Then you're lying!'

'Maybe,' I said. 'But anyway, executing you wouldn't be a good enough revenge. Because yes, I want you to feel remorse. I want you to feel the same pain as I do at losing someone you love above all others. And yes,

I want you to experience the same feelings of guilt as I do at having failed to protect your family well enough. I'm not above that, not as a human being. But we humans have the unique ability to renounce a short-term satisfaction in favour of something that has a higher goal.'

'Now you're talking like that book.'

'Read it,' I said. 'Then let's talk some more.'

I went out, locking the door behind me.

I entered the bedroom where she and Sam were playing with two Transformer figures Sam had got for Christmas from 'Uncle Colin', as it said on the gift label. Heidi and I had seen from Sam's reaction when he unwrapped them that it would break his little heart if we took them away from him and exchanged them for toys that didn't glorify violence in the same way.

'I gather you're having fun,' Heidi observed.

There was an edge to her voice and I realised she'd heard Larsen and me laughing.

'Well, I'm trying to anyway,' I said, hearing the same hard edge in my own voice.

'Have you talked to him?' she asked.

'Him' was Brad. She would no longer say his name.

'I checked on him,' I lied. As if laughing out loud wasn't bad enough, was I also supposed to tell her I had just had a meaningful conversation with our daughter's killer? Yes, I had said we had an obligation to get over Amy's death and try to look forward, for our sake and for Sam's sake. But in Heidi's view, sensitive people allowed grief to run its course; grief was the recoil after love, and if I didn't feel it then I had never loved Amy as deeply as I claimed. Her words had wounded me, of course they had. And she had seen it, and apologised. Everyone grieves in a different way, I had said, and maybe Heidi's was the better way, maybe she was dealing with something I was postponing. Even though I could see she didn't believe I meant what I was saying, I knew that she liked the way I was trying to compromise with her.

'Dad, look!' said Sam, running over and jumping into my lap. He held the Transformer figure up in front of my face and growled, 'I am Devastator! I can change!'

He twisted parts of the figure and a fork-like weapon appeared, before suddenly appearing to lose interest in the toy and looking me right in the eye: 'Can you change, Dad?'

I laughed and ruffled his hair. 'Of course I can.'

'Let's see then.'

I pulled a face, one that usually made him laugh. Now he just looked at me. He seemed strangely disappointed. Then he put his arms around me and buried his face in my neck. I looked up and Heidi gave me a tired smile.

'I think he thinks it's OK if dads don't change,' she said.

We kept strictly within the bounds of the property and tried not to get on each other's nerves too much. Even with four families there was more room than we had had in Downtown, but all the same it somehow felt more cramped. After the kidnapping Heidi felt she had to keep Sam close to her at all times. She wouldn't even let him play with the other kids in the large garden unless she was there with them. I tried to persuade her that we were safer here than anywhere else in the world right at that moment, but it didn't help.

'We will be attacked,' she'd said one day as we sat in the garden watching Sam playing with the two Larsen children. The mines and the booby traps had been deactivated and they were able to run around the garden in complete safety. It was a relief to hear their carefree laughter and know they really were enjoying the atmosphere of safety and security we were so desperately trying to encourage. Heidi had been raped but she still wouldn't talk about it. When I asked why and said it might be good for her to get it out in the open she replied that she really couldn't remember much about it. A girl had been there, and fortunately she had taken Sam out of the room, but after that she'd blanked everything out, all she thought about through the whole thing was Sam and Amy.

So there wasn't much to talk about. If the memories were somewhere down there in her unconscious then let them stay there – right now what mattered was that she function. My own understanding was that Heidi's ability to suppress these memories had something to do with the way great pain can, for a time at least, hide the distress of lesser pains, the same way it can with physical suffering. And the great pain was the loss of Amy. I realised that was why Heidi – that strong, caring, selfless woman who under normal circumstances would automatically have stepped in as a reserve mother for Larsen's motherless children – now almost avoided them. It was instead Chung's young wife who took on that role.

'They might try,' I agreed. 'But then they'll move on in search of something easier.'

'Not the gangs,' she said. 'Him. Colin. He'll find us.'

'Not if we lie low,' I said, with a worried look at the children. They were digging in the back garden where we had buried the young Black boy Herbert. Brad claimed not to know his surname; not that it really mattered, we weren't going to use it anyway. There was no cross to mark the grave that might have exposed the lynching.

'A father or a mother will always find a missing child,' said Heidi.

I didn't answer. Because I knew she was right.

I visited the police station the next day and heard some good news. Chief Inspector Gardell had traced a member of the gang, a guy named Kevin Wankel. It wasn't all that difficult since he was already in jail. Wankel had recently been arrested for killing and robbing a policeman, she told me. In his statement he had volunteered the information that he was a member of Chaos. But since the money Chaos shared out wasn't enough to pay for his methamphetamine habit he had gone out on his own to rob someone. He'd waited outside a strip club, approached the first man who came out, held a gun to his forehead and demanded his wallet. Witnesses described how the man had calmly said he was a policeman and that Kevin should be on his way, at which Kevin pulled the trigger, grabbed the wallet and ran off. He was arrested in the street an hour later as he tried to buy methamphetamine. His trial was already over and he'd been sentenced to life imprisonment.

She showed me Wankel's mugshot, but I didn't immediately recognise the face. He definitely wasn't one of those who had identified Brad as the killer.

'I've spoken to him,' said Gardell. 'He's more than willing to testify that it was Brad who did it. On condition that we get him some meth.'

'What?'

'Of course I said no. Adele Matheson won't bring a case that depends on evidence that's been bought with narcotics. But we can try offering him a reduction in his sentence.'

I looked at the photo and shook my head. 'He wasn't even there.'

'What?'

I pushed the mugshot across the table to her and pointed to the date. 'This was taken two days before the raid on our villa. He was already locked up. All he wants is dope. He'd sell his own mother for a gram.'

'Damn,' said Gardell. She looked as disappointed as I felt.

It's a strange thing when you're offered hope and then have it taken away from you. I left the police station the same as I'd come – empty-handed – and yet the day now seemed worse.

After Dumbo and I escaped from the villa that night we moved in with Maria.

She wasn't exactly over the moon about the fact that I'd brought somebody with me, but she accepted it as part of the deal. Because the deal wasn't just that we shared a roof, a table and a bed, it was also that I protected us and could – when necessary – go out and get us food. Maria didn't ask how and I never told her.

One trick was to find some quiet little road and get Dumbo to lie down in the middle of it. People didn't stop to help someone lying in the road any more, but at least they slowed down to drive round them. And as they did so I came riding up on the bike from the opposite direction, creating a little traffic jam. If we timed it right the car would come to a halt next to Dumbo, who would then get up, grab the shotgun he'd been lying on and shout 'Hands up!' – a line he loved and enjoyed shouting out whenever and wherever the notion took him. Motorists had no way of knowing whether I was part of the business involving the little guy with the shotgun or not and didn't automatically put their foot on the accelerator and mow me down, and those few seconds' hesitation were all the time I needed to produce my own shotgun.

This particular day we'd just played this trick. The guy was sitting in the car with his hands in the air and Dumbo's shotgun pointing at his forehead as I emptied the car of food and pushed one end of a plastic hose down into the fuel tank.

'Hands up!' shouted Dumbo for the third time.

'They already are,' said the motorist in a despairing voice.

'Hands up!'

'Dumbo!' I shouted. 'Calm down now.'

I closed my lips round the other end of the plastic pipe and started sucking to get the petrol moving up and into the jerrycan standing on the road.

I was concentrating so hard I never heard them coming, not until a voice that was way too familiar said loudly: 'Never knew the rug muncher could suck.'

I swallowed and coughed up petrol, spinning round ready to use the Remington rifle though I knew it was already too late.

There were three of them. One of the O'Leary twins had a gun pointed at Dumbo's forehead, the other a Kalashnikov pointed at me. The third – the one who had spoken – was wearing a red leather jacket on the back of which was, I knew, an embroidered sea monster.

'Ragnar,' I said. 'Long time.'

'But not long enough?' he smiled.

I started to get up.

'Stay on your knees, Yvonne, it suits you. And tell your dwarf to put down his shooter or we'll kill everyone.'

I swallowed. 'Do as he says, Dumbo. You're going to take what we got here?'

Ragnar swung his chain. 'Wouldn't you do the same?'

I shrugged. 'I guess that depends.'

'If, for example, someone ran off when the gang where she was second-in-command were under attack?'

'Wouldn't you have done the same?'

'You let us down. That's the first rule of Chaos, we don't let each other down. Am I right, boys?'

'Right,' the O'Leary twins answered in unison.

'The battle was lost,' I said. 'There was nothing I could do for you.'

'No? But you rescued this dwarf here.' Ragnar nodded towards Dumbo. 'You've trained him well, looks like he's learned how to make himself useful. We could use someone like that.'

'What happened up there?' I asked.

Ragnar peered into the bag of food I had set down on the road.

'They lynched Herbert and took Brad prisoner. Let the rest of us go, the idiots.'

'So then I guess you've already mounted a counter-attack.'

Ragnar gave me a puzzled look.

'Since they've got Brad, and one Chaos never deserts another Chaos in trouble,' I said. 'He's tried to rescue Brad, hasn't he, boys?'

This time the O'Leary twins said nothing.

Ragnar's small eyes were getting even smaller. But I couldn't stop myself: 'No? Ah, maybe you were happy enough to have me and Brad out of the way, so you could take over as leader?'

Ragnar's knuckles turned white as his grip on the chain tightened. 'You always did have a big mouth, Yvonne. No one ever tell you that's not such a good idea when you've got a Kalashnikov pointing at you?'

I swallowed. Thought of that girl, that Amy. Hadn't anyone told her?

'I've talked to Brad's old man and told him what happened,' Ragnar said, glancing over at the twins as though to make sure they'd heard him. 'He's going to handle it himself.'

'You saying you found Brad's father?'

He shrugged. 'It was more a case of him finding us. Anyway –' he took an apple out of the bag and bit into it – 'it's out of my hands now.' He made a face and threw the apple away. It bounced down the road.

'Did you know they still pay for dwarf sex down by the molo?'

I didn't answer.

'Remember, I let you live, Yvonne Big Mouth,' he said. Then he turned and started walking towards the corner where they must have left their bikes in order to sneak up on us. 'Remember the bags!' he called over his shoulder.

'OK!' shouted the twin who had the gun pointed at me. 'Shall we take the guns too?'

'Jesus, what do you think?'

Even though the O'Learys took our weapons they backed away after Ragnar, the Kalashnikovs still pointing at Dumbo and me.

I heard Ragnar's bike start; it had a special hoarse kind of sound. Then they rounded the corner. It took me a couple of seconds to realise what was happening, and before I could get up and yell to Dumbo to get out of the way I saw Ragnar swinging his hook. It made a sort of mushy sound as it caught in the back of Dumbo's shoulder, and I saw the point come out again on the other side, below his collarbone. The breath left Dumbo in a single, long-drawn-out gasp as he was dragged away from the window of the car he was trying to cling on to. He bounced twice, three times on the asphalt before he disappeared howling around the corner and was gone from my sight. I turned, ready to jump on my bike and follow them, and then the twins were roaring towards me and I heard the bullets strafing my machine.

And when they were gone too, and the fumes vanished, there I was, kneeling by the wheels of what had been my holy and damned machine.

'You need a lift?' asked the guy who was still there in his car.

I closed my eyes. I felt like crying. This isn't the town and this isn't the time for crying. It sure isn't. But I cried anyway.

It was late in the evening, and I was on my way home after yet another fruitless day's searching for members of Chaos. I needed an eyewitness, someone who could point the finger directly at Brad Lowe.

As I drove past the public prosecutor's building I saw lights on in a couple of the offices and on impulse parked in the almost deserted car park and rang the bell. Asked the voice that answered to call Adele Matheson's office. A few moments later she was on the speaker.

'I've been trying to get hold of you,' she said. 'I'm on my way home, can you wait five minutes?'

Four minutes later she came out the door. The outfit she was wearing, even the blouse, was the same as when we met the last time. She immediately began walking towards the car park. Her shoes were worn down on the inside, and that made her even more knock-kneed.

'Can you help me find Brad Lowe?' she said.

'But I told you –'

'You told me nothing I don't want to know, and I suggest we carry on like that. Can you guarantee that he will appear in a court case, yes or no?'

'Yes,' I said, surprised.

'Good. His next of kin have been informed of the charge and now you have been. It means that you and those who helped you when you found Amy must be willing to appear as witnesses.'

'Are you saying that . . . ?'

We stopped by a red Ferrari. I found it hard to believe the low, sexy sports car could belong to her until she unlocked it.

'I'm making no promises,' she said. 'All I'm saying is that after due consideration the public prosecutor's office has come to the conclusion that we have enough evidence to charge Brad Lowe with murder.'

IX

The attack came just before dawn.

They were well prepared, obviously familiar with the layout of the property, and counting on being met by force.

They were wearing camouflage and came gliding over the wall like porpoises across the surface of the water.

'These boys are pros,' said Downing as he leaned back in his chair and studied the monitors.

Less than two minutes had passed since the silent alarms on the outside of the wall had been triggered. Downing, who had been on watch, had roused us and we were now gathered down in the basement. The women and children were locked in the secure room directly opposite the cell where we were keeping Brad, while Downing, Chung, Larsen and I kept watch from the control room at the other end of the basement. On the monitors our camouflaged cameras – ordinary game cameras with night vision – showed the attackers gathering on the inside of the wall and then spreading out to approach the house from different sides.

'About thirty men,' said Downing. 'Various types of weapons but light, automatic rifles. I don't see any hand grenades or flamethrowers, so this looks like a surgical attack – the only ones to die will be those who are meant to die.'

All except Brad, I thought, but kept my mouth shut.

'Night vision, same old type as mine. These are experienced veterans, boys. The worst type of opponent.'

'There are so many of them,' said Larsen. His voice was trembling. 'Shouldn't we detonate the mines now?'

'That is scenario two,' said Downing as he drummed with his fingers on the side of the keyboard. 'What does that mean, Larsen?'

Larsen gulped. 'That we don't activate the mines and booby traps until they start the attack,' he whispered.

'Precisely. Chung?'

'Yes?' said Chung, who had just come in after making sure all the women and children were safely locked inside the secure room.

'When the mines and the booby traps start going off, switch on the current to the wall. I don't want any of them escaping.'

'OK.'

'Adams, you pilot the drone and give us overhead views.'

'Copy,' I said, using the military jargon we had just adopted.

'And, Larsen, you're ready with the machine guns, right?'

'Yep,' he said, adjusting his position in the chair and taking hold of the joystick on the remote control.

All of us were trying to sound a bit tougher than we actually felt. At the same time I think we also felt a sort of excitement that the thing we had been preparing and steeling ourselves for was finally happening.

'Right then, scenario two. When they start to move I'm going to count down to three and on zero we activate. Questions?'

Silence.

'Ready?'

Yes, in three voices.

A lot of things aren't the way they seem in films.

This wasn't one of them.

The next few seconds – because it lasted only a few seconds when we saw the recordings afterwards – were as unreal as anything I've seen on the big screen.

When they attacked and we switched on the floodlights, when the mines started to explode and the body parts were flying through the air, when the booby-trapped shotguns cut down one attacker after another, when several of them desperately tried to retreat and climb back over the wall that was now live, and I saw through the drone camera how the jerking bodies fell to the ground, how the bullets from Larsen's machine guns meant that they carried on jerking, it was really quite hard to believe it was all actually happening out there.

Then the explosions and the gunfire stopped and suddenly everything was very quiet.

Outside, some of the wounded began screaming for help. Larsen – who was sitting in a chair next to Downing and operating the machine guns through a joystick, the way you would in a computer game – had stopped shooting. Now he looked at the monitors, including the one showing the images from my drone. He used these to take aim. He fired only in short bursts, and with each burst there was one less cry for help.

Soon all was deathly silence.

We stared at the screens. There were bodies everywhere.

'We've beaten them,' said Chung cautiously, as though he didn't quite believe what he was saying himself.

'Yee-ha!' Larsen hollered, his arms stretched up in the air. It was as though a light that had been turned off in his head for a long time was suddenly switched on again.

I piloted the drone over the wall. A hundred metres down the hill three armoured trucks stood stationary, their engines turning over. And an SUV that I seemed to recognise.

'They've got more men on the outside,' I said. 'Shall we turn on the loudspeakers and tell them we're opening the gates so they can fetch their dead?'

'Wait,' said Downing. 'Look.'

He pointed to the alarm lights. One of them was on.

'Someone's broken the kitchen window,' he said.

I flew the drone back and sure enough, the shutter on the kitchen window had been twisted to one side, probably with a crowbar.

'A passed pawn,' said Downing. He put on his night vision and picked up his rifle. 'Adams, you take over here.'

The next moment he was out the door and had disappeared into the dark corridor outside.

We looked at each other. 'Passed pawn' was a term we'd learned. It meant soldiers operating independently of the unit. Without waiting for orders they could react at lightning speed to any opportunities that suddenly opened up. We listened but we couldn't hear Downing's footsteps. He had briefly shown us a ninja technique for silent walking but there hadn't been time to train in hand-to-hand fighting, we'd been so focused on making certain the walls were impregnable.

We heard a bang that made us jump.

Then a sound like someone falling down the basement stairs.

We waited. I was holding the automatic shotgun so tightly my forearm ached.

I counted to ten, and when Downing still hadn't knocked I turned to the other two.

'Downing's dead,' I said.

'This passed pawn will never breach the secure room,' Chung said confidently.

'Yes, but he can get Brad out,' I said. 'I'm going to take a look.'

'Are you crazy?' whispered Larsen. 'The passed pawn has night vision – you won't have a chance, Will!'

'That is exactly my chance,' I said, checking that my gun was loaded and the safety catch off.

'What do you mean?'

I pointed to the control panel, to the switch that controlled all the lighting in the house.

'Turn the light on when I go out, turn it off again in eight seconds, then on and off every five seconds.'

'But . . .'

'Do as he says,' said Chung, who I could see had got the idea.

I opened the door and slipped out into the darkness. The light went on. I ran towards the stairs, about as ninja-like as a rhinoceros. Downing lay there at the bottom. The night vision obscured his eyes but from the hole in his forehead I could see he was dead. I counted the seconds silently inside as I pulled the night vision off him. I sensed rather than heard the enemy approaching, hoping that the blinding of the light would delay him just long enough while he had to stop and remove the night vision.

Six, seven.

I had just got the night vision on when the light went again.

Now I heard the steps, heading away. He was retreating, had to get his goggles on again.

I followed the sound, trying to step more quietly but guessing he couldn't hear me as well anyway now that he was on the move himself.

I came to the T-junction with the security room to the right and Brad's cell on the left. Counted. Three, four. Flipped up the goggles and slipped round the corner to the right as the light came on.

Nothing.

I turned and there he was, standing seven, eight metres away from me, in front of the door to Brad's cell. Wearing black, not camouflage. He turned towards me, towards the light, for it was clear he could see nothing, and he lifted a hand to remove the goggles he had down over the balaclava.

Maybe the balaclava made it easier, I don't know, but I dropped to my knees, aimed and fired at him. To my amazement none of the bullets seemed to hit him. He tore off the goggles and tossed them away so they skidded over the floor and then he fired, the sounds echoing deafeningly around the stone walls. I didn't feel any pain, just a pressure in my left shoulder, as though someone had given me a friendly shove. But I lost all strength in that arm and the rifle slipped to the floor.

The passed pawn saw that I was helpless, but instead of firing wildly he took aim with the rifle steadied against his shoulder. It looked as though it was a point of honour for him to drop his enemy with a bullet through the forehead.

I raised my right hand, the palm towards him, and for a fraction of a second he hesitated, as though this universal and timeless gesture of submission touched some instinct in him. Because that's how I like to think of mercy.

Five . . .

Dark again, and I rolled from my kneeling position down and sideways as he fired. I pulled the goggles back down, saw the figure in the puke-green light, raised the rifle with my right hand and pulled the trigger. One shot. Then another. The second one got him. And the third. The fourth missed and ricocheted off the wall behind him. But the fifth hit, I think. And the sixth.

The lights came on and went off twice before I had emptied the magazine.

It was only later, after they had retrieved their dead and wounded, and I had taken off the night goggles, that it struck me: I no longer felt the dizziness and nausea I had felt earlier. On the contrary, I had never felt more balanced, more on top of things, clearer.

And at about daybreak, for the first time since Amy disappeared, Heidi slipped across to me in bed and put her arms around me. I kissed her and then – more careful with each other than we usually were – we made love.

X

A few days after we had repulsed the attack, I was back on Rat Island. Again Colin was waiting for me on the jetty. He looked wasted. Not thinner, wasted.

Rats darted back and forth in front of us on our way to the prison building.

'There are more of them,' I said, looking down at the sloping rocks which had been white the last time I was here. Now they looked black, not from the waves that broke over them as I had thought when I stood looking from the fishing boat on the way in, but because there were so many rats covering them.

'I think they swim over in the night,' said Colin, noticing the direction of my gaze. 'They're frightened.'

'Of what?'

'Of other rats. Those on the mainland are running out of food, they've started eating each other. So the smaller rats come over here.'

'Won't they start eating each other here too?'

'In the end, yes.'

We went inside, entering a part of the building that had been converted into a sort of mansion-type medieval castle. Liza was waiting at the top of the first-floor stairs and she shook my hand. Previously we would always hug each other. That was another of the customs that had vanished with the coming of the pandemic, although in our case now that wasn't the only reason: Amy's absence and Brad's absence made the children almost painfully present.

She excused herself, saying she had things to do, and disappeared, leaving Colin and I to enter the large and sparsely furnished dining room just in time to see an unusually large rat disappear through the door at the other end.

'Damn, that was big,' I said.

'But not so big that it doesn't run away from us and not the other way round,' said Colin. 'Although that's probably just a matter of time,' he added with a sigh.

We sat down and two servants approached, placed white serviettes in our laps and served us directly from a steaming saucepan.

'We can't even serve the food from ordinary dishes,' said Colin. 'They're everywhere and they'll risk anything once they pick up the smell of food. And they reproduce faster than we're able to shoot them.'

I looked at the stringy lumps of meat in the brown stew in front of me. I presumed it was meat from animals we're accustomed to eating, but once the thought had been planted the imagination wasn't easy to stop.

'It was good to come,' said Colin, who didn't seem to have much of an appetite either. 'All things considered.'

'You attacked us,' I said. 'You killed one of us.'

'You killed nineteen of ours and you're holding my son prisoner.'

'He's in custody,' I said. 'Awaiting a fair trial. The public prosecutor told you Brad was going to be charged, but you still attacked us. Because you know he'll be found guilty.'

'You're putting yourself above the law.'

'I thought you didn't believe in the law.'

'No, but you say you do, Will. And a man can only be condemned for betraying his own principles, not someone else's.'

'Or for not having any at all.'

Colin forced a smile. I knew why. These were the kinds of exchanges we used to have when we were growing up together, starting in the days when we dominated the school debating society and developing still further once it became my job to oppose his sometimes over-hasty thought processes. As usual he was the one who had the last word:

'Not having principles is also a principle, Will. As in, for example, adhering to the view that no principle shall be allowed to get in the way of your own survival and the survival of those closest to you.'

I looked down at my hands. Usually they were shaking. It started at about the same time as the pandemic. But now they weren't. 'What do you want, Colin?'

'I want Brad,' he said. 'And I want your villa.'

I neither laughed nor forced a smile. I just placed my serviette on the table and stood up.

'Wait.' Colin got to his feet too. Held up a hand. 'You haven't heard my offer.'

'You've got nothing I want, Colin. Don't you understand that?'

'Not you maybe, but what about Heidi and little Sam? What if I have something that can give them a new and better life, a chance to build a better society, one that follows the rule of law? Have you heard of the *New Frontier*? It's an aircraft carrier. It's sailing soon. There will be three thousand five hundred people on board. I've got three tickets on that boat. Bought them a while ago. Cost me a fortune. You can't buy tickets any more, no matter how much you're willing to pay. You get my three, and in exchange you give me Brad and the villa.'

I shook my head. 'Keep your tickets, Colin. Letting Brad get away unpunished would make a mockery of Amy's memory.'

'Ah, see how the noble Will Adams descends to our level. Suddenly it's not about keeping strictly to one's principles in the name of all mankind. Now it's revenge for your daughter.'

'It was a manner of speaking, Colin. Regardless of what I might think, Heidi would never agree to a trade-off like that.'

'Women are often more pragmatic in such matters than men. They see the benefit to the community, they laugh at our obsession with pride and honour.'

'So then I'll give you your answer before she has the chance to contradict me. No.'

*

On the way back down to the boat the rats didn't run out of our way quite so quickly.

'You weren't afraid I might take you prisoner and offer a swap for Brad?'

I shook my head. 'Everyone in the house is agreed that we won't give in to any form of blackmail if I don't return. Even though I left no instructions about what to do about Brad in that case, I think we both know what would happen to him.'

'He wouldn't get the trial you want to give him.'

Naturally he'd thought about it.

'Is it because of the rats that you want to get away from here?' I asked.

Colin nodded. 'Beth is ill. We think it's typhoid – she might have got it from a rat bite. We've tried everything we can think of to kill the damn things without killing ourselves at the same time. Did you know that rats and humans share ninety-seven per cent of the same DNA? One day the rat-human will appear. If it hasn't already.'

'She'll get better once she's on board the carrier,' I said. 'I hear some of the best doctors in the country were offered tickets at discount prices.'

'Yes,' said Colin. 'And yet you really are willing to deprive your family of those tickets because of a principle you know means nothing in the world of the rat?'

I didn't answer, just took the short step from the jetty and onto the fishing boat, turned and watched Colin grow smaller and smaller as we chugged away from the island.

But still something was bothering me. I knew him too well. He would never have let me get away so easily if he didn't have a backup plan. Some kind of alternative.

XI

It's night. I'm riding southwards and thinking back to the day Ragnar and the O'Leary twins took Dumbo. How different everything could have been. Or could it? Anyway, I'm headed for the slaughterhouse, and for the end of

280

this story. Behind me is a spike strip and a guy who tried to stop me; there's the house where I first met Will Adams, and the Lowe building where it looks like it won't be long before the mob gets inside. Maybe everything is preordained, maybe people like me just do the bidding of fate. The fuel gauge is on red. OK, let fate decide if I'm to run out of petrol and things don't end the way they were planned. Because something unexpected always happens. Like the way, for example, that Dumbo reappeared again a week after he disappeared.

I'd lost hope of seeing Dumbo again when my phone rang. Maria woke me, pointing to it almost in fear. It hadn't rung at all for the past couple of months because most of the networks were down and only one operator was still working.

I picked up and heard Dumbo's voice: 'They're allowing me one call.'

He was in the prison in Downtown. It was the last one still in operation and being used to hold people in custody as well as prisoners serving long sentences. An hour later we sat facing each other on different sides of a thick partition in the large visiting room, each with a telephone in our hand. He was wearing a striped outfit. I'd called it retro, which at least made him laugh, since he realised I'd said something that was meant to be funny.

Then he told me what had happened, and neither of us was laughing any more.

After Ragnar and the others had kidnapped Dumbo they'd taken him to Chaos's new clubhouse. From Dumbo's description I knew it had to be in the abandoned slaughterhouse down by the oilfield, on the road out to the airport. One evening Ragnar had brought a man back to the slaughterhouse and told those Dumbo shared the room with to get out.

'Ragnar pointed to me and said I was perfect,' said Dumbo. 'The man could have me if he got the gang somewhere decent to live, a new bike for Ragnar, twelve Kalashnikovs and fifty bazookas and fifty hand grenades. Plus one hundred and fifty grams of meth, two hundred tabs of Rohypnol, two hundred antabiato . . . no, anta . . .'

'Antibiotics,' I said.

'Yes, and –'

'That'll do,' I said. Sometimes Dumbo had a surprisingly good memory for details, especially insignificant details. 'But the man wasn't going to pay all that for just one night, was he?'

'No,' said Dumbo. 'For the rest of his life.'

'So he was from that club down by the docks.'

'No, he was from Rat Island, he said.'

'And? Did he say what he wanted you to do?'

'Yes. It was Ragnar said it.'

'What did Ragnar say?'

'Ragnar said I was to tell the police who would be coming soon that I hit that girl on the head with a golf club. And I was to say the same thing to the judge.'

I stared at him. 'And if you didn't?'

Dumbo's large eyes filled with tears and his voice trembled. 'He said they would feed me to the rats on Rat Island.'

'Then of course you had to say yes. But when the judge heard that . . .'

'I didn't say yes,' Dumbo said, his voice still choked. 'I said no. Because that would mean I would have to be in jail for the rest of my life, and I didn't want that.'

'I understand. But you told the police you did it – that's why you're here, isn't it? That was very clever, because they can't feed you to the rats before you tell the judge they threatened you.'

'No!' shouted Dumbo and beat his forehead against the glass screen. He sometimes did that when he got frustrated because he couldn't explain what he meant. I saw a warden making his way towards us.

'Easy, Dumbo.'

'They didn't threaten me. They threatened you! They said they'd kill Yvonne if I didn't do as they said.'

I took it in, piece by piece. Those bastards. All they need to know is what's irreplaceable for someone. Once they know that they've got them. Or got her.

Behind me the warden coughed. I put my hand to the glass screen.

'I'll get you out of here, Dumbo. I promise. I'll get you out. You hear?'

Dumbo pressed his hand up against mine on the glass wall and the tears came rolling down his cheeks.

'One minute. The helicopter will be landing in one minute!'

Of course it feels absurd to be standing here on top of a skyscraper twirling a glass of champagne while down below us civilisation as we know it is falling apart. On the other hand it wouldn't feel much less absurd without the champagne.

The lieutenant approaches, whispers something in Colin's ear, then runs back to the helicopter deck where the last of the rich and privileged wait to be lifted up and whisked away to a fresh start on board the *New Frontier*.

'He says the mob has got inside,' says Colin. 'But my people have cut the cable to the lifts so they'll have to fight their way up the stairs. Do you know, by the way, why staircases in old castles and cathedrals always run clockwise going upwards?' As usual Colin Lowe doesn't wait for an answer. 'It gave the defenders the advantage over their attackers because they could use their swords in their right hands.'

'Interesting,' I say. 'Incidentally, is there a way down that doesn't run the risk of getting your head chopped off? For those not travelling on the helicopter, I mean.'

'Sure. Relax, everything'll be fine. Look, there it is.'

A moving point of light comes swaying towards us. I look down into my glass, at the bubbles released from the bottom of it and rising up to the surface. Inexorable as a physical law.

'Tell me, Colin, were you infected with fear? Like the rats?'

Colin looks at me in some surprise. He hasn't yet raised his glass for the toast I know he's planning to make. To friendship, to family, to the good life. The three regulars.

'What are you thinking of?' he asks.

'When you bought Dumbo's confession. Did you panic?'

Colin shakes his head. 'I don't know to what extent a father is capable of rational thought when it comes to his own son or daughter, but when this Ragnar contacted me and said he had an offer I couldn't refuse, he turned out to be right.'

'Your conscience didn't bother you?'

'As you know, Will, mine is not as active as yours. So no, it didn't make too much noise. According to Ragnar, Dumbo was so severely mentally handicapped he was unfit to plead and by law couldn't be punished anyway.'

'It isn't that simple, Colin. And I think you know it.'

'You're right. It's probably that I wanted it to be that simple. Anyway, it seemed to me he deserves whatever punishment they can give him. Ragnar told me he raped Heidi.'

I grip the stem of the glass so tightly that for a moment I'm certain I'll snap it. Against the orange sky of evening I see the helicopter approaching between the skyscrapers. It makes me think of a grasshopper. Like that lovely, pea-green specimen I took home with me from my grandmother's farm one summer holiday. On the drive home I had it in a jam jar with a hole punched in the lid. But when we arrived it was dead, and for years afterwards my father would reminisce about it at family gatherings, about how inconsolable I had been, that I'd pushed a pin into my fingertip as a way of punishing myself. I could never understand why the grown-ups laughed.

'I'm thinking about what happened afterwards,' I say.

'You know very well I had nothing to do with that,' sighs Colin.

'But you could have prevented it.'

'The list of our sins of omission is infinitely long, Will. Of course you can accuse me of lacking the imagination to realise the extent of Ragnar's cynicism. But had he asked me I would never have allowed it to happen.'

By now I can just about hear the helicopter, the rotor blades whipping the air, the drone of the engine.

It was raining next day when I went to the courthouse. I wasn't allowed to see Dumbo but heard that his defence lawyer was someone named Marvin

Green, from the firm of Amber & Doherty. It took me the rest of the day to find the firm's offices; apparently they'd moved from the address I got at the courthouse and were now located in a graffiti-covered office block. I wasn't allowed in, just told through the door phone that Green wasn't there. When I asked where I could find him, said it was urgent because I had information concerning one of his cases, the person at the other end just laughed. She said I would either find Green at the pub on the corner or he'd gone home for the day. I went to the pub, heard from the barman that Green had just left, went back to the office block and after a lot of fuss and bother got Green's address. It was pouring with rain and riding up the hill was like riding up a stream.

The address wasn't far from the villa we'd been driven out of. But this was a small house, almost a bungalow, the type of place the artists who first moved up here long ago built for themselves. But it had steel gates and walls with embedded glass and barbed wire.

I rang the bell.

'Who is it?' said a hoarse, slurred voice though the speaker on the wall.

I looked up into the camera on the gatepost, gave my name and said I had information that could help Mr Green in his defence of Gabriel Norton, aka my friend Dumbo.

I heard the chinking of glass. 'Go on,' he said.

'You mean come in?'

'Go on, as in "talk". I don't let strangers in.'

So I said what I had to say standing out there in the rain. That Dumbo hadn't killed Amy but was the victim of a plot aimed at whitewashing the rich man's son Brad Lowe. It was a long speech and since I was neither interrupted nor given any other sign that anyone was listening I began to wonder whether Green had just hung up. But at least no one came out to chase me off so I carried on talking. Told him how Dumbo and I – back before we knew each other – almost by chance had saved each other's lives in a fire, and how we'd stuck together since then. We'd joined a gang, and that's how we managed to survive. I said there were probably a lot of things Dumbo was guilty of, but not the killing of Amy. I'd been in the house and could give him an alibi for the time the murder was committed.

I was finished, and so wet and cold my teeth were chattering as I stood there staring at that perforated brass plate below the bell. I had considered telling him that I had actually seen Brad killing Amy but decided that with Brad's father on the warpath it would endanger not just my life but Dumbo's and Maria's too. My goal was to get Dumbo out; what happened to Brad was a matter of indifference to me.

'Mr Green?' I said.

Silence. Then a wet coughing. And then that hoarse voice, a little less slurred now: 'I'll need your address if I'm going to call you as a witness.'

I gave the address where Maria and I lived, dictating the flat number so slowly and carefully that even a drunkard defence lawyer who'd long ago stopped caring about anything would be able to get it right.

'It'll be safest for you if you don't talk to anyone about what you know, or tell anyone you've been here,' he said. 'I'll contact you – don't contact me.'

On the driver down afterwards I had to stop on a bend. A coyote stood motionless in the middle of the road and looked at me. The eyes reflected light, and I almost thought it was a ghost. Coyotes usually run, but this one stood its ground. Like me. I thought of getting the Remington out and shooting it – we were out of meat, and maybe this would be edible if you cooked it long enough – then remembered that Ragnar and the twins had taken the gun. I waited for the coyote to move, but it didn't. Instead two more came slinking into the street light.

Just recently there had been more of them on the roads; not just coyotes but more animals in general. And fewer people. At night I could ride through one district after another and never see a soul. Were they all staying indoors, the way people did during the pandemic? Or had they left the city and moved out to the countryside?

I automatically checked the rear-view mirror to see if there were any coyotes behind me as well.

No. Not yet.

I revved the engine, opened the throttle and rode at them, horn blaring.

The coyotes didn't seem particularly afraid. They moved reluctantly out of the way. One of them snapped at me as I rode by.

XII

When I got back from Rat Island the last time I hadn't told Heidi I'd turned down Colin's offer of tickets on the *New Frontier* aircraft carrier. Not that I thought she would have agreed to the trade-off, because I felt sure she was as determined as I was that Brad should stand trial for what he'd done. But at least in not knowing there was a choice she was spared the dilemma, and the gnawing doubt about whether we had made the right decision in depriving Sam of what was perhaps – what was actually pretty definitely – his chance of a better life.

At the same time I was still waiting for Colin to make his next move. If he had an alternative plan to free Brad, and it succeeded, wouldn't I then bitterly regret that I had turned down his offer? Or would I continue to feel that I had done the right thing, responded the way a decent and upright person should respond? Maybe I wouldn't have the satisfaction of seeing my daughter's killer get his just punishment, but at least I hadn't lost my soul.

And then it came. The next move.

I was in the garden when Adele Matheson phoned me and told me the news over a very poor connection. That a certain Gabriel Norton, nicknamed Dumbo, had confessed to Amy's murder. And unless the confession was withdrawn, or evidence produced that exonerated Norton, then naturally she couldn't proceed with the case against Brad Lowe.

I said that this was Colin Lowe's doing. That either this Dumbo was taking one for the team, or else they were threatening him with something that was worse than life imprisonment.

'We can't exclude the possibility,' said Matheson. 'But . . .'

She didn't need to finish. As long as we couldn't prove that Dumbo was lying or being manipulated, then there wasn't much we could do.

I leaned against a tree, checked that Heidi and Sam were too far away to overhear anything, and tried to gather my thoughts. Adele Matheson waited patiently, but all I could do was open and close my mouth. Not a word came out.

'I'm sorry,' she said after a few moments. 'We must just hope that this Dumbo changes his story or fails to convince the court that he's a killer. I heard one detective say that they can't quite get the angle between the point of impact and the golf club to add up with the fact that Norton is a dwarf.'

'A dwarf?'

'I'm sorry, short. Or whatever the prevailing euphemism is. Anyway, circumstantial technical evidence like that doesn't count for much when there's a confession.'

I was only half listening. Thinking. So the one who'd confessed was the boy who'd rung the bell that evening with the girl. The same two I had let go the night we took the villa.

'I'll talk to him,' I said.

'By all means, try,' said Matheson.

'I mean it. I stopped one of ours from shooting him and the girl when they escaped on her motorcycle. He might be aware of the fact that I . . . well, that I saved their lives. Maybe I can get him to feel he owes me something in return.'

Matheson didn't reply.

'I'll keep you posted,' I said.

'Then goodbye.' She said it the way you say goodbye to someone you think it's unlikely you'll be seeing again.

XIII

I was searched before being allowed into the large visiting room. Four other visitors were already inside, talking on the phone to inmates behind the glass partition – it was just like when I visited Maria in hospital during the pandemic. The warden indicated my chair, number eight. Dumbo wasn't there yet.

I was looking forward to telling him I had spoken to his lawyer and that he would be calling me as a witness so that I could give Dumbo an alibi. We were just to say that we were together, nothing about how I'd seen through the keyhole that it was Brad. That way everything would be fine. We wouldn't be lying, we just weren't telling them everything.

As I took my seat I saw a familiar face behind the glass in number-one booth, in the far corner. It was Kevin Wankel. So it was here the stupid meathead was serving his life sentence.

I sat waiting and watching for Dumbo to come through the door.

It didn't look as though Kevin had a lot to say to his visitor. They sat in their respective chairs, her slumped, him with his greasy hair and the stubby brown teeth in his meths mouth.

Then the door at the back on the prisoners' side opened and Dumbo came in wearing the same striped prison outfit. His face lit up when he saw me, and I guess mine did too. The warden behind him said something I couldn't hear through the glass and pointed to the chair in front of me.

As Dumbo started walking towards me I sensed a movement in my peripheral vision. I didn't immediately react to it; Kevin had obviously suddenly made up his mind the visit was over and was heading towards the exit door and Dumbo. As he came closer I noticed he was holding his hand inside the back of his trousers.

I jumped up and yelled, but that damn glass wall reaching up to the ceiling choked off most of the sound.

There was a glint of steel as Kevin swung his hand in a low arc, caught Dumbo in the stomach and pulled the blade towards him. Dumbo doubled over. Both hands went to his stomach and I could see the blood running between the stubby fingers. Kevin grabbed hold of Dumbo's hair and pulled his head back, exposing the throat and cutting it with a sideways, arcing slash. Blood sprayed and splashed across the floor and Dumbo tumbled forward. Two wardens stormed in and Kevin dropped his weapon. It looked like a flattened piece of metal. He put up his hands in a show of surrender. Two guards pinned Kevin to the floor while a third came running in and pressed a hand against the gaping wound in Dumbo's neck. The pressure in the fountain of blood was gone and now it was just pumping weakly.

Dumbo's eyes were looking in my direction but they were glazed over. Of course I knew that with all the blood on the floor, blood that should have been circulating through his brain, he had to be unconscious already but I did it anyway. I picked up the receiver, put my other hand against the glass wall and said: 'It'll be all right. Just look at me, Dumbo. It'll be all right.'

Then it was as though another layer folded itself over the glassy stare, and I knew he was dead.

I had just arrived in the waiting room attached to the visiting room, taken a seat and was waiting to meet Gabriel 'Dumbo' Norton. Earlier in the day I had seen the mugshot and was able to confirm what I suspected, that it was the same boy who I had seen on the steps outside our house. Who had helped to tie me up. Who had . . .

I knew I mustn't think about that other thing, not if I was to be able to do what I intended to and establish a relationship with the boy that was based on sympathy and understanding and the sort of humanity and mercy I would need to discover for the most difficult thing of all – forgiveness.

I hadn't been told who the visitor before me was but I knew at least that it wasn't his defence lawyer – they didn't use the visiting room.

Suddenly from the other side of the door I heard screams, shouting and the scraping of chair legs.

The guard in the waiting room put his eye to a peephole and then checked that the door was locked.

'What's happened?' I asked.

'A stabbing,' he said without turning round.

A minute later he unlocked the door and the five visitors came out. They looked pale and shaken, but it was clearly not one of them who had been attacked.

One was crying. Or rather, there was no sound, but the tears streamed down her face. Maybe they blinded her so that she didn't recognise me.

I quickly joined the dots and a clear picture emerged.

I followed her.

She didn't notice me until we were out in the street and she was sitting astride her motorcycle. I stood directly in front of her.

'Is Dumbo dead?' I asked.

I saw how she automatically reached for something in a pannier on the bike, a weapon maybe, but it wasn't there.

'Was it you who killed him?' I asked.

I stared at him. Because it really was him, Amy's father, I saw that now. Was he asking if it was me who killed Dumbo?

'No,' I said, and I had no control at all over my voice. 'But maybe you did.'

'Then I would have been better off letting that shaven-headed guy with the laser rifle shoot the two of you up at the villa.'

I didn't know what to say. Or do. Because yes, I had wondered if it was his voice I'd heard when someone stopped the guy with the laser sight on his rifle from shooting. Shouting that they weren't murderers and – unless I saw wrong – pointing his own gun at the guy.

'So then who was it?' he asked.

'Dunno,' I said and started the engine.

'But you know it wasn't Dumbo who killed my daughter.'

What the hell was I supposed to say? Dumbo was dead, there was no one left to save any more. No one but myself.

'I don't know anything,' I said and revved the engine. He still kept standing there, the straight idiot.

'You know it was Brad,' he said. He rested both hands on my handlebars and stared at me, eyes burning like he was on speed.

I didn't answer.

'Come on,' he said. 'You aren't like them.'

'Like who?'

'Like those others in the gang. Chaos. You want something more than that, don't you?'

'I want my Remington rifle back,' I said. 'Apart from that I don't give a fuck about anything. Get out of the way, mister.'

'I'm living in the villa. If you want justice like me then come and talk to me. I think maybe we can help each other.'

I slipped the clutch and he jumped out of the way. Accelerated away. The exhaust popping and banging from the bullet-holes from when the O'Leary twins peppered the bike. I rode so fast I could feel the tears streaming horizontally into my helmet and across my temples.

It was Ragnar. I knew it was Ragnar, he was the only one who could get Kevin to do something like that. The only question was how did Ragnar know I was going to get Dumbo to withdraw his confession? I mean, it really wasn't all that fucking complicated.

The connection became even clearer when I got home and saw the ambulance parked in the street. Part of me was surprised because you so rarely see an ambulance these days; another part of me had been half expecting it.

I dismounted and walked over to the two men who were loading a stretcher into the back.

'Who . . .' I started to say, but they jumped in behind the stretcher, slammed the doors in my face and drove off, sirens blaring.

I turned and saw the trail of blood leading from where the ambulance had stood at the entrance to our block. I swallowed. It was my fault. My fault again.

I was the one who had given the address to Dumbo's drunken and corrupt defence lawyer.

No, it really wasn't all that complicated.

The street door opened and a pretty young woman came out.

'What happened?' I asked.

'It was a guy with the same kind of helmet as you,' she said.

'Red leather jacket with a monster coming up out of the sea?'

'Yes.'

'And?'

'He used a crowbar and broke into the flat at the end of our corridor.'

'But?'

'But when he got inside the man there had a knife and the motorbike guy had a Kalashnikov and shot him before he could use it. I spoke to his wife. She says they say he'll survive.'

She wiped away a tear and I put my arm around her shoulder and pulled her close.

'I'm scared,' she sniffled.

'I understand, Maria.'

It was so quiet I could still hear the ambulance, the siren rising and falling as though searching for a frequency it couldn't find.

I thought of the man. He looked like Amy, his daughter. I thought of when he sat tied up in the garage, the look on his face when he heard the screams from the house. Pain at the thought of pain in someone you love.

'So it wasn't you, it was Ragnar who arranged to have Dumbo killed?' I say. I have to raise my voice to be heard above the sound of the approaching helicopter.

'He didn't tell me about it until afterwards, and as I say, I would never have allowed it. Not murder.' Colin sighs and looks up into the sky. 'But of course, I'm not completely guilt-free.'

'Oh?'

'I'd been in touch with Marvin Green, Dumbo's defence lawyer. Good defence lawyers are in short supply now, most of them have left the city so people turn to the likes of washed-out alcoholics like Green who don't have the money to get out. And yes, he was easy enough to turn and he didn't ask for too much. He was told not to put a great deal of effort into defending Dumbo and not to put him in the witness box in case the poor bugger got mixed up about his confession. But then Green called me and said he'd had a girl come to see him who said she could give Dumbo an alibi. I got her address.' Colin took a deep breath. 'You know, before they turned off the power I never realised how beautiful the night sky is above the city.'

'Go on,' I say.

'So I got in touch with this Ragnar again and told him it was a condition of him getting the weapons and all the other stuff that Dumbo's confession stood, and that Brad didn't have to face a charge.'

'In other words you ordered him to kill Dumbo and the girl.'

Colin shook his head. 'It would have been enough if he'd threatened the girl to keep quiet and Dumbo had been sentenced, case closed.

Instead this Ragnar decided on drastic action because – as he said afterwards – the dead don't talk. He was pleased as punch when he came and told me what he'd done. No, he hadn't got the girl, obviously she didn't completely trust Green and had given him a false address. But that hardly mattered, he said, because he'd shut Dumbo up on a permanent basis, so now he couldn't retract his confession. He couldn't understand why I was so angry . . .'

'Don't you feel you have more than a little guilt in all this, Colin?'

He shrugs and sticks out his lower lip the way he always does when he's pretending not to understand the obvious.

'It wasn't my choice. He acted on his own free will.'

'You allowed his evil nature free play because you knew what the result would be. It was obviously you who gave him the girl's address. That was the choice of your own free will, Colin.'

'I thought he might have a word with her, not . . .' He spread his arms out wide. 'OK, so maybe I'm naive, but I do actually believe in people's ability to learn. To change and choose what is good.'

'That's good to know,' I say.

'Meaning what?'

'That you believe that free will combined with experience can turn someone who was previously bad into a person who will choose the good.'

'Don't you?'

'Oh, yes,' I say. 'That's why we release people from prison and hope it's safe. So for the sake of you and your family let's hope it is true, Colin.'

'Now what are you talking about, Will?'

By now I'm having to shout to be heard above the helicopter. 'I'm simply saying that your survival, like mine and like everyone else's, is in the final analysis dependent on our ability to learn the qualities of mercy, wisdom and forgiveness. And in particular the ability of those closest to us to learn them.'

'Amen to that!' Colin calls to the stars and the descending helicopter as he finally raises his champagne glass.

XIV

Within twenty-four hours of my meeting Yvonne outside the prison where Dumbo had just been murdered she was standing at our door.

'Thank you for coming,' I said.

She muttered something uneasy in reply. I had realised some time ago that certain people, certain sections of the population, are just not used to those who go around thanking each other for things.

She told me her name as we stood in the living room, looking out at Heidi playing Hawks and Doves with Sam. Heidi put on a deep menacing voice as she advanced on him, fingers hooked like a hawk's claws. I couldn't hear what she was saying, all that came through the window were Sam's squeals of delight.

'He's a nice boy,' she said. 'How . . .' She didn't finish her question.

'He seems to have forgotten everything,' I said. 'Can you understand that?'

Yvonne shrugged. 'I don't know, but for kids most of what happens is new and dramatic, even everyday things that seem trivial to us grown-ups. For example, I don't know if seeing someone in your family getting a beating is worse than being stung by a wasp, or your teddy bear losing an eye.'

I looked at the young woman. Something told me she was speaking from experience.

'So then why are children traumatised by sexual assault but apparently not by circumcision?' I asked.

'I don't know,' she said. 'But I would guess pain and humiliation are easier to take if the pain feels natural and necessary in some way. People can get tortured in a meaningless war and lose their minds, but not people who have a tooth taken out without an anaesthetic. Or a woman giving birth.'

I nodded. Now Heidi had caught Sam and they laughed as they rolled around on the grass. Heidi laughing; it struck me that was a sound I hadn't heard since that terrible night.

'Context,' I said.

'Eh?'

'I read somewhere that some people believe our minds can deal with pain better if we're able to put it in a context that seems to us to justify it.'

Yvonne nodded. 'Good. Then someone's written down what I think.'

'But . . .' I said, drawing a breath and folding my hands. 'The pain of losing Amy for me and Dumbo for you aren't things we can place in a meaningful context. So we need to find other ways of dealing with the pain, am I right?'

'Revenge,' she said.

I looked down at my hands. Colin used to say I always folded them before saying something important. And that when a lawyer is about to say something important that usually means bad news.

'That's one way,' I said. 'The human appetite for revenge distinguishes us from the animals, but from an evolutionary perspective it's still logical. If everyone knows that killing a child will lead to revenge, that will make the child's life safer. But if there's dispute over the question of guilt in the death of the child then any act of revenge is liable to give rise in turn to yet another act of revenge. Which in turn gives rise to yet another. It was spirals of bloodthirsty revenge like that that decimated the population of Iceland, for example. And the same thing happened in Albania. In Iceland they solved the problem by establishing a court consisting of the best minds in the community and they were charged with the task of deciding on questions of guilt or innocence, and where necessary passing sentence and carrying out the punishment. In so doing they eliminated the need for revenge. And this idea is not just the basis of the use of courts for dispensing justice but for the whole idea of societies in which the law is the same for everyone. This meant the end of a tyrannical system in which the strong were always in the right. Because when it is the state that is strongest the tyrannical and the barbarous must defer to the power of the law. Justice, common sense and humanity are the guiding principles. And that is what I want – that is why I have not executed Brad but intend to charge him in front of an independent court of law.'

I'm not sure I understood everything he said, but I think I got his point.

In the first place the rules of the road are for everyone who drives, and when there's been a crash it's not always best to leave it to the two hotheads involved to sort it out themselves.

'Fair enough,' I said. 'But how about when you realise the judge has been bought by the other side and that might is right after all? Should you just roll over and let it happen? Or should you stand up and fight?'

Will, as he insisted I call him, looked at me as he scratched his chin.

'My wife and son are coming in,' he said. 'I think maybe it's best if you don't meet. Come with me.'

I followed him down into the basement. Saw he'd made quite a few changes. He took me into a room that looked like a cross between the bridge of a ship and the control room in a recording studio.

'What do you need?' he asked. 'To get what you want.'

'A weapon,' I said.

'A weapon?'

'Ragnar stole my Remington rifle. But for this I'm going to need something heavy.'

Will nodded. He left the room and returned with a machine gun. He demonstrated for me how it worked. It could be used to mow down a small squad of men but was light enough for me to hold. He placed four hand grenades on the table in front of me.

'Enough?'

'Thanks,' I said. 'Why are you helping me? I was one of those who attacked your family.'

He looked directly at me. 'In the first place I'm going to ask you to do something for me in return. In the second place, I know you weren't a part of what happened when my wife . . . That you took Sam out of the room before . . .' His voice became thick and hoarse and he blinked twice. We could hear the two of them on the floor above us. He cleared his throat.

'And in the third place, because you remind me of Amy.'

There were tears and tenderness in his eyes and for a moment I thought he was going to stroke my hair.

'Same fighting spirit,' he said. 'Same sense of justice. When my generation is dead and gone and it's the turn of others to run the world I hope that it's people like you who run it, Yvonne. Not people like Brad and Ragnar.'

I nodded slowly. I hadn't done much to stop the rape, but it probably wouldn't do any harm if he thought better of me than I deserved. 'I'll do the best I can, Mr Adams. What is this thing that you want me to do in return?'

Slowly and in some detail, a look of pain and despair on his face, he told me. I realised this had been a very hard decision for him to take, and that he was still torn by doubt over it. And this time it was me who wanted to stroke his hair.

'OK,' I said.

He looked almost surprised. 'Yes?'

'Yes. I'm in.'

He checked that his wife and little Sam weren't nearby, then he followed me out to the bike.

'You don't think this is a gruesome plan?' I asked.

'Of course it's gruesome,' said Yvonne as she packed the stripped-down machine gun into the side pannier of the bike. 'Leaving the gruesome to the gruesome.'

She straddled the bike. 'I've no idea if your plan's going to work, Will. But if it does then it's probably the closest you're going to get to justice without one of those courts of yours.'

'It'll be your job to see that those are re-established once everything has totally collapsed and it all has to be built up again from scratch,' I said.

She rolled her eyes, put on the helmet with the image of Lady Justice executed, and the bike started up with a bestial roar.

I stood watching her until she disappeared from sight around a corner.

I didn't see a single coyote as I rode down through the valley. I've heard that they can smell danger. They're smart creatures.

XV

The day after I was up at the Adams villa I mounted the light machine gun on the front of my bike so that I could ride and shoot at the same time. Maria watched me wide-eyed and asked if I was going to war.

'Yes,' I said.

The slaughterhouse was in an industrial area south of Downtown, on a field surrounded by nodding oil pumps that looked like enormous ants raising and lowering their upper bodies over their front legs. It seemed as though the old pumps – again like ants – just kept on doing what they do regardless of whether the human race was going to hell or not.

The afternoon sun was low in the sky behind me as I turned into the forecourt in front of the slaughterhouse. The timing was carefully chosen. Dumbo had told me they would gather to eat in the main part of the slaughterhouse before heading out to raid after dark. And I needed them all to be together – that was going to be my only chance.

I'd made a reconnaissance trip earlier in the day and established that they didn't keep watch and that the big sliding door at one end of the hall was always left open, probably because they had no electricity to run the air conditioning. They must have thought that was OK; they probably didn't feel much threat out here.

I rode into the main hall. It was rectangular and big as two football pitches. Light fell from the windows in the ceiling high above. There were rails and wires with meat hooks up there too, but of course, no meat left hanging from them; anything like that had been consumed long ago. The smooth concrete floor inclined gradually towards the sluices, presumably so the blood would run away before it dried.

The bikes were parked at the far end of the hall and the gang was sitting in the middle at a long table, like in that painting of Jesus and the disciples. Only Jesus wasn't with them. It had taken me two seconds to count to eleven. Ragnar wasn't here.

Two of them jumped to their feet and ran towards their bikes. They were new. They didn't know who I was.

I opened fire, aiming just ahead of them so they could see the bursting showers of plaster and know they would never have time to reach the weapons on their bikes. They threw themselves to the floor.

'Stay down!' I yelled.

The walls echoed. They stayed down.

Then I rode slowly forward and stopped between two dangling meat hooks five or six metres from the table, so I was still covering everyone with the machine gun.

'What do you want?' asked one of the O'Leary twins – you can never be sure which is which until they're on their bikes.

'I want my rifle back,' I said. 'And my gang.'

'Your gang?' said the other twin.

'My gang,' I repeated. 'When Brad isn't here I'm the leader of Chaos.'

One guy laughed loudly. Another new one.

'Where's Ragnar?' I asked.

As though in reply came the snarl of an engine starting. A special, hoarse roar. I turned to the parked bikes and saw Ragnar riding towards us on his red Yamaha. He was steering with one hand. In the other he was holding what looked like a shiny new Kalashnikov with a pistol grip. Wonder how he'd come by that. I had my suspicions. He was fifty metres away when I turned the front of the bike towards him and fired off a short burst.

None of the bullets hit him but he braked sharply, only now realising it was a machine gun I had. And that meant superior firepower.

'Jump her!' he shouted. 'She can't take you all.'

'But quite a few,' I said in a voice so low only those at the table heard me.

'That's an order!' shouted Ragnar.

'The order is that you stay exactly where you are,' I said. 'I need you all alive.'

They stared at me. No one moved. Not that they thought I was the new leader. Not yet. But for the time being it was a machine gun giving the orders, not Ragnar. And it looked like he was losing.

But Ragnar knew the rules. He kicked out the stand, dismounted, and held up the Kalashnikov.

'You and me, no weapons!' he shouted, releasing the curving magazine and tossing it away so that it bounced and skidded across the floor. 'Or don't you dare, Miss Kickboxer?'

Of course I could have turned him down and just shot him there and then.

But I also knew that if the gang was going to accept a girl as leader then I had to show them something more than just that I was capable of pulling a trigger.

I dismounted, took the machine gun and walked over to the table, pulled out the bandolier and dropped it in front of them. Heard that hoarse roaring behind me, turned and saw that Ragnar was back on his bike and already on his way towards me, swinging the hook and chain around his head. I walked towards him, stopped between the meat hooks and waited. I'd seen it so many times. I knew his technique and I could read his body when he was about to throw. And when he did I held the machine gun up in front of me with both hands. The chain hit the top of the barrel, twisted round it once, the hook caught in the middle leaving me one second in which to act. I wedged the barrel down in two of the meat hooks, one on each side of Ragnar's hook, let go of the gun and took a step backwards. There was a rustling and juddering from the pulleys and wires up by the beam as they tensed, and then a straight line of steel connecting Ragnar's bike and the beam above. The engine of the Yamaha howled as it came to a sudden stop and the wheels had nothing to grip. Ragnar went flying over the handlebars in a perfect arc that threw him ten metres further down the hall, where he fell to the floor with a thud beneath a row of meat hooks.

I walked over to him.

He lay with his back to me, apparently unconscious. But as I got closer it was as though the sea monster on the back of his leather jacket flexed, and I saw his hand grab for something in the waistband of his trousers. I ran and kicked his hand as he turned. A glistening pistol – it looked like an expensive Glock – spun through the air. I could have let him get to his feet, I could have taken him anyway, but I had an audience. A gang wondering if this girl who said she was the leader was tough enough. Efficient enough. Merciless enough. So I gave Ragnar a simple but effective foot jab while he was still lying there. And before he'd recovered from that I was behind him with a so-called rear naked choke, my left arm around his throat, the right arm locking it, my forehead pressed against the back of his head as though comforting him. Then squeeze and cut off the supply of blood to the brain. Within ten seconds Ragnar was unconscious. I let go of him, pulled down one of the meat hooks directly above him. Glanced over at the table fifteen metres away and saw they were all watching. Rolled Ragnar onto his stomach, pulled up the red leather jacket and choked back the nausea as I drove the hook into the pale skin of his back. I crossed to the wall and turned the crank and Ragnar was hauled up into the air, the blood running evenly and steadily down his back towards the waistband of his trousers. I left him dangling a half-metre above the ground, walked over to his bike, unfastened the chain and then used it to tie his hands behind his back. Ragnar regained consciousness and began swearing and screaming at me, tried to twist himself loose but soon stopped, probably because he felt the meat hook digging into his muscles and tissue.

I walked back to the table and stood there. I could almost see the questions in their eyes. Who the hell was going to lead them now? Who was going to provide them with their next meal, with clothes, a roof over their heads and a place where they could be safe from their enemies? It wasn't going to be that loser hanging there on the meat hook, that much was obvious. But could it really be her – a girl?

'You took something that belongs to me,' I said. 'A Remington rifle. Which one of you has it?'

Of course they couldn't help themselves; everyone turned towards the guy who had it.

'You,' I said to him, a boy with big red pimples who couldn't have been more than fifteen. 'Go and get it. Now.'

He stood up and began to walk towards the bikes.

'Run!'

He ran.

'You others come with me,' I said, turning and heading back towards Ragnar. I heard nothing behind me and thought: shit, I've lost them. But then I heard the clinking of cutlery and the scraping of chair legs.

We stood in a semicircle around Ragnar. He was breathing heavily, his face twisted in pain, but he kept his mouth closed. Though it was nothing like when Dumbo got his throat cut, the blood dripped steadily from his boots and ran down the slope to the nearest sluice just the way it was meant to.

'This man here forced one of our own to confess to a murder he didn't commit,' I said, pointing up at Ragnar. 'After that he had him liquidated. There aren't many rules in Chaos, but the ones we do have are all we have.' I was talking loudly, louder than I had planned. Maybe it was to drown out the echo that made it sound as if I was standing in a church. 'Rule number one: one for all and all for one. If we follow that then we're invincible. If we don't, Chaos will be history inside a month.'

I looked round. A couple of them nodded.

I heard running footsteps. I turned and the pimply guy handed me my Remington.

'Ragnar,' I said. 'This is your jury. Do you plead guilty as charged?'

He groaned and kicked out with one leg, causing his body to half turn.

'No, all right then,' I said. I loaded the rifle and raised it. 'Then . . .'

He made a hissing sound and I lowered the rifle.

'I did it for us.' His whisper was almost inaudible. 'For Chaos. We wouldn't get weapons, nothing, if Dumbo withdrew his confession.'

'How much did you have to offer Kevin to kill Dumbo?'

'Not much,' he whispered.

'No, because Kevin's serving life already so he had nothing to lose.'

'Nothing to lose,' Ragnar repeated. His head was dangling now.

'I'm presuming you didn't tell anyone here you were planning to have a member of the gang liquidated?'

'All the weapons, the food . . .' Ragnar groaned, his chin on his chest. 'Without me we wouldn't have had anything.'

'We would have had Dumbo.'

Ragnar didn't reply. His body had rotated back to its original position.

'OK,' I said, addressing the others. 'Those who are against me sentencing this person to death, raise your hand.'

No hands.

'The condemned man gets to choose. Do you want to hang there till you die or do you want a bullet?'

Ragnar lifted his head slightly. His eyelids looked heavier. I had to make an effort to hear what he was saying: 'I'll take that bullet.'

I raised the Remington, pressed my cheek against the cool, good butt of the rifle. With an effort Ragnar lifted his head again slightly, as though to make my job easier. Aiming for his forehead I had the idea of trying to make the bullet-hole form a triangle with the eyes.

Then I fired.

XVI

I met Adele Matheson and Chief Inspector Gardell at the airport in the morning. It had been closed during the pandemic, when most of the privately owned airlines had gone bankrupt and never opened up again.

I'd parked out on the runway and could see the cars driving towards me like undulating spectres through the shimmering heat haze. As they got closer their outlines became clearer; one was a police car, the other a low, red sports car. They parked one on each side of me and we all got out.

'Thanks for coming,' I said.

'No need, but I don't have much time,' said Adele Matheson.

'Why here?' asked Gardell, who was still wearing sunglasses.

'The visibility's good,' I said. I knew they had noticed the Kalashnikov lying on my passenger seat. 'I just wanted to let you know that as from this afternoon Brad Lowe will be a free man. I've arranged for one of his relatives to fetch him.'

Matheson nodded. 'Chief Inspector Gardell and I take this as being simply information you possess and not implying in any way involvement in any potential case of false imprisonment.'

'I expressed myself in such a way as to allow of that interpretation.'

'Then you won't get any problems from us,' said Adele Matheson.

'What remains to be seen, of course, is how Brad Lowe interprets it. If he makes a complaint against me then you know where I am.'

'If that's all, then I have a case in court in an hour's time,' said Matheson.

I offered my hand. At first she just looked at it as though I had made a gesture that was obscene or at best old-fashioned. Then she shook it lightly. Gardell remained standing where she was as Matheson headed back to her Ferrari. 'Why?' she asked.

'Haven't I answered that question once before?'

'That business about respect for the courts and the rule of law? I don't buy any of that. Put it another way: I think you're as driven by revenge as the rest of us.'

'An eye for an eye, a tooth for a tooth,' I said as I watched Matheson's red wonder turning dreamlike in the haze. 'It's from the law of Moses, one of the earliest collection of laws we know of. It says the perpetrator must pay in kind for the harm done to others. But how can a perpetrator pay for having taken away a member of someone else's family? The greatest harm isn't necessarily to the one whose life has been lost but to those who have lost someone they love. The ones left behind who have to live with the loss, the pain and the guilt. The perpetrator should have to live with the same pain.'

'An eye for an eye,' said Gardell.

'It's a good law,' I said.

And once she had left I got back into my car and looked at the gun. I waited. Peering into the haze. Waited.

Then it came. A large black SUV, the same one I had seen driving away from the villa after the attack. Colin Lowe's car.

Brad wept when I told him I was setting him free and that soon someone I hoped he loved would come and pick him up.

'I don't deserve it,' he sniffled as the tears dripped down onto the mattress.

'You've been here for a while now.' Then I had to steel myself for what I said next: 'And everyone deserves a second chance.'

'You know what, Mr Adams? I've learned more from you in the short time I've been here than I did from my father during all of my upbringing.' His mouth opened and closed before a sob came out. 'I'm so sorry Amy's dead. I know there's nothing I can do for you, but . . .'

I laid a hand on his shoulder. 'There is something you can do. Chung and Larsen moved out yesterday and I need a strong man to help me move the ammo back here.'

He gave me a puzzled look.

'Heidi and I need somewhere in the basement to store food,' I lied. 'In here it'll just attract rats through the sewage pipe, so I'm going to have to use this room for ammo.'

'I'm ready.'

Brad didn't even ask me why I didn't simply block off the pipe but just got down to work carrying crate after crate of bullets, grenades, dynamite and petrol.

By the time we were finished we were both sweating and exhausted. Maybe there's something in the idea that hard physical labour creates a bond between men. I offered him a beer but he declined, saying he knew beer was in short supply and asked if he could have some water instead. It made me recall something a forensic psychiatrist told me once, how people will often say they made a mistake and were taken in by a man who devoted all his spare time to helping the poor and then turned out to have been a serial child abuser. But, said the psychiatrist, they hadn't made a mistake or been fooled. What was good in the man had really helped these people. It wasn't done as a cover for the other things he was doing. It's simply that people aren't either all good or all bad. Not Brad, not his father, and not me.

Night descends over the Lowe building as the enormous, insect-like helicopter prepares to land with a deafening roar. We stand watching in silence as the air is whipped up and the hairstyles and ties and dresses whirl about us. A few drops of champagne from Colin's glass sting my face like icy sleet and I taste the bitter sweetness in my open mouth.

And then the helicopter is down, the engine turned off and the rotor arms still spinning as the high-pitched whining gradually descends and decreases in volume and pitch.

Colin looks at me. Liza and Beth are standing by his side.

'Final group, board now!' shouts a voice from the helicopter door.

A dozen people swarm towards him.

Colin straightens his back, and I feel my eyes filling with tears.

The way they had done five days ago, when the Larsens and the Chungs took their few possessions and moved out. Larsen spent his money on a smallholding in the south, a place where they could grow their own food and be less affected by the collapse than in the cities. Chung had bought a fishing boat, and a lighthouse for his family to live in.

The way they had filled with tears when Brad left the villa four days earlier.

Why all these tears? Is it because what is inexorable, the certainty that there is no way back from here, always touches something deep in us? Whether it be farewells, or deaths, or just those ocean currents of time, happenings and life itself which separate us and pull us all apart from each other?

I hold out a hand to Colin.

'Farewell,' I say.

'Thank you.' Colin takes my hand and draws me close to him. 'Thank you for letting my son go.'

'Will!' shouts Heidi. She's standing by the helicopter door holding Sam by the hand. 'Darling, come on.'

'And thank you for letting me take over the villa,' says Colin.

'I'm the one who should be thanking you – for the tickets,' I say. 'It's just a pity there aren't enough for us all.'

'It's right that we should stay behind,' says Colin. 'I'm sure Brad will come back to us when he's had time to sort himself out. I think the way you treated him has given him a lot to think about, Will. You've given all of us a lot to think about.'

'Will, darling, they say they can't wait any longer!'

'I'm coming!' I shout back as I look into the eyes of my childhood friend. When choice is free, and yet inexorable. That false sense of freedom, contra to what has already been decided. The choice the brain would always make, based on the sum of all the information and every inclination available at the moment when the time for action comes. The absolute inevitability of the fact that I will never see Colin again, hear his laughter, smell his smell, feel the warmth of his handshake or his embrace. Of course I might be wrong, I can hope I'm wrong. But in the depths of my soul I'm afraid I neither hope nor believe I will see him again. But my eyes are as full of tears as his.

As the helicopter rises from the roof and wheels round I look down at the three people standing there waving, then I turn to Sam who tugs at my arm from his seat between Heidi and me.

'Where are we going, Dad?'

I point. 'There.'

'What's there?'

'West.'

'What's west?'

'The future.'

'What's future?'

'It's what's coming soon. Look . . .' I hold my hand in the air above him, flutter it down like a butterfly and tickle the pit of his throat. 'It's here now!' I shouted as he wriggles about, laughing away. 'And now it's over!' I say and stop tickling him. Hold my hand over him again. 'But there's more to come,' I say, and already he's giggling in terrified anticipation. As I'm tickling him my eyes meet Heidi's. They look dulled, but she's smiling. Again I raise my hand.

'And that was the end of that,' I say without taking my gaze from hers. 'But there's more to come . . .'

XVII

I'd found a shady place out of the baking hot sun while I waited for Will Adams to release Brad Lowe. Finally I heard their voices on the other side of the wall. Relaxed, good-humoured. Christ, they sounded like two old chums.

'So you're the one who's come to fetch me,' said Brad as the gates to the villa closed behind him. 'I thought he meant my father.'

For a few moments he just stood there looking at me and my bike.

'You ran out on us that night,' he said.

'It was all over by then,' I said. 'Getting out of there was the only option.'

Brad thought it over. Nodded. 'Sure. I would probably have done the same. So what happens now?'

'That's what we're wondering.'

'What do you mean?'

'You're the leader of Chaos. We're wondering what plans you've got for us.'

Brad stared at me in surprise.

I nodded at the bike. 'I'll ride pillion because I'm thinking you'll want to drive?'

Brad gave a big grin. He put his arm around my shoulder. 'I knew I could trust you, Yvonne. You know, if you hadn't been a carpet muncher I swear I would have had you for my girl. Where are we going?'

'To the funfair,' I said.

The reception had been a bit mixed when I told the gang I was off to fetch Brad and that from now on he was going to be leader. They were happy enough with me, they said, and couldn't quite understand why I would voluntarily give up tall privileges such as the best bike and first choice of weapons, food, room and girls.

But they did as I told them, painted WELCOME BACK, BRAD on a banner that was hanging above the gate as he and I rode into the abandoned little funfair the gang had taken over the day before. We had two generators with us, eight kilos of meat and ten litres of spirits.

To be honest the place was a bit creepy in the dark, but after dinner we lit the whole thing up in all its glorious bright colours and even got some tinny music going on the roundabout and the dodgems, shooting and loud cheers from the booth where the boys popped off airguns at little balloons, and even a scratchy voice on tape muttering scary stuff from what was left of a burned-out House of Horrors. Brad and I climbed up on horses next to each other on the roundabout. Creaking and out of sync they rose and fell as we shuffled round at an easy pace. Above the sounds of the barrel organs I asked him again: what plans did he have for us?

Eyes rolling, his voice slurred by alcohol, he said: 'We're going to kill that fucking Will Adams and the rest of his shitty crowd.'

'Why?'

'Why? Because he locked me up, that's why!'

'Not because he killed Herbert?'

Brad grunted and lifted the whisky bottle to his lips. 'That too. But nobody locks Brad Lowe up. Nobody talks to him like he was a snot-nosed kid. You don't act like you think you're a better person, that you're . . .' He made a face and gesticulated, but it wasn't easy to work out what he was trying to say.

'Holy?' I suggested.

'Yes. Will Adams talks like a priest, but he's just a fucking . . .' He waved the bottle about as though he was trying to catch the word in it.

'Hypocrite?'

'Yes!' He had to grab hold of the horse to save himself from falling off it. 'Him and those buddies of his, they didn't just kill, they slaughtered those men Dad sent to rescue me.'

'They defended themselves, you mean?'

310

Brad scowled at me and I bit my tongue.

'How are you going to kill him?' I asked. 'I hear he's turned that place into a fortress.'

'Yeah, but Brad Lowe has the answer –' he tapped the mouth of the bottle against his temple – 'in here.'

'And that is?'

'How many bazookas did Ragnar get from my father?'

'Fifty.'

'One.' Brad gave a loud laugh and tossed the empty bottle away; I heard it smash somewhere out there in the dark. 'One single one is all we need. We fire up through a sewage pipe that goes round into his ammunition dump in the basement. And – kaboom! – the whole house . . .' He balanced on the horse as he demonstrated with his hands, arms and puffed-out cheeks.

I nodded. 'How straight is that sewage pipe? If it's not straight the grenade will just blow up on the way in.'

'We'll find that out,' said Brad. Already he sounded a little less certain.

I sighed. 'I suppose you mean I'll find that out?'

'Can you?'

'Who's the one who always does stuff, Brad?'

'You, Yvonne,' he said, and even on a merry-go-round in motion I could feel his stinking alcohol breath on my face. 'You fix the stuff these other pea-brains here can't handle.'

'Give me four days,' I said.

'Four? Why . . . ?'

'Because the guy I know in the Map and Planning Department is away and he won't be back until then. I'll check to see if the pipe goes in a straight line and exactly where it empties out so we don't blow up the wrong house. OK?'

'What the fuck would I do without you, Yvonne?'

'You said it. But are you sure you want to go through with this?'

The lights around us went out, the barrel organ music began to drag, and then went hideously out of tune as the merry-go-round slowed down in the pale moonlight.

'What the hell?'

311

'We're out of juice,' I said. 'But I was asking . . . d'you really want to kill them? Adams did let you go, after all.'

'For chrissakes, Yvonne, don't you get it? That is exactly what pisses me off. I want –' he swallowed, a drunkard's tears in his eyes now – 'I want my father to know that I got the man who humiliated him. Because even if my dad is a bastard I love him. I love my mum and my sister too. But Dad . . . I've been a disappointment to him.' The horses had stopped completely now, with his in its lowest position, so that I was looking down at him. He straightened up. 'But once I've blown up that fortress and done what he wasn't able to do himself – then, at last, he'll see what I'm really capable of. Understand?'

There was a loud bang, a cheer, and the lights and music came back and the merry-go-round began slowly spinning again; Brad was up above me once more on his horse.

That night the whole gang slept inside the House of Horrors. Next morning, as I stood outside in the sharp daylight, Brad came over to me. He was pale and looked badly hung-over.

'I think I got a bit carried away last night,' he said as he stood tossing stones at the horses on the merry-go-round. 'Can we just forget about it?'

'You mean about Adams? Sure.' I was relieved.

'Not that. All that stuff about my dad. Forget it. That's an order. Just you find out about that sewage pipe.'

My bike and I are finally out of the city and riding along the deserted motorway. The asphalt swallows up all the light coming from the bike and from the moon. I pass the burned-out car wreck that's been there for the last couple of weeks. Several days pass before someone removed the charred remains from behind the steering wheel. I'm not sure what kind of story that was the end of, but of course the petrol tank was emptied a long time ago. It's been four days since Brad asked me to find out about the sewage pipe leading into the villa. That's all been sorted now. The fuel indicator is way over on the left now. It's finished its story too and is only waiting for the engine to realise it. There are the oil pumps. I slow down. High above me I hear the sound of a helicopter. I glance up and see a light in the sky moving in the direction of the bay. Long before I reach the slaughterhouse I can hear music. There's a party going on. Another party.

I pull up in front of the hall and see the twins holding up Eric, the guy who had my rifle. Eric's drunk, swaying about but keeping a tight hold on the bazooka pressed to his shoulder. It looks like the target is a rusting caravan about two hundred metres away.

I drive slowly into the hall. The sound blaring out from the single vast speaker is once again 'We are the Champions'. God, how I hate it. There are people sitting round the table and singing along. Others are dancing around beneath the meat hooks.

Brad sits alone at the end of the table with his feet up on a chair and a fat doobie in his hand. He looks up at me expectantly.

I take my time. Park my bike. Brush the thighs of my trousers.

'You're late,' says Brad when I sit down next to him.

'Met a few bumps along the way,' I reply, recalling the feeling of driving over a guy lying spreadeagled on a spike strip. I nod towards the exit. 'You've seen that the twins and Eric –'

'They've got permission. So?'

'I got the drawings from my pal in the maps department.' I open the zip on my leather jacket and hold up the papers I got from Will Adams when I was at the villa, where I got the machine gun, and where I said yes to what he asked of me in return.

'The sewage pipe goes up to the house in a straight line – all you have to do is stick the bazooka inside it and pull the trigger. I went and had a look around and I found the outlet for the pipe on the slope. The terrain is uneven and there's a bit of climbing, but we can get there and away again without being seen.'

'Perfect!' says Brad with a laugh. 'So what do you think?'

'About what?'

'About doing it.'

I shrug. Adams was insistent that I shouldn't lead Brad on or try to manipulate him. I was to make sure both options were open, so that his *choice really was free. Or as Adams put it: as free as we are to choose, being the people we are at any particular given moment in our lives. The point is – said Adams – the choice is Brad's: he can be his own punishment, or his own redemption.*

'You're the one who decides,' I say.

'We know that, but maybe you've heard it said that the sign of a good leader is that they ask for advice. Of course, it's then up to them whether or not to take the advice.'

'I can't offer you any advice when Chaos doesn't stand to lose or gain anything by this. You've got to follow your own heart and your own head, Brad.'

He seems irritated. 'OK then. I've already decided to do it, I just wanted to hear your opinion.'

There's a loud noise from outside and for a moment there's silence in the room; even the guy with his 'Champions' song keeps his mouth shut for a few seconds. Firelight flares outside the windows and I hear the cheers of Eric and the twins.

'I thought at dawn,' says Brad. 'What do you say?'

'Dawn sounds good.'

'But everyone knows that attacks always come around daybreak. Won't they be especially on the alert, don't you think?'

'Could be.'

'But you still think dawn is best?'

'Dawn is always best.'

Brad nods. Gives me a long scrutiny before he gets up and shouts: 'Party's over, Chaos! Drink up! We ride an hour before dawn!'

Cheers from the stoned gang members. The cheers turn into a foot-stomping chant of: 'Brad! Brad!'

He smiles broadly and holds his arms out wide in a gesture that both asks them to stop and at the same time accepts their tribute. He looks happy. Really happy. It was the last time I would ever see him look that way.

I wake up. Hear the steady, even breathing from Heidi and Sam. It's still dark in the cabin, but I can see a strip of grey along the edge of the curtain. It's no surprise to me that with Colin Lowe's tickets we've got a large cabin with three rooms on the upper deck. Heidi wept with joy. I look at the clock. Soon the sun will start its journey over the horizon.

Heidi snuggles up to me.

'What's the matter?' she whispers sleepily.

'Just something I dreamed.'

'What was that?'

'I don't really remember,' I lie.

I dreamed I was standing next to Brad and Yvonne. Brad was laughing and Yvonne looked serious as we stood and watched the burning villa. Brad laughed even louder when he heard the screaming and three people in flames came running through the garden and out towards us, down the slope.

'Burn in hell, Adams!' Brad cheered.

I turned and asked him if he couldn't see who it was who was burning, but Brad could neither see nor hear me. The flaming figures came closer, the tallest one holding two smaller ones close, and they fell to their knees in front of us.

'Brad,' said the tallest one. 'Burn with us. Burn with us.'

And I saw Brad's eyes open wide. His laughter stopped, his mouth fell open.

He turned. Now he could see me.

'You,' he said. 'You did this.'

'No,' I said. 'All I did was give you a choice. And you chose to start a fire.'

Brad ran forward. He fell to his knees and put his arms around the three of them as though trying to join them in the flames. But it was too late. Blackened and charred they crumbled in his arms. Brad stared at the ash on the ground. Buried his hands in it and screamed as though his very soul was in pain as the wind blew the ash away.

'But can you tell whether it was a good dream?' asks Heidi.

I think about it.

'No,' I say, and now I'm telling the truth. 'I can't. Come here . . .'

We're out walking on the deck. I'm carrying Sam, who's still sleeping. Everything is grey, it's all either sea or sky, there is no land, no horizon. Single-celled life, apparently that's how it all began. Then the sun rises up over the rim. As though by magic things acquire form and colour, and a new universe takes shape in front of our eyes.

'Our first sunrise,' I whisper.

Heidi repeats it: 'Our first sunrise.'

THE SHREDDER

A FLY LANDS ON THE back of my hand. I stare at it. The average lifespan of a fly is twenty-eight days. Does it know that? Does it perhaps wish that life could be longer? If it were offered a longer life in return for wiping out all memory of its loved ones, of all it has achieved, of its best days and moments, what would it choose?

I don't have time to worry about that right now. I move my hand and the fly takes off.

I need to forget, and I need to do it quickly.

I sit at the desk in front of the shredder. I close my eyes a moment and listen to the humming sound. It could be the fan in the ceiling. It might be coming from the suitcase. Or it could be the people outside on the streets. Then again it could be spy-drones. People say the military still have them.

Anyway, they've been on my trail for a long time, and I know that this time I'm not going to manage to get away. It stops here, in a stinking, baking hot apartment in El Aaiún. In the ceiling, between the bullet-holes and the shrapnel damage, a fan slowly rotates. It moves that scorching hot desert air around a bit after the sirocco has brushed aside the heavy Moroccan Berber rugs hanging in front of the windows and the balcony.

In a corner of the apartment, in front of the refrigerator, is a brown leather suitcase. It's a bomb. When it's opened, everything will be blown to bits, everything we know and aren't supposed to know will be gone. But before that can happen, whatever is inside it must be devoured, each brain cell must be consumed, must grow wings. Only then will it be time for the great flight. And before that I must forget everything I know.

But first I have to remember, call up the memories that need to be removed.

The white face on the screen of the shredder looks like a mask in a Greek tragedy. I try not to blink as I study my own reflection and manoeuvre my head so that my pupils are in line with the holes in the mask. Every trace that either directly or indirectly can lead them to the formula must be obliterated. I try to concentrate, because I know that only what I can remember now will be wiped out. Everything else they will be able to reconstruct from my brain, even when I'm dead. And I also know that the most efficient and complete deletion comes when the shredder is fed with memory pictures in chronological order, because then the associative memories are destroyed too. 'Think of it as like gutting a fish,' the sergeant who was instructing our research team said. 'Only the fish is *you*.'

OK. First the idea.

The Idea

It came to me in the middle of the night. I'd woken up beside my wife Klara needing to pee. I got up as quietly as I could so as not to wake her and made my way to the bathroom. We were living in Rainerstrasse, in that part of the city that still has electricity and running water. It was raining outside. I know that because I would have remembered if it *hadn't* been raining. Half awake, and about to urinate, I noticed I had the beginnings of an erection. I tried to remember what I'd been dreaming but there was nothing there that might have caused sexual arousal. My researcher's brain simply registered that my body had produced nitric oxide and norepinephrine. As I stood there my thoughts wandered on, created a new dream. I was dead, and my condition was what they referred to during the public hangings that took place directly after the Last War as *angel-lust*. As a medical student I learned that there was a simple physiological, not chemical, explanation for *angel-lust*, the fact that some of those on the gallows had erections visible through their trousers: the rope exerted an increased pressure on the cerebellum, and it was this that caused the priapism. Whoever invented the name *angel-lust* had probably been playing with the idea that there might be pleasure and joy, perhaps even some kind of liberation in death. But only playing. Death is, after all, the ultimate seriousness. The enemy who is always on our trail, whom we spend our lives fleeing from but who will, sooner or later, find us. It's just a question of when.

The reason my thoughts went looking that night for a connection between lust and extinction, desire and death, was obvious. For some time now our research team had been working to find a cure for hadesitt, the deadly sexual disease that had broken out just before the war, decimating the population of Africa before reaching us in both the western and eastern confederations, as HIV had done almost a century earlier. We had already managed to prolong the lives of certain patients with the medicine HADES1, and slightly lowered the mortality rate in other groups, but it was still up at 90 per cent and we were working with what we hoped was an improved version, HADES2. In connection with this we had been looking into the ways in which the disease spread. It came as no surprise for us to discover that those who had oral sex often, and frequently changed partner, ran a markedly greater risk of being infected with hadesitt than others. It was not until I began to analyse the second column of figures that a further – and quite remarkable – aspect of the study struck me.

We had assembled a smallish group of deceased prostitutes and porn actors, some of whom had died of hadesitt, others from different causes, in search of signs that the mortality rate and the danger of infection had fluctuated over time. The reason for this was that the hadesitt virus had not only developed a resistance to medicines but other survival strategies too, as every living organism does in the compulsive pursuit of eternal life. Since, as previously noted, the death rate from hadesitt was over 90 per cent, it was surprising to note that those who had more than the average amount of sex seemed also to have a longer average lifespan than the rest of the population. Bearing in mind both that this group was more vulnerable to hadesitt and the unhealthy lifestyles of many prostitutes one would have expected them to live shorter, not longer lives.

Of course, it's not unusual for researchers to see mystical connections and patterns in their data, often related to something that has no connection at all with the hypothesis being tested. Many of my colleagues have been quite properly ridiculed for pursuing research they've come across in this way. If you throw a dice to test out a hypothesis that you can influence telepathically to land on four, and it turns out that it lands with an unnatural regularity on five, then there is an obvious temptation to claim that what you were testing was whether the dice would land on the number you were thinking of, plus one. Ethically speaking, of course, that would be rubbish. The rule is: test what is to be tested, answer the question that has been asked. Any answer can be misused by changing the question so that it fits the result, thereby giving the researcher an apparently sensational breakthrough in a wholly different field. And that was exactly what happened to me that night.

I thought of nitric oxide and norepinephrine and in a dreamlike and yet clear-sighted moment spotted a connection. A connection I knew I could not dismiss, not even if it meant falling headlong into the classic trap. I also knew I could not tell anyone about the researcher's sin I was about to commit.

I flushed the toilet and went to the living room. Light from the last working street lamp on Rainerstrasse filtered in through the rain that ran down the glass. It fell onto the photograph of my brother Jürgen on the wall, onto the elephant rifle hanging above the fireplace, and on the pen Klara had given me as a birthday present one year. I picked up the pen, found a sheet of paper and noted down my wild ideas. Then I crept back to bed, where Klara was still sleeping in peaceful innocence. I looked at her face – calm and still beautiful – but ageing much too fast, before turning the alarm clock back an hour and a half, as though it were a symbolic act.

After I let myself into the laboratory the next morning, before anyone else had arrived, I at once began studying the figures more closely to test out my new hypothesis.

The Hypothesis

Three months after the night I had first thought of the link between sex and increased lifespan I was sitting in the office of my boss Ludwig Kopfer, the administrative director for Antoil Med. He had been listening to me for some two hours, almost without interrupting. Now he clasped his hands together and looked at me over the tops of his spectacles. They were without arms, the kind that just pinch over the nose; I think Sigmund Freud wore a pair.

'Correct me if I'm wrong,' Kopfer said, the way he always does, and without any suggestion that such an interruption would in fact be tolerated. 'But what this boils down to is that a compound of nitric oxide and norepinephrine can retard the ageing process and combat disease. And this is something that happens at the cellular level. That in theory this component can completely *halt* the ageing process.'

'We know that nitric oxide and norepinephrine affect the blood vessels in the genitals of both men and women during sexual arousal; but they're also important for the autoimmune system. It's the combination of norepinephrine and a couple of other substances that retards the ageing process. And I haven't found any reason why the right combination shouldn't be able to halt the process completely.'

'As in –' he whispered the word – 'immortality?'

I coughed. 'As in preventing the body from degenerating with age and ultimately dying from some otherwise harmless illness. There are numerous other ways in which to die.'

'Immortality,' Kopfer said again, as though he hadn't heard me, leaning back in his high-backed chair and looking thoughtfully through the window. 'The search for the holy grail!'

For a long time neither of us spoke. Outside, the smoke from Dusseldorf's factory chimneys rose silently into the air. It was strange to think how, fifty years ago, these had almost disappeared. Finally Kopfer spoke.

'You realise what you are asking for, Herr Jason?'

'Yes,' I said.

'You risk ruining the reputation of the whole company.'

'I'm aware of that.'

'So what if I say no?'

'Then I'll hand in my notice and take the material to one of our competitors.'

'You can't do that – the data you're basing this on is the property of Antoil Med and we'll sue not just you but the company you take this to.'

'Naturally, I won't use any of the material from here, I'll get new data. And now that I know what I'm looking for, better data. And no one can take the idea away from me, because that's in here.' I tapped my temple with my index finger.

I could see Kopfer muttering something inaudible, and then he sighed loudly. 'But *eternal life*. Good God, Herr Jason.'

'Of course, there are years of research remaining before we'll know whether I am right,' I went on. 'But I'm willing to stake my reputation and my career on it.'

'Of course you are, and if you are right then a Nobel Prize in either medicine or biology awaits you, probably both. And if you're wrong, then you can just start all over again. But for the company . . .'

'The company won't double its value times a hundred if I'm right, it will do so a thousand times. In other words, if there's a two per cent chance I'm right then it makes rational financial sense to go for it.'

'For the Eggen family and the other stockholders maybe. But to put the livelihoods of our workforce at risk like that . . .'

'The risk to workplaces here will be greater if a competitor gets to develop the medicine. It will replace between sixty and seventy per cent of all other medicines. The branch is facing a bloodbath. The only question is, Herr Kopfer, which side of the bloodbath will you be on?'

Kopfer had a way of rubbing the palms of his hands through his curly grey hair when he wanted to think, as though the static electricity activated his brain. And he did this now. 'If,' he sighed, 'if I allocate you the resources you're asking for, then it must be on terms of such secrecy that no one, not even husbands and wives, knows what it is you're working on.'

'I understand that.'

'I'll be talking to Daniel Egger, and he can decide whether or not the rest of the board should be informed. In the meantime, this has to stay between you and me, Jason.'

'Of course.'

Four days later I was summoned to Kopfer's office again.

'Egger and I are agreed that this must be kept under the radar for the time being,' he said. 'That goes for internally too. The fewer who know anything at all, the better. I can't hide a project as heavy on resources as this in the budget; we'll have to pretend it's about something else.'

'I understand.'

'It will appear to be a development of the hadesitt project, and for practical reasons be relocated to Africa.'

'Africa?'

'We own a building in El Aaiún, in the Spanish Sahara. It's Off-Broadway. Avoid the prying eyes of industrial spies and the media. We'll explain that it's closer to the source.'

'I see. Like the Manhattan Project, a lot of brains isolated in a desert.'

'Yes,' he said and looked out of the window. 'Only that was to invent a bomb capable of wiping out the human race. While this is –' he looked directly at me – 'the exact opposite, right?'

The Bomb

The smell of diesel and bars of white sunlight each time the wind moves the carpets. It's been many years now since the last electric car ended up on the scrapheap and they reopened the oil wells in the Sahara. Somewhere out there a siren is wailing; I don't know if it's an ambulance, a police car or one of the military emergency-response vehicles.

Two bangs, in quick succession. Fire and answering fire, or a double puncture at one of the roadblocks? Hopefully it's about the colonial overlords chasing the guerrillas, or the other way round, and not about me.

El Aaiún always has more questions than answers.

The watch on my wrist is ticking. A present from Klara on our wedding day. I know it's slow, but it's not slow enough.

Three months after the company's decision I, along with twenty-two hand-picked researchers and three semi-trailers filled with laboratory equipment, was in place in El Aaiún. Officially the project was known as HADES2, internally it was referred to as Ankh. Researchers are used to working under conditions of confidentiality, and no one knows more than they need to know to do their jobs, but I was aware that they knew the price they could ask for disclosing information about the project to one of our competitors might be temptingly high. For that reason I had, through the chairman of the board Daniel Egger, a former colonel who still had connections in the military, acquired a memory-shredder which had made the trip out with us. Each member of the team had signed a contract agreeing to subject themselves to it once they had submitted their final reports. The memory-shredder had been developed during the Great War, when the military were given exclusive rights to develop and use technology above the third degree. It was used by officers who possessed information they no longer had any use for, but which could be exploited by the enemy if the officer were taken prisoner. Because even if the officer could withstand the torture or followed standing orders and took his life with the cyanide pill they all carried, our enemies in the Russo-European Confederation had developed Exor, which was even then capable of extracting the memory from a dead and physically destroyed brain. The memory-shredder versus Exor. It was like an image of the technological warfare, move and counter-move, that had brought the world to such a wretched state, and led to the banning of technology in civilian life after the war. Yes, those of us in the health service are occasionally permitted to use the memory-shredder to remove memories in the psychiatric treatment of trauma patients, but this only ever applies to a member of the elite.

Research projects are like films or building projects; they're never finished on time, or within the budget.

But Ankh was.

That was chiefly because I, as head of the project, had at two critical junctions taken risky decisions concerning the way forward, and focused all our resources on these. If just one of them had turned out to be a blind alley it would have killed off the whole project. My assistant as head of research, Bernard Johansson, who was the only one besides me who had enough of a total overview to question my decisions, asked: 'What's your hurry, Ralph?'

He thought both times that we should have split into two groups at these crossroads, the way things had been done in the Manhattan Project. And he was right; we had the personnel, the money and the time for it. *They* had the time for it. The fact that I didn't have wasn't something I could share with Johansson. What I could share with him was the euphoria once we realised we had found it, the ultimate medicine.

It was – as is so often the case once you've got your answer – surprisingly simple. But complicated too, in that it demanded a new way of thinking. Evolution's way is for certain species to survive through producing new, healthier, better adapted individuals, with the older variants getting scrapped and dying out. But if the cell renewal in an existing individual is so comprehensive that the ability to learn is also updated then, metaphorically speaking, there is nothing to prevent an individual from giving birth to itself over and over again. Where normally a baby has to be taught everything from scratch, this reborn individual will appear complete with experiences that give it a crucial advantage in the struggle for existence. So why didn't such a species already exist? I think perhaps the answer is that it has taken time to develop a species intelligent enough to solve the mystery, but since all mysteries are solved sooner or later then we – meaning nature – have all along been on the right track. Intelligence is natural, the survival instinct is natural, ergo eternal life is natural.

That, at least, was what I was trying to convince myself of as I raised my head from the microscope at six o'clock one ice-cold morning in El Aaiún, looked at Bernard Johansson and whispered: 'We've found it.' And at the same time sublimated the question: 'Exactly what have we done?'

We pulled back the curtain and looked out over the desert. As the shimmering red rim of the sun rose over the horizon Johansson said that this was the dawning of a whole new day for mankind. While I thought how that sun must have looked like the flash from the first successful detonation of an atom bomb in the New Mexico desert in 1945.

'Nobel Prize?' said Johansson.

Maybe. Definitely. But a whole new day for mankind wasn't what I was looking for.

We dismantled the laboratory at top speed, left just a few things behind, including the shredder, crated up the mice and headed back home to Europe.

The Mice

'These,' I said into the darkness, 'are the twenty African pygmy mice used in the test.'

I depressed the lever on the projector and a new image appeared on the screen. 'When the experiment started they were all one year old, which corresponds to the average lifespan of the pygmy mouse. We gave ten of them injections. Two months later they were all still alive, while the ten who did not receive injections were all dead.'

There was a coughing from the darkness. Kopfer and I were the only ones in the company boardroom, the other eleven chairs for the time being unoccupied. And yet he'd seated himself some distance away from me.

'Correct me if I'm wrong, Jason, but what this boils down to is a chemical formula. A long one, certainly, but all the same, a formula.'

'The formula contains one hundred and fifteen symbols,' I told him.

'And this is not written down in some scholarly paper or on a computer, it's only –' in the darkness I caught a movement, as though he were tapping his index finger against his temple – 'in your head.'

'Everything from El Aaiún has been shredded, including the memories of those who did not have A-code clearance. Which means, everyone except me, Bernard Johansson and Melissa Worth.'

'Melissa . . . ?'

'Worth. The laboratory head.'

'OK. But I hope you realise the board is not going to stake the whole of the company's future on the fact that you have managed to prolong the lives of a handful of mice by a few months.'

'They're still alive,' I said. 'In human terms that means they're over a hundred and fifty years old. All ten of them.'

'Or risk ending up with nothing because you've forgotten the formula or been killed in a traffic accident. It is highly unusual not to have proper documentation of the work.'

'But we *do*, Kopfer. I have signed an agreement that in the event of something unforeseen arising, you can use the bio-memory downloader on me.'

He snorted. 'Bio-memory downloaders don't exist any more.'

'At least one does.'

'Exor?' He snorted. 'Do you know what it costs to use it, and how long it takes to do a complete search of even a single adult human?'

'Yes, and I know the rumours about it rusting somewhere in the ruins of Paris. But it works, and the army has people with the technological know-how to operate it. So as long as you have my brain, you'll find my formula in there. Actually, you don't even need the entire brain – a fragment will do.'

Ludwig Kopfer grunted something, and I saw him raise his arm to look at his watch. He'd gone back to using the kind of analogue watch with a radioactive content that had been banned in the 1960s once they discovered improved and less carcinogenic ways of making the hands luminous, a discovery that had since been lost. 'Let's see what the board has to say, Ralph. I'll call you after the meeting.'

At eleven o'clock that evening Klara and I sat on the sofa drinking white wine and watching *Titanic* on TV. It's strange to think that a ship that sank over a hundred and fifty years ago is still lying on the bottom of the ocean. And that there was once a time when it was still possible to make films like that. When progress in technology, knowledge and civilisation was something that was taken for granted. Most had obviously forgotten the dark middle ages, in which, among other things, we had forgotten how to make concrete.

Klara wiped away a tear, the way she always did every time Leonardo DiCaprio gave Kate Winslet that last kiss. Klara had told me that the reason she cried was because they had just met each other, the loves of their lives, and only had these few hours and days together as they headed towards inevitable catastrophe.

Klara had entered my life and our house when I was eighteen years old. She came with my brother Jürgen, three years older than me, who proudly presented his new love to the family. Klara had curly blonde hair, a lively personality and a smile that could melt a stone. Polite, helpful, sympathetic, easy company, the whole family fell for her at once. But not, of course, in the same way I did. Klara had an innocent charm, she had no agenda, she didn't play little games, and yet just occasionally I sensed a touch of some darker, passionate depth behind those flashing blue eyes when she laughed in my direction. But I never dared to think that it might be related in some way to me. In the first place, I was a loyal brother. Secondly, I was not the kind who was used to arousing this type of feeling in women. The exception had been a couple of colleagues who, I presume, fell for what they took to be a certain intellectuality and a pleasing calmness, perhaps allied to a degree of self-irony and an almost self-negating tendency to be of service. Whatever, throughout Klara's marriage to my brother she and I adhered strictly to our allotted roles as brother- and sister-in-law. For twenty years I hid my undying love for her, and she did the same. I offered my sympathies when it turned out she and Jörgen couldn't have children, and I exaggerated my concern when Jörgen fell ill. Just ten years earlier there had still been medicines on the market that could have saved him, and I know that through my connections in medical research, or via some illegal channel, I could probably have managed to get hold of something from the reserves stockpiled for central figures in the worlds of politics, research and the military. But I did not make the attempt, telling myself by way of an excuse that not only would I risk going to prison but that it would also be immoral and egotistical of me to take care of my own family like that when there were others in need who were much more important for the future of society.

In the days and weeks and then months that followed Jörgen's burial I hardly left Klara's side. We did everything together. Ate, read, went to the cinema, went walking. Travelled to Vienna and Budapest where we visited restaurants, cafes and museums, including the museums of technology that documented the naive faith of earlier generations that the future was heading only one way. During the evenings we walked the cobbled streets of these decaying cities, hand in hand, talking of everything and nothing. We were both approaching fifty, but while I still had a full head of dark hair, Klara's had turned silvery grey, and her bright smile and shining eyes were framed by deep furrows. I attributed the early onset of these signs of ageing to grief at the loss of her husband.

It was on the way home from one of these trips, standing alone in the bow of a riverboat, that I told Klara how I felt about her. How I had always felt about her. She told me she had always known, and she felt the same way too. When I kissed her it was with a deep, trembling feeling of happiness, accompanied by a curious melancholy. Melancholy because it had taken us twenty years, or almost half the expected lifespan in the Russo-European Federation, to find happiness.

Four years had passed since Jörgen's death, but still, out of consideration for the family, we waited a further year before marrying.

I was as happy as a man can be, at the same time as my research into telomeres, the white regions at the end of the chromosome that appear to determine the maximum potential lifespan of the human being, had come to a standstill. Maybe it was my frustration while working at the laboratory, in such sharp contrast to my joy at being with Klara, that meant I began working shorter days. Or did I have some premonition, did I recognise in Klara some of the symptoms we had encountered in the children with Hutchinson–Gilford syndrome whom we had studied, so-called progeria or hyper-ageing, in connection with our research? But I dismissed that thought; the syndrome is genetically determined, and something known about from the moment of birth.

When Klara began having problems with her hips and came home and said that the doctor who had examined her asked if she was really only forty-nine, I gave him a call. And he confirmed that the X-rays had shown him the body of someone he thought must be in her eighties. I arranged for Klara to see a specialist, who confirmed the presence of Werner syndrome, another cause of hyper-fast ageing, but one that can occur later in life. The specialist gave Klara another five years before she died of old age, just fifty-four years old.

Klara accepted her fate with resignation.

I did not.

'We get the time we get,' she consoled me, though it did nothing to stop my tears. 'And if we don't get the longest time, what we do get is the best, right?'

I gave up my job to spend more time with Klara, but then changed my mind after a couple of months. Longevity was my special field; surely there had to be something I could do beyond simply sitting and watching my beloved crumble away before my very eyes? So I began to work longer hours and with greater intensity than ever before, at one and the same time hunter and hunted. Then the board decided that the economic downturn meant the company could no longer afford to finance something that offered little hope of short-term profits, and I was diverted to the hadesitt research programme.

I had not told Klara about my discovery. Like the relatives of the rest of the research group, she believed I had gone to Africa to find a cure for a sexual disease. She was just glad to have me home again, and as we sat on the sofa and watched the unsinkable ship sink, I sent a stolen glance in her direction. Saw her lift the cup of tea I had made her to her lips as she wiped another tear from her lovely blue eyes.

The telephone in the hallway rang.

I went out and took the call.

'The board is giving you the go-ahead,' said Kopfer.

I exhaled deeply, only then realising I had been holding my breath.

'But they have certain concerns.'

'Which are?'

'They say that as long as the medical commission has no written documentation of the contents of the drug, the proceedings could be long-drawn-out, and it might take several years before they give us the go-ahead to begin testing on humans. Bearing in mind the size of the investment, the uncertainty and the time frame before the medicine starts to generate income . . .'

'They want me to tell them the formula?'

'Yes.'

I looked at Klara in the living room, her neck bent to drink her tea. Self-delusion, naturally. By now I was used to it. For Klara's neck was constantly bent, its elegance a thing of the past.

'And if documentary proof that it works on humans already exists?' I said.

'What do you mean?'

'What if I am already in a position to prove to you that the compound stops the ageing process in humans?'

I heard Kopfer stop breathing at the other end.

'Can you do that?'

Klara put down her cup. She loved the tea I made, especially the new flavour I had brought back from Africa.

'Soon,' I said, and hung up.

From the street below I hear loud, angry voices. Spanish, Arabic, Berber. But I can't think about that now. Should I have brought the elephant gun with me, now hanging uselessly over the fireplace back home? No. I'm alone and have no chance to defend myself, no chance of getting away. People want to live, no matter what the cost. Or so they think. For they don't know the price, they don't know what the consequences will be. And the humming from the suitcase is getting stronger, more insistent. Tick-tock, the seconds pass, the walking stick approaches. Everything they can take has to go. Scorched-earth policy. Not just for Klara's sake. Or for mine. But for humanity's sake. I'm ashamed of myself, but this act of betrayal is the only decent thing I've ever done in my life.

The Betrayal

Kopfer continued to press me to divulge the formula, excusing himself by saying that he was under pressure himself from the board. But I remained adamant that the risk of someone leaking it for financial gain was just too great.

'Ralph, making that assessment is not your call.'

'Maybe so, but I'm doing it anyway.'

'What I mean is that it is not your *right*. Your duty is to –'

'My duty is to God and to the human race, Ludwig.' I saw how Kopfer almost fell out of his chair at my use of his forename. 'Not Antoil Med. Not even REC. This discovery is bigger than any company or any individual country. The first to get hold of this formula will try to monopolise it and use it for political gain. The only place I could have gone with this would be the United Nations, if it still existed. I'd rather die than hand over the formula.'

Kopfer looked at me for a long time before rising from his seat and leaving.

I stayed where I was, nervous and shaking.

There had been something sorrowing, almost suffering in that look of his. The same look I had seen on the faces of those doctors who came to us with blood samples from their patients, and we had to tell them they were suffering from hadesitt.

I took regular blood and tissue samples from Klara, lying to her and saying I was sending them to a colleague who was working on a cure for Werner syndrome. In the laboratory I was able to see that the medicine was having the same effect as on the mice; the ageing process was not merely retarded, it appeared to have come to a complete stop.

But the medicine also had a side effect we had first observed in the mice. Melissa reported that they were less active, that they stopped visiting the communal cage, and seemed lethargic. The only lively reaction we got from the mice was the way they bared their teeth at the research assistants when they were being fed. I don't know to what extent African pygmy mice are disposed towards depression. Nor Klara, come to that. For a while I supposed that her abrupt changes of mood, her apathy and general lack of initiative were due to the thought that she would soon be dead. But I hadn't noticed any of this before I began putting the medicine in her tea, and if the change didn't exactly occur overnight it was nevertheless so rapid and obvious that I decided to reduce the dosage. With no apparent effect. On the contrary, it seemed as though her mood swings and her pessimism only increased, and that she had developed an addiction to the medicine. Melissa, too, reported that reducing the dosage of Ankh to two of the mice, which she had done on my advice, had had no effect on their behaviour. This only occurred once we started giving them antidepressants. Fortunately the same result was evident in Klara after I began putting a similar mixture in her tea.

One day Daniel Egger, the white-haired chairman of the board, came to my office. The Egger family owned 60 per cent of the shares in Antoil Med, and I had never seen the head of the family wearing anything other than a tweed suit and trainers and carrying a walking stick, the function of which remained unclear, since Daniel Egger trots rather than strolls when walking.

He sat down, placed his hands on the smooth top of his stick and just looked at me.

'Imagine,' he said after a while, smiling and displaying a row of teeth so pearly white you might almost think pearl was what they were made of. 'In the brain directly opposite me now lies the solution to the question that mankind has been asking itself since the dawn of time. How to avoid death.'

'Maybe so,' I said.

'But that is not the most surprising thing, Herr Jason.' Egger produced a handkerchief and began to polish the tip of his cane. 'The most surprising thing is that you are a scientist, a researcher who is prepared to betray the most important principle of science: that knowledge is there to be shared.'

'You think Oppenheimer and his research team should have shared their knowledge of the atom bomb with Hitler and Stalin?'

'Oppenheimer at least shared it with his superior, the president of the Western Confederation. And you are under the same obligation, Jason. It is the board and the head of this company which has provided you with the means to make your discovery and paid your wages. Your discovery is our property.'

'My obligation is to –'

'God and the human race. Kopfer told me what you said.'

'Of course, I will have to reveal the formula before I die. When that time comes.'

'That time –' said Egger, pushing the handkerchief back into the inside pocket of his tweed jacket – 'might come sooner than you imagine, Jason.'

I noticed that two large men, both wearing suits too small for them, were standing outside the door of my office.

I coughed. 'Are you threatening me, Egger?'

He looked blankly at me. 'I gathered from Kopfer that you are prepared to die in order to keep your secret.'

'Naturally I'm worried that the discovery might do more harm than good if it falls into the wrong hands. Three world wars have been fought for less, Herr Egger. One single life isn't so much.'

He sighed. 'God and martyr. Diametrically opposed, and yet mankind's two favourite roles. You're trying to play them both, Jason. It's not right. You're welcome to play God, but you're going to have to let someone else play the martyr.'

'What do you mean?' I felt a dark foreboding.

He smiled. 'I think Klara Jason would make a perfect martyr.'

It only took a second for my mouth to dry up. 'What are you talking about?'

'If the previous God could sacrifice His son to save mankind, you ought to manage to sacrifice your wife. Right?'

'I still don't understand . . .'

'I think you probably do,' said Egger, and pointed to the top of his cane. 'You know what this is? No, of course you don't. It's bone from the black rhinoceros. The black rhinoceros is –'

'I've seen pictures.'

'– extinct. This is from one of the last of them. I inherited the cane from my grandfather. He had no trouble walking either. Like me, he used it as a reminder that nothing has eternal life, everything disappears, for good and ill. Or *all things shall pass*, as the Jews said, at least those of them who lived in the USA. But now that death is no longer a certainty, an early death is all the more bitter. Whether it's your own or that of someone you wanted to spend the rest of eternity with.' He looked at me, and there was ice in his grey stare. 'You're going to give me that

335

formula, Jason. Here and now. If you don't, then you'll find when you get home to Rainerstrasse that your wife isn't there. When you eventually do find her – *if* you find her – she will be crucified. And I am *not* speaking metaphorically. She will be suspended in a forest, nailed to a cross of wood by her hands and feet, a crown of thorns on her head, the whole works, apart from that business about resurrecting on the third day. So what do you say, God?'

I swallowed. Looked at him, the way one poker player looks at another who has gone all in. Was he bluffing? I couldn't quite believe that Daniel Egger, one of the city's most prominent and respected citizens, a real pillar of society, was threatening me with criminal methods that might have come from a Mafia boss. On the other hand, he had been an officer during the war, and isn't that exactly what gives society's alpha males and females their positions? That they're willing to go further than others.

I nodded in resignation, took a sheet of paper from my desk drawer and began to write.

It took me almost four minutes to write down the formula using the chemical codes in which the world is boiled down to elements, molecular connections, pressure and temperature.

I handed him the sheet of paper.

His eyes scanned the symbols.

'The Holy Writ,' he said. 'But what's this?' He pointed to the title, a symbol like a T with a loop above it.

'The hieroglyph Ankh,' I said. 'The symbol for eternal life in ancient Egypt.'

'Elegant,' he said, as he folded the sheet of paper with infinite care and placed it in the inside pocket of his tweed jacket.

I watched him as he disappeared down the corridor. He was swinging his stick, and it made a cheerful clicking sound each time it hit the parquet floor. Like the second hand on a clock.

The countdown had started.

*

I didn't know how long it would take Egger to find out I had tricked him. Not even the researchers on my own team would be able to dismiss what I had written on Egger's sheet of paper as nonsense, since their knowledge was only partial. But given time, they would of course put two and two together and discover that the formula on the page did not add up to four.

It took me a week to find somewhere to hide Klara.

As a young medical student I had once, along with some other students, been shown round a mental hospital. It was a place in which the associations with hell could only have been matched by the nightmares and hallucinations of the inmates who lived there. The dark corridors reeked of sterilising fluids and excrement, and from behind locked doors came heart-rending shrieks and groans. Looking in through the food-delivery slots I saw pale faces, empty and terrified, gazing as though hypnotised into the darkness and confusion of their own souls. The person who showed us round, realising from our horrified expressions what we were feeling and thinking, told us that things hadn't always been this way, and that prior to the Last War the state had had the money and the technology to give the mentally ill a more dignified life.

The place I found for Klara seemed to offer just that. Dignity.

It called itself a convalescent home and was located on a hillside overlooking the sea. Clean, pure mountain air, spacious grounds, large, airy rooms, two nurses to each patient, and daily conversations with a psychiatrist. And – what was even more important – it was in the area formerly called Switzerland and had preserved a form of autonomy that gave it certain privileges. For example, the privileges of discretion, which meant they did not have to report the identities of their patients to the authorities or anyone else. Naturally, it was a service designed for the elite. And the elite were the only ones able to afford the price.

Even using all my savings I would not have been able to afford to keep Klara there for long. Then I thought of our house in Rainerstrasse. It had been in the family for generations, and Klara and I simply adored it. But it was large, and could and indeed *should* have been home to a family with children. Two rooms and a kitchen were all Klara and I needed. And each other.

'Now let me show you the gym,' the female superintendent continued.

'Thank you, Fru Tsjekhov, but I have seen enough,' I said. 'Let's get the papers signed and I'll bring her in tomorrow.'

The desert wind whispers a secret, a formula out there. The way Klara now and then could lean into me and whisper forbidden words, words meant for my ears alone, a formula of her own that opened up the gates and made the nitric oxide and norepinephrine start to flare inside me. That for a moment gave eternal life. I don't want to think about those other words of hers, the hate-filled ones she hurled at me when I came to fetch her. But I *must*. I must think of her rage, how she spat at me, scraped at the wallpaper with her fingernails and screamed that she had to get out, her eyes rolling wildly. Think how I finally managed to get enough sedatives down her to get her into the car. But also think of her peaceful face as she slept in the back seat while I drove through the night. The car began to overheat on the winding, uphill road leading to the home, but we made it. When I left Klara stood on the steps in front of the home, a nurse at each side ready to restrain her. But Klara didn't move. Her arms dangled by her sides. Big, heavy teardrops rolled from her eyes as she whispered my name, over and over again – I kept hearing it all the way back. Twice I was on the point of turning round and driving back to fetch her.

I need to think of all this. Think it so that it can be deleted from my brain, so there are no memory traces left to lead them to where Klara is. And I need to think it quickly, with no unnecessary digressions, complete in every respect, so that everything, absolutely everything, will be gone. Because my watch is ticking louder and louder now. Tick-tock. Daniel Egger's walking stick is getting closer. So I need to think about the visit.

The Visit

Late one evening, two weeks after I had driven Klara to Switzerland, there was a ring on my doorbell. Already it had been a bad day. Fru Tsjekhov had telephoned and explained that their own doctors wanted to stop administering the medicine that I, as Klara's doctor, had left them, with instructions that it be administered by injection every evening. I had explained that it was to counter Werner syndrome, but now they were of the opinion that it was in fact these injections that were the cause of her psychotic episodes, and that if they didn't stop dosing her with what was, for them, an unknown medication, then there was a real danger she would descend into a life of full-blown schizophrenia.

The endless acid rain poured down, etching itself into the roof tiles, eating up our house inch by inch. I had put the place on the market – there was even a board out on the lawn – and my first thought, as I heard the doorbell ring through the sound of the drumming rain, was that it must be a potential buyer. That Daniel Egger could not possibly have had time to work out that the formula I had given him was not genuine.

But when I opened the door slightly and saw Bernard Johansson standing there I realised that this was not, in fact, impossible.

'Well?' he said, rain dripping from his smooth and strangely egg-shaped skull. 'Aren't you going to let me in?'

I opened the door and he stepped inside, took off his coat, shook it lightly and I watched the drops fall onto the Turkish rug Klara had bought when we were in Budapest. We sat in the living room, he on the sofa where Klara and I used to sit.

'So, how can I help you?' I asked.

Johansson laughed. 'Christ, that sounds awfully formal, Ralph.'

'Maybe, but let's get to the point, shall we?'

He sat up straight. We could, of course, pretend that it was the most natural thing in the world for him to drop in just like that of a Friday evening, but given that neither this nor anything else remotely

339

resembling social intercourse had ever taken place between us in the fifteen years during which we had worked together, I could see just two possible reasons for his visit. One was that he – the only person on the planet who in under three weeks could have realised the formula was faked – wanted to warn me. The other was that he wanted to exploit it.

Naturally, it was the latter.

'I have a business proposition that could make us both rich.' His smile was strained, as though his discomfort was as acute as mine.

He explained to me that when Egger had come to him with the formula I had written down, he had initially – based on his almost complete knowledge of our research – been convinced that it had to be genuine and had told Egger so.

'But as I continued to work on this so-called formula, I began to realise that you had done what any good liar would do and kept as close as possible to the truth. The omitted elements, however, are so crucial to its success that only someone with my knowledge of the material would be able to fill in the blanks or correct the deliberate mistakes.'

'With all due respect I doubt it, Johansson.' I did not, however, see any reason to deny that the formula was defective. Chemistry is chemistry, after all, and Johansson was no idiot.

He nodded slowly. 'If I were to travel to Shanghai and offer an almost complete version of the formula to Indochina, they would not only give me unlimited resources and the best research team in the world, they would also pay me a fortune to solve the puzzle for them.'

'But you can't be certain you will succeed.'

'Give us time and sooner or later we will.' He sipped his tea. 'With you aboard things will move much quicker, and they will pay more. So what I'm offering you is a partnership. We split fifty–fifty.'

I had to laugh. 'Has it not occurred to you that if I wanted to get rich I would have done as you suggest, only gone it alone?'

'Yes,' said Johansson. 'And for that reason I know that temptation is not enough. I need threats as well.' His tone of voice was regretful, his expression hangdog.

'Oh yeah?'

'If you decide to reject my offer then, first of all, I will sell the project to Indochina. They will then make public what they are working on in order to stimulate the stock market, so that by an emission they can raise enough capital to fund the project. And once it is made public, I shall inform the board of Antoil Med that it is you who have sold the formula. And unlike you, who has shown no inclination to cooperate, I will be believed. Egger's response will be . . .' Johansson took another sip of his tea. Not just for effect – I think he actually enjoyed being as brutal as the situation demanded. He put down the cup as though he no longer liked the taste. '. . . quick, and not necessarily painless,' he concluded.

'You've thought it through thoroughly, Johansson. But there's one thing you've forgotten. Suppose I'm not afraid to die? Or more accurately: what if Ankh is as important for mankind as the splitting of plutonium was a hundred and fifty years ago, offering the chance to make a better world, but also the possibility of destroying it overnight? There isn't enough *dreyran* in the soil or the atmosphere to produce enough Ankh for everyone. So who is to decide who shall have eternal life? Who could accept not being among those chosen? With a population that dies only as a result of accident, suicide or murder, draconian legislation will be required forbidding the birth of children if the earth is not to be over-populated in the course of a single generation. And who is to decide who should enjoy the privilege of procreation, and who not? In short, if Ankh is not administered by a global authority then it will be not merely be confederation against confederation but every man for himself, the war of all against all in which neighbours and families turn on one another. My death is just a drop of blood in the ocean. But if I release the formula it's an ocean of blood. So go ahead, Johansson.'

He nodded as though all this had already occurred to him. Or at least thought that it must have occurred to *me*. 'Ralph, for as long as I've known you, you've been a utilitarian. And of course it's a noble idea, that the individual should sacrifice himself *for the greater good*, as they say in the Western Confederation. That's why I've always admired not just your intelligence but also your character and your ability to love others besides yourself. Where is Klara, by the way?'

I didn't answer, showed absolutely nothing.

'I see,' he said quietly. 'They will find her. And they will find the formula. They will use Exor on you. They will vacuum your brain.'

'Nonsense,' I said.

'Is it?'

All that could be heard in the room for the next few seconds was the rain beating onto the permanently brown lawn out there. Exor was controlled by the army. It was rumoured to be in a bunker where the Louvre had once stood, guarded by an entire squad. That it didn't need a whole brain to extract memories but that, using only microscopic fragments, it could interpolate its way to the whole memory bank. On the other hand this could take well over a year and cost the same as it cost to provide a big city with energy over the same period of time. Nevertheless, as was also usually the case in matters of technical research, Johansson was right. Offered the chance of a medicine that could give the generals eternal life, of course they would use Exor.

My brain approached the problem in the way prescribed by Descartes, using first intuition and then deduction. The conclusion that emerged was disheartening, but therefore also – strange as it may sound – liberating. Because there was so obviously only one solution there was no need to torment my brain with doubts, deliberations and procrastination.

'You know, in former times hunters used to bring trophies home with them from Africa,' I said as I stood up. 'They used to mount the heads of rhinoceroses, zebras, lions and antelopes up here,' I said, pointing to the wall above the fireplace. 'But since there are no longer any large mammals left in Africa, this is what I took instead.'

I lifted down the heavy old elephant gun I had bought in a bazaar in Marrakesh. 'The seller claimed that it was used to kill the last elephant in Africa. And I liked the irony of having a rifle above the fireplace instead of a lion's head. A dead rifle that no longer has any function, that has been overcome and now hangs on the wall, an object of general ridicule. We all die, but what if, before that, we are able to do something that is useful for the whole flock, for the community? Yes, I probably am a utilitarian. I really do believe that we have a duty to carry out any act that benefits rather than harms mankind, whether we want to or not.'

I pulled on the breech. The rusty mechanism obeyed with a grating reluctance. I stared into the barrel.

'Ralph,' said Johansson, his voice uneasy. 'Don't be stupid, shooting yourself won't help. You might mean it to be a utilitarian act, but Exor can extract data from your brain long after you're dead.'

'What I was trying to say,' I went on, 'is that the correct moral action does not necessarily need to be morally motivated. This action, for example, is primarily motivated by my egotism, my love for my wife, and my hatred of you.' I turned the rifle on Bernard Johansson, aimed at his head and fired. The report was loud, but the hole left in Johansson's forehead surprisingly small considering the heavy calibre of the bullet.

'And yet it is, from a utilitarian perspective, correct,' I said, walking round the body and registering the fact that Klara's sofa would never be quite the same again.

It's been a long journey back to the Spanish Sahara. For several days now I've been hearing the low, crackling sound of the larvae's hungry chomping, not knowing whether it came from the suitcase or from my own head. But then it fell silent, the way a coffee pot does just before the water begins to boil. Then a low rumbling. Rising and rising. And now finally it's boiling, Klara, my beloved. I hear voices and heavy, shuffling footsteps on the staircase. They aren't afraid of me, they know they have all the superiority they need, but not all the time. None of us has that. From the moment we're born we start to die.

These are the last thoughts, they're about the letter. About the mice. About Anton. About the decision. And so, Klara, I have to leave you.

The Decision

Waking in the bed Klara and I had shared as the day broke, my first thought was that it had all been a nightmare.

But Klara was gone, and the body of Bernard Johansson lay on the sofa in the living room.

I had thought about it all night and slowly begun to realise that getting rid of a body is a very difficult thing to do. That in preparation for obvious solutions such as dumping the body in the sea, or burying it in a wood, there are any number of practical logistical problems which can seem almost trivial but which, taken together, impose a dauntingly high risk of being caught.

What bothered me most was not being convicted of murder, but the thought that, lacking my brain, they could use Exor on Johansson's. Because even though that wouldn't give them the whole formula it would get them so close that – as he had correctly pointed out – sooner or later they would find the solution.

I looked at the clock. There was every reason to suppose that Johansson – who was, in most respects, a completely typical young researcher – had kept his criminal plans and his visit to me secret, so it would probably be a while before they started looking for him.

I dragged the body into the bathroom, hauled it up into the bathtub and covered it with the Turkish rug.

Then I headed off to work.

I sat in my office staring at the keyboard of my typewriter. Newspapers lay next to it, the headlines all about the planned meeting between the four confederations at Yalta. Of course the thought had occurred to me. I had dismissed it, thought it again, dismissed it. And now thought it yet again. I had even put paper in the typewriter and was ready. Because Egger had been right. It really is second nature for a researcher to want to share his knowledge. And if Ankh was to benefit all mankind then it could only happen one way: if everybody, absolutely everybody, was

344

given the formula at the same time, so that no one could exploit the knowledge to further their own power. Of course, there might still be war over access to resources such as *dreyran*, but if I were to give the world leaders the formula while they were gathered at Yalta, and they realised that the only alternative to chaos and violence was if they reached an agreement, passed laws and ensured a fair distribution of resources, then it still might end well.

It was just a question of faith in human nature. Like Kierkegaard's 'leap of faith'. You needed to persuade yourself to believe something that all experience and logic told you it was impossible to believe. Because there was actually no alternative. If I – a very good but not exceptional researcher – could stumble across the formula for prolonged and in theory eternal life, someone else would be able to also, regardless of whether or not I kept it secret. It's chaos theory. Anything that can happen, will happen.

So: one text, four copies, one to each of the four confederation leaders. One formula with an explanation of what it was, and why it was being sent out to everyone. It wouldn't necessarily get there quickly. Things weren't like they used to be in the days when the internet existed. But my letter-heading and my signature, Head of Research at Antoil Med, would at least ensure that it would be read by the confederations' experts. And they would immediately realise what it was they held in their hands, and that it was urgent. It would have to happen at Yalta.

I pressed down the first key. My office door opened.

Normally I would have reprimanded my subordinates for entering without knocking, but when I saw the distraught expression on Melissa Worth's face I realised it wasn't a simple oversight. I steeled myself. This could only be about one thing: Bernard Johansson's mysterious absence.

'The mice,' said Melissa, and now I saw that her eyes were brimming with tears. 'They. They're . . .'

'They're what?'

'They're killing each other.'

*

Melissa and I ran to the laboratory and found the other members of the team gathered round one of the large communal cages where we had allowed the mice to socialise, before they had started to show signs of aggression.

Six of the mice lay bloody and lifeless in the sawdust, the four others were locked in their individual cages.

'We were just following the programme,' said Melissa. 'We reduced the injections to a minimum, and because the mice had stopped showing aggression when we fed them in their individual cages we opened up the slides to the communal cages, just like we all agreed. They went straight for each other, all of them, as though they'd just been waiting. It happened so quickly we didn't have time to get them back in their cages before . . .' Melissa's voice cracked up. She had been there from the very beginning, one of those who had seen the miracle take place, who had given her time, her whole life to the project.

'Take them out,' I said. 'Freeze them.'

I returned to my office, intending to complete my letter to the confederations.

But instead I sat there, staring at the blank sheet of paper, seeing the dead mice in my mind's eye. I wasn't particularly surprised by what had happened – but why wasn't I? It was one thing that the aggression in the mice appeared to have been a side effect of Ankh, another thing altogether for the mice to continue to be aggressive even after the doses were reduced. Was it possible that the medication brought about a permanent change in the chemistry of the brain? Other questions arose: among mice there can hardly be a complex scale of aggression, and the difference between hissing at another mouse and killing it are probably minimal. What effects might Ankh have on the behaviour of humans? Klara's behaviour was an isolated case and could well be the result of completely different factors. Nor had she developed murderous tendencies. Or had she? What would have happened if I had stopped giving her the antidepressants along with the Ankh?

And so, as the sun sank below the rooftops, reddened by the factory smoke, I had still not begun my letter. Instead I started going back over our research material. Might it be something in the Ankh that was causing the aggression? And if so, could it be removed without affecting Ankh's power to retard the ageing process?

At ten o'clock that evening, after the others in the team had gone home, I went to the laboratory and took blood samples from two of the dead mice. I then took one from myself and ran tests. Read the results and concluded that it was as I had thought. The active ingredient that retarded the ageing process was the same as that which triggered the aggression. One and the same thing, two sides of the same coin.

But the blood-analysis machine showed something else too. That the level of Ankh in the mice's blood was lower than it ought to have been, given that they had been injected that same day. I took one of the capsules from the fridge and put it under the microscope. In less than a minute I had located the two holes in the lid, invisible to the naked eye but in the microscope enormous craters. Someone had punctured the capsules with a microscopically small hypodermic needle. Through one of the holes they had withdrawn Ankh from the capsule, and through the other replaced the stolen medicine with some other fluid, probably water.

As Head of Research I had access to my team's clock-cards and I checked these to see if there was a pattern, if the same person had been clocking out last from the laboratory recently. Because Ankh had a very limited shelf life and wasn't needed in large quantities for the African pygmy mice, the medicine was in continuous production, but in extremely small quantities. In other words, a thief would need to operate in the same way, continuously, and on a very small scale.

I found what I was looking for. A name. Anton, a quiet and shy individual who, although thirty-nine years old, still worked as a research assistant. I don't know whether it was lack of ambition or because he had never taken the last part of his biology exams. Or it could have been for health reasons – over the last couple of years he had been off sick for long periods at a time. Whatever, on account of his long tenure and responsibility for tidying the laboratory at the end of the day, he was a keyholder, and from the others' clock-cards I could see he had been alone in the laboratory for at least two evenings every week over the last year.

I mulled it over for a while before calling Kopfer and telling him what I had discovered.

Then I turned out the light and went home.

Two hours later I was sitting on the sofa with a beer watching the TV when it came on the news. A reporter standing in the street in front of a squad car with a flashing blue light said that the police had tried to arrest a thirty-nine-year-old man in his home, suspected of stealing from the company where he was employed, and that the suspect had attacked the two policemen with a knife, critically injuring one of them. The man had now barricaded himself inside his flat. Armed police had arrived and were trying to engage him in dialogue, but the thirty-nine-year-old had shown no willingness either to communicate or to give himself up. The excitable reporter pointed to a house and explained that the man had just been seen in a window, waving a bloody knife and shouting threats and obscenities. At this point the anchorman in the studio interrupted and gravely announced that they had just heard from the hospital that the badly injured policeman had been declared dead.

I stared at the TV pictures. The police stood sheltering behind their cars, their guns pointed in the direction of Anton's house. If they didn't already know it, they would soon find out that he had killed their colleague. It was as though I could see their fingers squeezing a little harder on the triggers. I didn't need to watch any more; the outcome was a foregone conclusion and I switched off the TV. I put the empty beer bottle on the table and looked at the syringe that lay there. That I myself had taken Ankh home was hardly a question of theft. It had been done to speed up the testing on humans, on Klara. And, after she had responded positively, although with what might look like unfortunate side effects, on myself. I had been taking Ankh for a month and a half now and hadn't noticed any sign of depressive thoughts or increased aggression. But of course, it could well be the case that the individual involved is not aware of his own feelings, that he or she rationalises them away and regards the situation itself as difficult or demanding of a violent response, that the cause is not to be found in his or her own psyche or behaviour.

I thought of the body in the bathtub.

I, who had never laid a hand on another person, not even as a child, had killed a man.

Ankh. If I hadn't seen it before it was clear enough to me now. Ankh was not a recipe for eternal life, it was a recipe for chaos and death. Fortunately, for the time being at least, the recipe was a secret, the formula that gave more than just the ingredients involved but also the correct procedures, pressures and temperatures necessary, and that could not be reproduced by an examination of the material itself; for that they would need to get hold of me, find the recipe in my brain.

The memory-shredder. It was still in El Aaiún.

I called the airport. And found I was in luck. If I could make it to Vienna the following day I could get a seat on board the weekly flight to London, and from there the Madrid plane that departed every other day. From then on I would have to improvise. I booked the ticket.

Afterwards I called Switzerland. I got Fru Tsjekhov on the line, apologised for ringing so late and explained that Klara should be completely taken off the medicine I sent them. That I had discovered it might be the direct cause of her mental condition. And that we could only hope the damage wasn't permanent, but that it would probably take some time before she was herself again.

I went up to the bedroom and packed a bag. Some clothes, the few roubles I had, and a wedding photo of Klara and me. If I drove all night I could make Vienna by daybreak.

When I entered the bathroom to get my toiletries I stood looking in the mirror at the bath behind me.

I turned, pulled away the rug and looked at Bernard Johansson. At the hole in the forehead. The coagulated black blood that had run over the bottom of the bathtub. I might perhaps manage to delete myself, but once they found the body of my closest associate they would definitely put his brain through Exor. How long would it take them to fill in the remainder of the formula? A hundred years? Ten years? One year? But it was too late to hide the body now.

The dead man appeared to be staring at a point in the ceiling above me, as though still waiting for the angels to come and take him away. Fly off with his soul.

Fly off.

I swallowed.

It had to be done.

I went back up to the bedroom and took out an old leather suitcase.

Then I went down to the cellar and fetched the saw.

The Journey

From out in the corridor a voice shouts my name.

Something hard pounding on the door. Could be the butt of a gun.

The journey. I must remember the journey. Vienna. London. Madrid. Then a transport flight to Marrakesh and from there hitched a ride on a lorry.

The driver spoke a little Russian and wondered what I had in the suitcase that smelled so bad. I told him it was a human head, that I had opened the cranium up with an axe and left it out in the sun for three days to attract the flies. That flies had crawled into every orifice and laid eggs that had turned into larvae and were now eating up the brain. The driver laughed at my joke, but still wanted to know why.

'So that he can get to heaven,' I said.

'So you're religious?'

'Not yet. First I need to see his ascent to heaven.'

After that the driver didn't speak any more, but when he let me off at El Aaiún and I gave him the last of my roubles he leaned out of his window and said in a quick, low voice: 'They're on your trail, señor.'

'Who is?'

'I don't know. I heard in Marrakesh.' Then he put his lorry in gear and disappeared in a cloud of black diesel smoke.

I let myself into the flat and the stuffy air hit me like a wall. For months I had lived and worked here. I had suffered, hoped, rejoiced, wept, taken wrong turnings and still achieved the miracle. But most of all I had longed to be at home with Klara. I opened the windows and doors and dusted off the memory-shredder. Switched it on and breathed a sigh of relief: the batteries were still able to provide power. I took the wedding photo out of the bag, put it on the table next to the shredder, sat down, took a deep breath, concentrated. The desert wind moved the heavy rugs in front of the windows. Then I began at the beginning.

So that's how it is. The snake bites its own tail and the circle is closed.

I shut my eyes. Everything's inside now. Everything that must be wiped out, deleted, vanished. Including Klara. My darling, darling Klara. Forgive me.

As the door crashes open I press the large button on which it says DELETE. After that I remember noth—

I'm staring up at a large fan in the ceiling. It's turning slowly, but I can't move. I hear two sounds: a low humming, and a regular tapping sound. Two faces enter my field of vision. They're wearing sand-coloured camouflage uniforms and pointing at me with machine guns. I have so many questions, and I know the answer to at least two of them. The humming I can't identify, but the tapping is easy to recognise. It has to be the walking stick belonging to Daniel Egger, chairman of the board at Antoil Med, the company I work for.

'Release him,' says a voice. And sure enough, it's Egger's.

I'm able to move again, so I sit up. Look around. I'm sitting on the floor in a room in semi-darkness. Light leaks in between the hanging rugs. Where the hell are we?

Egger sits in a chair directly in front of me. He's in uniform, like the others. It's a little too new-looking to be his old colonel's uniform from the days before he took over the family concern. The face is lightly sunburned. He leans his chin against the smooth, black top of the stick and directs his cold, intelligent gaze on me.

'Where is the formula?' he asks. His voice sounds hoarse. Maybe he has a cold.

'Formula?'

'For the medicine, idiot.'

He says it calmly, as though it's my name. Idiot? Have I done something wrong?

'But it's in the reports I sent to Kopfer,' I say.

'What reports?'

'What reports? The research reports on HADES1, they're submitted every week and –'

'Ankh!' snarls Egger. 'I'm talking about Ankh.'

I look at him, look at the armed men in the room. What's going on?

'Ankh?' I repeat, as my brain searches for a place where this word might have hidden itself.

Egger looks at me expectantly. And then my brain finds the word in there, in the drawer in which it's hidden.

A drawer from my childhood, when I read about Egypt. 'You mean the hieroglyph for eternal life?'

Egger's sunburned face glows even redder. He turns to the desk behind him. There's a machine there, I don't know what it is. It looks like one of those personal computers, from the days before the collapse of civilian technology. Egger picks up something next to the machine and holds it up in front of me.

'If you don't give me the formula we'll find her and kill her.'

It's a photograph in a wooden frame. I recognise myself, of course, but not the woman in the picture. We're dressed like a bridal couple and I try to recall the occasion. Perhaps it was at a carnival, or some kind of practical joke. I really try, but the pretty, if ageing, face of the woman doesn't excite any associations. And yet it seems as though Egger

352

is serious about his threat. Can't help wondering if maybe the man isn't quite all there.

'I'm really sorry, Herr Egger,' I say. 'But I'm afraid I have no idea what you're talking about.'

It's hard to interpret exactly what it is I see in his look. Rage? Hatred? Bewilderment? Fear? Like I said, it's hard.

'Boss,' says a voice. I look towards the end of the room where a man is standing with a sergeant's stripes on his chest. He points at a worn leather suitcase with his gun. 'There's a humming noise coming from this.'

I see that the other men start backing off towards the walls.

'Brown!' barks Egger. 'See if that's a bomb.'

'*Jawohl!*' A man steps forward. He's holding a metallic object that resembles what people used to call a mobile phone. Runs it along the side of the suitcase. And now I recognise the suitcase. It's the one I inherited from my brother Jürgen. Did I bring it here myself? And suddenly it dawns on me, why nothing dawns on me, why I have this feeling of staring at a jigsaw puzzle in which not just individual pieces are missing but the whole puzzle. Because that apparatus with a screen on the desk, doesn't that look like the apparatus I once saw used on a patient suffering from trauma, a so-called memory-shredder? A machine that shreds certain parts of the memory, eliminating specific thematically connected memories but leaving the rest untouched? Have I used such a machine on myself? Egger was asking about a recipe. Have I removed a recipe from my memory? For a bomb? Is that a bomb inside the –?

'The suitcase is clean,' says the man with the metallic object.

'Open it,' says Egger.

The men around him press their backs against the walls. My heart beats faster.

'We'll all die if we don't find the formula,' hisses Egger. 'Now!'

The sergeant steps forward, flips up both locks on the suitcase and looks to be taking a deep breath before he flips the lid open.

The humming is now deafening, and it is as though we are staring into a black storm, a night in motion. It takes a second for me to realise what this is. Then it rises up towards the ceiling in a single dense mass, there to break up into black sections that again divide into even smaller sections. Flies. Fat, heavy flies. And now that they're all over the room, attention focuses on what is revealed inside the suitcase.

A human head.

The skull has been split open. Eyes, lips, cheeks, all the soft parts are gone, probably eaten up by at least one generation of larvae now matured into grown flies. But all the same, perhaps because of the bare and unusually egg-like shape of the head, it seems to me that I recognise the extremely intelligent researcher I once employed as my deputy and assistant, Bernard Johansson.

A breath of wind causes the rugs to flap into the room, sunlight floods in, a puff of warm air strikes my face.

'The flies!' shrieks Egger. 'They're heading for the light! Catch the flies!'

The men stare at him in puzzlement. Look up towards where the swarm has already magically disappeared; only a few flies are left now around the slowly rotating ceiling fan.

One of the men opens fire on them.

'No!' Egger shouts. He's almost crying.

No one stops me when I get up, walk over to the window and lift aside one of the rugs.

I'm looking out on a hillside. There are roofs below me, and the settlement continues all the way down to a point where it suddenly stops, and desert takes over. And beyond that: just sand, and a sun that is either risen and on its way up through the sky, or setting and on its way down, it's hard to tell when you don't know which direction you're look-ing in. It's very beautiful. And speaking of the sky, I think of the flies which are now, for the first time in their short lives – the lifespan of the average fly is twenty-eight days – free and on their way up into the heavens, taking with them what they've consumed of Bernard Johans-son's head. I close my eyes and feel a remarkable freedom, in spite of the men with the guns behind me. I don't know what it is, only that I've unburdened myself of something, and now feel myself as light as a . . . well, as a fly.

If they don't intend to lock me up, are they going to shoot me now? Maybe, and if so then it's for something I've forgotten, something I found it necessary to shred; that at least is the only image that emerges when I join up the dots linking the few clues I find here in this room. And if I were to summarise my allotted span before they shoot, what could I say? That I have used my life, my twenty-eight days, to develop HADES1, a medicine that might be the start of something that will reduce the suffering of humanity. So no, it cannot have been a completely wasted life. That's fine. There's nothing I miss.

But still I feel a curious emptiness somewhere inside me. As though an organ has been surgically removed, I can't find any other way to express it. And there, in that emptiness, I feel that yes, there really is something I miss.

I miss having known love. Having had a woman in my life.

THE CICADAS

'READY,' I SAID.

'READY,' I SAID.

'Get set,' said Peter.

'Go!' we shouted in unison and started running.

The deal was that the last to cross the imaginary finishing line between Zurriola's beach and the lifeguard's chair two hundred metres away had to buy beers for us both. But it was also training and a rehearsal for our participation in the bull run at Pamplona in two days' time.

For the first few metres I didn't give my all. Not just because I could afford not to but because I was pretty sure I would win and at the same time didn't want to rub Peter's nose in it in a way that would put him in a bad mood. Peter Coates's genetic heritage hadn't given him much practice in losing. He came from a line of scientists, models and businessmen, all of them successful and affluent and – those I had met at least – with unusually white teeth. But they weren't a notably athletic family. I kept a couple of metres behind Peter and observed his energetic but not especially effective or elegant running style. He had muscles, powerful thighs and a broad back, but although he was by no means overweight there was something heavy about him, as though he moved through a heavier gravitational field.

I had to position myself directly behind him when the course narrowed between two sunloungers and some bathers making their way back up from the cooling waters of the Biscay, and the sand kicked up by Peter's bare feet sprayed across my stomach. We got a few choice Spanish oaths tossed after us but neither one of us slowed down. I pulled out to the right of Peter, closer to the water's edge, where the sand was firmer and nice and cool underfoot. When we planned our trip Peter had told me that not only did San Sebastián have some of Europe's finest restaurants but was also known to be relatively cool when the heat of the Spanish summer was at its most ferocious. That San Sebastián was the place where the more sophisticated and less sun-worshipping class of tourists took their vacation. And fortunately the cloud cover and the steady breeze we'd experienced since our arrival there the day before had been a welcome relief from the stifling heat of Paris and on the train journey.

I went up a gear and ran alongside Peter and could see the look of triumph already on his flushed face with the finishing line less than fifty metres away, and how it gave way to a look of desperation when he saw me next to him. I still had a choice, I could still let him win. A defeat would cost him more than victory would reward me, so it wasn't a case of what Peter had told me was called a zero-sum game in which the pluses and minuses all cancel each other out in the great reckoning. But the question was really whether it would hurt him more to realise I had let him win. Peter's laboured panting, and the fact that he was giving it absolutely everything, didn't they oblige me to show him respect by also giving my all? And wasn't there a tiny little part of me that really did want to rub his nose in it, for being so superior to me in every other way? Thirty metres to go. Choices. They feel so free; but are they really? Wasn't what I was about to do already written in the stars?

I sprinted and in a couple of seconds was past him. I could see him trying to respond but he didn't have enough left; his running got more and more ragged and he lost what little rhythm he had had to begin with. I simply maintained a steady speed so as not to beat him by too much, but still he fell further behind. Five or six more paces and we'd be over the finishing line. I felt something hit my leg, lost my balance and tumbled forward. I just about had time to break my fall and to see Peter gliding past me.

He walked back towards me, hands held above his head, his white teeth gleaming, and I sat up, still spitting sand.

'Cheat!' I coughed as I tried to summon up more saliva.

Peter laughed loudly. 'Cheat?'

I spat and I spat. 'Tackling from behind, that was an obvious trip.'

'So what? Was there anything in the rules against that?'

'Come on, that's a given.'

'Nothing is a given, Martin. Rules are constructions. Constructions have to be constructed. Before that happens the ability to be –' he held up his closed fist and raised a finger to accentuate each point – 'problem-solving, to take rapid decisions, to see past rigid modes of thought, to ignore counterproductive moral conceptions and –' he smiled as he held out a hand to help me up – 'as well as to tackle from behind are as admirable as the ability to move the legs rapidly.'

I took his hand and pulled myself to my feet. Brushed the sand off my body. 'Fair enough,' I said. 'I'll have to comfort myself that in one of your parallel universes right at this very moment I'm the one who's tackled you from behind, I'm the one who's giving you the lecture, and *you're* the one who has to go and buy the beers.'

Peter laughed and put his arm around my shoulder. 'I buy, you fetch, OK?'

'Parallel universes do exist,' Peter said again as he took a swig from the bottle and sort of wriggled himself and his towel deeper into the sand.

'OK,' I said, carrying out the difficult art of drinking lying down, and peered up into the grey sky above us. 'I understand that I don't understand your quantum physics and your theory of relativity, and that I'm sure what you say is right about there being enough dark matter to make a parallel universe, but that there's an infinite number of them, well, I have trouble with that.'

'In the first place these aren't my physics theories, they're Albert Einstein's. And his underrated and almost equally clever friend Marcel Grossmann.'

'Well, I'm no Grossmann, Peter, so if you want to convince me you can't use equations and numbers.'

'But the world *is* equations and numbers, Martin.' Peter opened his blue eyes beneath his sun-bleached fringe and smiled in my direction, showing his white teeth. A girl once asked me if they were real. Not that it was either Peter's scientific brain or his teeth that had attracted me to him in the first place and ended up as probably his best friend. I don't know what it was. Maybe that unforced, pleasant self-confidence that sometimes accompanies natural-born talents and inherited money. Because Peter was a boy who knew that, without any particular trouble, he would meet all expectations. It was curiosity that drove him, not his family's ambitions for him. And perhaps that brings us closer to an explanation of why he chose a poor art student from the wrong side of town as his best friend. He was the one who had been attracted to me, not the other way round. Probably because I represented something he was curious about, the only thing his family lacked: the sensitive, volatile artist mind that, despite being vastly inferior to his when it came to mathematics and physics, was able to transcend the boundaries of logic and create something else. The music of the senses. Beauty. Joy. Warmth. OK, I wasn't quite there yet, but at least I was working on it.

And it was perhaps also curiosity rather than respect that led him to accept the condition I laid down for our taking this trip together: that he wasn't to pay for anything for me. It meant that we travelled on a budget that was affordable for me. So it was Interrail tickets from Berlin through Europe, nights spent on the train or at cheap hotels, and meals at reasonably priced restaurants or in rooms where self-catering was available. Peter made just one exception. That when we reached San

Sebastián – our penultimate stop before the goal of our trip, San Fermín and the bull running in Pamplona – we should eat at the world-famous Arzak restaurant, and he would foot the bill.

'Will it convince you if I tell you that Stephen Hawking was doing work on parallel universes when he died?' said Peter. 'The physicist, you know, the guy in the wheelchair and –'

'I know who Hawking was.'

'Or *is*. If the numbers add up then he's still alive in a parallel universe. We all are. So in fact, we do live forever.'

'If *the numbers* add up!' I groaned. 'At least Christianity makes eternal life dependent on a belief in Christ.'

'What will be really interesting will be to check out this Christ figure when the time comes, when we can move in a controlled manner between universes.'

'Oh? Meaning that it's already taking place in some uncontrolled manner?'

'Sure. Ever heard of Steve Weinberg?'

'No, but I'm guessing he won the Nobel Prize for something or other,' I said. My bottle was empty and I turned my gaze from the lazily swaying sea in front of us to the bar behind.

'Physics,' said Peter. 'His theory is that we, as the collection of vibrating atoms we actually are, might find ourselves vibrating at the same frequency as a parallel universe, in the same way you can be listening to a radio station on one frequency and suddenly hear another in the background. When that happens universes split and you can enter either one or the other reality. Know who Michio Kaku is?'

I tried to look as though the name rang a bell but I was struggling to place it.

'Come on, Martin. That rather affable, Japanese-looking professor on TV who talks about string theory.'

'The cool guy with the long hair?'

'Him, yeah. He believes that déjà vu *might* be a result of the fact that we've had a peek into this parallel universe.'

'Where we've been?'

'Where we *are*, Martin. We're living an infinity of parallel lives. This reality –' he gestured with his hand towards the parasols, the sunloungers and bathers – 'is neither more nor less real than the alternative. That's why time travel is possible, because there's no paradox involved once you have parallel universes.'

'Temporal paradoxes, self-contradictions that make time travel impossible, that for example you could travel back in time and kill your own mother?'

'Yes, but think of it instead in this way. If you're travelling through time, then you have by definition split the universe in two, and in a parallel universe, or in some other universe, two of you can exist. You can be both dead and living at one and the same time.'

'And you understand all this?'

Peter thought about it. Then he nodded. It wasn't arrogance, just honest Coates self-assurance.

I had to laugh. 'And now you're going to find out how time travel can be accomplished?'

'If I'm lucky. First I have to get on to the research team at Cern.'

'And what are they going to say when a twenty-five-year-old says he wants to send people off time travelling?'

Peter shrugged. 'When Apollo Eleven landed on the moon the average age in the control room at Houston was twenty-eight.'

I got to my feet. 'Right now I'm planning a voyage to the bar and I'll be back with more beers.'

'I'll come with you,' he said and stood up.

Just at that moment there was a scream and Peter turned. He shaded his eyes.

'What is it?' I asked.

'Looks like someone's in trouble. Out there,' he said, pointing.

We'd gone to Zurriola because it was the surfing beach in San Sebastián. Not because we surfed, but because it meant young people. And that meant cooler beach bars. But also bigger waves. I saw a pink bathing cap bobbing up and down between the blue crests out there. Now I heard a woman behind us start shouting. I turned automatically towards the lifeguards' station, an overgrown stool on stilts a little further off down the beach. The chair was empty, and I couldn't see any lifeguard heading for the water. I can't remember making the decision; I just started to run without waiting for Peter who, for some obscure reason, was unable to swim.

I ran, keeping my knees high through the shallow water to get as far out as possible before I began swimming. The last thing I did before diving in – while I still had a clear view – was to fix on the direction of the person in the pink bathing cap out there. When I came back up to the surface and started doing my own version of the crawl, a self-taught but efficient enough technique, I said to myself that it was further out than it looked, and I would have to pace myself and find a rhythm that would let me breathe properly between strokes. How far out was she? Fifty metres? A hundred? It's hard to judge distances across water. At every tenth stroke I took a short break to check I was heading in the right direction. The waves weren't big enough to break out here, which was probably why there were no surfers in the water today, but they were still big enough for the girl to disappear – because it was a girl, I could see that now – every time I sank down into a trough. It couldn't be more than ten, maybe twenty metres now. She wasn't screaming any more; there had only been the one scream. So either she'd seen that help was on the way and was saving her strength, or else she didn't have the strength left to scream. Or else she wasn't in trouble at all, she'd just screamed, maybe a fish had brushed past her foot. This last possibility I dismissed as I was raised up by the next wave and saw the pink bathing cap disappear beneath the surface of the water in the trough below me. Up it bobbed again. Disappeared again. I filled my lungs, kicked out and dived down. I would probably have spotted her at once in sunshine and clear water, but because San Sebastián is famous for its clouds I saw only bubbles and shades of green in the dim light. I kept on swimming down. The water was darker and colder. I don't often think about death, but I did so now. It was the bathing cap that saved me. Or her. If it hadn't been such a striking colour I would probably never have seen her, because her swimsuit was black and her skin too dark. I came closer. She looked like a sleeping angel as she swayed there, weightless and swaying in the slight echoes of the waves that reached this far down. And it was so quiet. So lonely. Just her and me. I put one arm around her ribs beneath her breasts and pulled us back up towards the light. I felt her warmth against my arm, and what I persuaded myself was the slow beating of her heart. Then something strange happened. Just before we broke the surface she turned her head towards me and looked at me with large, dark eyes. Like someone risen from the dead, someone who had crossed over into a universe where people breathed water. The next moment, as our heads made the transition from the watery region to the aerial world, her eyes closed once more and she floated unmoving in my arms.

I heard shouts from the beach as I lay on my back in the water with the girl's head on my chest and kicked out for the shore. As we reached the shallows, Peter, the lifeguard and a man who said he was a doctor waded out to us and helped her onto dry land. I lay in the shallows, coughing up water and trying to recover my strength.

'Baywatch m-aaa-n.'

I opened my eyes. A man with a red beard and an equally red, sun-burned face was looking down at me. In a rudimentary way the wide grin was equipped with teeth, the kilt was dirty, as was the blue shirt which was – unless I was mistaken – in the colours of the Scotland football team.

'You're a true saviour,' he continued in his slurred but nevertheless comprehensible Scottish English as he helped me to my feet. Once we were on our feet, however, I was the one supporting him, for the man was roaring drunk.

'Question is, can you save me, *Baywatch* man? I need twenty euros to get to Pamplona.'

'I've got it, but I need the money myself,' I said, which was the truth.

I looked at the crowd of people further up the beach and noticed a middle-aged woman wearing an outfit that outdid the Scotsman's: hijab and bikini. She was standing bent over the doctor and Peter, whom I could just glimpse between the crowd of people as he knelt beside the girl. The woman alternated between sobbing and scolding, but no one seemed to be paying any attention to her. When I turned back to the Scotsman he was already on his way towards some of the other bathers. I walked over to join the crowd.

'How is . . . ?'

'She's breathing,' said Peter without looking up at me. 'We're waiting for an ambulance.'

He stroked the girl's face with his hand, partially obscuring it from me, so that all I could see was her forehead. On it, directly below her glistening black hairline, small downy tufts of soft hair that were already dry stirred in the slight breeze.

I felt a hand close around my arm and the woman in the bikini and the hijab spoke to me. It sounded Arabic, or Persian maybe, or perhaps Turkish. Or maybe I just thought that because she looked as though she came from that part of the world. Anyway, I didn't understand a word of what she said.

'English, please,' I said.

'Russkii?' she asked.

I shook my head.

'Daughter,' she said and pointed to the girl. 'Miriam.'

'Ambulance,' I said. She looked at me uncomprehendingly, reeled off several more words in the same foreign tongue and then squeezed my arm, as though the language barrier could be surmounted if only I concentrated hard enough.

'Hospital,' I tried, and mimed someone driving, but still got no response.

A distant siren sounded and faded on the breeze, and I pointed in the direction of the sound. The woman's face lit up.

'Aha, hospital,' she said, though I couldn't hear much difference from the way I had just said the word. The woman disappeared and came back carrying two bags just as the ambulance personnel came running with the stretcher from the ambulance parked in front of the line of bars. The doctor and the girl's mother walked alongside the stretcher. Peter and I stood watching them. Then, without a word, Peter grabbed up his phone from the towel and ran over to the ambulance. And there, to my great surprise, I saw him starting to talk to the mother. He entered something on the keypad, showed it to her, and she nodded in confirmation. Then the woman kissed him on the cheek and got into the ambulance which immediately drove off, this time without the siren.

'How did you communicate with her?' I asked Peter when he returned.

'I heard her ask if you spoke Russian.'

'Do *you* speak Russian?'

'A bit,' he smiled. 'Optional choice at my school.'

'And you chose Russian because . . . ?'

'Because at least half of all the really good research being done in physics is written in Russian.'

'Of course.'

'They're from Kyrgyzstan. Everyone from there over forty speaks a little Russian.'

'Anyway, she seemed pleased you could speak it.'

'Perhaps.'

'She kissed you.'

Peter laughed. 'My Russian is atrocious. From what I said she got the impression that I was the one who had rescued her daughter, and I –'

'You?'

Peter smiled again. He was a good-looking boy, but in the course of our trip – probably owing to what was, for him, an unusually spartan diet – his face had lost some of its childish rotundity, and the muscles were visible on the suntanned body that had, until recently, been slightly chubby.

'I didn't correct her.'

'Why not?' I asked, although I already had some idea.

'That girl's face,' he said, still smiling. 'And those eyes. When she regained consciousness and opened them ...' His voice had a dreamy quality that was quite unlike the Peter I knew who had, by his own account, no time for sentimentality. 'You should have seen her eyes, Martin.'

'I did,' I said. 'She opened them for a second or two while we were under the water.'

Peter wrinkled his brow. 'D'you think she saw you? I mean, d'you think she would recognise you as the man who saved her?'

I shook my head. 'Faces are very different underwater. I don't know if I would recognise her either.'

Peter turned his face up to the sun like a man who wanted to be dazzled. 'Do you have any objection, *old chap*?'

'To what?'

'To our pretending that I was the one who swam out to her.'

I didn't reply, because I wasn't sure what to answer.

'What an idiot I am,' said Peter, eyes closed and with that smile that seemed unwilling to leave his face. 'What does one dream of when one swims day in and day out, year after year, knowing that one will never be a world champion? Of course – that some day one will save someone from drowning and be celebrated as a hero. Perhaps even be awarded a medal so that, one day, one can tell one's children the story of how it was won. Am I right?'

I shrugged. 'Somewhere deep down inside there's probably some such stupid dream, yes.'

'And when at last it comes true, I ask you to let me take the credit. And all because of a pair of lovely eyes. Some friend I am!' He laughed, shaking his head. 'I must have got a touch of sunstroke. I asked the mother for her phone number so that I could call and make sure everything turned out all right the way the doctor said it would.'

'Jesus. You –'

'Yes, Martin! I must see those eyes again. Those eyebrows. That forehead. Those pale lips. And that body . . . my God, the girl's an absolute nymphet.'

'Exactly. A little too young for you, maybe?'

'Are you crazy? We're twenty-five. Nothing is too young for us!'

'I doubt she's more than sixteen years old, Peter.'

'In Kyrgyzstan they get married when they're fourteen.'

'You'd marry her if she was fourteen?'

'Yes!' He put his hands on my shoulders and shook me, as if I was the one who had gone mad. 'I'm in love, Martin. Do you know how many times that's happened to me?'

I thought about it. 'Two and a half. If you've been telling me the truth.'

'Never!' he said. 'Not that I was lying. I just thought I knew what love was. Now I know.'

'OK then,' I said.

'OK then what?'

'It's OK, you can be the one who saved her.'

'You mean that?'

'Yes, and if you'll stop shaking me and leave her alone if she's under eighteen then we've got a deal.'

'And you swear that you'll never, never tell her, or her mother, or anyone else?'

I laughed. 'Never,' I said.

That night I dreamed a strange dream.

Peter and I shared a room in one of the little hotels in old town, and the voices and laughter from the restaurants on the pedestrian street just below our open window, along with all the other street sounds and Peter's steady breathing from the bed on the other side of the room, mingled together and wove the stuff of which dreams are made.

I was – not surprisingly – underwater and had my arms around something I thought was a person, but when it opened its eyes I found myself looking into a pair of dark, bloodshot fish-eyes, like the ones Peter had been looking at on the fish counter outside the restaurant where we had eaten earlier in the evening. He had told me how the eyes told you most of what you needed to know about the fish we chose, but he was careful to squeeze the body, to get some idea of how fresh it was and its fat content, and then scrape his fingernail across the skin, because it seems that if they're factory fish, the scales flake off when you do that. Peter had taught me all sorts of elementary things about restaurant food such as this, and about wine too. Before meeting him it had never struck me that the background from which I came wasn't a particularly cultured one. I mean, in my family home we knew plenty about the latest trends in art, music, film and literature; but when it came to the classics and drama – which Peter had systematically made his way through since the age of twelve – he was way ahead of me. He could quote long passages from Shakespeare and Ibsen, although sometimes he showed a lack of understanding of their content and meaning. It was as though he employed the methodology of science to dissect even the most intensely emotional and aesthetically advanced texts.

I jumped when I saw the girl's fish-eyes; and as that slippery fish-body glided out of my arms, and she swam down into the darkness beneath us, I saw that the bathing cap was not pink but red.

I was woken by a light that came and went, as though someone were playing a torch back and forth across my eyelids. When I opened my eyes I saw that it was sunlight slipping between the curtains as they swayed in the morning breeze.

I got up, feeling the cool of the wooden floor against my feet in the large, sparsely furnished room, and pulled on my trousers and a T-shirt as I spoke to Peter's motionless back in the other bed.

'Breakfast time. You coming?'

The grunted reply suggested the after-effects of the wine the previous evening. Peter had no head for alcohol, or at any rate tolerated it worse than me.

'Want me to bring you something?'

'A double espresso,' he whispered hoarsely. 'I love you.'

I emerged into the sunshine and found an open pavement restaurant which, to my surprise, offered a good breakfast, unlike the usual tasteless Eurocrap you get in tourist joints.

I glanced through a Basque newspaper someone had left behind, looking maybe for some mention of the heroics on the beach the previous day, but since Basque is a language unlike any other I couldn't make out a word of it. Maybe Kyrgyz was too? Because that's what it would be called, wouldn't it? Kyrgyz or something like that? On the other hand, people say Pakistani, they don't say Pakis. Once I'd thought all this through without reaching any conclusion, eaten my breakfast and got a triple espresso to go in a paper cup, I returned to the hotel.

As I let myself into the room and put the cup down on the table beside Peter's empty bed I noticed that the rug on the floor was gone.

'Where's the rug?' I called in the direction of the bathroom where I could hear the unmistakable sound of Peter brushing his teeth. In case it contained the secret to white teeth, I had once considered making a closer study of his technique.

'Had to chuck it out, I puked up on it,' I heard from the bathroom.

Peter appeared in the doorway. And he did indeed look terrible. His face was grey, as though his tan had been washed off with chlorine, and there was a hint of dark rings around both eyes. He looked ten years older than the euphoric boy who had declared himself to be in love for the first time only a day earlier.

'Was it the wine?'

He shook his head. 'The fish.'

'Really?' I checked, but my own stomach seemed in good shape. 'Think you'll be better by this evening?'

Peter made a face. 'I don't know.'

We had booked the table at the Arzak four months ago. It had been a last-minute thing. We'd downloaded the menu and on the train through Europe eagerly planned our meal from start to finish in several different versions. It's no exaggeration to say I'd been really looking forward to it.

'You look as though you've just died,' I said. 'Come on, Lazarus, don't let a bit of rotten fish –'

'It's not only the fish,' he said. 'Miriam's mother just called.'

The serious expression on his face wiped the smile off mine.

'Apparently things aren't going as well as expected and she asked me to come to the hospital. No one there understands a word of Russian.'

'Miriam? Is she . . . ?'

'I don't know, Martin. But I've got to go over there at once.'

'I'll come with you.'

'No,' he said firmly as he stuck his bare feet into the kind of soft loafers people from his end of our town usually wore.

'No?'

'They only let visitors in one at a time, so they asked me to come alone. I'll call you when I know more.'

I was left standing in the middle of the floor, on the pale rectangle left by the rug, wondering whether he meant more about Miriam, or about our restaurant visit.

On my way out I saw the end of the rolled-up rug sticking out of a rubbish bin in the parking space behind the hotel. Thought of the stink of puked-up fish and hurried on by. I spent the day wandering aimlessly through the streets of San Sebastián. It was clearly a town for the rich. Not the Russian vulgarians, the importunate Arabs, the bellowing Americans or the smug nouveau riche from my own country. It was a town for those who take their wealth for granted, knowing at the same time that they are privileged. Who are neither proud nor ashamed of their position, who feel the need neither to hide nor to display the fact that they are wealthy. They drive cars that look like other people's cars and, in case you're interested, cost twice as much. In San Sebastián and other holiday towns they live in a kind of shabby, relaxed elegance in large summer houses hidden behind tall hedges, with rusting wrought-iron gates and facades that look as if they could use another coat of paint. Their clothes look comfortable and, to the uninitiated, nondescript, yet they have a discreet and timeless stylishness, bought in shops that Peter knows about, and can't understand that I don't, and that anyway I couldn't afford. The upper class can know a lot about the working class and the poor, and feel a deep fascination for them, especially if they can boast of great-grandparents who started out there. But they are often wholly ignorant of the upper-middle classes, those who are so keen to gain a foothold on the ladder that leads up to their own class. They're like city dwellers ignorant of even the most elementary aspects of life in their own immediate vicinity but fully conversant with all that is remote and exotic.

I walked through San Sebastián's broad streets, hearing the voices around me speaking Spanish, Basque, French and something that was possibly Catalan. But no Nordic languages. So I moved through the town as an outsider, the same way I had moved through Peter's social circle. His friends treated me with a courteous friendliness and hospitality and held open the doors to rooms they pretended not to know I had no right to enter.

'You must come to our Autumn Ball, Martin, absolutely *everyone*'s going to be there!'

The Stop signs began with what was correct 'attire'. The word simply means what you wear; but in their context it means not just a dinner jacket but the *right* dinner jacket. How to wear it, and all the other small and secret details that can – and do – expose you as the outsider you really are. The way that their glances – despite the welcoming exterior – can and do reveal that little touch of contempt they feel for outsiders whom, without thinking too much about it, they regard as pushy candidates to join their ranks, on the automatic assumption that everyone wants to be one of them. Because they know where their place is, and that is at the top of the food chain. That's to say, there's always room for someone even higher up, and that is where their attention is concentrated, on that next step up.

In that respect Peter was probably a little more laid-back than his friends. Not that he wasn't competitive once he'd set himself a goal. But he didn't seem driven by social ambition, more by curiosity and genuine enthusiasm. Of course, a person who is already accepted feels less need to be accepted, and I think that was what made Peter so classy and easy to like. Or so hard to dislike. And as his chosen one, some of this dripped onto me.

The girls in Peter's circle seemed to like me particularly. His accreditation was my entry ticket, at the same time as I was regarded as 'exciting', even a bit 'dangerous', which would have made the boys who knew me in my old neighbourhood laugh out loud. Though it was mild and pretty much smoothed out I still spoke with an East End accent, and Peter described me as an artist without the prefix 'wannabe' the word actually deserved. I'd spent a night or three with some of these girls without breaking any hearts. They seemed as satisfied with the no-strings brevity of things as I was. I'm guessing they referred to it as a 'fling' when they talked about it to their friends. Because that's exactly what it was: a slight sidestep away from their ordinary everyday reality. Because naturally they wouldn't want to get seriously involved with someone as unserious as a would-be artist from the East End of town, regardless of how cute and likeable he might be.

One of them had been an old flame of Peter's, a girl with an interest in horses. At a party at Peter's place she had – when I told her how I used to ride the old nag on my grandparents' farm – invited me to go riding with her. I told her I would have to ask Peter first if he thought it was OK.

Peter had just laughed. 'Go for it,' he said, giving me a punch on the upper arm. So I had. Perhaps at some point it had occurred to me that a romp in the hay with an upper-class girl wearing riding gear was an erotic cliché, but that didn't make it any the less enjoyable. Probably the opposite. But once I started enthusiastically relating what had happened to Peter I realised I had misjudged the situation. A slight tightening of the facial muscles, an almost imperceptible stiffness in his smile. So I lied, said I'd tried but that it hadn't worked out. I don't know why that seemed to make him like me better, because the way I told the story I hadn't had any qualms about trying to seduce my best friend's first girl-friend. I could only hope that she wouldn't say anything about that little 'fling' of ours. Because in that fraction of a second I had seen something, something in that stiff smile, something unknown and yet somehow also known, a Peter I didn't recognise, but who in some way or other I knew was there.

When I returned to the hotel I saw that the bin had been emptied. I went up to our room, lay down on my bed, closed my eyes and listened to the sounds coming through the window. It was something I'd noticed before, the way both natural sounds and the noises of cities and towns could change over the course of a day, as though following regular cycles ordained by routines, communal activities and daylight. Right now there was the shivering sound of a grasshopper or cicada, caused by the vibration of a membrane, a frenetic mating signal the male of the species was created to make and therefore could not help but make, a slave to his own sexual instincts.

When I awoke the room was in darkness, I had the taste of ashes in my mouth and what I had been dreaming slipped away from the grasp of memory. But there had been something about a flying carpet.

I looked at my watch. Eight thirty. The table was booked for nine. I checked my phone. Nothing from Peter. I called him, no reply. I sent an SMS consisting of a simple question mark. I waited ten minutes, then dressed and went out.

At five minutes past nine the taxi dropped me off outside the Arzak. It was on the ground floor of what appeared to be a residential block. The restaurant's name was on a narrow, arched awning above the entrance. There was no flashing sign, nothing displaying the three stars in the Michelin guide. I sent a text to Peter, said I hoped everything was OK, that I was outside the Arzak and was going to go in and wait at the table in case he was on his way.

This time the answer came at once.

Don't. Go back to the hotel now, I'm coming straight from the hospital and I'll meet you there. I'll treat you to the Arzak some other time.

I shoved the phone into my pocket and looked down the road for a taxi, but there wasn't a car in sight. I decided to enter the famous restaurant, explain the situation and perhaps get them to book a taxi for me. I was greeted by a maître d' wearing a red waistcoat. I offered my apologies for the fact that Peter Coates and companion were unable to come this evening, but that Coates had had to make a hospital visit. The maître d' glanced down at the evening's seating plan that was in front of him as I looked around. The restaurant was simply but tastefully furnished, stylish and homely at the same time. My parents would have liked it here if they could have afforded it, and maybe that's why I had the odd feeling of having been there before.

'But Mr Coates and companion are here, sir,' the maître d' said in a thick Spanish accent.

My mouth was gaping. He looked up at me.

'If there has been a misunderstanding, perhaps you want to talk to him, sir?'

'Yes,' I said without thinking. 'Yes, thank you.'

As I followed him I regretted it. The whole thing was obviously a misunderstanding; either the maître d' had gone cross-eyed or someone had taken our reservations. Anyway, there was nothing I could do about it now. I glanced down at my phone and Peter's message to make sure I hadn't misunderstood. When I looked up again and caught sight of her it seemed so obvious I was astonished it hadn't occurred to me before, at the same time as it was a complete surprise.

Peter sat with his back to me, and from his body language I could see he was talking animatedly about something, no doubt about our limited conceptions of space and time. She was silent. Her gaze wandered up past his shoulder and found mine. It was as though an electric shock passed through her. And through me. She was wearing a plain black dress. The eyes, or perhaps it was just the pupils, seemed almost unnaturally large and dark in the rather wide face. The mouth was wide too, with generous lips. But the rest was small. The nose, the ears, the shoulders, and there were no breasts visible beneath the fabric of her dress. Perhaps it was that slender, girlish young body that had made me suppose she was younger than I now saw she was. She was probably about the same age as Peter and me.

Her gaze held mine. Maybe I had awakened some dormant memory of the moment she looked at me under the water. She didn't look ill at all. Peter was still deep in his description of a reality he believed to be more real than the one which the three of us currently inhabited, but I knew it was only a matter of time before he noticed the expression on her face and turned.

I can't explain all the thoughts, the half-thoughts and beginnings of thoughts that then collided with one another and made me respond as I did, but I wrenched my gaze from hers, let it wander further as though it had not found what it was searching for, then turned on my heel and quickly left.

I pretended to be asleep when Peter let himself into our room at half past midnight.

He stood listening in the doorway, then silently undressed and got into bed without turning on the light.

'Peter?' I murmured as though I had just woken.

'Sorry,' he said. 'They wouldn't let me go.'

'Oh?' I said. 'How is the girl? Miriam, isn't it?'

'Still very weak, but she'll be all right.' In the darkness he made a yawning noise. 'Goodnight, Martin, I'm all in. Again, my apologies. We'll find a good restaurant in Pamplona.'

I was on the point of telling him. That I'd seen them in the restaurant. Expose him in triumph, make him laugh about it too, tell him that of course I appreciated his priorities, that naturally when he had obtained a table at the best restaurant in the world he took along the girl he was hoping to marry. Should bloody well think so too. That in potential life-changing situations like that, loyalty to your pals had to go by the board. And anyway this particular pal hadn't shown any particular interest in gourmet restaurants four months ago.

I would actually have said that, because Peter had shown more consideration than the situation required. Had he not, after all, been willing to lie to me and deceive me? Gone to all that unpleasant bother just so that I wouldn't feel hurt? But of course I didn't feel hurt! Well, yes, slightly. Hurt to think that he had so little faith in my consideration for him that I wouldn't completely understand when he preferred the company of the person who could be – if he played his cards right, in the small amount of time he had at his disposal – the love of his life.

But I didn't say it. I don't know why not. Maybe it was because I felt as though he was the one who should be doing the talking, and not leave it up to me to expose the lie. Anyway, the seconds ticked by. And at a certain point it was just too late. If I said something now it would no longer be something we could laugh about and he would lose face. Because in the course of those few seconds I had lied too. And in doing so, in pretending I knew nothing, I'd allowed him to develop the lie, to involve himself more intricately in it. If I exposed him now if I would drive a wedge of suspicion between us.

I closed my eyes. It was confusing. Very confusing.

I saw her eyes on the insides of my own eyelids. What did she know? About me, about Peter? Had she seen through the fiction that it was he who had saved her? Did she remember me? Was that what I had seen in her gaze? And if so – why hadn't she told him that she had seen me in the restaurant? No. No, she couldn't possibly remember, she had hardly been conscious. After a while I heard Peter's breathing, deep and even. And I fell asleep too.

Next morning Peter and I checked out, took a taxi to the railway station and boarded the train to Pamplona. It was packed, but fortunately we had tickets booked in advance. The journey inland and up to the heights took an hour and a half. We disembarked a little after nine, the air still cool, cooler than in San Sebastián though the sun shone from a cloudless sky.

We found the place where we were going to stay, a private house which, like so many others in the town, rented out rooms to tourists during the San Fermín festival.

The festival offered a wide range of activities, and I had read that for many Catholics and local people it was the religious processions, the folk dancing and theatre performances that were most important part of it. For aficionados of blood sports it was Hemingway's *Death in the Afternoon*, the bullfighting at the Plaza de Toros de Pamplona. For everyone else it was the bull running that took place every morning through the narrow, cobbled streets in the old part of town and ended up at the bullring.

Peter and I had agreed that we would do the bull running twice over the nine days the festival lasted, since we reckoned that the second time – when we knew what we were in for – would be very different from the first. Or as Peter put it: 'It'll be like two first times.' I hadn't thought about that, that there is also a first time for experiencing something for the second time.

After meeting our hosts and settling into our two small but clean rooms we went out to breakfast before Chupinazo, the ceremonial firing of a rocket from the balcony of the town hall at midday that marks the start of the festival. We stood in the square along with thousands of cheering, singing people, many of them wearing the white shirts and trousers and red neckerchiefs we had seen in photographs. The atmosphere was so electric that for a while I forgot all about what had happened in San Sebastián.

Our lodgings were less than a hundred metres from the town hall square, and yet it took us twenty minutes to make our way through the crowds that almost blocked the narrow streets. And we heard more languages here than we had done in San Sebastián. Outside a bar where the clientele had spilled out into the street we were offered wine for no other reason than that we had each bought our red neckerchiefs and Basque caps from a street vendor.

'I'm happy,' said Peter after we'd downed the sweet sangria, exchanged promises of eternal friendship with our new Spanish friends and moved on. I had, of course, noticed how he had been checking his phone every five minutes since early in the morning, but made no mention of it. After a short sleep we headed out again to eat churros and drink brandy. We followed the music, the stream of people and tried our hand at speaking all the languages we heard spoken around us. At some point around midnight we found ourselves in a small marketplace with a fountain where several young men formed a human pyramid from the top of which one of them dived, five metres above the cobblestones. He was caught by a human safety net consisting of six or seven other boys and girls. They repeated the feat, people cheering loudly every time, and suddenly I saw Peter standing up there. He spread his arms sideways, kicked off and dived. But when he crossed his own centre of gravity and his head was pointing directly downwards I felt as though the heart inside me stopped beating. There was a gasp from the watching crowd. Peter disappeared behind the ranks of people in front of me. Silence. And then once again the cheering rose up to the star-strewn sky.

'You're crazy!' I yelled as Peter appeared in front of me and we hugged each other. 'You might've been killed!'

'Peter Coates has already died a million times,' he said. 'If he dies young in this universe, he's still got countless others in which things can turn out well for him.'

I tried to hold on to that thought the next morning as, together with a group of other young men, most of them wearing white, we stood in front of a little statue in a niche in the wall of a house. We listened as a prayer was offered to the figure, who apparently represented the patron saint of San Fermín. It was now seven thirty, and on the way out of our house we'd seen people, young men mostly, sleeping off the night's drinking on the cobbles around the walls of the houses, huddled close to one another for warmth in the cool mountain air of the night. Now they were on their feet and ready for the day's bull run. The prayer consisted of a single sentence in Spanish and was for blessing and protection from the bulls. Peter and I joined in as best we could.

There was still half an hour before the run started, so we went to a bar – Jake's bar – for an espresso and brandy. On the counter I saw one of the newspapers that I had noticed several of the young men were carrying rolled up in their hands. I glanced through the paper, trying to pick up some of the Basque words, then gave in and studied the pictures instead. Most seemed dedicated to yesterday's opening ceremony and the day's bull run. Among them were photographs of what I assumed had to be the six bulls due in the streets that day, along with statistical information about them. To put it mildly they looked scary. I turned the page. As my gaze flitted across it, I stopped at one picture in particular. It was of a rug. Like the one on the floor of our room in San Sebastián. And I noticed the name of the town in the caption. I turned to Peter but saw his back disappearing in the direction of the toilet. I therefore leaned towards the man standing next to me and asked politely and in English if he could translate for me. He shook his head with a smile: 'I'm Spanish.'

The barkeeper – busy filling a glass with brandy – must have overheard us, because he turned the newspaper towards him and studied it for a few moments.

'The police have found an unidentified corpse at the municipal dump in San Sebastián. It was wrapped up in a rug.'

The barkeeper disappeared towards the other end of the bar, and I was left sitting there staring at the picture. It was obviously a very common type of rug because Peter had said that, when he paid the proprietor for it, it cost so little it wouldn't have been worth trying to have it cleaned anyway.

When Peter returned he looked pale.

'Stomach OK?' I asked.

He nodded and smiled. He was holding his phone in his hand. During the night, going back and forth to the toilet in the corridor, I had heard the low voice coming from his room. Since he had not once during the course of our trip spoken to anyone back home I assumed the call was with her. Miriam. And I made up my mind to tell him so, after the bull run. Just in a casual sort of way: 'Oh, by the way, I heard you talking last night. Who was it? Miriam?' It might be enough to get Peter to start telling the whole story. Or at least relax a bit and talk the way he usually did, spontaneously and openly. Sure, he was friendly, the way he always was. But there was a watchfulness there now, a caution. I had put it down to guilty conscience combined with the effort required to make sure he didn't reveal what had actually happened. But looking at Peter now I knew I wouldn't be asking him about Miriam. Nor about anything else either.

Peter exhaled, long and heavy, the way an athlete does at the start of a race. 'Shall we go?'

At eight precisely there came the distant boom of a cannon. That was the rocket being fired further down in the old town, the signal that the bulls had been released. Along with another fifty or so runners we were standing at a spot we had been told was well suited to first-timers. It was about halfway along the 800-metre route, and now it was a matter of keeping the nerves steady until we caught sight of the bulls, and not starting to run too early.

Two girls who had climbed up onto the barricade across the side street where we were standing started laughing down to us, showering us with sangria from two leather bottles and staining our white T-shirts red. I shouted: 'Jake's bar después' – afterwards – which made them, and those standing around us, cheer loudly and blow kisses in our direction.

'Concentrate now,' said Peter quietly into my ear. 'Listen.' He looked serious. And now I heard it too. A low throbbing, like the sound of approaching thunder. Some of the runners around us, probably first-timer tourists like ourselves, were unable to control their nerves any longer and started to run. Then we caught sight of the first runners as they rounded the corner fifty metres away from where we were standing. And behind them came the bulls. The runners pressed themselves up against the walls of the houses to let the great beasts rage past them. Behind them some had fallen, others on top of them, and I saw a bull butting into the helpless pile, saw even at that distance how the white horns emerged red, and the blood spouted from the human pile, like the sangria from those leather bottles. I had been told that the bulls will attack anything lying down that moves. So if you fell, you were not to move, not even if you got trampled.

I saw two men in white start to run.

'Now!' I said and set off. I ran along the walls of the houses on the left side of the street. Peter was alongside me. I half turned and saw a huge beast with enormous horns which I realised, from the white patches, was only a cow, sent out with the bulls to calm them down and show them the way. But then directly behind the cow came something else altogether. A black colossus. I felt as though my heart had stopped beating, though probably the opposite was the case and it was beating faster than ever. Half a ton of muscle, horn, testosterone and fury. And it struck me that if I gave Peter a push now, just enough to make him lose his balance, he'd slip on the smooth cobblestones, and no matter how dead he tried to play, in a matter of moments he'd be the target for the killing machine behind us.

'Here!' I shouted, pointing to the barricade across the side street next to us, jumping for the wooden wall and grabbing the top. Peter did the same. Eager hands held us and pulled us up and over onto the other side and down among the singing spectators. A leather bottle of wine was pressed to my lips as though it were first aid. I saw the same thing happening to Peter and we laughed, gasping for breath, laughing and gasping for breath.

We returned to our rooms to rest and wash off the sticky sangria, adrenaline-stinking sweat and dust. When I met Peter in the corridor to use the shower after him he was wearing only a towel around his waist and had a small tattoo on his left pectoral, an M with a heart round it.

'Hey!' I said, pointing. 'When . . . ?'

'In San Sebastián,' was all he said.

'So this is really serious?'

'Yes.'

'But shouldn't you have a plaster on a fresh –'

'I didn't want it to look fresh,' he said. 'I asked the tattooist to make it look as though I'd always had it.'

And looking closer I could see he'd done a good job, and that the tattoo did actually look a little faded.

Peter wanted to catch up on a bit of sleep, but I said I was going out for some breakfast and to see if those girls had turned up at the bar. As I squeezed my way through the narrow streets I picked up the news that two people, a man and a woman, had been gored during the bull run and were fighting for their lives in the hospital.

On the way past Jake's I heard a girl's voice: '*Hola*, Mister Bull Runner!'

I shaded my eyes. And sure enough – there in the dim interior were the two girls from the barricade. I went in, ordered a baguette and a bottle of water and listened to their eager chattering in a mixture of Spanish and English. They were local, from a country village just outside Pamplona. The one who spoke the best English, a well-built blonde girl with kind, sparkling eyes, was studying in Barcelona. She said she always came back for San Fermín but that a lot of the people in Pamplona – including their parents – were really tired of all the tourists, the drunken parties and general disturbance, and usually left town and stayed away until it was all over.

'During San Fermín the parties are even wilder in the villages,' she said. 'And the drink is much cheaper. Here the price for a beer is crazy when San Fermín. Come with us!'

'Thank you, I have to be somewhere,' I said. 'But maybe tomorrow?' I got the blonde's phone number, ate the breakfast baguette and left.

At the railway station I had to wait an hour for my train, and I arrived in San Sebastián in the middle of the siesta, so most of the shops and places to eat were closed. I asked the taxi driver to take me to the police station.

He dropped me off by the river, in front of two modernist – or maybe

I should say postmodernist – blocks that looked like slices of cake. Twenty minutes later I was sitting in the office of Imma Aluariz, a plain-clothes detective. She was older than me, in her mid-thirties maybe. Small, a bit stocky and with a severe face, and a pair of brown eyes that, it seemed to me, could turn soft if they saw something they liked. After listening to me for two minutes she called a number and at once a young man entered and explained that he was an interpreter. It took me a little by surprise, since Inspector Aluariz's English had been good. But as this was a murder case they probably wanted to avoid any possibility of misunderstandings.

I explained that my friend and I had had a rug identical with the one in the newspaper, that it had been tossed into the bin behind the guest house because my friend had been sick on it. The two of them looked at the address of the guest house and said a few words to each other in Basque. Aluariz put her fingertips together and looked at me.

'Why,' she said slowly and ponderously, as though to convey that the question demanded an equally slow and well-considered reply, 'do you come here?'

'Because,' I said, automatically echoing her slow rhythm, 'I thought it might help you in the investigation.'

Aluariz nodded slowly and seriously, and yet it was as though she were supressing a mocking smile. 'Most people would not come from Pamplona just to tell us they have seen a carpet that is . . .' She glanced at the interpreter, who was still standing.

'Similar,' he said.

'Similar to the one in the newspaper.'

I shrugged. 'I also came in case you found vomit on the carpet. Or bits of skin from my toes, because I walked barefoot on it. So . . .' I looked at them. Obviously they understood where I was going with this, but still they declined to conclude the reasoning process for me. 'DNA could have made us suspects, I suppose.'

'Have you or your friend had your DNA tested by the police?'

'No. I mean, I haven't. I also doubt if my friend have ever been in contact with law enforcement.' Too late – and to my considerable irritation – I heard that I had said *have* where I should have said *has*. On the other hand, I had used *law enforcement*, which seemed to me a pretty elegant phrase. But why did I think of that now? Why did it matter to me what sort of impression I was making?

'There was no *vómito* on the carpet,' said Aluariz.

'Oh,' I said. 'Well, in that case . . .'

'. . . there's no case,' she concluded for me.

What did I feel? Was it a mild sense of disappointment?

Imma Aluariz put her head on one side. 'But just to rule you out, would you agree to give us your DNA, Mister Daas?'

'Of course,' I said. 'If you can tell me about the case.'

'What do you mean?'

'The victim. Is it a woman or a man? Cause of death? Any suspects?'

'We don't make deals like that, Mister Daas.'

I felt myself blushing. And maybe she found the blushing a sympathetic trait, because for whatever reason she changed her mind.

'It's a man in his mid-twenties. Naked, no marks, no papers, that's why we can't identify him. Blunt force to his head. No suspects yet.'

'Thank you,' I said.

'Everything I just said was in the news,' she said.

'In Basque,' I said.

For the first time I saw her smile, and I had been right about the eyes.

It was siesta time at the forensic department where I was to give my DNA sample, so I arranged with Aluariz to return later in the afternoon. In the meantime I took a taxi to Hospital Universitario Donostia. It was an enormous place, but the queue at the reception desk was short. It took me some time, however, to persuade the woman behind the desk to help me. I explained that I had saved a certain Miriam from drowning, that she had been brought here, that I had met her directly after she was discharged, that she'd travelled on with her mother, but that she'd left a ring behind and that I needed her full name and hopefully a telephone number. I was able to tell her that Miriam hailed from Kyrgyzstan and give the date and approximate hour of her admission. The receptionist looked sceptical but directed me to the Casualty Department. Once there I had to repeat the lie, but did so with greater conviction this time, now that I'd had a little practice at it. But the young woman in the glassed booth just shook her head.

'Unless you can show me some proof you're her next of kin I can't give you any information about the patient.'

'But . . .'

'If there's nothing else, we are very busy here.'

She was wearing white trousers and a white shirt, and I could just see her running in front of the bulls. And getting gored. A second woman who had been looking through a drawer in a filing cabinet behind the one in white had obviously overheard us. She came to the desk, leaned over the first woman's shoulder and tapped on the keyboard. They both looked at the screen, the light from it reflected in the glasses worn by the second woman.

'It looks as though we did admit a patient from the Zurriola beach at that particular time, yes,' she said. I saw there was a *Dr* in front of the name on the ID card pinned to the breast pocket of her white coat. 'We're sorry, but our duty of confidentiality is very strict. If you'd like to leave a message and your contact details with us, we will send a message to the patient.'

'From here I'm heading directly off for a few days walking in Andorra, so I won't be contactable either by phone or mail,' I lied. 'I think among the admission details it might say that a Spanish doctor went with her in the ambulance.'

'Yes, and I know who he is, but he doesn't work at this hospital.'

'But you can give him the patient's details, and he can decide whether or not to give them to me. You can tell him I was the guy who brought the girl ashore.'

The doctor hesitated, studying me. I had the feeling she knew this wasn't just about a forgotten ring. Then she pulled out a phone and tapped in a number. A quick conversation in Spanish ensued as she continued to study me, as though describing me to the person on the other end. She hung up, tore a sheet of paper from the block next to the keyboard, looked at the screen, and wrote something down. Handed the sheet of paper to me.

'*Buena suerte*,' she said, and gave me a brief smile.

'Hello?'

I had never heard the voice before, and yet I knew it was hers.

I stood outside the hospital, a warm wind in my face and the phone pressed to my ear.

'I'm Martin,' I said. 'I'm Peter's friend.'

'It's you,' was all she said.

'I'm in San Sebastián and have a couple of hours before I have to be at the police station. Do you fancy a coffee?'

'Do I *fancy*?' she laughed. It was good, spontaneous laughter, the kind you want to hear all the time.

'Like,' I said. 'Would you *like* a coffee?'

'I would both like and fancy a coffee, Martin.'

'It's you,' she said again as half an hour later she stood at my pavement table outside the same bar where I had breakfasted the previous day. The gusting wind made her loose-fitting, hippie frock and raven-black hair sway around her. With one hand she made vain efforts to keep the hair out of her face, where it partially obscured the generous mouth and the dark eyes. I stood up and held out my hand. Her build was slight, but she was taller than I remembered. As I had watched her cross the open cobblestoned square towards the bar her slow, hip-swinging walk made me think that she had perhaps once worked on a catwalk.

'I'm so glad you were able to come,' I said.

We sat down. She sighed, smiled and gave me a long look, open and fearless. The skin was dark, lighter where it was slightly pockmarked. Her face wasn't quite as beautiful as I had recalled from the restaurant, although she had probably been wearing make-up then. But I saw what Peter had seen. The eyes. They shone with such an intense light, giving her a presence that was almost intrusive. And the white teeth, the front two crooked. And of course, the eyebrows. Heavy, with a natural, slanting pattern in them, like the feathers of a bird.

'We've seen each other before,' she said.

'So you remember?' I said, signalling to the waiter.

'Don't you?'

I looked at her again. 'You looked different on the beach. Your eyes were closed.'

'Not on the beach,' she said.

'*Si, señor?*'

I looked up and ordered two espressos, with a quick glance at Miriam to check the order.

'Triple,' she said.

'Mine too.'

The waiter disappeared.

'Why this place in particular?' she said.

'I ate breakfast here. Peter and I stayed over there.' I pointed to the guest house on the far side of the square. Saw that the window of our room on the fourth floor was closed.

Miriam turned. 'Wow, it looks nice. How was the breakfast?'

'Breakfast?'

'I love breakfasts. Unfortunately it looks like they're the same wherever you go in Europe. At least, they are in the towns we've visited. Expensive and taste of nothing.'

I nodded. 'It's good here. The coffee is too.'

She was still looking over at the guest house, giving me the chance to study her more closely. The neck, the throat. The shoulders, which were bony and reminded me of a skinny cat.

'Was it expensive to stay there?' she asked.

'No, it's cheap. At least, considering where it is. But the rooms are simple.'

'Simple is fine.' She turned to face me again. 'Mamma and I are looking for somewhere cheaper than where we're staying now.'

Yes, I thought. Simple is fine.

'Do you work as a model?' I asked.

'Wow,' she said, and rolled her eyes.

I laughed. 'Yeah, yeah, I know it's a corny pickup line. Do you want to know why I ask?'

'Because I'm skinny?'

'Because you walk like a model, and that's not an especially efficient way of moving from point A to point B.'

'So a bit like my swimming then.'

'And because models often dress badly. Not badly as in tasteless, but it's as though they want to show the world that they really don't care about appearances and all that superficial stuff. And also – of course – that they can make even boring clothes look good.'

'Are you implying that my dress doesn't look good?'

'Well, what do you think?'

'I think you're trying a bit too hard to convince me you're intelligent and interesting.'

'Apart from the *too hard* bit, how am I doing?'

The sun had discovered a gap in the clouds and she blinked her eyes shut and conjured up a pair of large sunglasses.

'As models, when we're at work we're forced to wear so many outfits that are uncomfortable to walk in that in our free time we prefer comfort to the wow factor. But of course we're also hoping the garment we bought at the flea market or took from Grandma's wardrobe will become the latest fashion after we've worn it.'

'Nice try, but now I know you're not a model.'

She laughed. 'I'm not?'

'You didn't get out your sunglasses to hide the fact that you were lying, but once you had them on it seemed like a good idea to take the opportunity to do so.'

She placed her elbows on the edge of the small, round and unsteady metal table, supporting her chin in her palms, and smiled at me. '*Now* you seem a bit smart and interesting.'

'Do you often lie?'

She shrugged. 'Not often, but it happens. What about you?'

'Same here.'

'You lie to friends and girlfriends?'

'That's two different questions.'

She laughed. 'True enough. Friends, then?'

I thought of Peter. About the fact that I had travelled in secret to San Sebastián, contacted Miriam and was now sitting here with her. If I had wanted to meet her, all I had to do was ask him for her number. Not that I would have got it. But he had lied, so why shouldn't I be allowed to lie a bit too?

'Always,' I said.

'Always?'

'I'm kidding. It's one of Socrates' paradoxes. About the man from Crete who says that Cretans lie all the time. Ergo it can't be true that all —'

'It wasn't Socrates who said that, it was Epimenides.'

'Oh? Are you calling me a liar?'

She didn't laugh, just gave a slight groan. And from the way my ears were burning I knew I was blushing.

'So what are you then?' I asked.

'Student.'

'History? Philosophy?'

'And English. A bit of everything. And nothing.'

She sighed, pulled out a shawl and tied it round her head the way her mother had worn it, though it looked as though Miriam was doing it to keep her hair under control. 'And refugee.'

'What are you fleeing from?'

The sun vanished again, and the next gust of wind was immediately cooler.

'A man,' she said.

'Tell me about it.'

The waiter put our coffee cups down in front of us. She took off her sunglasses and stared down into hers.

Miriam described how she had grown up with her parents in Almaty in Kazakhstan. I could remember my father talking about Almaty – or Alma-Ata as it was called in those days – and world skating records set thanks to the thin air and the special angle at which the wind came down from the mountains that meant you had it at your back all the way round the track. Miriam's father had been in the oil business, and they had been members of the new financial upper class in that large and sparsely populated land.

'Corruption and censorship, a dictator who renames the capital city after himself, the biggest country in the world without a coastline. And yet we were happy there. Up until the time my father disappeared.'

'Disappeared?'

'He'd threatened to blow the whistle on some Americans who got hold of oil rights by bribing government officials. I can remember him saying I should be careful about what I said on the phone. And then one day he didn't come home from work. We were told nothing, and we never heard from him again. My mother noticed how the privileges we used to enjoy started disappearing one by one, and we had to move from the house because they said it belonged to the oil company. We set off on what I thought was a holiday to Kyrgyzstan, where my mother's family come from, but we never returned home.'

Miriam described Kyrgyzstan as a more beautiful but poorer version of Kazakhstan. And more open. 'At least people weren't afraid to say something bad about the dictator,' she laughed. But more old-fashioned too, even in the capital, Bishkek. For example, *ala kachuu*, bride-kidnapping, was practised there. Even though it was officially against the law, people reckoned that a third of all marriages came about because the husband had kidnapped his future wife and he and his family forced her to marry him.

'Mamma's family had money. Not a lot, but enough to enable me to study in Moscow. And each time I came back home to Mamma, the life in Kyrgyzstan seemed more and more . . . far away. It's so . . .' She threw open her hands. Long, slender fingers with bitten nails. 'You know, a lot of people in Kazakhstan want to get rid of the "stan" ending, because they don't want to be associated with that type of land. Like these oligarchs who try to disguise their country accents. Well, in Kyrgyzstan they don't even try, people are just so smug and satisfied with who they are. I'd got used to all the comments from the men in the streets – I ignored them – and I hadn't even noticed this one little guy who just stood there at the bar staring when me and my cousins had a drink at the hotel bar. Then one evening as we were on our way in as usual two men grabbed me while two others held my cousins back and I was dragged away to a car and driven off.'

I could see she was trying to tell me all this in a matter-of-fact way, as though it was just a curious and even comical story, but the slight tremor in her voice betrayed her.

'I sat between two men in the back seat, and when I asked them what they were doing they said I was to marry the son of the man sitting in the passenger seat. I started crying, and the man turned and gave me what was supposed to be a comforting smile. He was all dressed up for the wedding, an overweight guy about fifty, with more gold teeth than real ones. And sweating, because it was a warm day. He said: "My boy will love you, and you will love him." Just that simple. When we arrived, we were led into a big house. There were men standing outside – they looked as if they were keeping watch. One of them had a rifle. I didn't know it at the time, but the man in the passenger seat was Kamchy Kolyev, head of the mafia that controls the cemeteries in Bishkek. If you want a grave you have to buy it from him.

'There was a thin young man standing just inside the doorway. He was wearing a black suit and a *kalpak*, which is a traditional hat men wear at weddings and funerals. He looked almost as afraid as me and just stared. There was a crowd of people behind him, obviously wedding guests, and an old woman – I think it was his grandmother – tried to put a white shawl over me. I knew that if I allowed her to do it that meant I agreed to the marriage, because I'd heard these horror stories about *ala kachuu* before, I just never thought it could happen to me. But just like in all those stories I'd heard, I was so scared I didn't dare to resist. All the guests clapped, I was given a glass of *arak* – vodka – and told to drink it down, and then the ceremony got under way. They had taken my mobile phone away, and someone was watching me the whole time, so it was impossible to warn anyone or run off. I cried and I cried, and the women tried to comfort me. "It'll be better when you have children," they said. "You'll have something else to think about. And the Kolyev family will look after you, they're good people, rich and powerful. You're luckier than many of the others here in this room, so dry your tears, girl." I asked the boy I had just that moment married why me. He actually blushed. "I saw you several times in the hotel bar," he said. "But you're so beautiful, so I didn't dare to talk to you." So when his father had forced him to pick out a girl he'd like to marry he'd pointed to me, and they checked and found I wasn't already married. As he was telling me this I felt almost as sorry for him as I did for myself. And then it got dark outside, and my husband and I were led up to the next floor, to our bedroom, like two prisoners being led to their cell.'

Miriam gave a little laugh and the two tears – one from each eye – that rolled down her cheeks were so clear that I almost didn't see them.

'We were locked in, and a guard and three women – relatives of the boy – sat outside, obviously to follow what was going on inside. I pleaded with him to leave me alone, but the boy held me down on the floor and tried to take my clothes off. But he couldn't do it, partly because he was a little shrimp and not much stronger than me, and partly because he was so drunk. But when he whispered in my ear that if I didn't let him do it he would have to get help, I let him do it. We got into the bed, and he tried to penetrate me, but he was too drunk. He was almost in tears himself, the poor thing, said his father would kill him. So I comforted him and whispered that I wouldn't say anything, and he thanked me. Then I made a few passionate noises for the benefit of the people outside, and he started to laugh so I had to hold a pillow over his face. When I took it away again I thought for a moment I had suffocated him. But then he began to snore. I waited until I heard the women leaving and then I sneaked out of bed. I put on the boy's dark suit – like I said, he was small – and only the shoes were too big. I opened the wallet and took out a few *soms*, enough for a taxi home. Then I put his *kalpak* on, hid my hair inside it, opened the window, dangled from the sill and dropped down onto the grass. It was dark and had started to rain and several of the other guests were leaving. Kyrgyzstan is Muslim, but the prohibition in the Koran against alcohol isn't taken as seriously as, for example, the marriage vow, if I can put it like that. Luckily for me. So I just walked out of the gate through the drunken guests and guards without anyone reacting. Further down the road I hailed a taxi and got home. The following day my mother and I each packed a suitcase and with the little bit of money we had we took an early flight to Istanbul.'

'You fled?'

Miriam nodded. 'The Kolyev family would never have accepted it if I didn't live with the boy I had married. It's a question of honour and respect. Without respect even Kolyev is nothing. They really have no other choice.'

'But you'd been kidnapped! Why not report it to the police and ask for protection?'

Miriam gave a short laugh. 'You live in another world, Martin. They are Kolyev and Mamma and I are two penniless women from Kazakhstan. In the eyes of the authorities I'm a runaway who was legally married in the presence of Kyrgyzstani witnesses and they would say it was done freely. So I would be trying to get out of my matrimonial vows.'

I was about to protest that she could also produce witnesses to the kidnapping, but realised that, of course, she was right: I was the one living in another world, the one where might is not right – at least, not always.

'How long ago was all this?' I asked.

'Three months. Fled. Survived. Moved on every time we felt Kolyev's people getting close.'

'A lot of towns?'

Miriam nodded.

'And how long will you be able to finance this flight?'

She shrugged.

'It must be hell,' I said.

'The worst thing is,' said Miriam, 'that I've ruined my mother's life. For the second time. Sometimes I've even wished that she'd taken the easy way out and encouraged me to accept the marriage – then at least I could have fled on my own and taken my chances. But then, of course, she knew that if she'd stayed behind, Kolyev would have used her to get to me. Whatever, the way things are, I'm a millstone around her neck. So I feel as responsible for my mother as she does for me.'

Maybe it was the association between a millstone and drowning, but a crazy thought occurred to me. That Miriam had swum out into the waves so that she wouldn't be a millstone around her mother's neck any more. But it wasn't something I was going to ask her about. I looked up into the sky. We were some distance from the sea, and yet the air tasted salty.

'You look upset,' she said, raising her cup to her lips. 'Hope I haven't given you a guilty conscience or something. I didn't mean to.'

'Guilty conscience?'

'I know you can't help us. That isn't why I said yes to the coffee.'

Of course I had a guilty conscience. But that was on account of other things. Not only had I neglected to tell Peter of my plans in San Sebastián, but I also wouldn't be telling him when I got back either.

'Why did you say yes?' I asked.

She put her head on one side. 'Because you're Peter's friend.'

'Because you think Peter can help you?'

She nodded. 'He says he wants to.'

'Is that why you went to the Arzak with him?'

She nodded again.

'Not because he saved you from drowning?'

She didn't reply, merely brushed a lock of hair from her face and looked at me.

'Did you recognise me when I walked into the Arzak?' I asked.

'From where?'

'Yes, from where?' I asked. I had no intention of breaking the promise I had given to Peter, that I would let him be the one who had rescued her. But if she remembered me, remembered those seconds under the water when we had looked at each other, then that wouldn't be breaking any promise.

'But you remember seeing me there?'

'There was something familiar about you,' she said. 'But it was more like . . .'

'Déjà vu?'

'Exactly. As though you were someone I had met in exactly that way, only I'd never been at that restaurant before.'

'Like a glimpse into a parallel universe.'

'Does that sort of thing interest you too?'

I laughed. 'Peter says he's going to study it. We'll see how far he gets. But you said something on the phone. You said, "It's you." As though you'd been expecting me to show up. Was that another déjà vu?'

'Perhaps. Your voice . . .' She glanced out over the square, watchful. 'I honestly don't know. It's really quite confusing, isn't it?'

I took out my wallet. 'I have to go to the police station,' I said. 'Want to come with me?'

'Why?'

'To give a –'

'No. Why should I come with you?'

I shrugged. 'Peter doesn't know that I'm here. Can we agree to leave it that way?'

'No,' she said. 'I don't lie. Not to friends, at least.'

'Is that what he is? A friend?'

'Yes.'

'And if he's in love with you?'

'If he is then it's his problem.'

'But then what would you do? Let him help you and your mother anyway?'

She looked at me with a kind of surprised indignation. 'I'm not sure you and I know each other well enough for you to ask me that kind of insinuating question, Martin.'

'You've just told me your most intimate personal story, Miriam. If I want to, I'm thinking I can sell the information to this Kolyev for a pretty good price. But you trust me. Do you know why you trust me?'

'No, I don't,' she said, shoving her chair back from the table as though about to get up and leave.

'You don't trust me, or you don't know why?'

'The last one,' she said curtly.

'Instinct,' I said. 'You might have suspected that Peter sent me to find out what your motives are, but you know that's not why.'

'Then why are you here?'

'Because I love you.'

It was as though the sky had fallen inside my head. Not because it wasn't true – I had loved her from the moment I looked into her eyes under the water. Or before that. Yes, before. What happened under the water happened for the second time. I can't put it any other way, it was my own déjà vu. The reason that the San Sebastián clouds and sun and sky came tumbling down like that was because I said it out loud. It was like stepping outside present reality, like breaking through a glass ceiling or a fake sky, like emerging from this *Truman Show* reality into another one. Maybe no more real than the false one – maybe this one too had its fake sky and its hidden audience – but the two of them together were a little bit truer than just the one by itself, of that much I was certain. Miriam stood up, and when I lifted my gaze to look at her face I was blinded by the low sun and saw nothing until she was gone.

'That's that,' said Inspector Imma Aluariz as she accompanied me from the forensic laboratory back along the corridor to the lift. 'You should be back in Pamplona before the festival gets going again.'

I nodded. It hadn't taken long. A long cotton bud held by a man wearing latex gloves, a swab in my mouth and – as Aluariz had summed things up – that was that.

'Only one other thing,' she said as she pressed the lift button. 'You asked who the deceased was.'

'I was just curious to . . .'

'Shall we take a look at him?'

The lift doors parted in front of us and she gestured with her hand for me to enter first. She followed me in and pressed the button with (– 1) on it.

'Forensics are down in the basement, so this won't take long,' she said.

'I really don't need to –'

'Just to confirm whether or not the victim is someone you've seen before. It would be helpful for us.'

We stood in silence as the lift descended with a low rumbling sound, the kind of sound effects that, as Peter had once pointed out, people accept in films from space, even though they should know that absence of atmosphere means absence of sound.

Down in the basement we headed along a corridor. There were fewer lights, fewer people. The ceiling was lower, the temperature lower. And yet I began to sweat. My hands were clammy, my heart beating faster.

We passed through a couple of doors, Aluariz placing the card hanging on a cord around her neck against the card reader, and suddenly we were in an ice-cold room. Standing in front of us was a man dressed like a surgeon, obscuring the view of a steel bench with a light blue sheet covering what I realised must be a corpse. The way he was standing, and the short, wordless nod the two exchanged, made me realise that our entry was something they had planned. And when he jerked the sheet aside as though it were an unveiling I saw that their eyes were not on the body, they were watching me. In other words, the encounter had been set up in order to observe my response. And perhaps because I realised this I was able to moderate and hide at least some of my surprise.

'You seem shocked,' said Aluariz.

'Sorry,' I said. 'I've never seen a corpse before.'

'Have you seen this person before?'

I pretended to be thinking about it. Then I slowly shook my head.

'Never. Sorry.'

I left the police station after giving them my address in Pamplona and a promise to keep them informed of my whereabouts if I moved on over the next fourteen days, until the results of the DNA test were in. In the taxi on the way to the railway station I looked at my hands. They were still shaking.

The last train to Pamplona had already gone, but I knew there were plenty of buses around the time of San Fermín. But when I approached a ticket kiosk at the bus terminal I was told that all the buses were full and that the first available seat was on an early-morning bus leaving in time for the start of *el encierro*, the bull run. Out in the street I hailed a taxi, asked the driver how much to take me to Pamplona. He quoted a price that was way beyond my means, and when I tried to bargain he just shrugged apologetically and said: 'San Fermín.' So instead I asked him to take me to a reasonably priced place in San Sebastián where I could spend the night, and he waited while I bought a ticket for the 05.30 bus.

I tried two places. Both were fully booked, both said that every other place they knew of was full too. So I got the taxi driver to drop me off at the place where Peter and I had stayed. Though it had been a large double room it hadn't cost any more than the singles I'd been looking at. I stood in the back yard, and as the proprietor opened the door of his flat he showed no signs of recognising me. Maybe that's what happens when you see hundreds of new arrivals every year.

'Full,' was all he said.

I explained which room I'd been in, that just an hour earlier it had appeared to be vacant.

'Yes, but guest looking now,' he said in his broken English.

'I'll take it,' I heard a familiar voice saying behind me.

I turned round.

Miriam was standing with the proprietor's wife.

'For how long?' asked the proprietor.

'Indefinitely,' said Miriam, and looked at me.

'*Perdón?*'

'Sorry,' she said without taking her eyes off me. 'A long time, I think.'

'I hadn't expected to see you again quite so soon,' Miriam said as we walked along the bank of the wide river that winds through the town. Its name, she had told me, was the Urumea.

'Were you expecting to see me again at all?' I asked.

Miriam had called her mother and they had agreed they didn't need to move in until the next day, so I would be able to spend the night there.

'Well, you say you're Peter's best friend, so yes,' she said.

I smiled. '*Say?* You mean a real best friend doesn't tell his pal's girlfriend that he's in love with her?'

'Peter and I aren't a couple.'

'Or his chosen one.'

'I don't like to be chosen.'

'But maybe they're right this time, those voices whispering in your ear that, after all, you *have* been lucky, and there's no need for tears. Peter's a nice lad. And he's rich enough to be able to help you and your mother.'

She stopped, turned towards the river and looked across to the other side.

'It's not that simple,' she said.

'I know it isn't,' I said. 'You've got a responsibility to your mother as well as to yourself. It's a moral dilemma. If you want his help you have to give him hope that there might be something between the two of you. In other words you need to lie.'

She snorted. 'Why is that lying? I can't know right now whether or not I can love him.'

'Oh yes, you know.'

'Oh?'

'Because you love me.'

She laughed, shook her head and carried on walking. I quickly caught up with her.

'You do,' I said. 'You just don't know it yet.'

'You know what the difference is between you in the West and us out here? We can't get enough of romantic books and films, but where you come from you think they're true.'

'Maybe,' I said. 'But now and then you get a story like that which actually turns out to be true. And this is one of those stories.'

'How many girls have you used that on, Martin?'

'A couple. I probably wasn't lying, but I was mistaken, they weren't one of those stories. This time I'm not mistaken. *We're* not mistaken.'

'*We?* You know nothing about me, Martin. Do you realise how long we've known each other?'

'No,' I said. 'I've thought about that, but I don't know. Do you?'

She slackened her pace. Then stopped completely. 'What do you mean?'

I shrugged. 'From the first time I saw you, the first time I spoke to you, I've had this constant feeling of déjà vu. It's as though everything that's happening has happened before.'

'Oh yeah? So what's going to happen now?'

'Now you're going to ask me about this, and I'm going to reply that my advance knowledge is so short that it's like when you sing a song you don't know the words to if you think about it – all you know is that the words will come to you just before you get to them, all you need is the music to lead you along. And even before I said this I knew just before I said it that I would say it.'

'Air, nothing but hot air, not good enough,' she said with a wave of her hand. 'You're just talking it away. Give me something concrete.'

'We'll sleep together tonight.'

'You wish!' she exclaimed and took a swipe at me.

'No, not like that,' I said. 'With our clothes on. We won't even kiss each other.'

'Exactly. So now you're giving me an excuse to say yes to sleeping with you? Thanks, but I've met boys like you before. You're so creepy.'

The phone in my pocket vibrated and I knew it was Peter trying once again to get in touch with me. I hadn't answered because I didn't know what to tell him, at least not now that I wouldn't be coming back this evening. Before leaving for San Sebastián I had planned to explain my absence by saying that I had simply got caught up in Pamplona's noisy *moveable feast* and hadn't realised the phone had been ringing.

Miriam folded her arms and shivered. The wind hadn't dropped and now the cloud cover was so dense it completely blotted out the evening sun.

'I have to get back to Mamma,' she said.

'Are you sure? I was going to offer you dinner as a way of thanking you for the room tonight.'

She gave an exasperated little groan and shook her head.

'I can't afford to take you anywhere like the Arzak,' I said. 'But if the tapas in that bar is anywhere near as good as the breakfast then you'll be missing out on something.'

She put her head on one side, pulled the hair back from her gorgeous eyes and looked at me. 'Missing out?' There was something about the way she looked at me, as though she was searching for something. Or recognised something.

'I might be exaggerating,' I admitted. 'But it's probably . . . a pretty good meal.'

She nodded.

'Yes?' I said in disbelieving surprise.

'I'm very hungry,' she said. She had already turned and was on her way back.

Over dinner I told her everything I could think of about myself. About my impracticality, my indiscipline, my limited capacity for analytical thinking. About my slightly too vivid imagination and my desire to be creative, at the same time as I doubted that my artistic talents matched my ambitions. About how clumsy I was in matters of the heart. About my fling with Peter's girlfriend when we were younger. As though it was important for me to put it all out there, the good and the bad, while I had the chance.

'So then, in a nutshell, you're stupid and egotistical,' she said, and took a sip of her red wine. She sat with her long thin legs twined around each other, her back bowed and the narrow shoulders projecting forwards, as though she was mildly disabled. A while ago it had seemed to me she was less beautiful than when I had seen her at the Arzak. Now I thought she was even more beautiful. Maybe it was the softer light. Maybe because she was more relaxed. Or perhaps it was me.

'Yes, I am stupid and egocentric,' I confirmed.

'Are you saying that because you think it makes you more interesting? Because I'm not seeing a *bad* boy here, Martin.'

'So then what do you see?'

'A boy who's actually quite nice.'

'How come you make that sound as though it's you that's five years older than me and not the other way round?'

'We're the same age.'

'How do you know?'

'Peter told me you two are the same age.'

'I see. What else did he say about me?'

'Not a lot, actually. Your name didn't come up until I asked if he was really travelling completely alone to San Fermín.'

'And did he say he was?'

'No, not in as many words, but it's as if he wanted to give me that impression. That you didn't exist. At any rate, he avoided talking about you.'

'Strange,' I said, lifting my own glass.

'Not if he's made up his mind that he's going to have me, and the two of you usually end up liking the same women.'

'And you still think I'm a nice boy?'

'I think you do things you know are wrong, but at least you have a guilty conscience afterwards.'

'Yes, well, that's always something. And what about your bad sides?'

'I steal,' she answered without hesitating.

'You steal?'

'Yes. It's a kind of habit. I'm not a kleptomaniac, but I think I need the excitement. That's probably why I mostly steal things I don't really need.'

'Like the hearts of naive boys?'

'That's cheap,' she laughed, and we toasted each other.

It had grown dark and there were ominous rumblings from the clouds as we ate the last pieces of tapas and she talked to me about herself. About the boyfriends she'd had in Moscow, about her plans to move to Singapore, maybe get a job as a journalist on an English-language newspaper. But nothing about why she had swum out into the waves and almost drowned. At one point she picked up her phone; the screen lit up her face in the dark and she frowned.

'Your mother?' I asked as she laid it aside without answering.

'Yes,' she said flatly.

'Uh-oh,' I said.

'Uh-oh?'

'You might be good at stealing, but you're an even worse liar than me. Was that Peter?'

She sighed. 'He must have texted me twenty times since yesterday.'

'And you think that's too many?'

She made a face. I wanted to ask how many messages she had sent back but managed not to.

'Thank you,' she said, with a nod towards the empty plates. 'That was good.'

'Something else to drink?'

'Definitely not. Mamma is waiting for me.'

I gestured for the bill. She watched as I signed the credit card receipt.

'Christopher,' she said.

I looked up.

'I thought your name was Christopher,' she smiled.

'When?'

'When I saw you.'

'Did Peter say that –'

'*Baywatch m-aaa-n!*'

The bow-legged man in the kilt and the Scotland football shirt was standing by our table. He swayed about, and his breath smelt like fresh windscreen-washer fluid.

'My hero! I need ten euros to go to the *encierro* tomorrow. I'll play you a love song.'

'*Vete!*' snarled the waiter, pointing towards the square.

I gave the Scot a five-euro note and he staggered off and disappeared into the darkness.

'Let's hope he sobers up before the bull run,' I said.

'Oh, he is not going, he is here all the time,' said the waiter, rolling his eyes.

We stood up. Miriam shivered as the wind suddenly rose, and this time it wasn't just a gust – the soughing in the trees around us grew louder and louder.

'We'll take a taxi,' I said, and glanced up as lightning flashed. It was as if the heavens had literally burst open: the bolt looked like a thin, glowing crack that revealed something behind it, some other world. And then, tumbling from the crack, came the rain. It hit the parasols, the table, the cobblestones, and everyone was on their feet and running. By the time Miriam and I found shelter a few seconds later in a gateway arch between the square and the back yard of the hotel we were drenched.

'We're not going to get any taxi now,' I said.

'It'll stop soon,' she said.

I glanced up at the sky. 'Maybe. You're shivering.'

'You too.'

I held up the room key. 'Come on up, we'll dry off in the meantime.'

We unlocked the door and I turned on the light. The rug hadn't been replaced.

'Have a shower, that'll warm you up,' I said.

Miriam nodded and disappeared into the bathroom, and I sat down on the bed in which I had slept two nights previously. The sounds of the rain and the shower mingled with each other, just as my own feelings of happiness and frustration did. The phone rang again. It was Peter. I knew I had to call him. I'd changed my explanation; now my story was that I had gone out to their village with those two Spanish girls from the barricade, that me and the blonde one had really hit it off and it looked like I would be spending the night there. He'd buy that. Wouldn't he? I thought of the corpse in the mortuary. I wasn't sure of anything any more. I heard the shower being turned off and put the phone back in my pocket. I couldn't feed the lie to Peter with Miriam listening in; I knew I quite simply wouldn't be able to handle it.

She emerged from the bathroom draped in one of the white towels, hurried across to the other bed and crept shivering in under the blanket.

'Suddenly there was only cold water,' she groaned. 'Sorry.'

'That's OK,' I said. 'Since I'm already wet I'll go out and buy something. Anything you want?'

'You're going out to ring Peter,' she said.

'That too.'

'Lie,' she said quietly.

'Why? We haven't done anything.'

'But you will lie. I'm just saying that it's OK by me.'

I went out and descended the stairs. Stopped in the gateway and took out my phone. Had tapped in Peter's name and was about to press Call when I realised something. The sound of the pouring rain was so loud that Peter would be bound to hear it, and it was by no means certain it was also raining in the area around Pamplona. In fact it was unlikely; before setting out we had read that even though they were so close to each other, it rained twice as much in San Sebastián as in Pamplona at this time of year.

I looked out across the square. It was deserted, but through the rain I heard a cracked voice singing – 'Mull of Kintyre' unless I was very much mistaken. And there, on the far side, alone beneath the awning over a closed shop, stood the Scot, thrashing away on his guitar.

I ran across the square, ducked beneath the same awning. He gave a big smile and stopped playing.

'*Baywatch m-aaa-n*, what d'ya wanna hear?'

'Can you play anything Spanish or Basqueish?'

By way of reply he at once began bellowing 'La Bamba'.

'Keep going until I've finished this conversation,' I said. He nodded. I pressed Call and Peter answered before the second ring.

'Martin! I was beginning to think you were dead!'

'I thought *you* were dead,' I said. I couldn't stop myself. But he ignored it. Instead he started going on about how worried he'd been. And I told him my story.

'So I gather,' he said. 'Sounds like a real party, I can hardly hear you.'

The Scot looked as though he was about to finish and I gestured for him to continue.

'Wish me luck, Peter. And I'll see you tomorrow!'

'You don't need luck, you bastard.' He gave a short laugh, but it wasn't as sincere as he usually sounded. 'And make sure you're back in time for the bull run.'

'Sure.'

'You promise?'

'Yes.'

Pause. The rain splashed around us, and I could only hope the Scot's hoarse 'La Bamba' was drowning it out.

'Are you in love, Martin?'

I was taken aback. 'Maybe I am,' I answered, swallowing.

'Because you sound as though you are.'

'I do?'

'Yes. Now that I know what that sounds like, it's what you sound like.'

I swallowed again. 'See you,' I said.

'See you.'

I shoved a soaking ten-euro note onto the end of one of the strings sticking out from a tuning peg on the Scot's guitar and headed back across the square.

'What did he say?' asked Miriam once I was back in the room. She'd pulled the blanket right up to her nose.

'That I sounded as though I was in love.'

'Well, you look cold anyway. Go and dry off.'

I went to the bathroom, took off my clothes and with the last remaining towel tried in vain to rub myself warm. As I was standing there I saw a large insect walking along the wall by the toilet bowl. It looked injured, limping and dragging its leg along behind it. I moved closer, thinking to put it out of its misery, and then saw that the legs were stuck together and had left a thin trail behind them. I bent down and peered in behind the toilet bowl. There, beneath the pipe, in a place that would be hard to reach with a cloth, lay a small pool of some dark, dried matter. I put my finger into it, already with a pretty good idea of what it was. Beneath the blackish coating it was damp and sticky. I examined my fingertip in the light. There could be no doubt about it; it was blood.

'You look pale,' said Miriam as I returned to the bedroom with the towel wrapped around my waist.

'I've been using factor fifty.'

She laughed softly. Lifted up the blanket. 'Come here and warm yourself.'

I got under the blanket and snuggled up to her.

'Keep your hands to yourself,' she said, turned on her side and pressed her nose into the pit of my neck. She was like a little oven, and the warmth she radiated gave me more goose bumps than the cold outside.

I lay completely still, not daring to move for fear of breaking the spell. Or of waking from the dream. Because that was what it felt like. Like being in a dream that was partly sweet and partly nightmarish. The blood, the rug, the corpse in the mortuary. And there was another thing.

'Listen,' I said. 'Did you know that Peter got himself a tattoo that day he met you at the hospital?'

'No. What kind of tattoo was it?'

'He didn't mention it?'

'No. Why do you ask?'

'It doesn't matter,' I said. 'This business about my name being Christopher, was that something he told you?'

'No. Is it?'

'It's my middle name.'

'Is it?' she laughed. 'But that's fantastic.'

'Yeah,' I said. 'Fantastic.'

I didn't know if it was just my imagination, but it felt as though she had wriggled a little closer to me. And neither of us was cold any more. But I didn't move. Nor did she. Outside, the rain had changed from a hammering to a steady drizzle. The hoarse, suffering voice of the Scotsman was still audible – he must have been the only person out there. His song must have been one with many verses.

'I've heard that song before,' I said. 'I just can't remember where.'

'He told us it was an old Irish song,' said Miriam. 'About the merrow with the red cap.'

'Merrow?'

'It's Irish for mermaid.'

The mermaid in the red cap. I thought of my dream. Of rising up through the cold dark water to the surface and the light. Something else rose to the surface too.

'When you say he told *us*, do you mean you and your mother?'

'Me and Peter. We walked past him as he was playing not far from the restaurant we'd eaten at. Peter gave him fifty euros and asked him to sing "The Red Capped Merrow" again.'

I closed my eyes and cursed inwardly.

Even though Peter wasn't especially musical he must have heard that the guy who was singing 'La Bamba' was the same person he and Miriam had been listening to. OK, but if he had noticed then I could perhaps convince him that the Scot had moved on to the little village and started busking there. Anyway, if the jig was up then the jig was up. Oddly enough the thought made me calmer.

'Of course, fifty euros was far too much,' said Miriam. 'But I don't think Peter did it to impress me. I think he did it out of . . . how shall I describe it? A sense of duty?'

I nodded and folded my hands behind my head. 'I think you're right. Peter understands that money can help, that it's practical to have money, but not that it can impress, or make others feel small. In fact, he can be embarrassed about the fact that he's so privileged. And I know he sometimes experiences it as a burden and an obligation. He told me once he envied me.'

'Envied?'

'He didn't explain it, but I think he sees in me something he can't have, the naive innocence of the ordinary person, the freedom of not having enough money and power to feel obliged to take responsibility. Just the same way I see in him the naive innocence in the fact that he actually believes he has a moral responsibility for the rest of the world, that he's one of the chosen ones, that his inherited wealth is proof that a guiding hand is at work in this world.'

'But you don't believe that?'

'I believe in chaos. And in our ability to see connections where none exist, because we find chaos intolerable.'

'You don't believe in fate?'

'Should I?'

'You predicted that you and I would lie in the same bed together.'

'You heard the prediction, maybe subconsciously that was what made you invite me into your bed. Anyway, I said that we'd be clothed.'

'We're wearing towels. And we're not kissing.'

I was about to turn towards her, but then noticed the slight resistance in her body and desisted. Stared instead up at the ceiling.

'Maybe we always do that,' I said. 'Try to make sure that some prediction or other we believe in will actually come true. Maybe that's what our lives are about.'

We fell silent and listened as the sound of the falling rain grew even lighter. Soon people would be back on the streets again. The taxis would be driving round. Miriam would go to her mother. I glanced at the clock. In a couple of hours' time I would have to get up for my bus, but that was fine, I wouldn't be getting any sleep tonight anyway.

Now the rain had stopped completely. The Scot was no longer singing, but other voices were raised here and there across the square. Miriam changed position. I thought she was going to get up, but then she lay still. It was so quiet we could hear the drops of rain from the gutter as they hit the cobblestones beneath the open window with a sound like a deep, heavy sigh. I made up my mind.

'What I'm going to tell you now isn't to frighten you off Peter,' I said. 'It's just something I think you ought to know.'

'And what is that?' she said, as though she'd been expecting this.

'I think,' I said, and swallowed, 'that Peter has murdered someone.'

'All right,' she said. 'But that doesn't necessarily make him a bad person.'

'It doesn't?' I said, astonished.

'I hope not. I've murdered someone too.'

The people had all gone home and the birds were not yet awake, so all was still outside by the time Miriam had finished her story. She told me she had been telling the truth when she said she didn't lie to friends. 'But you weren't a friend then, Martin. You are now.'

It wasn't true that the man she had married hadn't managed to consummate the marriage. Once he threatened to call for assistance she had allowed him to take her. Rape without violence, that was what she called it. She'd blocked the details from her memory and recalled only the vodka stink of his breath. And when they got into bed he had fallen asleep at once. What really happened next was that she had held a pillow over his face. And didn't take it away again. She'd sat on top of the puny boy, trapped his arms beneath her knees and kept on pressing until she felt his resistance stop, and then carried on pressing.

'Until all the tension was gone from his body and I was certain I was a widow,' she said.

The rest of her story was true enough.

'I was convinced the police would stop us at the airport the following day. But I guess the Kolyev family never goes to the police. But if we'd taken a later plane, I'm certain they would have caught us.'

Miriam and her mother had then lived with friends in Istanbul.

'Until the day there was a knock on the door and someone was asking about us. Mamma's friends knew it must Kolyev's people and said they didn't dare to hide us any longer. Since then we've travelled back and forth all across Europe. It's expensive, but the advantage is that as long as we're within Schengen we don't have to show our passports. We never take planes or other forms of transport that keep passenger lists. But twice they've turned up at the hotels we were living at, and we've only just managed to get away. Now we stay in cheap hotels where they don't keep a digital record of the guests. But it's impossible not to leave any traces at all, so it's just a matter of time before they catch up with us. The one thing that could stop them looking is if they realise there's nothing to look for any more. That I'm dead. So that's why . . .' She swallowed. 'That's why I told Mamma we should go to the beach at Zurriola.'

I swallowed hard. 'You wanted to drown yourself.'

She nodded slowly.

'So that your mother would be free,' I said. My voice was thick.

Miriam looked at me, and from the expression on her face I realised that I had misunderstood.

'It was supposed to *look* as though I'd drowned,' she said. 'I'm a good swimmer. I was on the university swimming team in Moscow. The plan was to make a lot of noise so that we had witnesses to the fact that I was in difficulties, and then disappear. I was going to swim for a long way underwater – I'm good at that – and then continue on out to the point on the eastern side, where there's no road and it's completely deserted. I had a bag with clothes and shoes hidden behind one of the rocks there, and then I was going to take a bus to Bilbao where I'd booked a room under a false name and stay there a week. Mamma was going to report me missing, so that it would be in the newspapers.'

'And Kolyev would give up the chase.'

She nodded. 'But you came so quickly. I dived, and thought, well, now we have at least one witness to the drowning. But then you found me down there, in the darkness.'

'It was your bathing cap.'

'I wasn't quite sure what to do. The plan was ruined. So I thought I should just let myself be rescued, and then try to disappear again some other day.'

'But you've given up that idea now?'

She nodded.

'Because now that you've got Peter to help you, you don't need it.'

She nodded again.

'And he knows nothing about the Kolyevs, is that correct?'

'I told him about the abduction and the forced marriage.'

'But he doesn't know you killed your husband.'

'Don't call him my husband!'

'OK. So this means that you knew all along it was me and not Peter who rescued you.'

She gave a quick, bitter laugh. 'You didn't rescue me, Martin, you screwed things up for me.'

'But you played the rescued maiden for Peter.'

'*He* played the hero!'

'Yeah, everyone's lying. But . . .' I felt a hand touching my face. Fingertips against my lips.

'Shh,' she whispered. 'Can't we just be quiet for a few moments?'

I nodded and closed my eyes. She was right, we needed to take a break. Gather our thoughts. How could so much have happened in such a short space of time? Just two days ago Peter and I were pals on our way to the bull run in Pamplona, where his father and his uncle before him had been, so even though he would never admit it, it was understood to be a male rite of passage in the family. For me it was pure romance, living out Hemingway's *The Sun Also Rises*, a book which, according to my father, has to be read and enjoyed when you're young, because Hemingway is a young man's writer, a writer who has less appeal the older you get. But instead of a short, three-minute sprint through the streets of Pamplona I had the feeling now of running all the time, with all the side streets barricaded, and the horns of the bulls getting closer and closer. It was like Peter said, everything that can happen happens all the time, all at the same time. Time both is and isn't an illusion, because in an infinity of realities it is just as irrelevant as everything else. I was dizzy. I fell. I fell into a chasm and had never felt happier.

I could hear how her breathing had fallen into rhythm with mine, how her body rose and fell with mine. It was as though, just for a moment, we had become one; it was no longer her body giving warmth to mine or the other way round, we had become *one* body. I don't know how much time passed – five minutes, half an hour – before I spoke again:

'Have you sometimes wished you could travel back in time and change something?'

'Yes,' she said. 'But you can't. We might feel as though we have free will, but if you're the same person you were, carrying the same information in the same situation, you'll just repeat yourself all over again. It's obvious.'

'But what if you can travel back as the person you are *now*?'

'Aha. The idea that you can take revenge on your old psychopath of a schoolteacher in front of the whole class, or invest money where you know for certain what the outcome will be?'

'Or score the penalty you missed in your earlier life,' I added.

'It's fun to fantasise about,' she said. 'Until you come up against the paradox of time, that by changing the past you also change the future. And then it doesn't work out.'

'What if you travel back in time in the universe you inhabit now, but at a certain point which you've decided on yourself you slip into a parallel universe? One that up until that point is identical to the one you've been living in? A universe in which you already exist as another person.'

'Meaning that there are two of you?'

'Yes. In that case there is no paradox of time involved.'

'But a completely crazy reality.'

'Isn't every reality crazy?'

She laughed. 'Oh, yes!'

'The problem is that if you want to take that penalty kick again the earlier edition of yourself is already there, all geared up to miss. So you have to get that person out of the way first.'

'How do you that?'

'If you want to take that person's place without anybody noticing, the best way is to do what you did. Get the main character to disappear for ever.'

'Drown yourself?'

'Put a pillow over his face while he's sleeping.'

'Er, right. Martin?'

'Yes?'

'What are we talking about now?'

'We're talking about Peter having travelled here from another reality which was identical with this one until two days ago. And in this reality, which is here and now, he killed himself while I was out at breakfast.'

'Here? In this bed? With a pillow?'

'I think it happened in the bathroom, perhaps while my Peter was showering or using the toilet. The Peter who has just arrived hit him with something heavy, and there was bleeding, because there's blood beneath the toilet bowl. The new, but older, Peter cleaned up as far as he could, wrapped the body in the floor rug and dumped it in the wheelie bin behind the building, which he knew would be emptied later the same day.'

'I love it,' she laughed. 'But why? Why has he come back?'

'To change something that happened in the universe he's arrived from.'

'And that is?'

'That he didn't get you. I think you're the penalty kick he missed.'

'This is so good! You should make a film about it,' she said, apparently not noticing that she'd lain a hand on my chest.

'Maybe,' I said, and closed my eyes again. It was OK. OK to leave it there. Outside, it had started raining again. Miriam sighed heavily. Without opening my eyes I noticed the light from her phone.

'I need to tell Mamma I'm spending the night here,' she said. 'It's OK, all she knows is that I've rented a room here. She doesn't know you're here.'

I mumbled something in response. On the interior of my eyelids I saw once again that naked corpse. The mark on the temple. The white, unblemished skin. No tattoo. Peter. Who had just fallen in love for the first time in his life. Who had not yet had time to make his first mistake, the one that would ensure he never got her. He just looked like a happy boy sleeping.

I was mistaken.

I *did* manage to sleep.

When the alarm on my phone woke me it was still dark outside.

I looked at her, lying with her back turned to me in the bed. The black hair spread out across the pillow.

'I've got to go,' I said.

She didn't move. 'Will you tell Peter that we met?'

'No, I promised, remember.'

'Sure you promised, but you're best friends. I know how it is. Anyway, we've established now that all three of us are liars.' She turned in the bed and smiled at me – at least I saw teeth in the darkness.

'I don't know if the guy in Pamplona is any friend of mine,' I said. 'But I do know that I love you.'

'*That's what I call respecting the girl in the morning,*' she muttered, and turned her back on me again.

Once outside I discovered I hadn't enough cash for a taxi, but at least, as I ran to the bus station, my body built up enough warmth to dry off my clothes, which had been damp and ice-cold when I put them on in the dark.

There was a strange atmosphere on the bus to Pamplona. The passengers fell into three categories. In the first were those who were gearing themselves and their pals up for the bull run, shouting to each other from their seats, laughing loudly to hide their nervousness, punching one another on the shoulder and already on the sangria and the brandy. Then there were those who slept or else tried to. The third group was me, the guy on his own who sat looking out across the landscape, thinking. Who tried to understand and make sense of it all, and each time had to give up and start again. Finally the thinking was interrupted by a phone call from Peter, which I couldn't take, otherwise he would have known I was sitting on a bus. There was still over an hour until we arrived, and that wouldn't fit in with the story about it being a local bus.

I didn't call back until we reached the outskirts of Pamplona.

'And here was me thinking you'd overslept,' he said.

'No way. Meet at Jake's in fifteen?'

'I'm there already. See you.'

I pushed the phone down into my pocket. Had there been something in his voice? Something not quite right, some sign that he knew? I had no idea. Had it been Peter I would have known. But the man I had just spoken to was a stranger. I felt as though my brain were about to explode.

Jake's was so crowded I literally had to force a way between all the men – and the few women – wearing red and white. Peter – or the man calling himself Peter – was seated at the bar. He must have started early. He was wearing a cap and a large pair of sunglasses I hadn't seen before.

'Enjoy,' he said, pointing at a full glass of brandy.

I hesitated. Then I picked up the glass and drank it in one.

'Scared?'

'Yes,' I said.

He nodded at the newspaper on the counter. 'The bulls today are from the Galavanez farm. People say the bulls from there are real killers.'

'They do?'

'What they probably don't know is that they're the ones who are going to get killed. This afternoon.'

'I guess it's better not to know,' I said.

'Yes.' He looked at me. I looked at him. It was easy to see now. When he'd emerged from the bathroom in San Sebastián and said he'd thrown up, I'd thought the reason he'd lost his tan and looked older was that he was ill. Where had he come from? Which time? Which place?

'The hour is late,' he said without looking at his watch. 'Let's go.'

We stood in the same place as we had done the day before. That was the plan, that as far as possible the second time should be a replica of the first. *Sticking to as many of the variables as possible,* as Peter had described it. So that we could focus on the experience itself, not just spend the time processing everything that was new and unknown. Experiencing the same thing, but in a different way. Was that what this Peter had done over the last two days? In the universe he came from, had he and I – or the self I was in that other universe – stood in this same place waiting for the bulls? Of course, things had started to change from the moment he entered this universe, the sequence of events had stopped running in parallel. But how much had he changed? And how much did he want to change? It was unbearable.

Next to us a boy began sobbing convulsively. I recognised him as one of the noisy Americans from the bus. No, it was unbearable and I turned to Peter intending to tell him that I knew who he was – or more accurately, who he *wasn't* – when a sound told us that the bulls had been released.

My mouth went dry. I hunched over in a sort of starting position. I don't know why the runners didn't spread themselves out more evenly along the route, because actually one place seemed as good as any other. Instead we were gathered in groups. Maybe the idea is that there's safety in numbers.

'I'll run directly behind you,' said Peter. 'Between you and the bulls.'

The noise and the shouting got closer, and I seemed to smell panic and blood in the air, the same way the rain on the street the day before had pushed the air in front of it, causing the trees to sway and rustle out a forewarning. A couple of the tourists broke from our crowd and started to run, like those drips falling from the guttering outside the room during the night.

And then there they were. Rounding the corner. One of the bulls slipped on the cobblestones, fell onto his side but rose to his feet again. A body lay in the road where the bull had landed. A shaven-headed man in white ran directly in front of the lead bull, seeming to be steering it with the rolled-up newspaper he held in his hand, using it now to strike the bull on the forehead and now to keep his balance. The swarm around us began to move and I wanted to run, but somebody held me back by my jacket.

'Wait,' said Peter calmly behind me.

My mouth was so dry I couldn't respond.

'Now,' he said.

I ran. A little to the left of the middle of the street, as on the previous day. Concentrating on what was in front of me. Not falling. Everything else was beyond my control. Just feeling my way forward. But there was nothing there, white fear blanked out everything else. And then the legs went from under me. A clear and obvious trip. That was all I had time to think before I hit the cobblestones.

I knew I should lie still. But I also knew there was half a ton of bull directly behind us, so I rolled sideways to the left. A shadow crossed over me, something big, like a ship blotting out the sun. Then it had passed and looking up I saw the narrow black buttocks of the enormous creature.

It stopped. And turned.

Suddenly everything around me went quiet, so quiet that the solitary scream – maybe it was a girl up on the barricade who saw what was about to happen – chilled me to the bone.

The bull looked at me. The eyes were dead, expressed nothing other than that it saw me. He snorted. Scraped his front hoof against the cobblestones and lowered his horns. I didn't move. But that tactic was no longer the right one. I had been seen. Separated out from the crowd. That black train of muscle flexed and then exploded in my direction. I was as good as dead. I closed my eyes.

Someone grabbed hold of my foot and started pulling, sweeping me round as my chin bounced and scraped against the stones. The back of my head hit something, for a moment everything went black, and then I opened my eyes again. I had hit the wall of a house. Peter was standing above me, still holding on to my foot. A few metres away from us the man with the shaven head and the newspaper was dancing round the bull, busily distracting it with the aid of another man, also carrying a rolled-up newspaper. Peter positioned himself between the bull and me. A cow passed, and the bull seemed to lose interest and chugged off after her. The rest of the group, five bulls and cows, passed us directly afterwards, but ignored us. In truth they seemed tired of the whole business and just wanted to get away and find somewhere quiet and peaceful.

I sat up with my back against the wall of the house, and Peter squatted down beside me. I breathed. In, then out. And then again. In, then out. Let my pulse gradually slow down as I saw the street emptying as people made their way towards the stadium.

'Was that the plan?' I asked after a while.

'Was what the plan?'

'This. For me to fall in front of the bulls and you to rescue me. Was that the plan all along?'

I could see that he was on the point of saying something like: 'What are you talking about?' or: 'I don't understand.' But maybe he knew that I had understood.

'No,' he said. 'That wasn't the plan.'

'No?'

'Not to rescue you, no.' He rested his head against the whitewashed wall of the house. I did the same thing, looking up into the cloudless sky between the rooftops.

On the side streets up and down the route they had already started to dismantle the barricades.

'So you went to San Sebastián?'

'Yes,' I said.

'Why?'

'I needed to find out what had happened there.'

'And did you find out?'

'I saw your body.'

'That isn't me. At least not completely.'

'Then what is it?'

'It's hard to explain. It is me, but without my feeling of a self.'

'Is that why you were able to kill him?'

'Yes. But it wasn't easy. It was painful.'

'But not so painful that you couldn't do it?'

'The pain of not getting Miriam would have been worse. The way I look at it, it was a necessary suicide.'

'You had to kill yourself in order to win her?'

'Two Peters would have been very confusing, don't you think?'

'Got a cigarette?'

He straightened out his legs so that he could reach into his pocket and took two cigarettes from the packet. Lit up for us both.

'What was it the first Peter did wrong?' I asked.

'He failed to see that you and Miriam might have been made for each other.' He drew on his cigarette. 'Drop the *might have been*: you two *are* made for each other. Did you meet her in San Sebastián?'

'What do you think?'

'You're two cicadas. Of course you found each other.'

'I found her.'

'Yes, only the male cicada sings.'

I looked at him again. He seemed older now than when we had stood waiting for the bulls. As though he'd aged ten years over a couple of minutes.

'What happened?' I asked, dragging on my cigarette. 'Did you find out how to travel through time?'

'It took me eleven years,' he said. 'Me and a small group of researchers in Switzerland. And you don't travel through time, you travel between parallel universes or sequences of events. We discovered a way to slip in the back door of a parallel universe, but the problem was in finding which universe to enter, since there's an infinity of them, and most of them are dead, cold worlds. You can't change anything in a universe – the sequence of events is fixed – but you create new universes by moving something, even if it's just an atom, from one universe to another. If you discover a universe that is, up to a particular point – for example, up to the morning after you rescued Miriam – identical to the one you inhabit, and you transport yourself there, a new universe is created in which you *feel* as though you've changed the sequence of events, but actually it's simply a new one. Although actually it isn't even really new, it's just that you're experiencing it for the first time. Understand?'

'No.'

'I discovered a way of finding universes that resemble the one you inhabit. We call it a synchronised habitat. In the universe I come from I'll be awarded the Nobel Prize for it.'

I laughed. I couldn't help it.

'So you slipped into this universe directly after I rescued Miriam. But why not before?'

'Because the perfect starting point is that I saved her life. That is, that she *believes* I'm the one who saved her life. So I needed you first.' He took a breath. 'As you know, I'm unable to swim.'

I shook my head. 'But good God, why didn't you simply discover a universe where you get Miriam without doing anything?'

'They exist too, of course, but they're impossible to find, since a synchronised habitat contains only other universes that are similar. So I had to enter one of these and start to create, or to experience from within it a new one, which would hopefully be the one in which I end up getting Miriam.'

'You really give a whole new dimension to the phrase "searching for love",' I said, and regretted at once my attempt to be funny. Peter didn't seem to notice.

'Love is the greatest,' was all he said, following the drifting cigarette smoke with his eyes. 'There is an infinite number of universes in which you and I sit together and have this conversation, and in which the smoke curls away in exactly this particular way. And yet another infinity with exactly this same conversation but in which the smoke curls away in a *slightly* different direction, or in which one particular word is replaced with another. But there is no room for these universes in my synchronised habitat. So in all of those for which I have room, *you* are the one who gets Miriam. And to create a happy ending for myself I need to go via them.'

'Because love is greatest?'

'Greater than anything else.'

'Love is only a sensation fostered by evolution to ensure that the human race will procreate and protect its genes and its closest family members in an efficient way.'

'I know,' said Peter, stubbing out his cigarette on the cobblestones. 'And yet still it is greater than that.'

'So great that you're willing to kill this universe's version of yourself?'

'Yes.'

'And me, your best friend?'

'In theory, yes. But in practice, evidently not.'

'First you tried to kill me, then you rescued me. Why?'

He looked down at his dead cigarette which he carried on grinding into the ground. 'Like you said. You're my best friend.'

'You couldn't bring yourself to kill me.'

'Let's put it like that.' He looked up and smiled. 'Shall we go and get some breakfast?'

We went to Jake's. I ordered an omelette, Peter ham and coffee.

He must have thrown away the sunglasses and cap once we started running. Now, without them, I saw his hair was a slightly different shade of blond, and he had bags under eyes that had been as white as hard-boiled eggs but were now slightly dull and yellowish, with a fine tracery of veins running through them. Those teeth, however, were as white as ever.

'Then if I've understood you correctly,' I said, 'I get Miriam and you're unhappy for the rest of your life.'

'That is highly likely but remember that this is a new universe I'm experiencing. All I know is that it has been the same up until the point at which I boarded it. Now, because of my transfer, there's been a split.'

'Is that why there's an infinity of universes? People began moving between them, and that caused them to start splitting and —'

'We don't know. But it's possible. Everything that can happen has happened. Perhaps originally there were only one or two universes, and then people discovered the passageways and the process of expansion began.'

'In that case these universes are the creations of human beings.'

'As opposed to?'

'Natural creations. Or the result of physical laws.'

'Humans are created by nature, which is created by physical laws. Everything is physics, Martin.'

I could feel the phone vibrating in my pocket but let it ring.

'So what are you going to do now?' I asked.

'I'm putting together a research team with the aim of finding out how to move to another universe. The research will go ahead more quickly now since I'm already familiar with most of the other research fields.'

'And then you'll travel to another universe and try to get Miriam there?'

He nodded.

The food arrived.

Peter picked up the sharp steak knife, but then just looked down at his ham without touching it. 'I really hope you get her, Martin. And I regret that I almost killed you.' He put a note down on the table with his free hand. 'Now I need to disappear. Good luck, my friend.'

'What are you going to do?'

'What do you do after a bull run?'

'You sleep.'

'Then I'll sleep.' He moved the knife to his left hand, stood up, took hold of my right. 'One more thing: don't wake me. Stay away from the room at least until after dark, OK?'

He squeezed my hand, let go of it, weaved his way out past the other guests and was gone.

'Hey!' I wanted to run after him, but a big, loud-mouthed American drunk wearing a panama hat was in my way. And when I finally reached the street Peter was nowhere in sight.

When in doubt, go left. That was my father's motto and I followed it. I ran, bumping into people, calling out Peter's name. I passed the market square where they dived from the statue in the evening, not stopping until I reached the alcove by the statue of San Fermín.

Peter was gone.

I was so out of breath I had to support myself against the wall. That mean bastard. *Regret*, he'd said. He didn't say he was sorry, he just *regretted* he had almost killed me.

The phone vibrated again. I took it out, hoping it was Peter. A foreign number. Two SMSs.

Do you really love me?

And: *Really, really?*

'*Hola*, Mister Famous!'

I looked up from the phone and saw my two Spanish girlfriends from the village, arm in arm. The blonde came up and kissed me on both cheeks.

'You must have been very afraid,' she said. 'And so lucky!'

'Sorry?'

'When you were saved from the bull.'

'Oh . . . You were there?'

'No, no. You are on TV. You are famous, Martin!'

The girls laughed at what must have been the astonished look on my face before dragging me back to the bar I had just left. There, on the wall-mounted TV screen, highlights from the day's bull run were being shown.

'I didn't even know they were filming it,' I said.

'Officially, running in front of the bulls is illegal, but it is of course understood that the police look the other way. But the national TV will broadcast the run. Welcome to Spain!' They laughed until the tears ran down their cheeks and poured from their own sangria bottle into the bar's glasses without the bartender seeming to object. I, meanwhile, was staring at the screen and watching myself run, with Peter in his sunglasses and cap right behind me. Suddenly I stumbled, but there were so many others in the line of fire it was impossible to see what it was that had tripped me. The camera was on the bull and I was no longer in view. Up until the point at which the bull stopped. And then I saw it: two men clambering up onto the top of the barricade behind the bull. One of them was Peter, still wearing the sunglasses and cap. And he jumped over to the other side and disappeared!

The camera followed what the bull was looking at: me. And then a person who had been standing pressed up against the wall of the house right where I had landed, and who now stepped forward, grabbed round my leg with both hands and – as the bull charged towards me, horns lowered as though in search of something – swept the ground with me, and swung me round in an elegant semicircle, much as a matador swings the cape at such a sharp angle the charging bull hasn't time to alter course.

It was Peter. The other Peter. No, the third Peter. One who was even older than Peter the second. As I watched the distracted bull moving away and Peter the third and I disappear out of the picture I realised something. The reason Peter the third had said he *regretted* – the way you use that word when you're apologising on behalf of others – was because Peter the second, absolutely and completely and with no regrets at all, had tried to kill me. Peter the third had not come to win Miriam but to save me.

I swallowed.

The bartender gave me an enquiring look.

'Brandy,' I said.

'Where are you?' asked Miriam.

'At a party out in the country,' I said, peering up at the sky. But the sun had just set and it was still too early for stars. I had made my excuses and left the market square where a local dance band was now playing. Stopped beside an olive tree with the houses and the distant hubbub behind me, and in front of me vines stretching in rows all the way to the mountains. And there in the dusk I had called her.

'Are you drunk?'

'A little,' I said. 'Have you spoken to Peter?'

'He called Mamma, the crafty thing. She took the call, and because I was sitting right beside her she handed it to me. She doesn't know anything. All she knows is she wants him for a son-in-law.'

'What did he say?'

'He knew I'd met you in San Sebastián. Asked if we'd had a good time. Said he'd lost sight of you during the bull run and that you still hadn't returned to the hotel. I started to get worried when you didn't answer my text messages. That's why I called you.'

'I noticed that.'

'Why didn't you ring back earlier?'

'It's been a . . . a hectic day. I'll tell you about it later, I've got people waiting for me.'

'Oh yeah? That's what Peter said.'

'What did Peter say?'

'That you'd definitely end up at a party with some *chicas*. So I guess he was right . . .'

Her tone of voice, half amused and half rebuking, made me smile.

'Are you a bit jealous?' I said.

'Don't be stupid, Martin.'

'Say you're a bit jealous. Just to make me feel good about myself.'

'You *are* drunk.'

'Say it. Please.'

In the ensuing silence I listened. The song of the cicadas had ceased with the setting of the sun. Either that or they were singing the way they do where I come from: at such a high frequency the human ear can't pick it up. I thought about it, about vibrations, about all the things going on around us that we neither see, nor hear, or even know about.

'I'm a tiny bit jealous. Just for you.' I closed my eyes. A warmth – maybe it was happiness – washed through me.

'I'll come back to San Sebastián again early tomorrow,' I said. 'Breakfast?'

'A good breakfast?'

'I'll call you when I'm on the bus or the train.'

'OK.'

'Goodnight.'

'Goodnight.'

'And you?'

No answer. She'd hung up. But I said it anyway.

'I do. Really, really.'

I had just put the phone back in my pocket when it rang again.

'Yes?' I answered, still smiling, but instead of Miriam it was a different female voice:

'Mister Daas? This is Imma Aluariz with the San Sebastián police. Where are you right now?'

My tongue felt dry, and I only just managed to resist the impulse to end the call at once.

'I'm in Pamplona,' I said. Vague enough, and not exactly a lie.

'Me too,' said Aluariz. 'We need to talk to you.'

'About what?'

'You know about what.'

'Am I . . . a suspect or something?'

'Where exactly can we find you, Mister Daas?'

Two policemen – one in plain clothes, the other in uniform – led me from the car, past two other police cars in the direction of the house where Peter and I had rented rooms. The one in uniform lifted up the crime-scene tape, and we walked through the gate and then into the house. Instead of my own room they took me to Peter's. They stopped me in the doorway. There were a number of people inside, two wearing white from head to foot. The bed was hidden by a short, stocky figure standing at the end of it.

The plain-clothes policeman – who had introduced himself as a detective when they picked me up earlier – coughed and the stocky figure turned.

'Thank you for coming so quickly,' said Imma Aluariz.

I felt like saying it was *they* who had come quickly but just nodded.

'First I would like you to identify the body, Mister Daas.' She stepped to one side.

I don't know whether it's the brain protecting itself or the brain in flight when it starts to follow quite irrelevant trains of thought in situations like that. Because what I thought at the sight of the white duvet cover and sheet against the pillowcase that was soaked in something red that had to be blood was that it was a very apt combination for San Fermín. The same way the steak knife sticking out on one side of Peter's neck was an apt image of the bull with the handle of the matador's sword sticking out between his shoulder blades.

'It is my friend,' I said, my voice shaking. 'It is Peter Coates.'

I could feel Aluariz's eyes on me, but knew I had no need to act shocked because I *was* shocked. And yet I wasn't.

'What happened?' I asked.

Aluariz's gaze moved from me to the policeman in plain clothes. He nodded and said something in Basque.

'What did he say?' I asked.

'That both girls say you have been with them since this morning,' said Aluariz. She seemed to be weighing something up before she continued. 'It looks as though your friend has committed suicide. According to the pathologist it must have been some time between ten and twelve o'clock. The landlady found him.'

'I see,' was all I said. 'How do you know it was suicide?'

'We fingerprinted the handle of the knife and the only print we found was identical with his own.'

Identical, I thought. And yet not his own. The knife was from Jake's.

'What's interesting is that he looks very like the corpse in San Sebastián. Could almost be his twin, don't you think? And if that's the case, why didn't you say anything?'

I shook my head. 'I never heard anything about Peter having a twin brother, and actually I don't think they are very similar. I mean, the body in San Sebastián was younger, you can see that for yourself. And the hair was longer and fairer. And it didn't have that tattoo.' I pointed to the faded M on the chest.

'They could still be twins even if they don't have the same tattoo.'

I shrugged. 'I can understand why you think the two of them look alike. It's not easy for me to tell one Basque person from another.'

She gave me a sharp look.

I shrugged.

She took out a notebook. 'Can you think of any reason why your friend would want to take his own life?'

I shook my head.

'Could it be a guilty conscience because he killed someone in San Sebastián?' she asked.

'Is that what you suspect?'

'The rug the body was found in is from the rooms you shared. We found your DNA there.'

'In that case I should be a suspect too.'

'Killers – unless they're mad – don't get in touch with the police and provide them with conclusive evidence but no confession. And you are not mad, Mister Daas.'

Oh yes, I thought. I'm mad all right. And if I told you my version of what's happened you would think so too. And in parallel universes maybe that was exactly what I was doing now, and in many of them – in an infinity of them – I would be locked up in a mental hospital.

'I need to hear exactly what you know of Peter Coates's movements from the time you arrived in San Sebastián,' she said.

'If you want a statement from me I must tell you, I'm very tired,' I said. 'And not completely sober either. Can we do this tomorrow?'

Aluariz exchanged looks with her plain-clothes colleague. His head bobbed about a bit, as though he were weighing it up. Then he nodded.

'OK,' she said. 'We've no reason to detain you, you're not a suspect in either of these cases. And since our prime suspect is now dead, there's no rush. Ten o'clock at the police station here in San Sebastián, does that sound all right?'

'Fine.'

The sun was shining and the reflection from the water blinded me as I took off the sunglasses and wiped away my tears.

From where I was sitting on the hill on the deserted point of land I could see the whole of the Zurriola beach. I thought of my best friend. And of the one who was swimming in the sea below me. The woman we both had to have at any cost. Maybe he would have left her. In some universes at least he would have done. Same goes for me. But that didn't matter, not now and not in this universe, not in this story. So once I had dried my tears I went back to this story, to *my* story. I picked up the binoculars and located the pink bathing cap out there in the water. I couldn't hear her screams but training the binoculars on the beach three hundred metres further in I could see the mother – as before – running around and alerting the sunbathers to her daughter's cries for help. I turned the binoculars to the lifeguard's raised seat. Just as before, Miriam and her mother had waited to give their performance until the lifeguard on duty had taken a trip to the booths at the back of the beach to use the toilet.

A surfer ran down to the water, lay flat on his board and began paddling out towards Miriam. But this time she'd swum further out and he wouldn't make it before she disappeared. And now she ducked down below the surface and was lost to sight. I counted the seconds. Ten. Twenty. Thirty. Forty. Her lung capacity was really impressive – I'd been astonished when we ran through the whole operation the day before. The surfer reached the point at which he'd seen her disappear, slipped off his board and dived down. I moved the binoculars fifty – sixty – metres closer, to the shore directly below me, where the sea washed calmly over the parallel rows of stone that ran down from the deserted and uninviting water's edge and out into the sea. She'd removed her bathing cap, and I could only just make out the head with the dark hair breaking the surface for a couple of seconds as she drew breath before vanishing beneath the waves again.

I lay back in the grass. Soon she would be here. Disguised as someone else. And yet the same person. And we would try to sneak out of the country and enter another reality. A fresh start, with fresh opportunities. I realised I was still counting, but that now I was counting down. Counting down what was left of my old life. A high, piercing sound reached my ears, too high for a grasshopper or a cricket. A solitary male cicada looking for a female, with a sound that could carry for miles. That's a long way for such a small creature, I thought.

Soon, I could imagine I was already hearing her footsteps. I closed my eyes. And when I opened them again, I saw her. And for a fleeting instant the thought struck me: that I had been here, just like this, before.

THE ANTIDOTE

SOMEWHERE THERE'S A HARSH CRY from a bird. Or maybe it's some other kind of creature, Ken doesn't know. He holds the test tube up against the white sun, pushes the tip of the needle down through the plastic cap and draws the clear, yellowish liquid up into the barrel. A drop of sweat finds a way down between his close-set eyebrows and he curses under his breath as the salt stings his eye.

The constant and already deafening droning of the insects seems just to get louder. He looks at his father, sitting with his back against a grey tree trunk, the skin almost blending with the bark. Light flickers across his face and his khaki shirt, as though he were sitting beneath a disco ball in one of Ken's favourite London clubs. But he is actually sitting by the bank of a river in the east of Botswana and staring up into the lattice of trembling leaves that filter the sunlight through what Ken Abbott does not know is an acacia xanthophloea, a fever tree. Ken Abbott doesn't know very much at all about the burning hot, green and nightmarish world around him. All he knows is that he has very little time to save the life of the person who means more to him than anyone else on earth.

Emerson Abbott never had great ambitions for his son. He had seen too many examples of the tragic results the pressure of such expectations in upper-class families could have on the children. He didn't even need to look far. Not even as far as those public-school friends of his who had failed to achieve the successes expected of them, and who drank until every bottle in the world was dry before plucking up courage for the great leap, from penthouse apartments in Kensington or Hampstead and five floors down to where the asphalt is just as hard as it is in Brixton and Tottenham. Not even as far as Archie, the nephew whom he had last seen among bloodstained sheets and disposable needles in a hotel room in Amsterdam, with the mark of the angel of death's kiss already shaped on his lips, who had refused to go home with him and carelessly pointed a revolver in his direction in a way that told Emerson Archie didn't much care which way it was pointing when he pulled the trigger.

No, Emerson didn't need to look far. Only as far as the mirror.

For nearly thirty years he had been an unhappy publisher who published books written by idiots that were about idiots and that were bought by idiots. But there were enough of these idiots for Emerson in the course of his professional career to have tripled the already considerable family fortune, a fact that gave greater pleasure to his wife Emma than it did to himself. He could well remember that warm summer day in Cornwall when they got married, but he had forgotten why. Perhaps she was just in the right place at the right time, and from the right family, and in a very short while he no longer knew which interested him less: the money, the books or his wife. He had hinted at the possibility of divorce, and three weeks later she had told him, radiant with joy, that she was pregnant. Emerson experienced a deep and sincere happiness that lasted for about ten days. By the time he sat in the waiting room at St Mary's Hospital he was unhappy again. It was a boy. They named him Ken after Emerson's father, got a nanny for him, sent him to a boarding school and one day he was standing in his father's office and asking if he could have a car.

Emerson had looked up in surprise at the young man standing in front of him. He had inherited his mother's equine features and almost lipless mouth, but the rest came undoubtedly from him. The long, narrow nose with his father's close-set eyebrows formed a T-shape in the middle of the face with two pale blue eyes on each side. They had expected that his blond hair would gradually turn into his mother's mousy grey, but that hadn't happened. Ken had already developed the blasé and the would-be self-irony that gives the British their reputation for charm, and his blue eyes twinkled when he saw his father's confusion.

Emerson realised that even though he had intended to make ambitious plans for his son he would probably never have had time to realise them. How could his son have become an adult without his having noticed it? Had he been too busy being unhappy, of being the person everyone in his circle thought he ought to be, and if that was the case, why didn't that include being a father to his only son? It pained him. Or did it? He thought about it. Yes, it really did pain him. He raised his hands impotently aloft.

Maybe Ken had counted on his father's guilty conscience, and maybe not. At any rate, he got his car.

By the time Ken was twenty he no longer had the car. He lost it in a bet with another student over who could get back to the college fastest from one of those boring Oxford pubs. Kirk was driving a Jaguar, but Ken had still thought he had a chance.

The year after that he lost the equivalent of an annual grant from his father's educational fund in the course of a single evening's poker and drinking with the heir to Roland's fortune. He had three jacks and thought he had a chance.

By the time he turned twenty-four he had thanks to some miracle or other acquired documents showing that he had some knowledge of English literature and history and without any great difficulty got a job as a trainee in an English bank of the old school, meaning that the board knew how to appreciate an Oxford graduate who knew his Keats and his Wilde, and took it for granted that carrying out a credit valuation of a customer or analysing financial transactions were talents people from his social background were born with or could pick up along the way.

Ken ended up in stocks and shares and was an unqualified success. He called the most important investors each day to tell them the latest dirty jokes, took the more important ones out to dinner and strip clubs, and the most important ones of all down to his father's country place, where he got them drunk and, on the rare occasions when the opportunity arose, screwed their wives.

The board were debating whether to kick him upstairs and make him a head trader when it emerged that he had lost almost £15 million of the bank's money on unauthorised dealings in futures on the orange juice market. He was summoned to appear before the board where he explained that he had thought he had a chance and was at once kicked not upstairs but out of the bank, the City and the whole of London financial life.

He began drinking but couldn't quite make it work and instead started going to the greyhound races, though he'd never been able to abide dogs. It was then that the gambling really got out of hand. Not in pounds and pence, because Ken, despite his name, no longer had a credit rating. And anyway, it would have been difficult for him to top that orange juice deal. But the compulsive gambling consumed all his time and all his energy, and before too long he was tumbling headlong down a dark pit and on his way to the bottom. Or presumed bottom. Because so far, the falling hadn't stopped, and looking on the bright side of things that might well mean there was no bottom.

Ken Abbott funded his accelerating addiction to gambling by turning to the only person he knew who still didn't seem to have realised what was going on: his father. For the son had discovered that Emerson Abbott had the most wonderful talent for forgetting. Each time he knocked on the door to ask for money his father would stand there, looking at him as though it were for the first time. In fact, looking at him as though it was the first time he had ever stood there at all.

Ken pulls the needle up out through the plastic cork.

'Do you remember how to do it?' By now his father's voice is no more than a hoarse whisper.

Ken tries to smile. He had never been able to stand needles, or else he would never have stopped taking cocaine but gone all the way with it. Not that he wanted to join the 27 Club like Jimi Hendrix, Kurt Cobain and Jim Morrison but, alas, he's like Oscar Wilde in that he can resist everything except temptation. What he has to resist right now is the desire to throw up at the sight of the needle. But he has no choice. This is a matter of life and death.

'Remember and remember,' mumbles Ken. 'Remind me. I have to locate a vein?'

His father shakes his head. He's rolled up his trouser leg and points to his leg where two small holes puncture the skin. Blood is beading on one of them.

'Forget about veins. Just inject the syringe close to the bite. Small injections, three or four pricks. Then one in the thigh.'

'The thigh?'

Despite his condition the father manages to give Ken one of those exasperated looks he hates so much. 'So it's closer to the heart than the bite.'

'Are you certain it was an Egyptian cobra, Father? It can't have been one of those thingummies . . .'

'Thingummies?'

'I don't know . . . a boomslang or something like that.'

Emerson Abbott tries to laugh but all that comes out is a cough.

'A boomslang is a small green bastard that hangs in the trees all day,

Ken. This one was black and it was wriggling along the ground. And the boomslang is haemotoxic, so the blood would have been pouring out of my mouth, my ears and my arse by now. Don't you remember how we went through all this?'

'I just want to be completely sure before I give you the injection.'

'Of course. I'm sorry.' His father closes his eyes. 'I just hope you don't feel these weeks have been a waste of time.'

Ken shakes his head and he means it. Sure, he's hated every second of the twenty-seven days he's been here, hated the long hot days trudging round the snake farm behind his father and the grizzled old Black foreman whose parents, in a darkly humorous moment, had named Adolf. Those voices have gone in one ear and out the other, about the green and the black mambos, about the fangs at the front and the back of the mouth, about the ones that can bite even when you're holding them up by the tail, about which ones are to be fed mice and which ones birds. He doesn't give a shit about whether cobras come from Egypt or Mozambique, all he knows is that there are a hell of a lot of them, and that his father must have been off his trolley when he bought the farm.

In the evenings they sat on the veranda in front of the house, his father and Adolf both sucking on pipes as they heard the cries of the animals out there, with Adolf describing the legends and beliefs related to each one of them as they announced themselves in this way. When the moon rose and the cold laughter of the hyenas made Ken shiver, Adolf told stories about the Zulus, who believed that snakes were the spirits of the dead and let them come into their houses; and about how the tribes in Zimbabwe would never kill pythons because a long drought was certain to ensue. And when Ken laughed at these superstitions his father talked about certain remote regions of the north of England, places in which people still observed an old ritual involving snakes: if you saw an adder you had to kill it at once, draw a circle round it with a cross inside and then read over it from Psalm 68. And as Ken watched in astonishment his father stood up there on the veranda and declaimed into the pitch-black jungle night:

'Let God arise, let his enemies be scattered:
let them also that hate him flee before him.
As smoke is driven away, so drive them away:
as wax melteth before the fire,
so let the wicked perish at the presence of God.'

The bird shrieks again. Perched at the top of the tree the white, long-legged bird with the red comb on its head looks almost like a cockerel.

'Isn't it funny how little we know each other, you and I, Ken?'

Ken jumps. It's as though his father can read his thoughts. His father sighs.

'I don't suppose we ever got to know each other really. I . . . was never really there, was I? It's a pity when fathers aren't there.'

The last sentence lingers in the air and seems to demand an answer, but Ken doesn't have one.

'Do you hate me, Ken?'

The buzzing of the insects suddenly stops, as though all of them are holding their breath.

'No.' Ken holds the point of the needle up and ejects the air until a drop runs down it. 'Hate's got nothing to do with it, Father.'

Emerson Abbott had woken at first light, looked at his sleeping wife as though trying to remember who she was, risen and crossed to the open window, looked at the trees in the park whose black branches reached starkly up towards the grey winter skies, at the asphalt far down below that glistened wetly in the light from the lamp posts, swaying in the wind.

Times were hard, people needed comfort, escapism, cheap lies and dreams, and since he sold these cheapest his publishing business was humming along. An American company had made an offer. The business had been in the family for three generations. Emerson Abbott had smiled. He stepped up onto the windowsill, a gust of wind had wrapped the curtain around his foot and almost made him fall. Holding on to the guttering he raised himself to his full, shivering height. The rain drove in from the side, prickling like icy nails against his skin. He opened his mouth. It tasted of ashes. He knew the time had come for the great leap. He closed his eyes.

When he opened them again he was divorced from Emma, whose surname was now Ives, which was not her maiden name but the name of her new husband, who had moved in after Emerson moved out because by the terms of the settlement she kept the house. The Americans had taken down the Abbott sign above the publisher's door. They had decided they would use their own name, and in truth Emerson was happy that the family name was no longer associated with the products that emerged from behind that door. Through a friend he bought a snake farm in Tuli in the west of Botswana. He knew nothing about the business of farming snakes, only that they delivered snakes to reptile parks and to laboratories that produced serums that could prevent humans dying from snake bites, and that it wasn't particularly profitable.

Three weeks after he had opened his eyes he shut them again as tightly as he could. The sun hung like an oversized reading lamp above the taxi rank outside the international airport in the not quite so international capital of Botswana, a country town the name of which was, his plane ticket told him, Gaborone. He took a taxi to the government offices, and after a week of running up and down the corridors of bureaucracy he left with all the necessary documentation, the licences, the signatures and rubber stamps, and had not since that day been back to Gaborone. And since Gaborone was the only international airport that meant he hadn't left Botswana either.

Because why should he? As quickly and instinctively as he had hated Gaborone he fell in love with Tuli. The farm consisted of three old but well-maintained brick buildings where the staff of four lived alongside the eight hundred snakes, all of them with bites that were in greater or lesser degree fatal. The buildings were situated on a high plain surrounded by buffalo bushes and mongongo trees on gently sloping hillsides. The place was rarely visited, save by elephants taking the wrong route down to the riverbank, jackals in search of offal or discarded shoes, or the weekly jeep that came to fetch snakes and snake serum and brought in supplies along the almost impassable roads. Across the green-rimmed horizon dead trees pointed spectral black fingers up towards the sky, but apart from that there was nothing here to remind him of London.

When the dry season came, herds of impala gathered on the plains where they could be close to water, along with their regular fellow travellers, the apes. After them came the zebras and the kudu antelopes. The lions hunted day and night – it was party time for the savannah's predators – and in the brief dusk they could see the sun flare up in the west before it disappeared, and later on hear the deep growl of the lions rolling through the night as moths swarmed around the outside lamps like snowflakes in a blizzard.

Only once had he doubted that here was where he belonged, and that was when a *Naja nigricollis*, a black-necked spitting cobra, gave birth to her young and he saw the father start to eat them alive, one after another, before they managed to get him out of the cage. Adolf had told him that small snakes were a natural part of the cobra's diet – but its own young? It excited a disgust in him, a distaste for the nature of the creature that left him for a time wondering whether or not he could face carrying on. But then one evening Adolf showed him a dead tiger snake, bitten to death by its own young, and explained to him that the way of nature did not recognise ties of kinship, that it was always and everywhere a case of eat or be eaten. That it wasn't evil or immoral to eat one's own offspring or one's parents – on the contrary it was simply living out nature's imperative, and that was what Africa was about: survival, survival at any price. And in due course Emerson Abbott was able to accept this and even admire it as part of the pitiless system of things, the remorseless logic that kept nature in balance and gave the animals and the humans their right to live. And gradually he rediscovered what he had been missing for so long: the fear of dying. Or more accurately: of not being alive.

And then came the rainy season. He would never forget that first time. He fell asleep to the first rain at night, and when he looked out across the plain the next morning it looked as though some insane painter had gone berserk on the grey and yellow canvas. Within a day or two the plain was transformed into a billowing field of pungent smells, wildly psychedelic colouring and insects that flashed low above a carpet of petals and the swelling brown waters of the river.

And he thought: where else could he possibly want to be?

Six months after his arrival he sent a letter home to Ken, and then, having waited six months for a reply, a second letter. He concluded his monologue the year after with a Christmas greeting and, since he'd heard in a roundabout way that Ken hadn't settled to anything meaningful in London, the offer of a job on the farm.

He wasn't expecting an answer and he didn't get one either. Not until three years later.

Ken liked almost everything about cocaine. He liked the effect it had on him, the people around him liked the effect it had on him, he didn't get hangovers, and he didn't notice any signs of dependency. The only thing he didn't like was the price.

That was the reason, after two terrible weeks at the dog track had brought on a minor financial crisis, he'd turned to the poor man's version – amphetamines. And he met Hilda Bronkenhorst. An ugly and surprisingly stupid health freak he'd slept with a few times in the hope that she'd loan him some of her father's money. Each time he watched her open her legs and demand to be served he thought that at the very least he would have earned the money. Anyway, she was the one who told Ken that amphetamine is a synthetic product. That the body never manages to completely break down synthetic products. Meaning: once you've taken amphetamine there will always be traces of it in your system. And since there were two words that put Ken in an absolute panic – *never* and *always* – he stopped at once. He swore that from that time onwards he would never take anything but healthy, organic compounds like cocaine, and realised that he needed money. And quickly.

His chance came when he called in at the office of a former colleague in the City with the intention of refreshing the friendship so that the next time they met he could ask him for a loan. Just for fun Ken's former colleague showed him an illegal betting ring on the World Cup final between France and Brazil which a couple of the big stockbrokers were running though their own encrypted pages on the Reuters screens. When his ex-colleague left the room to get more tea without logging out Ken didn't hang about. He closed his eyes, saw an image of Ronaldo's dinosaur-thick thighs, typed in his own name and address, navigated across to the stakes column, closed his eyes again, saw Brazil's gold-clad heroes raising the trophy aloft and wrote '£1 million sterling'. Enter. He held his breath as he waited for a response, knew his name wasn't registered, that the stake was too high, but also that in the Reuters world people dealt every second with obligations for ten times that amount without asking who was at the other end. He thought he had a chance. And the message came back: 'CONFIRMED'.

If only Ronaldo hadn't suffered an epileptic fit that night following a protracted PlayStation session then Ken might not have had to worry about how he was going to keep on paying for his cocaine habit nor – as the situation then unfolded – felt any anxieties concerning the immediate state of his health. Two days later, early in the morning, which in Ken's case meant shortly before eleven o'clock, his doorbell rang and a man was standing there wearing a black suit and sunglasses and carrying a baseball bat and explaining to Ken the consequences for him if he wasn't able to get his hands on a million pounds within the next fourteen days.

Four days afterwards, late in July, Emerson Abbott received a telegram in which his son returned his Christmas greetings, accepted the offer of a job and asked him to meet him at the airport in Gaborone in five days' time. Plus details of the bank account for the money for the plane ticket, to be transferred as soon as possible. Emerson was delighted with this turn of events and annoyed only that it meant he would have to go back to Gaborone again.

Ken looked at his watch, a Raymond Weil in South African gold that ticks its way towards Judgement Day with Swiss precision.

This day had started the same as the twenty-six others. Ken woke up wondering where the hell he was and why. He remembered why first. Money. Which should have turned his thoughts in the direction of his creditors in London but which instead turned them to that white powder, which was now like a woman he was no longer quite so sure he had a platonic and no-strings-attached relationship with. The symptoms were classic, but it seemed to him the irritation and the bouts of sweating were just as likely the effects of being in this godforsaken place full of poisonous bugs, insects that were everywhere, and the disrespectful Blacks who seemed to have forgotten long ago just who it was that colonised and attempted to civilise this land. But the depressions were new. Those sudden, dark hours when he seemed to lose his grip on reality, the floor vanished beneath him and he fell down into a bottomless pit, and all he could do was wait until it passed.

'Snake hunt,' said his father at breakfast.

'Fantastic,' replied Ken.

Ken had tried to show an interest, he really had. For twenty-six days he'd sat up straight in his seat as his father lectured him. About everything you should and shouldn't do when dealing with snakes, about which snakes produced which venom, the mortality rates associated with each one and the various symptoms. This last thing was important if one didn't know the type of snake the patient had been bitten by and had to be able to choose the right kind of serum among the forty that were kept on the farm. But if Ken were being honest – something he tried as far as possible to avoid – the poisons, the serums and the symptoms all got jumbled up into one big litany of terrible ways in which to die. Though at least he'd understood that the test tubes of serum had codes and blue caps, and the ones containing the poisons codes and red caps. Or was that the other way round?

When Ken's concentration failed, when his thoughts drifted off and his pen ceased to take notes, then his father would just glower at him.

After breakfast they drove for thirty minutes along something that was vaguely reminiscent of a road, passing variously from thick green scrubland to mudholes half a metre deep and through a desiccated and yellowish lunar landscape. At a certain point, that seemed to Ken to be quite arbitrarily chosen, his father stopped, jumped out and retrieved three cloth sacks and a long pole with a metal loop at the end.

'Put these on.' His father tossed a pair of swimming goggles to him.

Ken gave him a baffled look.

'Spitting cobra. Nerve poison. Can hit you in the eye from eight metres away.'

Then they started searching. Not along the ground but up in the trees.

'Pay attention to the birds,' said his father. 'If you hear them screeching or see them hopping from branch to branch you can be pretty sure there's a boomslang or a green mamba close by.'

'I don't think –'

'Shh! Hear those clicking sounds? Those are polecats, hunting. Come on!'

His father ran in the direction of the sounds with Ken reluctantly trailing along behind him. Suddenly he stopped and signalled for Ken to come closer and be careful. And there – on a large flat rock – sure enough, a long black brute of a thing lay basking in the sun. Ken guessed it must be at least two metres and, maybe, thirteen centimetres long. He wished he could have placed a bet on it. His father made his way stealthily around the rock until he was directly behind it, lifted the pole up high and looped the wire carefully down over the snake's small, distinctive head. Then he tightened it. The snake gave a jerk and opened its jaws wide as though yawning in some incredibly dangerous way. Ken stared in fascination down into the pink gullet and was at once reminded of Hilda Bronkenhorst.

'Can you see how the poison fangs are located at the front of the mouth?' his father shouted enthusiastically.

'Yes?'

'So then what do we have here?'

'Please, Father, let's just get this over with first. It's making me nervous.'

He dropped the snake into the sack that Ken was holding open.

'Black mambo,' said his father, shading his eyes as he peered up into the trees.

Whatever, Ken thought, and shivered as he felt the snake wriggling about inside.

After half an hour in the baking sunlight Ken allowed himself a smoke break. He leaned up against one of those trees his father had tried to teach him the names of, and he thought of the rifle in the car, that this was probably about as good a time as any, when he heard his father's scream. It wasn't really much of a scream, more a short bark, but Ken knew at once what had happened. Maybe because he'd dreamed about it, thought about it or just unconsciously hoped it would happen. He stubbed out his cigarette against the tree trunk. If he was lucky this might turn out to save him a whole lot of bother. He shaded his eyes, and there, over by the riverbank, he saw his father's back, bent over in the waist-high, stiff grass.

'Dammit, Ken! I've been bitten and I didn't see what kind of snake it was. Help me look for him!'

'On my way!'

His father hesitated a moment, perhaps taken aback by the tone of his son's voice.

Ken remembered his father saying that if you couldn't identify the snake and were left to make a choice between the forty different antidotes there was no use in trying to cover every option by injecting all of them; do that, and the antidotes would kill you quicker and more certainly than the poison. He also remembered something his father said about moving your feet quietly when you were out hunting snakes, that they leave as soon as they pick up the vibrations through the ground. Ken put his feet down as heavily as he could.

'Got it!' his father shouted as he dived down into the grass. Another of his lessons: the risk of being bitten a second time is less than not knowing what it was that bit you the first time.

Ken swore inwardly.

Poor bastard, thought Ken as he saw his father swinging the sack over and over again against the nearest tree trunk. And he wasn't thinking of the snake or of his father. The image of the guy in his doorway in the suit and with the baseball bat had appeared on his retinas again. As usual, Ken Abbott was thinking of Ken Abbott.

His father slumped to the ground by the tree trunk as Ken approached. His skin was red and his breath came in hoarse gasps.

'Find out which one it was,' he whispered as he tossed the sack over towards Ken. The cloud of dust whirled up from the ground made Ken cough. He opened the sack and gingerly poked his hand inside.

'Don't . . .' was all his father had time to say.

Ken felt the rough, dry fish skin against the palm of his hand. Over the past few weeks he'd touched more of them than he cared to think about. This one hadn't been any different. Not until he realised that the movement he had felt beneath the scales was muscular and that the animal wasn't dead. Not even close to dead. He screamed, more out of fear than pain, as he felt the fangs penetrate the skin of his arm. He pulled his arm away quickly and saw the two circular puncture marks just below his elbow and screamed again. Then he put his arm to his mouth lightning quick and began feverishly to suck at the holes.

'Cut it out.' His father's voice was weak and despairing. 'That only works in Westerns, I told you that.'

'Yes but –'

'And the other thing I told you was never to stick your hand down into a sack of snakes whether you think they're dead or not. You turn the sack upside down and empty it, being careful about your legs. Always.'

'Always' and 'never' in the same didactic utterance. No wonder Ken hadn't registered it.

'Empty the sack.'

The snake fell to the ground with a soft thud and coiled itself, paralysed by the sunlight.

'What do you think, Ken? A Cape cobra?'

Ken didn't reply, just stared wide-eyed at the snake.

'Sandslang? Gabon viper?'

The supersensitive tongue slid out of its mouth, absorbing tastes and smells in a way that gave it – at least, according to one of his father's lectures – a complete picture of its surroundings within a single second.

'Don't let it get away, Ken.'

But Ken did let it get away. He had neither the strength nor the nerve to touch a snake again, still less one that had just shortened his lifespan down to twenty-seven years.

'Damn!' said his father.

'You must be joking!' said Ken. 'You saw it as clearly as me and you know how to recognise every snake in the whole of this damned continent. Are you telling me you don't know –'

'Of course I know which snake it was,' said his father, looking at Ken in a strange and enigmatic way. 'And that's why I said "Damn". Hurry up and fetch the brown bag from the car.'

'But shouldn't we get back to –'

'It was an Egyptian cobra. Our central nervous systems would be paralysed before we got halfway. Now do as I say.'

Ken's brain tried desperately to assess the situation and the options. It couldn't. He even poked the tip of his tongue out of his mouth, but that didn't help either. So he did as his father told him.

'Open it,' his father said when Ken returned with the large brown buffalo-hide doctor's bag. 'Hurry.'

His body writhed; his mouth was open as though he couldn't get enough air.

'I'm feeling fine, Father, why –'

'Because I was the one who got bitten first. It's got five times as much poison as the second time. Which gives me about half an hour and you two and a half. What do you see?'

'There are a lot of test tubes attached to the sides here.'

'We always take supplies with us of the antidotes for bites we know we won't have time to get back home for. The Egyptian cobra, can you see that one?'

Ken's eyes raced over the names on the labels on the test tubes.

'Here it is, Father.'

'I need to take it at once. Hopefully I'll still be alert enough to show you the way when we drive back to the farm so that we get there well before you start to have problems. The needles are in the bottom. You know what you've got to do, son.'

Ken looks across at his father. It's clear he is no longer able to move. He just sits there, eyes half closed and watching his son. Then Ken concentrates on the needle again. Tries to ignore the nausea. Takes a deep breath. Knows that this is something he'll remember to his dying day, the moment when he took things into his own hands and saved the life of the man he loved above all others. He places the point of the needle between the two bite holes, sees how the skin dips a little under the pressure, and then moves back out again once it's been penetrated and the point enters Ken Abbott's arm. It stings, and he breathes deeply through his nose as he pushes the plunger down. He watches the changing level of the yellow fluid until about two-thirds of it are left, and then pulls the plunger back up a tiny bit, removes the needle and repeats the procedure a little higher up the arm. A thought strikes him: so he won't be joining the 27 Club after all. Quite the contrary; he's going to be rich, happy and have a long life. All thanks to an injection. You could die of laughing.

'How are you feeling?' he asks cheerfully.

'Sad,' whispers his father. His chin is now down in his chest.

Ken withdraws the needle and uses a ball of cotton wool to dry the small bead of blood left behind by the injections. No nausea. No guilty conscience. Just sunshine and joy. In a word – the jackpot, at last.

'Well, my dear Father. If it's any comfort, that actually hurt quite a lot.' Ken looks at his watch. 'Comfort for the last few remaining minutes of your life.'

With a great effort the father lifts his head.

'Why, Ken? In God's name, why?'

Ken sits down beside his father and puts an arm around his shoulder.

'Why? Why d'you think? Same reason I've been going around with that rifle just waiting for a situation to arise in which I could blame a hunting accident, a stray shot or whatever you call it. Money, Father. Money.'

Emerson's head droops down again. 'So that was why you came? For your inheritance?'

With his free hand Ken slaps his father on the back. A throbbing pain has now started spreading in the area around the bite and the needle marks in the other arm.

'I read a depressing article about the age wave in the *Guardian*. You know the life expectancy of middle-class men between fifty and fifty-five who haven't yet had a heart attack or got cancer? Ninety-two. I've got a few creditors who aren't willing to wait that long, Father. But I think it will ease their minds considerably when I return as the sole heir and with your death certificate in my hand.'

'You could have just asked for the money.'

'A million pounds? Even I'm not that cheeky, Father.'

Ken gives a loud laugh. Instantly his laughter is answered from the other side of the river where a pack of grey-brown hyenas have arrived and are observing them with curiosity. Ken shivers.

'Where did they come from?'

'They can smell it,' says Emerson.

'Smell? Surely you haven't begun to smell already.'

'Death. They recognise the smell of it. I've seen it before.'

'Well. They're ugly, they're stupid and they're on the other side of the river. I hate them.'

'That's because they're morally superior to us.'

Ken looks on in surprise as his father continues:

'No freedom of choice, no morality, you're probably thinking. But if freedom of choice means being able to force your nature, and morality is to will it, then why are we so unhappy?'

Emerson Abbott raises his head again and smiles sadly.

'Well, it's because we fool ourselves into thinking we could have done things differently. We think having souls gives us the ability to act in ways that are not just designed to benefit ourselves. But we can't. And the proof is that we are here, we still exist. We eat our fathers and sons when we must, not from hate but out of love of life. And yet we think we'll burn in hell for it. And maybe we will. That's why the cobra which chooses to eat its own young is morally superior to us. It doesn't feel a moment's shame, because there is no sin, just the consuming will to live. Understand? You are your only redeemer. And redemption comes only when you do what you have to do to survive.'

Ken's on the point of replying when a sudden pain in his chest causes him to lose his breath.

'Something wrong?' asks the father.

'I . . .'

'You have a pain in your chest,' said his father. Suddenly his voice is normal again. 'That's how it starts.'

'Starts? What . . .'

'The Egyptian cobra. You do remember how we went through this?'

'But . . .'

'Nerve poison. First, burning pains around the site of the bite that gradually spread to the rest of the body. The skin around the bite becomes discoloured, the arms and legs swell up, and then comes a feeling of drowsiness. And then, towards the end: accelerating heart rate, discharges from the mouth and eyes, paralysis at the back of the throat making it difficult to speak or breathe before the advent of the final stage: the nerve poison paralyses the heart and lungs and you die. It can take hours and is extremely painful.'

'Father!'

'You sound surprised, son. Weren't you paying attention in class?'

'But you . . . you seem . . . better.'

'No, you can't have been paying attention,' says the father with a thoughtful look on his face. 'Or you would have noticed the difference between an Egyptian cobra and an African rock python.'

'African . . . rock python?'

'Aggressive and unpleasant, but not poisonous.' His father sits up and rolls his neck. 'You're right, I'm absolutely fine. But how are you? Do you notice how your throat is beginning to constrict, son? In a little while the cramps will come, and that really isn't something to look forward to.'

'But we . . .'

'Were bitten by the same snake. Mysterious, isn't it? Maybe what you took is a little different from what's in me.'

Ken's mind clouds over. He looks at the empty test tube on the ground, tries to get up but his legs won't carry him. His armpits have started aching.

'If you'd been paying attention in class you would have checked the cork on the test tube before injecting yourself, Ken.'

Red, thought Ken. Red cork. He's injected poison into his own arm.

'But there were no other test tubes for the Egyptian cobra, I checked them all. None with a blue cork, no antidote . . .'

His father shrugs. Ken gasps for air. The buzzing of insects has become a steady pressure against his eardrums.

'You knew it all along. You knew . . . why . . . I came.'

'No, I didn't know. But I'm not stupid so I didn't completely exclude it either. And of course, I would have stopped you had you tried to inject me with it.'

Ken can't feel the tears coursing down his cheeks.

'Father . . . drive me back now. Time is . . .'

But his father seems not to have heard him. He is on his feet now and peering across to the other side of the river.

'Adolf says they're good swimmers, though I've never seen it myself.'

Ken slides down and remains lying on his back, staring up at the sky. The sun is still high above the trees on the hilltop, but he knows that come seven o'clock it will be as though someone cuts an invisible thread, and the sun will tumble in free fall below the horizon and within fifteen minutes all will be pitch-black. The white bird screeches again. It flaps its wings and two seconds later Ken sees it crossing his field of vision. It's so beautiful.

'Time to be getting back,' says his father. 'Adolf will have dinner ready soon.'

Ken hears his father pick up the bag with the serum inside and then hears him move away. For a few seconds there is silence. Then he hears splashing sounds from the water. Ken Abbott knows he hasn't a chance.

BLACK KNIGHT

Part 1: The Opening

'YOU CAN FEEL YOUR EYELIDS getting heavy,' I said.

The pocket-watch – maker unknown but weighted by sufficient gold to keep it swaying steadily for some time – had been in the family's possession since 1870.

'You are feeling tired. Close your eyes.'

The silence was complete. The street-facing windows were triple-glazed, so that not even the chiming from the mighty bells of the Duomo di Milano penetrated. It was so quiet that the absence of ticking was noticeable. The hands were splayed out on each side from the moment the watch breathed its last. Now the mute object was minus the function a watch is meant for.

'When you wake up you will not remember that you were gravid or that you've had an abortion. The child never existed.'

I felt suddenly on the verge of tears. When I lost my own child I also lost what we psychologists call my affective control, meaning that I could whimper and blubber over the slightest thing that reminded me of it. I pulled myself together and continued: 'It will seem to you as though you came here to be cured of a nicotine addiction.'

Ten minutes later I carefully woke Fru Karlsson from her trance.

'I don't feel any craving at all,' she said as she buttoned her mink coat and looked at me.

I was sitting behind my desk and taking notes with the Montegrappa pen I had come across many years ago in an antiques shop. Patients like to see you making notes, it makes them feel a little less like something on a conveyor belt.

'Tell me, Dr Meyer, is hypnosis difficult?'

'It depends what you're hypnotising,' I said. 'As film directors say, the hardest to work with are children and animals. And it's easiest with a receptive and creative spirit like yours, signora.'

She laughed.

'There are rumours that you once managed to hypnotise a dog, Dr Meyer. Is that true?'

'Just rumours,' I smiled. 'And even if I had, I have a vow of confidentiality as regards all my patients.'

She laughed again. 'But what power it gives you!'

'I'm afraid I'm as powerless as anyone else,' I said, searching through the desk drawer for an ink cartridge to replace the one in the pen, now empty. The leader of a local chess club I used to belong to once said to me that the reason I always lost was not that I didn't know what I was doing, but that I sabotaged my own chances of winning through my bewildering weakness for the weak. He suspected that I would prefer to sacrifice a castle rather than a knight because I *liked* the knight better. Or because I thought of myself as a knight.

'They're pieces, Lukas,' he said. 'Pieces! The knight is the least valuable, and that is a fact, not preferences.'

'Not in every position. The knight can get himself out of some pretty tight situations.'

'Knights are slow and always arrive too late to save anyone, Lukas.'

I found the ink cartridge, a narrow metal sleeve the same length as the pen, and with a thin steel tip like a hypodermic syringe. I realised it would be my last one, that Montegrappa pens and cartridges were no longer produced. Like so many other uselessly beautiful quality products it had vanished beneath the merciless pressure of global competition.

I wrote slowly, reverently, careful not to waste my words. Fru Karlsson would start smoking again. And she'd tell all her friends that Dr Meyer was no good so I'd spared a rush from that quarter. She wouldn't remember she'd had an abortion. If she ever did it would be because something had overridden the hypnosis. A special word, a mood, a dream, it could be anything. As in my case. At times I've thought I might like to obliterate Benjamin and Maria from my memory. At other times not. Anyway, it's been a long time now since I had the ability to hypnotise myself. One learns too much about it. Like the conjuror no longer able to enjoy being fooled, even when one wants to be.

Once Fru Karlsson had gone I packed my beautiful black leather Calvino bag. I'd bought it because it had the same name as the anti-Fascist rebel Italo Calvino. And, of course, because I could afford it.

I knotted my Burberry scarf and walked into the reception area. Linda, who was the receptionist for me and the two other psychologists in our joint practice, looked up.

'Have a nice day, Lukas,' she said with an almost inaudible sigh and a scarcely noticeable glance at her watch which showed, as usual, that it was still only three. She used this Americanism not, primarily, to bless the remaining hours of daylight, or until I went to bed, but to point out the injustice in the fact that my working day was so much shorter than that of my two colleagues, and therefore hers. I think she believed – or thought she believed – that my not taking on more patients showed a lack of solidarity, but there was no way she could know that in recent years the psychology practice had become secondary and functioned more or less as a cover for my other, real job. Which was to kill people.

'Have a nice day, Linda,' I said as I strolled out into the lovely December sunshine.

I've never quite been able to make up my mind whether or not Milan is a beautiful city. It has been in the past, you only need to look at the pictures from back then, when Milan was a city in Italy, and not in Capitalia, as I call the stateless condition the world is in today. Of course, before the last of the physical world wars it had been almost supernaturally beautiful, but even after the bombs the city has preserved a discreet but distinct elegance in which the fashion houses in particular had influenced the style and taste, and vice versa. In the days before the sixteen giant business cartels assumed control of Europe, North America and Asia, factory emissions were subject to central authority regulations, which meant that even in Milan, with one of the worse air-pollution problems in Europe, one could still on a good day see all the way to the white peaks of the Dolomites. Now it lay over the city in a constant veil, and those who could not afford the overpriced air conditioners now in the hands of a monopoly lived lives that were short and sickly.

The cartel-run media tell us that people are richer than ever before and prove it by presenting us with statistics showing the real income per inhabitant. The reality is of course that the creators and directors of the cartels earn a thousand times more than the average worker. Eighty per cent of them are on temporary contracts with no chance to plan for the long term. They have to live in the ever-expanding slum that surrounds the city on all sides save in the north.

After Milan became the centre of European finance, with the Borsa Milano and the headquarters of seven of the cartels, the population exploded. The city was now not only the largest in Europe but also harboured the world's third-largest slum. I'm no socialist, but you don't need to be one to feel a longing for a time when incomes were lower but distributed more evenly, and there was a functioning state which did its best to help those who were struggling.

I passed the Duomo di Milano. In front of the imposing cathedral, queues of the tourists and the faithful extended into the large square of the Piazza Duomo. At the other end of the square I passed the tables of what those of us working in the business call Café Morte, Café Dead. The men sitting there – and they were exclusively men – had newspapers and phones in front of them while their eyes swept the square in search of possible employment. The market for contract killing had grown exponentially once the cartels and an unregulated open market took over, and those offering the service could principally be divided into two classes, a bit like prostitution. Café Morte was the outdoor market, for the street-walkers. Customers using the place could get a job done for a fee in the region of 10,000 euros. The quality was variable, as was the discretion offered; but in a society in which both the police and the authorities were drastically reduced and institutionally corrupt the risk of being caught was acceptably low. So the response of the family members or the employers of a target was quite commonly to arrange a contract killing. It meant that the business – like gun running or drug smuggling – was expanding.

The first cartel killings, in which personnel from rival cartels were killed in order to weaken their competitors, were carried out by taxi drivers, and it's generally believed that that's why we're referred to as 'drivers'. But you've got those who wait for their fares at a taxi rank like the Café Morte, and then you've got the limo drivers, the ones who work the indoor market, the luxury prostitutes, the ones you need to approach through a middleman called a 'fixer'. Drivers like that have reputations and can cost as much as ten times what they charge at the Café Morte, but if you want to take out some well-protected employee from one of the cartels then these are the ones you need to hire. People like me.

I had no idea I had a talent for work of this kind, would even have thought the opposite. But a high degree of empathy can also help in understanding how an opponent thinks. In the two years I'd been in the killing business I'd become one of the most in-demand names. Income from my psychology had been sinking from the day my son turned eight years old and died, and after Maria committed suicide it dried up completely. But money wasn't the reason I became a driver. As a psychologist I'm used to deducing people's simple and often banal motivations, and that includes my own. And my motive was revenge. I was able to live with the fact that my child had been born dumb. That was just mere chance, no one's fault, and it didn't spoil anyone's happiness. But I couldn't live with what had taken Benjamin's life: human greed, businessmen who had worked out that if they took a few discreet shortcuts around the expensive fire regulations required for their electrical products they could sell them cheaper than their competitors and still increase the profit margin. I realise it might seem a bit strange to claim that a defective bedside lamp could be the cause of a man abandoning his humanity and embarking on a career as a spreader of death. And I use the word 'spread' advisedly; because I didn't have one name to focus my anger on I had to take revenge on all of those who ran the cartels and took those kinds of decisions, those whose unscrupulous worship of Mammon had taken Benjamin and Maria from me. The way a terrorist whose family has been killed by a bomb will fly a plane into a skyscraper full of people he knows aren't personally responsible for his loss but who are still complicit in their death. Yes, I knew exactly why I had become a man who murdered prominent members of the cartels. But such knowledge doesn't change anything; insight like that doesn't necessarily lead to a change in behaviour. Spreading death did nothing to slake my thirst for revenge – I had to keep going. I could of course have ended my own life, but the sudden realisation that life is meaningless doesn't necessarily mean that people want to stop living. People like Maria are, after all, the exception.

I carried out a test which I did at regular intervals, letting my gaze sweep across the pavement tables outside the cafe. Noted that I still did not register any flicker of recognition in the gazes that met mine. They simply recorded the fact that I was not a customer and moved on. Good.

To carry on making a living in the limousine trade it was imperative that no one – not even the customer – should know your face. The fixers took twenty-five per cent of the fee and they were worth it, if for no other reason than that we could hide ourselves behind them. Among those who got taken in the limo branch – and by 'taken' I don't mean by the police – there were more fixers than drivers. You only had to look at the gravestones in the Cimitero Maggiore to know that.

In addition to my unquenchable thirst for revenge I had certain other advantages as a driver. One of them was Judith Szabó, known simply in the business as the Queen. She was one of the three or four best fixers and her abilities were legendary. People said the Queen never left a boardroom meeting without a deal, and at this moment in time I was her only regular client. And only lover. I think. Of course, I can't be certain – her previous steady client also believed he was her only lover. Another advantage was that unlike many of the other drivers I had a credible cover, at least I did as long as I had enough patients not to make it seem odd that I should keep on turning up at the office. My third and most important advantage was that I had a murder weapon the others didn't. Hypnosis.

I stopped at a pedestrian crossing and waited for the light to change from red to green, all senses on the alert. I no longer like standing still in a public setting without knowing who the people around me are. A rifle with a telescopic sight and silencer behind one of those French balconies, a knife in the back as the lights change to green, the blade up into the kidneys so the initial pain is so great the victim is unable to make a sound but is left lying there as the crowds move on.

There was a time when drivers were at the top of the food chain, or at least had no need to walk in fear of their lives. This was before the cartels began employing the best of them on a permanent basis, so that the drivers themselves became key employees and, as such, legitimate targets. The cartels had organised their own militia which were in practice above the law, and competition for the markets – meaning principally technology, entertainment and medicine – was becoming more and more reminiscent of old-fashioned wars than old-fashioned capitalism. I had recently read an article that compared the situation with that of the Opium War of 1839, when the British East India Company, with the support of the British government, went to war against China to defend their right to export opium to the Chinese, on the basis of the mercantile principle of free trade. Today it was no longer about opium but technology, entertainment, a kind of mild stimulant known as *artstimuli*, and medicines that extended one's lifespan. The strange thing was that while the markets were deregulated and the competition in every way tougher, the number of actors had fallen, not risen, and the incidents of mono- and oligopoly more frequent as a result of the acquisitions. Because as they say in the world of the sharks: size is everything. Or rather, size won't help if you've got no teeth. The teeth were the best brains, the best inventors, the best chemists, the best business strategists, and in due course these rose to the same status and wage levels as the top footballers. But after a while those companies that were unable to afford these wages – and were unscrupulous enough – began to kill the best brains of the others as a way of lowering the standards and enabling themselves to compete. The best companies had to respond in kind in order to remain market leaders, and the best chemists, inventors and leaders were replaced by a new aristocracy: the best contract killers. It looked as though the company with the best killers would, in the long run, turn out winners. And that's what started the cannibalising process we're in the middle of now. Companies hired killers to kill their competitors' best contract killers.

And that's why I froze when I heard the voice behind me, and a little to my left, in what is so aptly called the driver's *blind spot*. It wasn't because I recognised the voice – I didn't – and yet I knew it had to be him. Partly because he spoke the Neapolitan variant of the Calabria dialect, which was why they called him 'il Calabrese' (Broccoli). Partly because I had been halfway expecting him to appear sooner or later. Partly because no other driver but Gio 'il Calabrese' Greco could have sneaked up on me like that. And partly because I could see, reflected in the windscreens of the passing cars, that the man behind me was wearing a white suit, and Greco always wore a white suit when out on a killing.

'Now that's quite an achievement,' said the voice into my ear.

I had to steel myself not to turn. I told myself there would be no point, that if he was going to kill me he would already have done so or would do before I could do anything about it. Because what we are talking about here is the best driver in Europe. This is not a matter of opinion. For several years Greco had been the highest paid driver in Europe, and we live in an age in which it is generally accepted that the market is always right. According to Judith, when she was Greco's fixer she could get double what Thal, Fischer or Alekhin were paid.

'Think you're better than me, Lukas?'

I stepped back half a pace as a trailer whizzed by in front of my face and made the ground shake.

'To the best of my knowledge they pay you three times what they pay me. So no.'

'What makes you think I'm talking shop, Lukas? I'm wondering if you think you fuck her better than me?'

I swallowed. He laughed. A hissing laughter that began in a T and then turned into a long, jerking S.

'I'm joking,' he said. 'I am talking shop. The killing of Signor Chadaux. The board of his company couldn't decide whether it was a traffic accident or a suicide. So they called in an expert on death. Me. Because on the footage from the traffic-monitoring camera –' he pointed up towards the facade on the other side of the road where I knew the cameras were mounted – 'you see Signor Chadaux standing with the other pedestrians waiting for the red light right where we're standing. But when the lights changed to green and everyone began to cross, Signor Chadaux was left standing here alone. He looks like he's asleep on his feet as another crowd of pedestrians comes up alongside him. But then the lights change to red, he closes his eyes and moves his lips, as though he's counting inwardly. Have you seen the recording?'

I shook my head.

'Then perhaps you saw it when it actually happened?'

Again I shook my head.

'Really? Then let me describe it for you. He steps straight out onto the pedestrian crossing. Know how many cars ran over him before they managed to stop the traffic? No, then you probably don't know that either. Let me tell you something they didn't put in the newspaper, and that is that Signor Chadaux had to be scraped off the asphalt like chewing gum.'

'Did they find out whether it was an accident or a suicide?'

Greco laughed that thin, hissing laughter of his. Softly, but so close to my ear I could still hear it above the traffic.

'Chadaux's company is a competitor of one of the companies you're working for. You believe in coincidence, Lukas?'

'Sure. They happen all the time.'

'No, you don't.' Greco wasn't laughing any more. 'I studied the video a few times, then I came down here to take a closer look. In particular I checked that traffic light that you can see in the video Signor Chadaux has his eyes fixed on.'

Gio Greco pointed to the set of lights directly opposite us. 'It has screwdriver markings on it. And when I checked the security camera it turns out it was down for about an hour the previous night, not that anyone could explain why. How did you do it, Lukas? Did you install a screen in the traffic light which you could use your phone to communicate with to hypnotise Signor Chadaux? Did you tell him when to step out into the road, or was there a trigger? The red light, for example?'

Through the winter cold I could feel the sweat breaking out over my whole body. I had only ever spoken to Greco twice before, and I was afraid both times. Not because there was anything to be afraid of – this was before drivers were used to liquidate each other out. It was just his aura. Or rather, the absence of an aura, the way cold is just the absence of warmth. The way pure evil is just the absence of mercy. As I see it, a psychopath is not a person possessing a special quality, but someone just lacking something.

'Have they put you on to me?' I asked. 'Chadaux's company?'

On the traffic lights in front of us the red figure gave way to the green, and on either side of us people streamed across. If I moved, would I get a bullet in the back?

'Who knows? Whatever, you don't sound as if you're all that afraid to die, Lukas?'

'There's worse fates than leaving this vale of tears,' I said as I watched the retreating backs of the pedestrians who had left us alone on the pavement.

'Better than being left – I think we can agree on that, Lukas.'

The first thing that occurred to me was, naturally, that he was talking about how Judith had left him. It would have been naive to suppose that he wouldn't find out somehow or other that I had taken his place as both her client and her lover. But something in the way he said it made me think he might have been referring to me. That it was me who had been left by my son Benjamin and by my wife. I had no idea how he might have come by such information.

'Hello, I'm . . .' he said in English. The words came slowly, rhythmically. I stiffened.

'Relax,' he said with a soft laugh. 'I'm not going to shoot you here right in front of the security cameras.'

I forced one foot forward, then the other. I walked on without looking back.

The most obvious reason Milan has become the capital for Europe's drivers is, of course, that it has become a centre for technology and innovation. The best brains are here, the richest companies. The city is a watering hole on the savannah where animals of every kind congregate; apart from the handful of herbivores so large they've got no need to worry, most of us are hunters, prey or scavengers. We live in a symbiotic relationship of fear from which none of us can escape.

I walked along one of those narrow cobbled pedestrian lanes that twist slightly so you can't see far ahead. Maybe that's why I always choose this route to my office: I don't have to see everything that lies ahead.

I passed the small, exclusive fashion shops, some of the less exclusive, and the workshops housing the craftsmen who experienced a renaissance after the mass production of so many goods came to a standstill as a result of the shortage of raw materials.

My chessboard was waiting at home for me, set up for my favourite game, Murakami versus Carlsen. It was a game from the years after Carlsen peaked, but well known because in the very early stages Carlsen wandered into a trap so obvious and yet so cunning that it was afterwards called the Murakami Trap and became as famous as the Lasker Trap. Murakami would later use a brutal variation of the trap in an even more celebrated game of lightning chess, against the young Italian comet Olsen, from right here in Milan.

My heart was still pounding after the encounter with Gio Greco. I knew, of course, that murder in the street wasn't his style; he left that kind of thing to the drivers. But when he had said 'Hello, I'm . . .', I had felt certain my time was up, and I would soon be meeting Benjamin and Maria again. I don't know whether it's because Greco is a fan of Johnny Cash, but his calling card, his farewell to his victims is, according to legend, 'Hello, I'm Greco.' I know some people say he only began saying that *after* the legend arose. If he wasn't actually present, that is. Because he was capable of remote killing too, as the case of the spectacular attack on the Giualli family in the Sforzesco Castle the previous year showed.

I knew no one was following me, but naturally I couldn't help wondering why he had suddenly appeared like that and given me just half of his famous line. Because Greco had been right; I didn't believe in coincidences. Was it a threat? But why should I take the threat seriously when both he and I knew he could have done the job there and then; it would have been a perfect opportunity. What was he planning? Maybe he just wanted me to believe he was planning something, maybe that was just an old lover wanting to make sure the new one didn't sleep too well at night.

My thoughts were interrupted by loud voices and shouts ahead of me.

A crowd of people were gathered in the narrow street, standing with their heads looking upwards. I looked up too. Black smoke was belching out from a French balcony on the floor below the top. Behind the balcony bars I saw something, a pale face. A boy. Eight maybe? Ten? It was hard to tell from below.

'Jump,' shouted one of the onlookers.

'Why doesn't someone run up and get the boy?' I asked the man who had shouted.

'The gate's locked.'

Others came running. The crowd doubled, trebled in size and I realised I must have arrived just after the fire had been discovered. The boy opened his mouth, but no sound came out. I should have realised at once, and maybe I did. It probably wouldn't have changed anything; I could feel the tears welling up inside.

I ran to the gate and hammered on it. A small aperture opened and I was looking into a bearded face.

'Fire on the sixth!' I said.

'We're waiting for the fire brigade,' the man answered, his voice suggesting a line already learned and rehearsed.

'That's going to be too late – someone has to rescue that boy.'

'The place is on fire.'

'Let me in,' I said quietly, though everything in me wanted to scream.

The gate opened slightly. The man was tall and broad, with a head that looked as if it had been beaten down between his shoulders with a sledgehammer. He was wearing an ordinary driver's uniform, a nondescript black suit. So when I pushed my way in and past him, it was because he allowed me to do so.

I sprinted up the stairs, the toxic air scorching my lungs as I ran, counting each floor. When I stopped on the sixth there were two doors. I grabbed the handle of the one on the left. It was locked, and I heard the furious barking of a dog within. Then I realised the balcony was on the right side of the front of the building and tried the handle of the second door.

To my surprise it opened and smoke came billowing out. Behind the black wall I glimpsed flames. I pulled a piece of my woollen coat up over my face and went in. I couldn't see much, but it seemed to be a small apartment. I headed in the direction the balcony had to be and banged into a sofa. I shouted, but there was no reply. Coughed and headed on. Flames licked from an open fridge door and on the floor in front of it lay the twisted and charred remains of something. A bedside lamp?

As I say, I don't believe in coincidences, and this was an orchestrated replay, arranged for my benefit alone. Yet I still had to do what I knew I was expected to do – I could see no alternative.

A sudden gust of wind briefly wafted the smoke away from the balcony door and I saw the boy. He was wearing a dirty blazer with a badge on it, a stained, threadbare T-shirt and trousers to match. He stared at me with wide-open eyes. His hair was fair, just like Benjamin's, but not as thick.

I took two quick steps forward and wrapped my arms around the boy, lifted him up and felt the small, warm fingers grab the skin at the back of my neck. I raced towards the front door, coughing smoke. Found it after feeling my way along the wall, tried to locate the handle. Couldn't find it. I kicked at the door, put my shoulder to it, but it wouldn't budge. Where the hell was the door handle?

I got my answer when I heard the hissing from the fridge, like the sound of air escaping from a punctured hosepipe. Gas streamed out, igniting the flames and illuminating the whole apartment.

The door had no handle. No keyhole, nothing. Directed by: Gio Greco.

Without letting go of the boy I ran back to the open balcony door. I leaned over the wrought-iron railings on the shallow balcony.

'Breathe,' I said to the boy, who was still staring at me with his wide-open brown eyes. He did as I instructed, but I knew that no matter how far out I held him, we would both soon die from carbon monoxide poisoning.

I looked down at the crowd in the street below, the faces staring up open-mouthed. Some were shouting, but I heard nothing, their words were drowned by the raging of the flames behind us. Just as I didn't hear the sirens of the approaching fire engines. Because there were none.

The man who had opened the gate for me, he wasn't just wearing the same suit as the others at the Café Morte; his face also had the same cold, closed expression, as dead as his victims.

I looked to my right. There was an ordinary balcony there, but it was too far away, there was no chance of reaching it. No balconies to the left, but there was a small ledge leading to the nearest window in the neighbouring apartment.

There was no time to lose. I held the boy a little bit away from me and looked into his brown eyes.

'We're going there, so you're going to have to sit on my back and hold on tight. Understand?'

The boy didn't answer, just nodded.

I swung him over onto my back and he held around my neck and wrapped his legs around my stomach. I stepped over the railing, holding fast to the rail as I placed one foot on the ledge. It was so narrow there was room for only a small part of one shoe, but fortunately they were my thick winter shoes, stiff enough to provide some support. I let go of the railing with one hand and pressed it against the wall.

People down below were screaming up at us, but I was hardly aware of them, or of the height. Not that I'm not afraid of heights, because I am. If we fell we would die, no question. But since the brain knew that the alternative to balancing on the ledge was burning alive it did not hesitate. And because balancing requires more concentration than the summoning of desperate powers, the brain temporarily closed down the fear side since that served no useful function in the current situation. In my experience, both as a psychologist and as a professional killer, we human beings are surprisingly rational in that respect.

With infinite care I let go of the railing. I was standing with my chest and cheek pressed in against the rough plaster and felt myself in balance. It was as though the boy realised he had to remain quite still on my back.

There was no longer any shouting from the street below; the only sound was that of the flames that were now outside on the balcony. In a sort of slow shuffle I started to move carefully to my right along the small but hopefully solid ledge. Solid it wasn't. To my alarm I saw it disintegrating in gel-like pieces beneath my feet. It was as though the pressure from the shoes created a chemical reaction in the ledge, and I could see now that it was a slightly different colour to the rest of the facade. Since I was unable to stand in the same place for more than a few seconds before the ledge began disintegrating I kept moving. We were already so far from the French balcony that retreat had become impossible.

When I was close enough to the window in the neighbouring apartment I carefully loosened my Burberry scarf with my left hand while holding on with my right to the protruding windowsill. I had been given the scarf by Judith as a fortieth birthday present, along with a card on which she had written that she liked me a lot, a joke referring to the strongest word I ever used to express devotion to her. If I could manage to wrap the scarf around my hand I could break the windowpane, but one end of it was trapped between the boy's arm and my neck.

The boy gave a start and moved as I jerked the scarf free, and I lost my balance. With my right hand gripping round the windowsill and only my right foot on the ledge I swung out helplessly from the facade like a barn door on hinges, almost fell, and then at the last moment managed to grab hold of the window ledge with my other hand.

I looked down and saw the Burberry scarf gently drifting down towards the ground. The height. The hollow feeling in my stomach. Got to keep it out. I raised my bare right fist and punched the windowpane with all my might, trying to tell myself that by hitting so hard I was reducing the risk of cuts. The glass shattered in a shower of shards and I felt the pain race up my arm. It wasn't from the cut but because my fist had hit something hard. I grabbed hold of whatever this hard thing was, leaned to one side and saw that my punch had landed on a metal grid. It was hinged on both sides and locked in the centre with a large padlock. Who puts wrought-iron bars on a sixth-floor window?

The answer was obvious.

Through the bars I looked into a small, bare, dimly lit apartment. No furniture, only a large fire-axe hanging on the wall directly facing me, as though on exhibition. Or to put it another way, as though Greco wanted me to see it immediately.

Scrabbling, scraping sounds. A dark figure ran over the floor snarling and jumping. I felt the wet jaws and the teeth across my fingers holding round the bars. Then it dropped down to the floor and began howling furiously.

Instinctively I leaned backwards as the dog jumped up at me, and now I could feel the boy's small hands slipping down my neck. He wouldn't be able to hold on much longer. We had to get in there, quickly.

The dog – a Rottweiler – sat on the floor directly below the window, slathering from its open jaws with white, glistening teeth. It stood up on its hind legs and leaned them against the wall, but its snout kept butting up against the bars and it was unable to reach my fingers. As it stared at me with a cold, expressionless hatred I noticed something dangling from the collar around its thick neck. A key.

The dog gave up. Its forepaws slid down and it sat on the floor, barking up at me.

The boy tensed his legs and tried to ride higher up my back. He was whimpering softly. I stared at the key. At the fire-axe. And at the padlock.

Greco was willing to sacrifice a piece.

That's what the great chess players do. Not to give the opponent an advantage but to improve their own position on the board. At that exact moment I couldn't see what his plan was, but I knew he had to have one. During a chess tournament in Nottingham in 1936 Emanuel Lasker, the German world chess champion, watched his opponent think for half an hour before finally offering him a major capture. The German declined the offer but went on to win the game. When he was asked afterwards why he hadn't taken the piece he replied that when an opponent as good as his thinks about a move for half an hour before deciding that the sacrifice is worth the reward, then he certainly wasn't going to respond by making the exact move his opponent had been expecting of him.

I thought about it. Ran through it. And made the move my opponent had been counting on.

I squeezed my left arm between the bars. It was so tight the sleeves of my jacket and shirt were pulled up exposing the naked, bloodied skin. My offer to the dog. Which responded silently and at lightning speed.

It twisted its lips and I could see the teeth sink into my underarm. The pain didn't come until it clamped its jaws. I pushed my right arm through, but as my hand stretched for the key around its collar the dog pulled my left arm down towards the floor in an attempt to get away from my free hand.

It isn't true that certain breeds are able to lock their jaws, but some bite harder than others. And some are more intelligent than others. Rottweilers bite harder and have a higher IQ than most. So high in fact that I chose a Rottweiler when I made a bet with two other psychology students that I could make an animal perform simple tasks – such as nodding several times, for example – under hypnosis. But the only thing I managed was to get it to sit quite still, and there was nothing new in the fact that a few simple techniques can get animals – everything from dogs and chickens to pigs and crocodiles – to lie motionless and apparently under deep trance. The hypnotist can only take partial credit for this catatonic state, which is due as much to the instinct to 'play dead' in situations in which flight is impossible. The aim is to arouse the predator's reluctance to eat something that is already dead and possibly diseased. But it was obviously new enough for my two friends, who handed the money over and earned me an undeserved reputation as the great animal hypnotist. And at that stage of my life I couldn't afford to turn down either one.

I forced my right hand in between the bars until I could reach down to the dog and let my hand rest lightly on the animal's forehead. Moved it slowly and rhythmically back and forth while keeping up a stream of low talk. The dog looked up at me without releasing its jaws. I don't know what it was feeling. A hypnotist is not, in virtue of his trade, any kind of sage. He's just someone who's learned certain techniques, an average chess player lacking in any particular insight who makes the opening gambits he has seen praised in some book. But obviously there are both good and bad hypnotists, and I was, after all, one of the good ones, perhaps even one of the best.

Even in humans, what hypnosis does is leapfrog over the slow cognitive processes, which is why it works so surprisingly quickly, quickly enough for a man waiting at a pedestrian crossing to be manipulated by simply looking into a traffic light for a few seconds and seeing there some previously implanted trigger.

I saw the dog's eyelids half close and felt the jaws relax. Continuing to speak slowly and calmly I moved my right hand to the chain-collar, released the key and pulled it towards me. At that same moment I felt the boy's grip loosen and his body start to slide down my back. I reached out behind me, grabbing across the little body and caught him by the lining of his trousers before he fell off. I held on to him but knew I wouldn't be able to do so for long.

I had managed to hold on to the key by pressing my thumb inside the key ring; now I had to work it out and get it in the padlock in the middle of the bars. It couldn't be done with one hand. The bite was almost completely relaxed now and carefully I pulled my arm away, feeling at the same time how I was also pulling at the dog's head. The teeth of a predator incline backwards, I reflected. It's logical, so that they can hold on to their prey. So very carefully I pushed my arm a little further inwards before lifting it, and this time my hand came free. The blood ran down my forearm and into my palm so that I almost slipped off as I gripped round one of the bars with my little finger and ring finger.

'Hold on tight for ten seconds,' I said loudly. 'Count out loud.'

The boy didn't answer but renewed his grip around my neck.

I let go of him and using the other three fingers and my right hand I managed to get the key in the padlock and turn it. The hasp sprang up. I pushed one side of the grid open and turned so that that the boy could climb off me and get in through the window.

From the street below came the sounds of applause and bravos. I entered the apartment. The dog sat quite still, staring off into space, or perhaps deep into itself, who knows? I don't read the professional journals any more, but I do recall a listing once of animals believed by researchers to experience an 'I', and that list didn't include dogs.

The door was lined with a blank metal plate and like the door in the neighbouring apartment it had no handle. To make sure it was actually locked I gave it a little shove with my foot before lifting the fire-axe down from its two hooks on the wall. I tested its weight and studied the door.

Blood from my arm dripped onto the wooden floor below me with a deep, sighing sound. I heard another sound and turned to the window.

The boy was standing directly in front of the dog. He was stroking it!

I saw the muscles tense beneath the dog's smooth dark fur, saw its ears prick up. The trance was over. I heard a low growling.

'Get away!' I shouted, but I knew it was too late. The boy managed a half-pace back before his face was splattered with blood. He sank to his knees, a look of shock in his eyes. The blade of the axe was wedged into the wooden floor directly in front of him, and between the blade and the boy lay the decapitated dog's head with its twisted lips. The heart pumped two final spurts of blood from the mutilated body.

For a second or two I simply stood there. And only now did I realise that so far not a sound had come from the boy's lips. I dropped to my knees, right in front of him. Took off my coat and wiped the blood from his face with it before placing a hand on his shoulder and making eye contact with him, then shaping my words with my hands:

You're a mute, is that right?

He didn't respond.

476

'Are you a mute?' I asked in a loud, clear voice.

The boy nodded.

'I had a son who was a mute too,' I said. 'He used sign language, so I can understand that. Do you know sign language?'

The boy shook his head. Opened his mouth and pointed in towards the gap. Then he pointed to the axe blade.

'Oh Jesus,' I said.

The phone rang.

I took it from my jacket pocket. It was a FaceTime call, unknown number but I had a hunch who it was. I pressed the answer button and a face appeared on the screen. It looked like a Guy Fawkes mask, the mask once used by idealist revolutionaries the world over to protest against the powers that be, the nation state. With the thin moustache, the goatee beard and the unfailingly ironic smirk that contracted the eyes, Gio Greco looked a bit like a pig.

'Congratulations,' said Greco. 'I see that the two of you have made it to the torture chamber.'

'At least there's no fire in here,' I said.

'Oh, when you see what I've got lined up for you'll be wishing you'd died in the fire.'

'Why are you doing this, Greco?'

'Because the Abu Dhabi cartel are paying me two million. You should feel honoured, it's a record price for a driver.'

I swallowed. Acquiring a reputation as a top driver carries its own risks, greater and smaller. Greater, because the price on your own head goes up; smaller, because other drivers won't take a job where they know there's a good chance they'll be the ones that end up in a grave. I'd been relying on that smaller risk to give me some protection.

'I could actually have pushed the price even higher,' said Greco. 'If they'd been the ones who approached me.'

'So you were the one who went to them?'

'The job was my suggestion, yes. And I knew I could offer them a price they couldn't refuse.'

The sweat was prickling all over my body, as though it thought that getting rid of liquid like this would improve my chances of survival.

'But why . . . all this? You could have just shot me at the pedestrian crossing.'

'Because we had the budget for something a little more extravagant than a bullet, something that would get us talked about in the business. Creating a reputation is, after all –'

'Why?' I had shouted, and saw the boy looking at me with frightened eyes. There was silence at the other end, but I could almost hear his contented smiling.

'Why?' I said again, struggling to keep my voice calm.

'Surely you must know that. You're a psychologist, and you're fucking the Queen.'

'Is it jealousy? Is it as simple as that?'

'Oh, but jealousy isn't simple, Lukas. See, after Judith left me I sank into a pretty deep depression. I ended up seeing a psychologist, and he told me that in addition to depression I was suffering from narcissism. I don't know whether it makes sense to say someone *suffers* from having a well-founded self-image, but I told him anyway I'd come for some happiness pills, not to get a fucking diagnosis about completely different things.'

I said nothing, but what Greco told me was classic narcissism, where the narcissist refused to recognise the personality disorder or seek treatment for it, and that it was typically through depression that those of us in the health service got to meet the half per cent of the population the diagnosis applied to.

'But he wouldn't stop, the idiot,' Greco sighed. 'Before I shot him he managed to tell me that a characteristic of narcissists is they have a highly developed sense of envy. Like the first narcissist in literature, Cain. You know, the guy in the Bible who killed his own brother out of jealousy. Well, I guess that just about sums me up in a nutshell.'

I didn't know whether this shooting his psychologist was a joke, and I had no intention of asking. Nor did I propose to point out the futility of taking revenge for something you know you can never get back. Maybe because that was exactly what I was doing with my own life.

'Now do you see, Lukas? I am the victim of a personality disorder that makes me want to see you suffer. I'm sorry. There's nothing I can do about it.'

'I suffer every day, Greco. For God's sake, kill me and let the boy go.'

He smacked his lips three times, the way a teacher responds when a pupil gets the addition wrong on the blackboard.

'Dying is easy, Lukas. And your suffering is less now, because the Queen is good medicine, don't you think? OK, I want to open that wound up again. I want to see you squirming on my fork. I want to see you trying to save the boy. And failing again. I hear that when your son had smoke poisoning you drove him to the hospital but you got there too late.'

I didn't answer. When we smelled the smoke in the middle of the night and ran into Benjamin's room where he was lying next to that smouldering bedside lamp, he'd already stopped breathing. I drove as fast as I could, but I'm no racing driver and the hospital was too far away and as usual I was a knight on the wrong side of a chessboard.

'The boy's vocal cords,' I said. I had to swallow. 'Was it you who cut them?'

'To make him more like your son. So blame God for the fact that your wife gave birth to a mute.'

I looked at the boy.

Where had Greco found him? Probably in a slum on the outskirts of the city, a place where the sudden disappearance of a small child wouldn't excite much attention.

'I can just jump out of the window,' I said. 'And put an end to the whole game.'

'If you do the boy's guts will be destroyed by gas.'

'Gas?'

'Just one touch on the keypad.' Greco held a small remote control up to the camera. 'It's a new invention by one of the cartel's chemists. A type of mustard gas that slowly corrodes the mucous membranes. It is extremely painful and can take several hours. You puke up your own guts before you bleed to death internally.'

I looked around the apartment.

'Forget it, Lukas, it'll come through the ceiling and the walls, you won't be able to stop it. In one hour exactly I'll press the start button. Sixty minutes, Lukas. Tick-tock.'

'Fire engines are on the way – the firefighters will hear us shouting.'

'The fire's already out, Lukas. It was only a thin coating of spirits across a fire-retardant plus a burning fridge. No one's coming. Believe me, the two of you are alone.'

I believed him. I looked at my watch and coughed. 'We are all alone, Greco.'

'You and I are alone at least, now that she's been taken from us both.'

I looked up at that Guy Fawkes face of his again. *Taken from us.* What did he mean?

'So long, Lukas.'

The connection was broken and I was staring at a blank screen. Things freeze from the outside, but the cold I felt came from inside and was spreading outwards. He couldn't have . . . ?

No. It had to be something he wanted to trick me into believing.

But why?

So I'd get on the line to Judith at once to check that she was safe, so that he could trace the signal to her hiding place? No, he knew enough about things to know that, like him and like Judith, I had a phone that could switch arbitrarily between such a large network of the cartels' satellites and private base stations that it would make the signal impossible to track.

I stared at the ceiling and the walls. Looked at my watch, at the second hand that jerked remorselessly onwards.

Tried to think clearly, to work out my next move, but it was impossible to know if my brain was functioning rationally, like the climber on Everest, knowing that the lack of oxygen at altitude enfeebles his powers of judgement and yet not being helped by that knowledge, confusion is confusion.

Sixty minutes. No. Fifty-nine.

I had to know.

I called her number, my heart pounding furiously as I waited.

One ring. Two.

Pick up. Pick up!

Three rings.

Part 2: The Middlegame

In another of Murakami's games his opponent lost it all in the middle-game. Not because Olsen played badly, but because he was under pressure after falling into the Murakami Trap in the opening. The pleasant-mannered but always silent Olsen had used up valuable time in trying to work out his response and it left him struggling against the clock as well as Murakami's strongly positioned and numerically superior major pieces. A frequently rehearsed argument revolves around the issue of whether Olsen sacrificed his queen, or Murakami took it. Most people, myself included, think it obvious that Olsen would not voluntarily have sacrificed her, and that all he achieved when Murakami took the piece was a post-ponement of the inevitable. In an ordinary game Olsen would have resigned and handed the victory to Murakami, but in lightning chess there's always the chance your opponent will be stressed into making a catastrophic mistake. So Olsen chose to suffer on and allow himself to be cut up, piece by piece; all the while his one remaining black knight hopped about like a headless chicken. Playing that game over again, move by painful move, was like enduring a Greek tragedy. You know how it's going to end; the object is only to find the most beautiful way of getting there, what the drivers call *the scenic route*.

I met Judith Szabó while she was still Gio Greco's fixer and girlfriend. It was at a ball at the Sforzesco Palace that Luca Giualli, head of the

Lombardy cartel, had purchased from the commune and turned into his own private fortress. In addition to hiring a small army to take care of the family's security he had employed me to look for holes in the security routines and pick up signs of any imminent planned attacks.

I was standing by the piano in the atrium looking out across the crowds of the rich and the powerful in their tuxedos and ballgowns. I noticed her, even though she tried to carry herself just like any other guest. Not only because she was so strikingly beautiful in her bright red gown and long, raven-dark hair, but because she had been unable to resist approaching me like a professional.

'You're not doing your job especially well,' was the first thing she said to me.

She was a couple of centimetres taller than my 175.

'You must be Judith Szabó,' I said.

'See, that's better. How did you work that out?'

'I hear things. And you walk around like a queen and look around like a driver. Your name isn't on the guest list, so how did you get in?'

'I am on the guest list. As Anna Fogel, from the Tokyo cartel. There's an invitation in the same name. It was just too easy to hack the system, and the check on my fake ID was embarrassingly feeble.' She flashed a bank card at me.

I nodded. 'And why wouldn't I just sound the alarm now and have you cuffed?'

She smiled briefly before nodding in the direction of Luca Giualli, who stood conversing with the mayor of Milan, a man who had spoken enthusiastically of returning to the city-state model of Italy.

'Because –' said Judith Szabó, and I knew more or less what she was about to say – 'to do so would reveal that you had allowed a potential assassin to get so near your employer that she – had she so wished – could have killed him.'

'Then why are you here?'

'To deliver a message. From you know who.'

'The Greek. Broccoli head.'

She smiled thinly. 'He just wants to find out whether you're as good as they say you are.'

'Better than him, you mean?'

Her smiled broadened. Her eyes were so lovely. Cold and blue. And I thought at the time, she has a psychopath's pulse, her heart would beat slowly in a life-or-death situation. Later I would discover I was mistaken, that she was simply a consummate actress. And that the reason she was able to act the psychopath so well was that she was living with one.

'And now at least we know you aren't the best, Herr Meyer.' She looked into my eyes as she brushed something from the lapel of my Brioni tuxedo, though I knew there was nothing there.

'Excuse me, Herr Meyer, I've got someone waiting for me.'

She must have seen how I lifted my gaze above her shoulder and slowly shook my head, because she tensed, turned and looked up at one of the interior balconies in the atrium. It was too dark for her to see whether there was anyone in the darkness behind the open balcony door, but when she lowered her gaze she saw the red dot of a laser beam dancing across her gown.

'How long has that been there?' she asked.

'Red on red,' I said. 'I doubt whether any of the guests have noticed it yet.'

'And how long have you known that Anna Vogel doesn't exist?'

'Three days. I asked for every name on the list to be double-checked, and when Anna Vogel cropped up and there's no one of that name in the Tokyo cartel it naturally made me curious about who you might be. And it looks as if my guess was right.'

That smile of hers was no longer quite so steady.

'What happens now?'

'Now you go back to the person waiting for you and tell him that he's the one who's been sent a message.'

Judith Szabó stood there, studying me. I knew what she was wondering about. Whether I had planned to let her go or had made my mind up on the spot.

Whatever, two weeks later I would have reason to regret that decision.

Fourth ring.

She always has a phone close by, always. Please, Judith.

Fifth ring.

Don't be dead.

I called her two weeks after that meeting at the Sforzesco Palace.

'Hello,' was all she said.

I recognised her voice at once. Probably because I'd been thinking about her.

'Hi,' I said. 'I'm calling because you rang this number. Can I ask how you got it?'

'No,' she said. 'But you can ask if I'm free for dinner this evening.'

'Are you?'

'Yes. The table's booked. Seven o'clock at Seta.'

'That's early. Will I survive?'

'If you're punctual.'

I smiled at what I took to be a joke.

But I was on time. And she was already seated at the table when I arrived. As before, I was struck by the austerity of her beauty. No sweetness, just healthy, symmetrical and properly proportioned. But then those eyes of hers. Those eyes . . .

'You're a widower,' she said, once we had got a little shop talk out of the way without revealing any secrets.

'What makes you think that?'

She nodded in the direction of my hand. 'No driver wears a wedding ring. It tells you something about them. It makes them potentially vulnerable, knowing that there's someone they love.'

'Maybe I wear it as a distraction. Or maybe I'm divorced.'

'Maybe. The pain in your eyes tells me something different.'

'Maybe that's from all the victims I have on my conscience.'

'Is it?'

'No.'

'Well then?'

'Tell me something about yourself first.'

'What do you want to know?'

'There's probably quite a difference between what I want to know and what I'm permitted to know. Start anywhere you like.'

She smiled, tasted the wine and nodded to the wine waiter who, without asking, had known who would be doing the tasting.

'I'm from a well-to-do family. My every material need was met, but none of my emotional needs. The closest to that was my father, who abused me regularly from the age of eleven. What d'you think a psychologist would make of that and my ending up in this business?'

'You tell me.'

'I've got three university degrees, no children, I've lived in six countries and always earned more than my lovers and my ex-husband, and I was permanently bored. Until I started in this business. First as a client. Then as . . . a little more. Right now I'm Gio Greco's girlfriend.'

'Why not the other way round?'

'What d'you mean?'

'Why don't you say Gio Greco is your boyfriend? You use the passive form.'

'Isn't that what strong men's women usually do?'

'You don't strike me as someone who's easy to dominate. *Right now*, you say: that makes it sound like a purely temporary arrangement.'

'And you sound like a person preoccupied with semantics.'

'The mouth overflows with what the heart is full of – isn't that what they say?'

She raised her glass and we drank a toast.

'Am I mistaken?' I asked.

She shrugged. 'Aren't all relationships temporary arrangements? Some end when the love is gone, or the money, or the entertainment value. Others when there's no life left. What happened in your case?'

I twirled the thick-bellied wine glass between my fingers. 'The latter.'

'Competitors' drivers?'

I shook my head. 'It was before I entered the business. She took her own life. Our son died in a fire the year before.'

'Grief?'

'And guilt.'

'And was she? Guilty?'

I shook my head. 'The guilty one was the maker of the Mickey Mouse lamp in the bedroom. It was made of a cheap and highly inflammable material in order to undercut the competition. The maker denied any guilt. He was one of the richest men in France.'

'Was?'

'He died in a fire.'

'We aren't by any chance talking about François Augvieux who burned to death on board his yacht in the harbour at Cannes?'

I didn't answer.

'So that was you. We always wondered who it was. There was no very obvious client. An impressive debut. Because it was your debut, wasn't it?'

'The world doesn't need people who refuse to use their power to do something good.'

Again she put her head on one side, as though to study me from another angle. 'Is that the reason you're in this business? To kill unscrupulous profiteers and revenge your son and wife?'

It was my turn to shrug. 'You'd have to ask a psychologist about that. But tell me, what would the Greek make of you and me sitting here and dining together this evening?'

'What *would*? What makes you think he doesn't know?'

'Does he?'

She smiled quickly. 'He's out on a job. And I'm on a job too. I'd like to have you in my stable.'

'You make me sound like a racehorse.'

'You got anything against that?'

'Not the analogy. But I don't need a fixer.'

'Oh, but you do. You're too easily outmanoeuvred without one. You need someone who's got your back.'

'The way I recall it, you were the one who got outmanoeuvred.'

'I hope you don't take this personally, Lukas, but you shouldn't be here right now, you should be with your client.'

I could feel my pulse quicken.

'Thanks, Judith, but Giualli's safe enough in his fortress; and there are no traitors in our crew, I've made sure of that personally.'

Judith Szabó took something out of her Gucci bag and placed it on the tablecloth in front of me. It was a drawing or a print. It showed a cat running with something that looked like a lit explosive charge fastened to its body. In the background was a castle.

'This is a 500-year-old illustration of an offensive tactic used by the Germans back in the sixteenth century. They would capture a cat or a dog that had found its way out through one of those little escape routes animals always find as a way out of the fortress or village they come from, then tie an explosive charge to it and drive it home. And hope the animal would get back up through its tunnel before the fuse burned down.'

I felt a prickling between my shoulder blades. I already had a pretty good idea of what was coming next. It was something I hadn't – and should have – thought of.

'Gio is . . .' She seemed to be looking for the words. And as well as not being weak, Judith Szabó didn't strike me as a person who had trouble finding her words. When finally she did, she spoke quietly, and I had to lean forward to hear.

'I've got no problem with the method as such – it's our job, after all, and we do what we have to do. But there are limits. At least, there are for some of us. Like when that boy who lives with his mother at Sforzesco, Anton . . .'

The name made me jump. Paolo Giualli and his wife, twenty years

487

younger than him, were good people. Good, at least, considering how rich and powerful they were. They had three well-brought-up children who treated me with a distant courtesy which I reciprocated. Things were a little different with Anton, the five-year-old son of the cook, who lived in one of the service flats below stairs and was so like Benjamin I had to make a conscious effort to control my feelings for him. Judith Szabó stopped, maybe noticing that the name had a particular resonance for me. She coughed before continuing: 'So Anton is going to be the cat,' she said.

I was already halfway out of my seat.

'It's too late, Lukas. Sit down.'

I looked at her. Her voice was steady but I thought I could see tears in those blue eyes of hers. I knew nothing. Only that I was, once again, the knight.

Several days would pass before the testimony of witnesses and forensic examinations revealed what had happened. The Giualli children were accompanied by bodyguards wherever they went – at home, at school, at ballet, at karate, visiting friends – but the same thing didn't apply to children of the staff. All employees were searched on arrival and departure – for treachery is, after all, a part of human nature. But the chances of their being kidnapped were regarded as remote, especially since all employees had signed a contract which clearly stated that, in any such eventuality, their employer was absolved of any responsibility.

When Anton returned home from school that afternoon, an hour later than usual, he was in a state of exhaustion and told his mother how he'd been stopped by a man on his way through the Sempione Park. The man had held a cloth against the boy's face, everything went black and Anton said he had no idea how long he'd been out before waking up beneath one of the bushes in the park. His neck and throat were hurting, but apart from that he was feeling as well as could be expected. When asked to describe the man all Anton could remember was that, in spite of the heat of the day, he had been wearing an overcoat.

His mother had straight away spoken to Luca Giualli who at once rang the police and the doctor. The doctor had said the pains and the swelling around the neck could indicate that something – he declined to speculate on what it might be – had been forced down the boy's throat. But he couldn't say any more until he had taken a closer look.

According to the police report, four officers had been approaching the entrance to the fortress when the explosion occurred. The charge contained in the gelatine bag in the boy's stomach would not have been powerful enough to kill Luca Giualli and his wife had they been in their part of the fortress and Anton in the service flat. But they were – as we said – good people, and they were not merely close by but actually in the same room, so that there was little left of any of them once the police and the fire brigade had made their way through the ruins.

These details were still unknown to me as I sat that evening in one of Milan's best restaurants looking into Judith Szabó's blue eyes. What I knew for sure was that Anton was dead, and probably Luca Giualli too. That I had failed to do my job, and that it was now too late. I realised too that Judith Szabó had not been joking when she said I might be dead if I turned up late.

'At that ball,' I said, 'I should never have let you go.'

'No, you shouldn't have. But you wanted to send a message to Greco, didn't you?'

I ignored that. 'You invited me here so I wouldn't be at the castle when the boy came home. Why?'

'At the ball I realised you were good. You would have smelled the fuse and possibly saved Luca Giualli.'

'Was it Greco's decision to get me out here tonight for this meal?'

'Greco takes all the operational decisions.'

'But?'

'But this was my suggestion.'

'Why? As you see, you've overestimated my ability to sniff out

489

anything at all. When you invited me here, I thought –' I stopped and pressed my thumb and index finger into my eyes.

'Thought what?' she said quietly.

I breathed out heavily. 'That you were interested in me.'

'I understand,' she said, and laid her hand over mine. 'But you aren't mistaken. I am interested in you.'

I looked down at her hand. 'Oh?'

'The main reason I got you out of the way is because I didn't want you to die too. You let me go the last time we met. You didn't need to – I don't even think it was something you planned. So it was my turn to show a little mercy.'

'Showing mercy is not the same as being interested.'

'But I'm telling you I am. I need a new client. I think I've just lost the one I had.'

She looked down without moving her hand from mine. With her other hand she lifted the serviette from her lap and held it out to me.

'You're crying,' she explained.

That was how things started between me and Judith. With tears. Was that the way it was going to end too?

Six rings.

Seven.

Eight.

I was about to hang up.

'Hey, lover boy. I was in the shower.'

As I breathed in hard I realised I had been holding my breath.

'What's up?' she asked, worried, as though she'd read my silence.

'I'm in a locked apartment with a mute boy –'

'Gio.' She said it before I'd finished my sentence.

'Yes,' I said. 'I was afraid he'd traced you too.'

'He can't find me here, I've already told you that.'

'Everybody can be found, Judith.'

'Where are you?'

'That's not important, you can't help me. I just wanted to hear that you're OK.'

'Lukas, tell me where –'

'Now you know he's trying to reach you by using me. Stay hidden. I . . .'

Not even now, in this situation, could I make myself say it.

Love.

That was a word reserved for Maria and Benjamin. Over the course of the year in which Judith and I had been together it had occurred to me that maybe one day I would be able to say it and mean it. But no matter how much Judith fascinated and interested me and in all sorts of ways made me happy, that was one door that seemed locked shut.

'. . . am so fond of you, my darling.'

'Lukas!'

I hung up.

Leaned against the wall.

Looked at my watch. It was working against me, that much I realised. But why had he given me all this time? Why run the risk of my calling up my allies and summoning them to come to my assistance, rescue me? Or perhaps even the police?

Because he knew I had no allies, or none willing to go up against someone like Gio Greco. As for the police, when was the last time they got involved in a stand-off between drivers, with or without an innocent boy as bait?

I beat the wall with the palm of my hand and the boy looked startled.

'It's all right,' I said. 'I'm just trying to think.'

I put my hand to my forehead. Greco wasn't crazy, not in the sense that he acted irrationally. It was just that with his particular personality disorders – a more precise diagnosis would probably be *malign* narcissism, which isn't far away from psychopath – he operated with a rationale that was completely different from that of so-called normal people. If I was to predict his next move then I needed to understand him. We were revengers, both of us, but that was where the similarity ended. My crusade against the cartels was not just a form of spiritual cleansing, a way of muting my own pain; it was also principled: I wanted to tear down a world order in which the greediest and most unscrupulous profiteers had all the power. Greco didn't want to torture me as a matter of principle, but for the brief, passing and sadistic pleasure it gave him. And in pursuit of that pleasure he was prepared to sacrifice the lives of innocent people. That was it. That had to be the reason why he didn't just start the torture or the killing straight away; the pleasure would have been *too* brief. He wanted first to enjoy the knowledge that I knew what lay in store for me. This – my fear – was just his starter.

I went over my reasoning again.

There was something there that didn't quite add up.

The direction in which I was thinking, that he just wanted to see me suffer – that was something he'd planted, it was exactly what he *wanted* me to think. It was too simple. He wanted something more. What does a narcissist want? He wants affirmation. He wants to know he's best. Or, even more important, he wants everyone else to know he's best. Naturally. He wants to show the whole business, the whole cartel world, that he's better than me.

So far he'd managed to make me go along with everything he'd planned. I had run up the stairs to rescue the boy. I had managed to get us over to the other apartment. I had used the axe the way I was supposed to use it. I had . . .

I froze.

I had called Judith. He'd arranged it that way. He wanted me to call her. Why? Phone calls couldn't be tracked and phones located the way people once could be. Silence.

I took the phone out again, tapped in her name. Pressed the phone to my ear. Silence.

The phone wasn't ringing. I looked at the screen. The symbol showed not just a bad connection, it showed no connection at all. I crossed to the window, held the phone. Still no connection. We were in the middle of Milan, it wasn't possible. Or, of course, it was possible. If someone installed a jamming apparatus in a room they could turn the jamming signal on and off at will.

I stared at the walls, trying to see where Greco might have hidden the box. On the ceiling, maybe? Was the box there to ensure I couldn't call anyone once I had – predictably enough – called Judith? Greco probably thought that after all there just *might* be someone I could call who could possibly do something to upset his plans.

Accept. I had to accept that that possibility no longer existed. And I had to stop thinking about why it was he might possibly have wanted me to ring Judith, because there was nothing at all I could do about it. At least now she knew he was on the warpath, and I had to believe her when she said that she couldn't be traced through the phone, and that he didn't know where her apartment was, because not even I knew that.

I looked at my watch. And at the boy.

I had no doubt at all that Greco would use gas; he'd done so before. When the most brilliant inventor in the largest of the three electro-cartels took his vehicle in for repairs Greco had bribed a mechanic, entered the place by night and simply installed a gas pellet in the gearbox that would break open when the inventor put the gear lever into overdrive. The cartel's security people had come for the car the following day, checked it for any explosive devices and then driven it through the heavily trafficked city streets to the house where he lived. It wasn't until a few days later, when the inventor drove to his country home by Lake Como, that the car was out on a motorway and in due course he moved up into overdrive. The car went off the road close to one of the large bridges, rolled over and was crushed against the cobbles of a village square directly below. The death was recorded as a road accident. Not that insiders didn't know gas was involved, for the death of everyone who is important for a company's competitive success is always regarded as suspicious and involves an autopsy. But according to Judith the electro-cartel was anxious to play down the vulnerability of its security system as being bad for its reputation. The irony of it all was that within the drivers' world I was the one given the credit for the attack, merely because on one occasion I had answered a query from another limo driver about how to eliminate this chemist who had an army to guard him and who rarely left his fortress home, and then only in a bulletproof car with his own personal driver and bodyguards for a skiing trip to the mountains at Bergamo. I suggested that one should track down the personal driver and hypnotise him without his knowing it, simply prime him with a trigger word which – when he heard or read it – would immediately put him into a trance. This type of hidden hypnosis leaves the person apparently exactly the same, and he feels exactly the same too. I suggested the trigger word should be a place name he would be bound to see along one of the fastest and most dangerous stretches of road between Milan and Bergamo.

I don't know whether Greco was ever told of my suggestion and that was what inspired him, or what he thought about me being given the credit for the attack. The point is, I would never have carried out such a mission; I never do jobs in which innocent people can die.

Again I looked at my watch. The problem wasn't that time was moving too fast. It moved slowly, but I was thinking even slower.

I had to get the boy out of the apartment before the gas was released.

If I could get the people down in the street to tear down one of the shop blinds, might they possibly be able to use it as a jumping sheet?

I crossed to the window and looked down.

A man in police uniform stood down there. Apart from him the street was empty.

'Hey!' I suddenly shouted. 'I need help!'

The uniformed man looked up. He neither responded nor moved. And although he was too far away for me to see his face clearly, I noticed that the big man's head seemed to have been beaten down between his shoulders. The pedestrian precinct was closed at both ends of the block by security tape, presumably fake too, like the uniform. I closed my eyes and cursed inwardly. Big as he was, and wearing that uniform, he probably had little trouble telling people to move on. The drama moreover was at an end; the fire had been put out and the boy and I presumably rescued. I looked across to the other side of the street. Tried to estimate the distance in metres. The fake policeman crossed the street and disappeared through the gate directly below me.

I stepped back inside and studied the apartment again. With the same result. There was just us in here, the four walls, a fire-axe and the decapitated body of the dog. I walked round the walls, hitting them with my fist. Brick.

'You know how to write?' I asked.

The boy nodded.

I took the Montegrappa pen from my inside pocket and handed it to him.

'What's your name?' I asked, pulling up the sleeve of my coat so that he could write on the cuff of my white shirt. But it was saturated with blood from the bite wound, and before I could pull up the other sleeve he had turned to the wall and was writing on the pale blue wallpaper.

'"Oscar, eight years old",' I read aloud. Then I said: 'Hi, Oscar, my name is Lukas. And you know what, we're going to have to get out of here.'

I'd worked it out already. It was about eighteen metres down to the street. Tying together the coat, the shirt and my trousers I would be able to lower Oscar four metres down. Using his own clothes would make that six metres. I could probably let Oscar go from a height of four metres without him getting seriously injured. But even for that I would need another eight metres. And where was I going to find that in an apartment that had been completely stripped?

I stared at the dog. We had not had much anatomy during our psychology studies, but one of the things I did notice – apart from the paper-thin bone between the eye socket and the brain – was that the human body contained eight metres of intestines. Or intestine. Because from the anal aperture to the throat is one long tube. How much weight could an intestine bear? I thought of my uncle in Munich who served sausages linked in their skins and how as a kid I used to try to pull them apart. In the end I always had to use a knife.

I picked up the axe.

'Think you can help me, Oscar?'

The boy looked wide-eyed at me but nodded. I showed him how I wanted him to hold the dog's body between his knees and hold the front paws out to the sides and back, so that the dog's stomach lay open and distended in front of me.

'Close your eyes,' I said.

It's remarkable how delicate we mammals are. All I had to do was draw the sharp edge of the axe up through the fur and the belly opened, and the guts tumbled out. So did the stench. I immediately began to pull the intestine out, concentrating on breathing through my mouth.

It was hard to see in all the blood and slime, but I located what looked to me like two ends and cut them off. Tied a knot in each end to seal off the openings. It didn't look like eight metres, hardly even five. But the material seemed flexible, so maybe with a little weight on one end it would stretch to eight?

I took off my clothes and tied them together using a reef knot. It took a while, since it was a long time since I had practised the knots I learned from my father, in the days when I thought I was going to go in for competitive sailing, as he had done.

After several failed attempts I finally got it right, but when I tried to secure the intestine to the sleeve of the coat the two wouldn't connect; the sleeve simply slipped out through the knot. I tried to think hard as I sat there on the floor in only my underwear, shivering in the cold draught coming from the window. It just didn't work. I swore out loud and looked at my watch. It was now more than half an hour since Greco had begun his countdown.

I had another go, this time using a longer section of sleeve; but again the slippery, slimy gut just glided out through the knot. I threw the gut and the coat aside, lay back on the floor, pressed my stinking bloody hands to my face and felt the tears welling up.

He had me exactly where he wanted me.

A small hand lifted my own from my face.

I looked up and there was Oscar holding something up in the air. The gut and the coat sleeve. Knotted together. I took hold of it and pulled at the two ends, but they held fast. I stared in disbelief at the knot. And then I recognised it. It was a sheet bend. And I remembered what my father had said when I told him that Maria and I were going to get married. That with certain women the knot to use was a bowline, easy to tie and easy to untie. But getting married, the knot to use then was a sheet bend; the harder you pulled, the tighter it got.

'Where did you learn . . . ?'

Oscar saluted with two fingers held to his forehead.

'Cubs?'

He nodded.

Just then the phone – which I had placed on the floor, along with my keys and wallet – began to vibrate. I picked it up. FaceTime again, and once again I had a full-strength signal.

I pressed Take Call and again Greco's face filled the screen.

'Hi, Lukas. She's on her way. Look, she's just parked outside.'

He held the phone up to a computer screen. I saw a street, obviously in a fashionable residential area, and the door of an Alfa Romeo opening. I felt as though someone had injected iced water into my chest. The woman who got out and crossed the road moved like a pro. And like a queen.

Greco spoke from behind the phone: 'When you can't find them, the thing you have to do is make them come to you.'

Judith was wearing the red coat she always wore when attending business meetings. When she was going to war, as she used to say. She removed it before the meeting started and wore beneath it a snowy white blouse. That symbolised a blank sheet of paper, she said. A willingness to compromise. And before she put her coat back on again she had always got a deal for her client. *Always.* It was so obvious when I thought about it now, the way you understand every genius chess move once it's been shown to you.

Gio Greco had been Judith's lover longer than me, he knew her better.

He was also a better chess player than me. He knew I would call her when he said those words: *'You and I are alone at least, now that she's been taken from us both.'* And he knew what she'd do once she realised Greco had me in his power; go and see him and do what she was best at doing: negotiate a deal.

Greco's grinning face filled the screen again: 'You look like you realise what's happening here, Lukas. The Queen is going to die. All is lost. Or is it?' He lowered his voice dramatically, like a game-show host on one of those franchises spewed out by the Tokyo cartel. 'Maybe you can save her after all. Yes, you know what: I'm going to give you one last chance to stop me. You can use your weapon.The great Lukas Meyer will hypnotise the terrible Gio Greco and save the day. Come on. You've got about fifteen seconds before she gets here.' Greco opened his eyes wide as though to show how ready and responsive he was.

I swallowed.

Greco raised a slender, shaven eyebrow. 'Something wrong?'

'Listen –' I began.

'Can't do it, Lukas? Performance anxiety? Do you get that too when she needs fucking?'

I didn't answer.

'OK, that wasn't really fair,' said Greco. 'See, that psychologist I was telling you about, he suggested hypnosis as a cure for depression, but when we tried it, it turned out I'm not a good subject. He said it was because of my so-called personality disorders. I'm immune to it. I mean, there must be some advantages to being insane.'

Laughter. The T and the long S again, like the hiss of a punctured bicycle tyre. Then he was gone from the screen. The phone appeared to be placed on a shelf or suchlike, and I saw something that looked like a hallway and an oak door with an entryphone. There was a jarring, ringing sound. Greco appeared on the screen again, his back to me, his white suit gleaming. He seemed to be holding something up in his hand so that I couldn't see. He picked up the entryphone with his free hand.

'Yes?' Pause. Then, in a surprised voice: 'No, is that you, darling? How lovely, it's been such a long time. Well, well. So at least you still remember where you used to live.'

He pressed the button on the entryphone. I heard a distant buzz and then the sound of a door opening. I was clutching my own phone so hard I thought I might crush it. How could Judith, who was so intelligent, who knew Greco so well, fail to see that he had smoked her out from her hiding place by using me? The answer came back as quick as the question. Of course she knew. And still she'd come. Because there was no alternative – this was her only chance to save me.

I wept. No tears came, but my whole body was sobbing. I wished I'd lied to her. Told her I loved her. Given her that at least. Because she was going to die. And I was going to watch.

Greco turned his piggy face in triumph towards me. And now I was able to see what he was holding in his hand. A karambit. Curved handle and a short blade bent like a tooth. A knife with which to slash, chop or stab. And which, once it's in, does not let go.

I wanted to break the connection but couldn't bring myself to do it.

Greco turned towards the door and opened it, holding the knife in the hand behind his back so only I could see it. And then she came in. Face pale, her cheeks a feverish pink. She embraced him, and Greco let her do it without taking his hand from behind his back. Now I could see them both in profile.

'Run!' I shouted into the phone. 'Judith, he's going to kill you!'

No response. Greco had probably put his phone on mute.

'How nice,' said Greco in a voice that sent a short, hard echo round the hallway. 'To what do I owe this visit?'

'I regret it,' said Judith, out of breath.

'Regret?'

'Regret leaving. I've thought about it for a long time. Will you have me back?'

'Wow,' he said. 'Even before you've taken off your coat?'

'Will you?'

Greco bobbed up and down on his heels.   •

'I –' he said, and sucked on his upper lip – 'will take Judith Szabó back.'

She breathed quickly and put a hand against his chest. 'Oh, I'm so happy now. Because I want you, Greco. I know that now. It's just that it's taken me some time. And I'm sorry about that. I hope you can forgive me.'

'I forgive you.'

'Well. Here I am.' She took a step towards him, her arms wide. Greco stepped back. She stopped and looked at him in confusion.

'Show me your tongue,' he said quietly.

For an instant Judith looked as though someone had just slapped her. But she recovered quickly and smiled.

'But, Greco, what –'

'Your tongue!'

It looked as though she had to concentrate, as though this involved a highly complicated locomotor operation. She half opened her mouth, and then out came her pale red tongue.

Greco smiled. He looked almost mournfully at the exposed tongue. 'You know very well I would have taken her back, Judith. Her. The one you were. Before you turned into someone else and betrayed me.'

The tongue disappeared.

'Greco, darling . . .' She reached out to him, and he took another step back.

'What's the matter?' she asked. 'Are you afraid of me? Your people searched me at the door.'

'I'm not afraid. But if there was anyone I was afraid of, it would be you. All I can do is admire your courage. But then, you have always defended the one you love. That's why I was certain you would come. That's your method, after all: *go directly to the root.*'

'What do you mean?'

'Come on, Judith. You're a better actress than that.'

'I've no idea what you're talking about, Greco.'

But I did. That was her mantra as a fixer. *Go directly to the root.* When she was contacted with a commission, something which, for obvious reasons, almost always happened via a middleman, she always made it her business to find out who the real customer was and pay a visit to that person. It was always a risky business. She might lose the commission, or expose herself to danger, but she insisted on going *directly to the root* in order to fix a price and agree on the conditions. She always got a better price, she maintained, because she could do without all the middlemen taking their cut, and there were no misunderstandings about what was included in the service and what was not. And I supported her tactic of going *directly to the root* method because I wanted to know the reason for the commission, what the intended result of it was. My road to heaven was paved with the evil intentions of others, and I just wanted to make sure that the greater evil didn't win out.

'Maybe, *maybe* I want this, Judith Szabó. I like your tongue. You've come to negotiate. So make a start. What are you offering to spare his life, your psychologist?'

She shook her head. 'He's been out of my life a long time, Greco. But yes, of course, I expect you not to harm him.'

Greco put his head back and laughed his T and S laugh until his piggy eyes disappeared behind his round cheeks. 'Come on, Judith, a negotiator has to lie better than that. You know what I wish?'

I shuddered as he reached out a hand to stroke her cheek.

'I wish you'd have loved me enough to do what you're doing for him.'

Judith stared at him, her mouth open. One hand continued towards her cheek. The other tightened its grip on the handle of the knife behind his back. I could see the tears welling up in her eyes, the way her body seemed to collapse inside; she was already moving her hands up to protect herself. She knew pretty well what was about to happen. That this had always been the likely outcome. And that now it was too late for regrets.

'Hello . . .' he said.

'No!' she shouted.

'No!' I shouted.

'. . . I'm Greco,' he said.

He swung the knife in a tight arc so swiftly it seemed to leave a trail of silver through the air.

Judith stared at him and at the knife. The blade was clean. But her throat had opened. Then came the blood. It splashed out, and she raised her hands as though to prevent it falling onto her coat, her present. But as she pressed her hands to her neck the pressure increased and blood sprayed from between her fingers in thin jets. Greco backed away but not quickly enough; blood splashed on the sleeve of his white suit jacket. Judith's legs gave way and she fell to her knees. Already her eyes were glazed; oxygen was no longer reaching the brain. The hands fell lifelessly from the neck, already the volume of blood had diminished. For a second or two her body balanced on the knees, and then she collapsed forwards, her forehead hitting the stone floor with a soft thud.

I screamed into the phone.

Greco looked down. Not at Judith, but at the sleeve of his jacket as he tried to wipe away the blood. Then he walked over towards the phone, and I didn't stop screaming until his Guy Fawkes face filled the whole screen. He looked at me without saying anything, with a sort of mild solemnity, like a mourner. Was that what he was? Or was he acting the sympathy in a parody of the undertaker's professional solemnity?

'Tick-tock,' said Greco. 'Tick-tock.' Then he broke the connection.

I tapped in the police emergency number and pressed Call. But of course I was too late, I no longer had a signal.

I collapsed onto the floor.

After a while I felt a hand on my head.

It was stroking me.

I looked up at Oscar.

He pointed to the wall, to the words he had written there.

It wil soon be beter.

Then he put his arms around me. It was so unexpected I didn't have time to push him away. So I simply closed my eyes and held the boy. The tears came again, but I managed not to sob.

After a few moments I held him a little away from me.

'I had a boy like you, Oscar. He died. That's why I'm so sad. I don't want you to die as well.'

Oscar nodded, as though to convey that he agreed with me, or understood me. I looked at him. At the dirty but fine blazer.

And then, as we carefully made our knotted rope of clothes and guts, I told him about Benjamin. The things he had liked (old things like big picture books, gramophone records with funny covers, Grandad's toys, especially marbles; swimming; Daddy's jokes), the things he didn't like (fried fish, going to bed, having his hair cut; trousers that made him itch). Oscar nodded and shook his head as I went through the list. Mostly he nodded. I told him one of Benjamin's favourite jokes and that made him laugh. Partly because it's stupid not to laugh when there are only two of you, but mostly, I think, because he thought the joke was pretty funny. I told him how much I missed my boy and my Maria. How angry it made me. The boy just listened, responding now and then with facial expressions, and it occurred to me that now he had taken over my job as the mutely listening psychologist.

I asked him to write something about himself on the wall while I tightened all the knots and got our rope ready. He wrote in keywords.

Brescia. Grandad blazer factory. Nice house, swimming pool. Men with guns. Daddy Mummy dead. Run. Alone. Doghouse. Dog food. Football. Black car, man in white clothes.

I asked questions. Joined up the dots. He nodded. Large, shiny child's eyes. I gave him a hug. That warm little chin nestling in the pit of my neck.

Looked at the dog's head lying on the floor behind him. Dog's eyes. Child's eyes. Pig's eyes. Tick-tock, tick-tock. I closed my eyes.

Opened them again.

'Oscar,' I said. 'Get out the pen. We're going to try something a bit weird.'

He took out the Montegrappa pen. The kind of beautiful thing they don't make any more.

Part 3: Endgame

Once Olsen's queen was off the board and the decision had been taken it was as though Murakami gave his opponent a short breathing space. He could afford it – Olsen was the one running out of time – and it looked as though Murakami, instead of bringing matters to a quick conclusion with a *coup de grâce,* preferred instead to take the opportunity to show off to his audience, the cat's last sadistic moments of play with the mouse. The even-tempered and silent Olsen had completely abandoned his bloodied defence of the king and instead moved his black knight to the other end of the board, as though in denial of the grim reality of his situation, a general playing a round of golf as the bombs rain down around him.

'Don't be afraid, Oscar. You won't fall.'

I spoke calmly. Established eye contact. My heart was beating hard, probably as hard as his was. The gut was fastened around his chest in a bowline knot. He'd taken off his outer clothes and we had attached them to the end of the line, and now the half-naked child's body, still wearing his shoes, was dangling above the cobblestoned street below, his hands holding tight around the balcony railings.

'Now I'm going to count to three,' I said, struggling to keep my voice calm. 'And you let go on three? OK.'

Oscar stared at me, panic in his eyes. He nodded.

'One, two . . . three.'

He let go. Brave boy. I stood with one foot braced against the wall by the window and felt his body-weight stretching the intestine downwards. It held. We'd tested it inside the apartment and I knew there was no reason it wouldn't hold now, just because it was eighteen metres above ground. I'd wrapped the gut around my wrist twice in order to brake, but still I could feel it begin to slip. That was all right – the idea was to lower him down, only it mustn't happen too fast. I would have to brake when I reached the join with the coat, and if that was too abrupt then the whole gut might snap.

Oscar slipped down and away from me. All the time we kept our eyes on each other.

At the junction with the coat I had to brake and saw how the gut stretched like an elastic band. I was certain it wouldn't have held my eighty kilos, but the boy can't have weighed more than twenty-five. I held my breath. The gut swayed and stretched. But it held. I continued paying out the rope, quickly, before it could change its mind. On reaching the last item of clothing, the boy's blazer, I leaned out as far as I could to make the drop to the street as short as possible for Oscar, holding on to the sleeve with one hand and with the other around a railing.

'One,' I said loudly. 'Two, three.'

I let go.

Oscar landed feet first, I heard his shoes hit the cobblestones. He fell over. Lay there a moment or two, as we had agreed on beforehand, to check that he was uninjured. And then he stood up and waved up at me.

I hauled up the rope and untied his clothes. Dropped them down to him, and he quickly put them on. I saw him checking the blazer pockets to see if everything was there; the pen, the money I had given him, and the key to my apartment. I knew it was a vain hope, but at least that was what it was: a hope.

It didn't last long.

Two men in black drivers' suits emerged from the gateway, one of them the big man with no neck. They started chasing Oscar and caught up with him before he reached the security tape. They carried him, jerking and struggling, over to an SUV that stood illegally parked in the pedestrian street.

I didn't shout. Just watched in silence as the car disappeared.

I had done what I could. At least the boy wouldn't die breathing in Greco's hellish gas. He might even let Oscar go. Why not? Once the king has been checkmated, the other pieces can stay there untouched. And drivers – most of them at least – don't kill just for the sake of it.

I went back inside the apartment, untied my own clothes from the gut and started to dress. The dog's head looked up at me, one eye gouged, the other one whole.

Did I believe that? That Greco would take pity on Oscar?

No.

I looked at my watch. Twelve minutes to go before the gas came billowing out into the apartment. I sat on the floor and waited for the phone call.

Outside, it was growing dark.

Greco rang two minutes before time was up.

The phone was probably mounted on a tripod and the screen showed what appeared to be his room. Bricks, wood. Large white surfaces. Outside, on a large terrace, a Christmas tree with its lights lit in the evening dark. At the veranda door two armed guards, muscles bulging beneath tight-fitting black drivers' suits. Greco sat on a white leather sofa, and beside him, legs dangling, was Oscar. His blazer was buttoned up wrong, the Montegrappa pen visible, clipped to the breast pocket. He looked frightened and exhausted from crying. On the coffee table in front of them was a chessboard that looked, from the position, as though it was nearing the endgame. Next to it lay the karambit and the remote control for the release of the mustard gas.

'Hello again, Lukas. An eventful day, don't you think? And that's probably a good thing, since it's your last.'

Greco rubbed the sleeve of his jacket with a cloth. That bloodstain. He couldn't seem to get rid of it.

'I just hope it's over soon,' I said.

'Actually, I had thought of putting our boy here in a bedroom with a bedside lamp and pressing the button. But it was too much . . . bother. And I like this knife.' He reached out for the karambit.

'Don't you understand how sick you are, Greco?' My voice was tight and hoarse now. 'This is a child. An innocent child.'

'Precisely. That's why it surprises me you didn't take your own life while you had the chance. All this –' he gestured broadly with his hands – 'would have been completely unnecessary if you'd had the brains and the balls to jump out the window.'

'But you would have killed the boy anyway.'

He grinned broadly. 'Why on earth should I do that?'

'Because you are who you are. You have to win. If by taking my own life I had saved the boy the victory wouldn't have been yours alone, it would have been a draw.'

'Now *that*,' laughed Greco, 'is sick. And you are, of course, absolutely right.'

He picked up the knife and turned towards Oscar, who sat with eyes closed, as though the light were too bright, or to shut out the world. Greco put his other hand on the boy's head. Long S-sound. Then he coughed and began:

'Hello . . .' he said, in that familiar, slow, clear, sing-song voice.

I forced myself to keep my eyes open and watch the screen.

A spasm passed through Oscar and his hand went up to his breast pocket, took out the Montegrappa pen clipped there and opened it in a single, fluid practised movement. Greco observed him with an amused smile.

'. . . I'm Greco,' he concluded, stressing each syllable.

Oscar had taken out the needle-shaped cartridge and was holding it upside down in his little hand. The whole thing had taken less than three seconds, same as the last few times we'd rehearsed the sequence of moves. And now he swung his hand. He was a bright boy and by the time we'd finished he was hitting the eye in the dog's head every time, even when I held it high above him and moved it about. Hit it again and again, as calm and collected as a robot, the way hypnotised people are. Until we were down to two and a half seconds from when I gave him the trigger words, 'Hello, I'm Greco,' to him taking the pen out of his breast pocket, removing the cartridge and stabbing.

I saw the point of the cartridge penetrate Greco's eye, and could sense how it slipped through the paper-thin bone at the rear of the socket and on into the brain. Oscar's small, balled hand against Greco's face like a growth, like broccoli. Greco was staring with the other eye, not at Oscar but at me. I don't know what I saw there. Astonishment? Respect? Fear? Pain? Or perhaps nothing. Perhaps those muscular spasms passing across his face were the result of whichever centre of the brain the cartridge point penetrated, as I recalled from my student days how we could get dead frogs to move their legs by stimulating the nervous system.

Then Greco's body suddenly relaxed, and he exhaled in a long gasp, his last S, and the light in the remaining good eye went out, like the red light on a piece of sloppily produced electronic equipment. Because in the final analysis perhaps that's all we are. Frogs with conduits that transmit impulses. Complex robots. So advanced we even possess the power to love.

I looked at Oscar.

'Hi, I'm Lukas,' I said.

He emerged immediately from his trance, dropped the cartridge and looked at me. Next to him, his head lolling on the back of the sofa, lay Greco, the cartridge sticking out of his eye as he stared up at the ceiling.

'Keep looking at me,' I said.

I saw the men behind Oscar who had raised their machine guns but who now stood as though frozen to the spot. No shots had been fired. For there was no longer any danger to be averted. No longer a boss to be protected. And, their brains were telling them, though they could not have formulated the thoughts themselves: no one left to pay them for killing this boy, this child whose body would haunt them for the rest of their nights were they to kill him.

'Stand up slowly and walk outside,' I said.

Oscar slid down from the sofa. Picked up the two parts of the Montegrappa pen from the floor and put them in his pocket.

One of the men had approached the rear of the sofa. He lay two fingers against the corpse's carotid artery.

Oscar headed for the hallway and the front door.

The men exchanged quizzical looks.

One of them shrugged. The other nodded and spoke into the microphone on his lapel.

'Let the kid go.'

A short pause as he adjusted his earpiece.

'The boss is dead. What? As in finished, yes.'

Greco lay staring up at the heaven he'd never get to. A solitary red tear ran down his cheek.

It took me almost three hours to cut my way through the metal-reinforced door, by which time the blade of the axe was so dull it functioned more as a sledgehammer.

I saw no one either in the entrance or outside as I walked into the street. They had probably been informed the operation was cancelled. Were probably already on their way to other jobs for other bosses, other cartels.

I made my way through the dark streets without looking over my shoulder. I thought of the chessboard on my table back home, where Carlsen had just stepped into the Murakami Trap and in eighteen more moves would resign. As I walked along there I couldn't know that in twelve years' time I would be watching that famous game in which Olsen, who has likewise fallen into the Murakami Trap, moves his black knight to F2 and looks over in silence at the disbelieving and despairing Murakami.

Reaching the block where my apartment was I rang the bell. There was a click from the entryphone, but no voice.

'It's me, Lukas,' I said.

A buzz. I pushed the door open. Going up the stairs I thought of all the days after Benjamin and Maria were gone, when I had dragged my feet up these steps and dreamed they would be standing in the open doorway waiting for me. As I stopped on the final landing, suddenly so tired it was like a pain in my chest that almost dropped me to my knees, I looked up. There, in backlit silhouette in the doorway, I saw that little figure, I saw my son.

He pointed to his eyes and looked at me. I smiled and felt those lovely warm, wet tears rolling down my neck and in beneath my shirt collar.

Oscar and I walked through the ruins of Brescia, hand in hand. It had been a poor city, actually one of the poorest in Italy, although being in a rich part of the country it wasn't easy to tell from the outside. But Brescia failed to survive the collapse of the nation state and in time had become a slum.

We stood in the street and looked through the fence at the old clothing factory, which was now just an abandoned site, a burned-out shell that appeared to be home to a pack of wild dogs. I had had to fire a warning shot towards them to keep them away.

We walked through the gateway of a house that had clearly once been beautiful. Not ostentatiously large, and built in a tasteful art deco style. The white walls had brown damp stains on the outside, the windows were broken, and a sofa dragged halfway out through one of them. From within came the echo of a dripping sound, as though from a grotto. We walked round the back, where snow still lay in patches on the grass, faded brown after the long winter.

Oscar stood at the edge of the empty swimming pool full of snow and rubbish. The tiles were cracked and the rim of the pool a dirty brown.

I saw Oscar's eyes fill with tears. I pulled him towards me. Heard the quick, short snuffles. As we stood there the sun broke through the mingled clouds and smoke and warmed my face. Spring was on its way. I waited until he'd finished snuffling, then held him away from me and told him in the sign language we'd been practising that the summer wasn't far away, and then we'd go to the coast and swim in the sea.

He nodded.

We didn't go into the house but I saw the name plate on the door. Olsen. Despite the adoption we'd decided that Oscar would keep the name. In the car driving back to Milan we ate the panzerotti I had bought in Luini, and I turned on the radio. They were playing an old Italian pop song. Oscar drummed away energetically on the dashboard, miming the words to the song as he did so. The news came on afterwards. Among other things there was an item about how the now forty-year-old Murakami had once again defended his world title. We could see the outlines of Milan as Oscar turned towards me. I had to slow down to read all the signs he was making, concentrated and careful:

'Can you teach me to play chess?'

Jo Nesbø is one of the world's bestselling crime writers, with multiple books including *The Son, Macbeth* and *Knife* topping the *Sunday Times* charts. He's an international number one bestseller and his books are published in 50 languages, selling over 50 million copies around the world.

Before becoming a crime writer, Nesbø played football for Norway's premier league team Molde, but his dream was dashed when he tore ligaments in his knee at the age of eighteen. After three years of military service he attended business school and formed the band *Di Derre* ('Them There'). They topped the charts in Norway, but Nesbø continued working as a financial analyst, crunching numbers during the day and gigging at night. When commissioned by a publisher to write a memoir about life on the road with his band, he instead came up with the plot for his first Harry Hole crime novel, *The Bat*.

Sign up to the Jo Nesbø newsletter for all the latest news: jonesbo.com/newsletter

Robert Ferguson has lived in Norway since 1983. His translations include *Norwegian Wood* by Lars Mytting, the four novels in Torkil Damhaug's Oslo Crime Files series, and *Tales of Love and Loss* by Knut Hamsun. He is the author of several biographies, a Viking history and, most recently, *The Cabin in the Mountains: A Norwegian Odyssey*.